Death Stalks Kettle Street
by
John Bowen

For Elaine
(my big sis)

Cosy /ˈkəʊzi/ (US cozy) – adjective (-ier, -iest) snug, comfortable, relaxed, homely, intimate and friendly, safe and secure.

Cosy: A subgenre of crime fiction mystery, where sex and violence are commonly downplayed and the crime and subsequent investigation are confined to a contained social group or location.

Chapter 1

Each season sang its myriad demands. Bernard Brocklehurst ignored none of them.

His beautiful garden enjoyed constant year-round grooming, diligent care and dedication. Before retirement, gardening had been pushed into the weekends, but the last few years had permitted him to indulge himself fully in his passion. If Bernard's garden was his mistress, then few beaus were as patient and attentive, few more familiar with their beloved's idiosyncratic charms, seductive sweeps, curves and cheeky bumps.

The 30-by-80 square feet of backyard received lavish attention; Bernard studiously trimmed, scarified, fed and aerated his immaculate lawn, diligently weeded the borders, turned and nourished their soil with decadently rich compost. Plants and flowers were pruned and pampered from delicate off-cuts to brilliant blooms. Slugs and winged pests were kept at bay, cuttings harvested and nurtured.

Bernard lived for his garden, risked his life for it, he liked to joke occasionally. A medical blood test some years back to rule out a food allergy had identified him as being violently allergic to wasp and bee venom. A single sting could risk plunging him into anaphylactic shock, a fatal physiological reaction that could end not just his gardening days but his days, full stop. In reality, such an event was extremely unlikely, even if Bernard were reckless (which he was not; his brand of living dangerously was indulging in a second sherry during the Strictly Come Dancing finals); he took great care to check for wasps and bees when pruning. He wore sturdy gardening gloves, long trousers, and even kept an EpiPen handy, just in case.

On this particular balmy afternoon he was down on his aging knees planting daffodil bulbs, unhurriedly scooping out pocket-sized craters in the rich soil before thumbing a knotty ball into each. A quick brush of the trowel, followed by two firm pats, and they were covered, ready to erupt like buttery yellow trumpets, rude as ruffians in a few brief months.

Bernard had just reached behind him into the paper bag for another bulb when a long shadow fell over him. He would have turned, but was not afforded the opportunity. A hand seized the back of his head, and with a brisk violence which took him completely by surprise, drove him forward, smashing his face into the dirt. For a few moments a struggle ensued; he fought, but his assailant had been prepared and he had not. He tried yet again to lift his face from the soil, strained a wild eye back. In the periphery of his vision he glimpsed a gloved hand holding a small jar, empty but for some whizzing and bobbing winged dark spots—

The gloved hand gave the jar a vigorous shake, and the grip on his head was exchanged for an equally powerful elbow which swiftly jammed itself behind his neck, immobilising him just as effectively.

Bernard tried to scream, but only succeeded in inhaling a mouthful of nutrient-rich soil. He felt something pressed against his neck followed by a sharp stab—

No, not a stab. A sting.

Pinned down, unable to move, he felt the sting's cruel chemistry poison his body.

His throat began to swell and close.

Then his assailant broke away, released him. Bernard rolled over, pulling his face from the dirt, and stared at the brute through rapidly swelling eyes, vainly trying to suck air though the pinhole-sized aperture which only a moment ago had been a perfectly adequate airway. The shadowy figure stood over him, ballooning in and out of focus until the darkness now crowding Bernard's vision swelled large enough to blot everything out.

The shadow stood and watched for a spell, until Bernard's chest rose and fell for the final convulsive time.

Then the shadow reached into his jacket pocket and removed a mobile phone. It was scuffed and cheap, purchased along with several others from various car boot sales, SIM card abandoned with a small amount of credit remaining. He thumbed in a number and hit dial.

Chapter 2

Greg Unsworth stood at the sink, looking through his kitchen window out into the garden in a vain effort to divert his attention away from the cupboard, to avoid acknowledging how the space was rapidly becoming two square feet of intolerable anarchy and chaos.

He took another cup from the draining board, carefully began to dry it. He had a method. Greg dried the lip first, then the handle, then the body, then the bottom, then the interior and finally around the lip again. Still hot from the scalding washing-up water in which it had been scrubbed, the cup squeaked against the tea-towel, audible reassurance that every last vestige of grease and dirt had been removed. Satisfied, Greg moved to put the cup in the open cupboard with the rest. He girded himself, set it down with the handle oriented in the direction it was presently facing, in this case toward the kitchen doorway.

His fingers hovered over it momentarily, before drawing away. As with the last cup and all those before it, he was required to fight an urge to rotate the cup so its handle pointed in the right direction, toward the window.

It looked wrong. The window was the right way—

No. He heard his therapist Martin's voice in his head. There was no right way. Cup handles were free to point any direction. Nothing would change. The ground would not heave, shake and split open beneath his feet, nothing terrible would occur. The cup would just happily sit where it had been placed. There was no right way. The whole concept of a right way for cup handles to face was an 'irrational construction'. If Greg was to make progress, this was just one of the many battles he must win, one cup handle at a time. He wondered, not for the first time, how other people saw the world. To him it seemed marked in invisible lines, degrees of symmetry and ratio. Placing cups randomly in the cupboard was like parking a car not just across two spaces, but diagonally across two spaces, with one wheel up on the kerb, all the doors left open.

Drawing a deep breath, he plucked the final cup from the drainer, dried it to the same thorough and exacting standard as those before and set it in the cupboard. This time the handle happened to point toward the wall. He exhaled and closed the cupboard door. He drained the washing up bowl, rinsed the suds away and filled the sink with hot water from the tap. Drained it once more, half-filled it again, and then drained this. He checked the tap.

Off.

He turned it a little more to test.

Off, but the feeling wasn't right.

This was tricky, because Greg had to be certain not only that the tap was off, but that it was aligned symmetrically with the sink. The quarter revolution required to orient it correctly would either mean a counter-clockwise turn, which might then risk a drip, or a clockwise turn which might mean it was twisted too tight. He had stripped the thread of many a fitting this way.

He risked a further clockwise quarter turn.

Off.

Off.

Definitely off.

He leaned forward so that his eye-line was level with the tap's mouth, counted to sixty, just to make sure no drip was slowly forming. He saw nothing, no slow-forming belly of liquid. Satisfied, he left the kitchen.

On his way into the hall he spotted something sitting on the mat beneath his letterbox, a white bubble-pack envelope. He fetched it. There was no address on the front, no markings at all. He tore it open, tipped the item inside into his palm, and frowned. It was a small tube of cream.

He was still frowning when the phone rang. He padded into the front room and picked up. The phone was an old rotary-style one. Greg had issues with buttons, keypads and keyboards.

"Hello?"

There was a moment's silence and then the caller spoke. The voice was low, almost whispered.

"Six minutes and I'll be gone. Lawn. Blue door. Window boxes."

The line went dead. Greg set the phone down.

What was all that about? The tube of cream was still in his hand. He stared at it. There was the silhouette of a winged insect on the front. It was a tube of Insect Bite & Sting Relief cream. He checked the envelope again, puzzled, but there was nothing on the package, no address, no stamp. It had been hand-delivered then, a free sample of something perhaps, simply one more thing stuffed through his letterbox along with the pizza leaflets and junk mail? He returned to the kitchen and tossed it into the bin.

He was about to exit the kitchen and stopped in the doorway. There followed a short spell during which he stood gripped with indecision. He turned, stared at the cupboard door, behind which the cups lay, handles in disarray.

He backed up, opened the cupboard and carefully adjusted the handle of every last one to face the window.

Chapter 3

Jeremy smiled, a big, confident smile with a pinch of cheeky thrown in, a smile a writer might describe as wolfish.

"I'm not sure I understand. How can you resist me, Beth? I'm irresistible."

Beth Grue studied him as he lounged behind the gym's reception counter and leaned back on his chair, fabric of his leisure centre branded T-shirt drawn taut over his over-developed shoulders, chest and biceps. He could probably have done with the next size up. It would, without doubt, have been more comfortable, but lacked the 'look at my amazing muscles straining to burst free' thing he had going on. Jeremy clearly had no intention of spending all his free time in the gym and living on a diet of chicken breasts and brown rice to hide his beauty under an L sized shirt.

The grin still beamed from his handsome tube-tanned face.

His comment about being irresistible was a joke, of course; by acting out the caricature of someone monstrously vain and over-confident he was actually being self-effacing. I'm not conceited and ridiculous enough to believe I'm really irresistible, he was saying. Yeah, I'm handsome, but I'm not one of those guys...

Only in this case, Beth rather suspected maybe he did think he was irresistible.

"Hm... I'd check the label of those protein shakes you drink about recommended consumption," Beth said. "I think one too many may have addled your brain."

"Irresistible," he repeated, still grinning. "Okay, forget about a drink then. We could go for a meal. What do you like? Italian, Indian, Chinese, Thai?"

Beth shook her head, her smile benign, as far from flirtatious as she could manage. She only hoped the accompanying tilt of her head and slight wobble would be misread as nonchalance, rather than iffy muscle control. The subtle subtexts of body language could get murky when your body didn't always do what you wanted it to.

"I don't think so." She returned her locker key, sliding it across the counter. Without breaking eye contact Jeremy scooped it up and exchanged it for her one pound deposit.

Despite Beth having attended this gym for a year now, she hadn't attracted Jeremy's interest until a month ago, seemingly from out of nowhere. She had politely made it clear she wasn't interested, but this only seemed to have made him keener. She had unwittingly made herself a challenge, which she found both unwelcome and irritating. She liked this gym, and given it only had seven staff on rotating shifts, Jeremy was a frequent fixture.

This brand of sudden interest from nowhere wasn't a new phenomenon. It was something Beth had experienced enough times previously to have eventually got a handle on. The process went, she felt, like this: When men first encountered her they saw the surface stuff first, the wobbly walk, the stiffness, the sometimes errant muscle control. When she talked, they heard the characteristic slack, that spooly soft quality of her speech before they paid any attention to the content of what she said. They saw someone disabled, and all too often assumed she was more disabled than she actually was. There might even follow an awkward spell where she would be spoken to as though she possessed the mental age of a pre-schooler.

Soon (although occasionally, depressingly, not quite soon enough) they would grasp she was not simple-minded and begin to actually see her. And what they often saw was this: a pretty face and a body with curves in the right places, well-toned from years of physical therapy and sessions in the gym.

She wasn't conceited or vain, just acknowledging simple objective facts. Apart from keeping herself in good physical shape, her contribution to these attributes was limited. They were mostly the result of random genes and dumb luck, something she'd had no more say in than having been born in a breech position and getting her umbilical cord twisted around her neck, resulting in her brain being starved of oxygen for a short spell.

Things were what they were.

Fate, life's ever-present spinning roulette wheel, had dealt her good looks, great legs, perky boobs, a nice backside and mild cerebral palsy.

There were guys, like Jeremy, who following this reappraisal became interested in her. They tended to quickly forget their initial assessment of her, but she could not. Knowing someone was capable of that kind of ignorance, prejudice, short-sightedness… it lingered. What was the saying? You only get one chance at a first impression?

Such guys, after reappraisal, committed the further error of assuming she would be an easy conquest. Had Jeremy? She thought maybe he had. He was a good-looking guy, and quite charming in his way, but the assumption irked her, nearly as much as her disinterest making her all the more alluring.

True, there was a time when she might have indulged in a single serving of Jeremy, one or two nights of mindless fun, but those days were behind her. She had nothing to prove, to herself or anyone else.

"You can't keep this up for too much longer," he continued, thoroughly unabashed. "You'll crack eventually you know. Treat yourself to some sweet, sweet Jeremy…"

The grin was back, full beam. Had he had his teeth whitened? She thought maybe he had, or perhaps they just looked florescent beside his tanned skin. The over-confident dickhead act wasn't completely ineffective, though. In fact she very nearly smiled.

Good effort.

Wrong girl.

Chapter 4

Seams, cracks…those divisions between one discrete section of paving and another: Stepping on them was not allowed.

To the casual observer, Greg's daily pilgrimage to the corner shop might not appear unusual. After all, it wasn't like he skipped, tiptoed or hop-scotched down the path. He had become too familiar with the terrain now to call for anything but minor adjustments in his stride. Only an attentive watcher might actually notice his feet never, ever, ever, set down on places where the paving met.

Preet Hanif's shop lay at the foot of Kettle Street, where it intersected with Badger Street, although few locals and customers called him either Mr Hanif or Preet. Most, at his request, called him Pete. Pete ran the shop with the help of his family. Evenings or weekends his son or daughter could often be found manning the till, earning and contributing while they studied at university.

Greg made the trip every morning. Well, almost every morning: there were those grim days where nothing went right, felt right, where everything conspired to prevent him doing almost anything, the days where his compulsions were strong enough to defeat him; but mostly the trip was a fixture. He made a point not to bulk buy certain items, or to buy some things in small quantities, so he always had something that required him to leave the flat to get. Teabags, which he got through rather a lot of, he deliberately bought in packs of 40, enough to last two or sometimes three days. After six years, he and Pete knew each other well, and this made things easier. He didn't have to explain, feel the quizzical gaze of someone unaccustomed to his habits.

Mid week, the street was quiet, traffic light. Kettle Street sat in a suburban area twelve miles from the city centre. The bottom half of the street's housing was council-owned or previously council-owned, and subsequently bought by its former council tenants under the right-to-buy scheme. The upper half was made up of newer developments, where a couple of pebble-dashed concrete tower blocks had once stood.

In the main, dwellings in the street were well-kept. Many still retained front gardens due to the road being a generous width, wide enough to park a vehicle on either side without obstructing through traffic. Kettle Street was spared the hard, bare look which afflicted many neighbouring streets, where most gardens had been tarmacked or block paved into driveways. It felt greener and cosier. Kettle Street was Greg's home, and had been for six years. It was a nice, ordinary street, a street largely free of trouble or dramas, predominantly home to long-term tenants. It was a common criticism of twenty-first century life that people frequently had no contact with their neighbours, but Greg knew many of his, if only to share a word or two with in passing. One, Mr Cooper, even headed a residents' association group and distributed a newsletter once a month.

It was a safe, regular, orderly place, was Kettle Street, and orderly was how Greg liked things.

The bell dinged as Greg entered the shop. He had often considered rigging his own front door with one. He liked the ding. It was definitive. Ding! The door was open. Ding! Closed.

Pete was at the counter. Greg caught his eye and raised a hand in greeting. Pete responded with his usual hearty, "Hello Gregory, my friend!"

Greg collected a litre carton of milk, a packet of Yorkshire Tea teabags and a Warburton's thick-sliced loaf and took them to the counter. Pete began to ring them up on the till.

Pete shook his head. "Very sad news. Did you hear? Mr Brocklehurst passed away yesterday."

Greg felt oddly shocked. Old Mr Brocklehurst was dead? It seemed impossible. They had spoken just the previous morning, on Greg's way home from the shop.

"How? What happened?"

"Stung by a bee, or a wasp, not sure which. An allergic reaction, would you believe? Fatal." Pete seemed incredulous the two things could be connected. "Mrs Boon spotted him from her upstairs window. He was lying in his garden...He could have been there for hours." Pete shook his head sadly. "Such a nice gentleman. Never missed his Gardeners' World Magazine. Not once in ten years."

Greg couldn't claim to have known Bernard Brocklehurst all that well, just the occasional morning conversation in passing, just a minute or two here and there, commenting on the weather and such, but he found he already missed him. It was a strange kind of familiarity, but all those scattered minutes added up. Mr Brocklehurst would never again ask Greg how life was treating him, or comment on how his garden could do with the rain even if his joints could do without it...

And one morning, just like that, dead. One less friendly face in the world.

Greg counted out the correct change for his milk, bread and teabags, and checked it, and then checked it again. Someone was standing behind, waiting to be served too, but he couldn't hurry. He had to be sure before handing it to Pete.

"Perfect," Pete declared after carrying out his own deliberate, unhurried and methodical count, which Greg knew full well was for his benefit rather than Pete's own. Both of them knew Greg would fret he'd have cheated Pete out of something if there was any doubt. Return trips to the shop to confirm there had been no discrepancy in some transaction, that Pete hadn't been short-changed, had once been common, and still occurred now and then. Pete knew a thorough check now might afford Greg peace of mind later.

The man standing behind Greg exhaled impatiently.

Pete ignored him. "And check all items are on the receipt?"

Again Greg nodded.

Now the man let out a second audibly annoyed grunt. Greg glanced around to find a hulking bruiser of a figure standing there. Greg had seen the man before, just enough to know who he was. He was new to Kettle Street, moved in over the road around a month ago. Broken nose, bald head, neck thick enough to be engaged in a dispute with his shoulders as to where one ended and the other began. All in all, he looked like something sprung from the primates' enclosure of the nearest zoo, clippered, and wrestled into a pair of stone-washed jeans and a black t-shirt in a hopeless attempt at disguise. An aggressively ugly blue-black India-ink prison-style tattoo decorated one side of his neck-shoulder: a web, and in its centre a large spider…eating a smaller spider.

He stared Greg down, growled, "In your own time. I've got all day."

Greg quickly averted his gaze.

"So, Gregory," Pete said, eyes flicking past him to the man, making it clear neither rudeness or intolerance would result in swifter service, "what plans might you have today, my friend?"

"Oh, not much really. Just see how things go, you know?" Greg replied, trying to hurry things along.

Pete unhurriedly tore off Greg's till receipt, checked each item on it against Greg's purchases, wrote 'checked' on it and then handed it to Greg.

The man stepped forward to take up Greg's place at the till, tossed down a copy of The Racing Post and a packet of extra-strong mints.

Pete served the man briskly but silently, and made a point of chirping "Goodbye Gregory!" as Greg slipped out of the shop door.

Greg emerged to find frail Rose Gordon, who lived a few doors up from him, passing by. She was making her way to the road, looking distinctly unsteady on her feet. As she approached the kerb, the shopping caddy she was pulling along beside her wobbled and threatened to tip over. Greg hurried over and managed to right it before it could topple. It settled back onto two wheels with a muffled clink of bottles.

Belatedly, the elderly lady seemed to realise what had almost happened. A look of alarm ghosted across her face, swiftly followed by relief.

"Ooh, good save."

Rose Gordon smiled; a nice big wrinkly smile that travelled all the way to her eyes and lit up her face. Greg tried not to stare at her nose, which was an orgy of burst capillaries. The tip was crimson, a drinker's nose. This, together with the shop she had just exited, the local off-licence, and the clink of bottles? The scene didn't call for Sherlock Holmes to deduce Mrs Gordon liked the odd tipple. Her unsteady passage suggested she liked one so much these days she possibly started early. Like, breakfast early.

"You might need to think about getting yourself a new trolley, Mrs Gordon. The wheels on this one look a bit wobbly. They might be worn out."

Rose smiled again. "Aren't we all, my dear?"

Greg smiled back, until he noticed the man with the spider neck tattoo. He was standing outside Pete's shop, staring at him, observing Greg with an unashamed look of study. Greg averted his eyes, wondered for a moment if the man were purposely trying to intimidate him. After a few seconds he glanced back. The man was walking away up the road, The Racing Post tucked in his back pocket.

"That's the chap who moved in a few weeks ago isn't it?" said Mrs Gordon, who had evidently been following Greg's gaze. The man entered the betting shop on the corner.

"Yes."

"Looks a bit of a one, doesn't he?"

He did indeed, thought Greg.

—

Adrian spied his brother coming down the road long before Greg saw him. Greg was walking beside an elderly lady pulling a tartan shopping caddy. They shared a few words and then the old girl slowly crossed the road while Greg watched after her, letting herself into a house a few doors down. He looked like a regular guy in his late twenties. Adrian only wished he was.

He had been reasonably confident his big brother hadn't gone far, or for long. Compared to most people, Greg's world was tiny. As someone who commuted around the country for work, loved to travel, and had spent an entire year backpacking after university around the US, Asia and Europe, Adrian found the scope of Greg's existence difficult to imagine. Greg had never set foot on a boat or a ferry, let alone a plane. Greg required familiarity, and his comfort zone was suffocatingly small. As kids, the brothers' family holidays had always been spent in the UK, reached by car, their dad at the wheel. A string of days in some guest house where the room always required lengthy organisation before Greg could settle. Relocating Greg was a sure way to remind everyone in the family how much they did and didn't do to accommodate him.

So while school friends returned berry-brown from Spain and Greece, the Unsworths explored the exotic delights of Torquay, Weymouth, Tenby, Skegness...

He watched his brother's approach.

Greg was doing his pavement thing. Adrian's brother's ambulation lacked the unconscious rhythm of a simple stroll; there were odd pauses or lurches as he took pains not to tread on cracks on the paving, or seams where the slabs met.

Adrian knew he should feel nothing but compassion for his older brother, but some degree of irritation always lurked below, the old undercurrent. Thirty-one years old and Greg still hadn't managed to get a grip on this shit. Adrian refused to accept he would always be messed up, even if offered precious evidence to the contrary.

Where there was life there was hope, so he continued to foot the bills for yet another therapist. Who knew? Perhaps this Martin Mangham might succeed where the others had failed. Neurolinguistic Programming. Adrian had encountered the impressive-sounding methodology via a recent management team-building seminar.

Greg spotted him, raised a hand in greeting.

Adrian gave him a tip of the head, smiled.

"Corner shop?" he asked, when Greg neared.

"Milk, bread, teabags." Greg jiggled the carrier bag he was holding.

"Ah."

They walked up Greg's path together and Adrian waited while Greg opened up. Once inside, he dutifully removed his shoes as Greg had, and set them on the mat beside the door, aligning them exactingly to the mat's orientation, knowing if he didn't Greg would faff about placing them 'right'. He was about to enter the kitchen when he noticed Greg was still hovering in the hall.

"Everything good?"

"I've just got to…" Greg jerked his head ever so slightly at the door.

"Of course," Adrian said, tried to keep the sigh out of his voice, tried to remember Greg hated this stuff more than anyone else ever could. "I'll wait in the kitchen."

He smiled, hoping to conceal his quiet exasperation. There was always something with Greg, some pointless ritual or rule that stymied the simple flow of everyday life. When they had lived together he'd been accustomed, conditioned to them, all the Gregisms. Once, living with them had almost seemed normal. Well, not normal, perhaps, but not so abnormal.

He continued through into the kitchen, clean as an operating theatre, tidy as a drill sergeant's sock drawer, and sat at the table, waiting and listening as Greg repeatedly opened and closed the front door, and opened and closed it. Getting it to it 'feel right' took several minutes and more than fifteen attempts. Adrian didn't mean to count but it was hard to ignore the repeated bump and click of the latch.

Greg finally joined him and set the kettle to boil. Adrian watched him pluck two pristine white mugs from a cupboard full of identically arranged ones, handles uniformly pointing to the window. Again Adrian experienced the familiar brew of pity and irritation: the mug handle nonsense, another long-standing Gregism.

Greg dropped a teabag carefully into each mug.

Adrian couldn't help himself.

"Dad's having trouble with the neighbours again. They're threatening to call the police. They think he's poisoned their trees, some evergreens they planted along the fence. The needles are brown and shedding and look post-apocalyptic now."

Greg turned. "Oh?"

"He was afraid they'd grow massive," Adrian went on. "Those are Leylandii, I told him. Most evergreens don't all grow that fast, or big."

Their father's current quarrel had been running for three months now. Since retiring he had found even more time to get annoyed about things. The new family who had moved in next door had been making 'improvements' to the place. First Dad had complained about the noise resulting from installing a new kitchen and bathroom, and then the garden had become the battleground. They had planted a row of evergreens which threatened, at some point, theoretically, to throw shade on his garden. His

27

response had been to immediately drill holes in their trunks and pack them with root killer. The neighbours either suspected or had outright rumbled his act of sabotage. It was just the latest episode of the long running series of Dad vs The World.

Adrian wondered why, though, he bothered telling Greg. Their father and Greg hadn't spoken for nearly five years now, and reminding Greg how pig-headed their father could be seemed an unlikely path to reconciliation. Just venting, then? He did occasionally feel somewhat put upon, saddled, left alone to deal with their dad's nonsense. How much of this was Greg's fault? Honestly? Not much. Even if things were different, how much use would Greg be in dealing with their dad's shenanigans, when just shutting his own front door was a challenge?

—

They drank tea, chatted. Greg enquired what Adrian had been up to, how things were at work. Adrian asked how therapy was going with Martin. Greg lied, and said well. Adrian stayed long enough to feel like he'd done his duty, then suddenly noticed the time and pretended he had to get going. Who knew, maybe he did?

Greg waved him off at the door, feeling as he often did following his brother's visits: worse about everything.

Adrian had a good job, something involving software systems and finance that appeared to defy simple explanation. It also seemed lucrative, enough for Greg not to feel guilty about letting him pay for the therapists. They, at least, allowed Adrian to live in the hope his only sibling might not one day be so fucked up. Martin Mangham, with whom he had another session arranged tomorrow afternoon, was the fourth such therapist on the conveyor belt of potential Greg-fixers.

Feeling tired, useless, a pinch of wretched and one heaped spoonful of guilty, Greg closed the door on his little brother.

Seven more tries and his infernal, internal arbiter agreed it was properly closed.

Chapter 5

Beth walked to work. She had rented a local flat specifically to spare herself the grind of a commute. It was one of the advantages that came with moving to another city. She had secured the job first and accommodation second. That had been five years ago. She still liked both her flat and her job.

Northcroft Library was a lovely old Victorian building, set within a row of residential housing. It wasn't huge, just large enough to serve the surrounding community, but it was busy enough in that capacity. With its ornate plasterwork and old red brick construction, it looked venerable and villagey, even though Northcroft had long since spread into a town. Perhaps as recently as the 1930s the area would have looked quite rural, but since then houses had been built, once green spaces and fields gobbled up, roads widened and junctions added to cope with the burgeoning traffic. If someone were to cup her hands around her eyes, though, form makeshift blinkers, plug her ears, view the library just in the context of its neighbouring cottage-style houses, she could easily imagine how things had once been. A more open vista revealed a shopping centre a short walk up the road, and a YMCA in the opposite direction.

Beth gripped a lovely big brass handle and pushed one of the building's twin, royal-blue painted doors open, slipped into the blessed atmosphere of 'Shushhh!' unique to only libraries or churches.

As she passed the leaflet carousel by the door in the tiny foyer, she spotted a small poster pinned to the notice board. It was new. Hailey must have put it up. The text read:

IS THERE A NOVEL INSIDE YOU?
Creative writing for beginners.
Limited numbers.
No fee (but commitment essential).

Hailey, head librarian at Northcroft, was on the front desk.

"What's this?" asked Beth.

Hailey smiled enigmatically, mimed pulling a zip closed across her lips. "Can't say more than what's there. I'm sworn to secrecy, on pain of death."

Beth raised an eyebrow. The poster had suddenly grown considerably more interesting. Fortunately Beth knew exactly how to extract the requisite information. Hailey may have sworn a vow of secrecy, but her mouth liked the taste of mutiny.

"Oh," Beth agreed breezily, "probably safest not to say anything then."

She wafted past, heading for the staff room to stow her coat and bag. It took perhaps four minutes for Hailey to crack. She appeared at the staff room door.

"Well," she said slipping inside and pointedly closing the door behind her, "I suppose it wouldn't hurt to tell just you. There should be some perks to being an employee after all. You might be interested in signing up once I tell you, but you have to swear to keep it to yourself. If it gets out, that class will be signed up and full by this afternoon."

Beth was twice as curious now.

"You heard of Dermot O'Shea?"

Beth had. O'Shea was a detective fiction writer, cosy murder mysteries, author of the Jacob Lumiere series. The BBC had even made a two-part drama based on the first novel. As far as Beth knew O'Shea had been quiet of late. In fact she couldn't recall a book from him in ages.

"The Jacob Lumiere series?"

Hailey nodded. "He's the course tutor. We're not supposed to say. He wants it to be a surprise."

"Dermot O'Shea is going to teach a creative writing course here? Why? I mean that's great, but..."

"He said he wants to give something back. He used to live around here. It was where he wrote Murder Most Murderous. His first published work."

"And he's going to teach a bunch of amateurs to write, here?"

Hailey nodded. "You're always saying you'd like to write a novel. Why not sign up? There are only eight places. Just think, being taught how to write fiction by a proper big-name author."

Beth thought about it, but not for long.

"Put me down for it."

—

Beth spent a quiet lunchtime with Google, looking up Dermot O'Shea. O'Shea had lived in Northcroft, and indeed written Murder Most Murderous here. He had a dozen novels to his name, ten in the Jacob Lumiere series, and two stand-alone novels that hadn't done nearly as well. That had been eleven years ago. He had published nothing since. She found a couple of fan sites, where the common theory was he had been struck silent with writer's block, but it seemed just as likely O'Shea had lost interest, run out of creative juice or just cashed out. He had been successful, a number of international bestsellers and the BBC drama, maybe successful enough not to have to write again if he chose not to,

Beth supposed. Perhaps that was it. Perhaps he had eventually developed the itch to teach instead.

What Hailey had said was true, Beth loved books and like many of those who do she had often entertained the idea of writing one of her own. She'd dabbled in short stories at school but the prospect of tackling a novel was something else. There was something daunting about the scale of a novel, but then wasn't this the very thing which made the adventure so alluring? Maybe with a little expert help she could really do it? She definitely wanted to try.

The afternoon passed quickly. Mr Cooper popped in to run some photocopies off of his periodic residents' newsletter. Beth saw him reading the notice about O'Shea's writing class.

Before she knew it 4 p.m. had rolled around, and the end of Beth's shift. Getting ready to leave, Beth found Hailey tackling the Contemporary Romance stack. It was a popular section, subject to frequent lends, but keen browsing also messed things up. Hailey had pulled a whole bunch of books off and had them on the cart. She was now methodically setting them back in alphabetical order, no doubt to receive more ravaging, pawing and fondling over the following week than the heroines within them could dream of.

Beth looked down at Hailey squatting near the bottom shelves. "Shouldn't you be locking up?"

"I should, but I just want to finish up here first. You heading straight home?"

"I am."

"Rose Gordon's book has come in. You usually pass Kettle Street on your way home don't you? Would you be a mega-sweetie and drop it in to her?"

"Be happy to."

"It's under the front counter with the other reserves."

"No problem. See you in the morning."

Beth fetched Mrs Gordon's book from the reserved pile. It was second from top, under a gardening book being held for a Bernard Brocklehurst. It was a large-print clean romance titled The Broken Pledge, featuring a dashing, Victorian velvet-suited character brooding on the cover. The library didn't generally do deliveries, but Rose Gordon was a special exception. She had worked as a volunteer until a few years back and it had become a little too much for her. A lovely old lady, she still made regular use of the library though. Beth was happy to save her the trip to collect her book.

Mrs Gordon's husband Ralph had passed on a few years back; Rose's nose suggested she may long have been fond of a drink, but Hailey said she thought the occasional evening whisky had found its way into other parts of the day. She had also voiced the opinion that at age 84, Rose had earned the right to do whatever she damn pleased. If a drink and a good book kept a twinkle in her eye, where was the harm? Where indeed, conceded Beth.

She left and took her usual route home, via Kettle Street. Beth checked the address again. Mrs Gordon lived half way down the street. She found the house and pressed the doorbell. A minute later the door opened on a chain, but only for a moment. It soon opened wide; Rose Gordon smiled at Beth.

"Beth? The new girl?"

Beth nodded. "The very same. Hello, Mrs Gordon. The book you had on reserve? It came in. Thought I may as well drop it off as I was passing."

Even though Beth had worked at the library for close to five years now, the old lady had stopped helping out a few months after she started, which, Beth guessed, would always make her the new girl to Rose Gordon. Beth handed her the book.

"That was very nice of you."

"No problem, really."

"I don't suppose you'd like to stop and share a pot of tea with me." Perhaps sensing hesitation, Mrs Gordon sweetened the deal. "I think I have some chocolate digestives, custard creams too." She smiled, a big, lovely, warm one that instantly tripled the crinkles on her face. Beth wondered how much company Rose Gordon got these days.

She smiled back. "What kind of idiot says no to a chocolate biscuit?"

—

Rose Gordon's home had a tired look to it, like the ghost of a house which had once been better cared for. Did she have local authority carers come by to help her out? Perhaps, but from Beth's experience, even if she did, they rarely had time to do a great deal. It wasn't a case of not wanting to help, just that they had lots of oldies to see and not much time to see them in. When the pay is likely minimum wage to boot, well, there just aren't enough saints to go around.

Rose Gordon returned from the kitchen carrying a small tray with a pot, two cups, a little jug of milk and a small bowl of sugar on it. She poured two cups and invited Beth to add milk and sweeten to her liking. For her part, Rose fetched a bottle of Bell's Whisky from a nearby cabinet and poured a tot into her own tea. Rose caught Beth's eye, and tipped her a naughty wink.

"You need something to loosen the joints and ease the aches at my age dear, a drop of Bell's. You really can't beat a drop of Bell's."

Again the lovely crinkly smile brightened her face. Where was the harm, indeed, thought Beth? At a certain age anything which pleases you and doesn't harm anyone else is surely fair game.

Rose pointed to the plate of biscuits. "Help yourself, dear."

"Thanks." Beth reached out to take a custard cream. A spasm thwarted the attempt for a moment. She had hemiplegia; her left side was weaker and prone to stiffness and dyskinesia. It wasn't acute, rarely more than a momentary irritation. Rose noticed though.

"What is it you have again my love?" she asked. "I don't recall…"

"CP," said Beth. Met with Rose's puzzled expression she added "Cerebral palsy?"

Still nothing.

"I'm a spastic."

At last the old woman understood. She nodded, oblivious to the fact that the world's chosen terminology had moved on. Beth cut her some slack. Spastic, a once acceptable way to describe people with cerebral palsy, had eventually transformed into a playground insult. The words spastic, and spaz, had both grown so toxic they were thoroughly abandoned by the leading charity founded to help people with CP. After nearly half a century, in the nineties the charity had been rebranded from The Spastics Society to Scope. Beth wasn't sure cutting the pejorative free had changed much. Like how the term 'handicapped' had given way to 'disabled'. They both communicated the same thing; you weren't supposed to be able to do what other people could. Except Beth usually found she was capable of a good deal more than most. She had issues related to her CP, but overcame them. In most instances her cerebral palsy didn't disable her. She was able, totally bloody able.

Spaz.

To the old lady the word was just a word, a descriptor, not an insult. Having been on the sharp end of the word in its mode as a playground insult, Beth felt less inclined to cut her childhood peers the same slack.

She completed the remainder of the custard cream's journey to her mouth without too much trouble.

"My Ralph loved a custard cream he did." Rose had turned to look at a framed photo standing on a nearby sideboard; it featured a picture of a friendly, elderly man.

"Your husband?" Beth asked.

Rose nodded. "Been gone three years now." She reached a spindly hand over and gave the frame of the photo a squeeze, smiled again, although this time the accompanying crinkle didn't make it to her eyes. Beth wondered how many people Rose had in her life. She saw no pictures of children or grandchildren. How many of her friends were still around?

When the old woman waved her off at the door twenty minutes later, Beth had already decided she would drop in on Rose again in a few days. Just to say hi, and maybe share a custard cream or two.

Chapter 6

Martin slowly paced the front room. Greg sat on the sofa, as requested. Martin's pacing made him uncomfortable, and a small part of him couldn't help but wonder if this was intentional; his new therapist was an odd individual, with, in Greg's opinion, an even odder outlook on life.

With his short, waxed and styled hair, replete with meticulously neat and tapered sideburns, a designer t-shirt under charcoal grey suit jacket, designer jeans and tan shoes combo, Martin Mangham was male grooming personified. The look was an aggressively smart-casual style that obviously demanded anything but casual effort to achieve.

"We have a saying in Neurolinguistic Programming, Greg: *The map is not the territory.*" Martin paused momentarily. Despite having just made a statement, he nevertheless fixed Greg with a quiet questioning stare, unwavering beneath a set of studiously shaped brows.

"You do?" Greg responded, annoyed that he had cracked under the fast burgeoning weight of Martin's silence.

"Do you know what we mean by this?"

"Um, not really."

"It means, Greg, that the way we each see the world is no more reality than the most detailed map or model of the world could be. We think we see the same world others do, but that simply isn't true. *Perception is projection.* Carl Jung said that, Greg."

"He did?"

"Yes. What he meant is the world we see is unique to each and every one of us, filtered, shaped by our hopes, fears, preconceptions, desires, our limited understanding of existence, constructed of chosen fragments, themselves often inaccurately collected through our senses."

"Right…"

"Scientific studies prove we attempt to take in something approaching two million bits of information per second. Two million. Think about that, Greg. Consider what a colossal task that represents…so colossal as to be impossible. Thankfully, evolution has equipped us with a central nervous system which attempts to tell which information we take in is important and which is not. We focus, and in tandem with our brain sift and sort the bits we most need, discarding the rest. Our senses are continually forced to sift, sort, and delete in order to attempt to capture the massive scope of reality, whatever that is, with the hopelessly inadequate bandwidth available. The picture, though, is always woefully incomplete, so we seek to patch in the missing parts. But how do we do this?"

Greg promised himself he would not respond this time. He felt much surer this was a rhetorical question.

"We use our past experiences, the world view we've formed," Martin continued. "The problem with this?"

Another rhetorical; Greg waited. Did Martin pluck his own eyebrows, he wondered, or go to a beauty salon? If so, how often? Once a week? More?

"We frequently misinterpret experiences, inaccurately gauge their threat, impact or meaning, lend them more weight and importance than they deserve. Take phobias, for instance. Personally I'm completely fine with spiders. There's really no logical reason to fear them. They are most often small, fragile and in the British Isles not at all poisonous.

So why do so many people fear them? It's a learnt response, commonly inherited through observation, Greg. A child sees a parent or some other trusted figure overreact to one, beyond all proportion to the real threat at hand. Lacking experience of his own, the child accepts the small fragile creature as a genuine danger. The lesson slips into his unconscious mind with the same weight as a genuine hazard."

Greg wondered. Were all phobias really learnt? Surely some had to just be there all along, instinctive, primal, quirks some people are born with. Were all maladies so easily paired with reasons? In Martin's world it seemed so; each and every one assigned an unambiguous cause.

"These intrusive thoughts you have?"

"Yes?"

"They are an example of what I'm talking about. You fail to perform some action, the consequences of which are either non-existent or trivial, and you have thoughts that tell you something dreadful will occur as a result. Your subconscious mind is sending you a warning, but why?"

Greg feared he had lost Martin's thread.

"Fear, dread, anxiety," Martin ploughed on. "These things are all vital levers in the machine of self-preservation. They seek to drive us to action, to escape the threat which ignites them. Only I believe in your case the stimulus threat matrix has become wired up all wrong; we're going to change that."

"That would be nice."

Martin smiled. Like many of his mannerisms, though, there was the whiff of something calculated about it. Martin seemed far too aware of himself and his movements. Greg often got the impression Martin sometimes adjusted his posture in response to a movement Greg himself had made. In their initial meeting, when outlining some of the methods and techniques used in NLP, he had mentioned something about matching, mirroring then leading as a way to subliminally achieve rapport. If this was what he was doing, thought Greg, it wasn't quite subliminal enough, just vaguely unnerving. He wondered where Adrian had found Martin Mangham, and maybe if he wasn't getting a bit desperate. Greg knew Adrian only wanted to help, and Greg wanted to get better too, believe there was a way to fix what was wrong with him. In all honesty, though, he wasn't so sure there was anymore. The closest thing to a real fix had been pharmaceutical. A couple of years ago, after much experimentation, his GP had appeared to find a cocktail of drugs that really worked. For a short spell Greg had almost known what it felt like to operate like a normal person. The intrusive thoughts grew less frequent, lost their power over him, but then his hands and feet had started to feel cold. In another couple of weeks they grew numb and chalky pale. The drugs were screwing with his circulation even while he'd effortlessly opened and closed doors and stepped on sidewalk seams and binned his receipts without more than a glance. Greg had been forced to stop taking the drugs. Several unsuccessful attempts to find an alternative seemed to confirm that medication wasn't going to be the magic bullet it had briefly promised to be. The side effects were always too severe, or the benefits too minor in comparison to the problems they brought. Adrian had been very excited, and the drugs' subsequent failure a huge disappointment. It was at this point Adrian had really begun to instigate his own Let's Fix Greg with Therapy project. Psychotherapy.

41

Hypnotherapy. Cognitive Behavioural Therapy, and now this Neurolinguistic Programming malarkey…

Greg wondered if Adrian recognised the blaring subtext of his Fix Greg project: that his disorder wasn't just hard on Greg, but Adrian too. It always had been, Greg supposed. As children, Adrian had taken pains to prove that although he and Greg were brothers, they were not alike. Adrian was confident, capable, popular…

After their mum had died and things had got complicated, Adrian somehow ended up caught in the middle of that too. Trying to keep the three of them, sons and father and painful empty hole where mum used to be working the same as it had before. Perhaps even with the three of them trying it wouldn't have worked. Greg wondered if Adrian thought fixing him would magically fix that mess too.

Martin was still in full flow.

"The crucial thing to accept is that reality, whatever that is, is unimportant. What is important is what we or others believe. Reality is meaningless. If someone believes drinking tap water causes them to feel more confident they will behave appropriately. Ergo, belief and a glass of H20 equal confidence. The result is all that matters.

"What we *think* or *believe* is happening is what drives our actions. If we *believe* a problem is solvable it may be; if we believe the opposite, that is equally true. We're going to reprogram your subconscious mind to believe *your issues are not only solvable*, but that *solving them is inevitable*. Others function perfectly well without performing these rituals of yours; biologically they are no different to you. We must apply simple logic: if 99.99 per cent of the population can do something that suggests *it is easy.* If they can do it, *you can do it.*"

Greg nodded. This was another thing Martin did. He put emphasis on aspects of his speech. Greg wondered if this was also supposed to be subliminal.

"Ah, well. I see our hour has come to an end. We'll continue where we left off on Wednesday. In the meantime, continue to *resist unwanted behaviours.*"

Greg stood up and followed Martin to the door. Something lay on the mat below the letterbox, a white bubble-pack envelope. Greg saw Martin off then bent and collected it. Once his therapist had gone and the front door was closed to his satisfaction he tore it open and upended it, tipping the contents into his hand.

A small bottle, a miniature shot of spirit. Grant's whisky.

Greg studied the envelope. Plain. No address. A free sample? Were companies even allowed to distribute free samples of alcohol? And with no accompanying literature? And he didn't drink anyway. He dropped the envelope and bottle into the kitchen bin.

Chapter 7

In the room on the library's second floor Dermot O'Shea stood at the head of the class, facing his assembled students, and swept his tornado grey eyes over them. Beth thought immediately of his most famous character Jacob Lumiere about to reveal the identity of a killer in the final pages of a mystery.

Instead, O'Shea said, "Fiction is not life."

O'Shea had a good voice, deep and musical. English father, Irish mum, O'Shea was born in Belfast and moved to England in his early twenties according to his wiki page. His musical growl suited him. He was tall, solidly built, Beth reckoned somewhere in his mid forties, and really rather handsome for an older guy, if a little intense and serious.

O'Shea had paused a moment, seemingly to allow his declaration to breathe a little in the library's study room, to sink in.

One of Beth's fellow students scribbled the four words into the note pad in front of them. Like many of her classmates, Beth recognised him as being a regular patron of the library.

O'Shea continued, "Not only is fiction not life, never should it strive to be. Life is random, shapeless, woefully lacking in definitive beginnings and endings, and full to the brim with coincidence and dumb luck. Fiction must be better than life, in every respect. Fiction is life given shape, bequeathed balance, afforded symmetry, lent boundaries. Fiction offers us a window through which to view the human condition in a way real life rarely does. Fiction is life given meaning."

When O'Shea had walked into the class and introduced himself (with just a cursory mention of his work) Beth wondered if she was the only student to know who he was. If so, she doubted she would be by the following lesson. The rest would surely Google him, and thereby discover the same information about their 'secret' tutor she had days ago, that after a period of success he had not published a novel in over a decade, or appeared to engage with the media to any extent either. This latter aspect, she supposed, was not so unusual. Most media interviews existed to sell something, if only a point of view, but with no forthcoming book to be seen, O'Shea had nothing to promote.

O'Shea continued his theme. "The purpose of a story is to say something. To that end it requires a shape, a structure that takes the reader on a journey. The writer charts the course and the reader follows. The writer should know the ultimate destination, the places he wants the reader to visit along the way, the experiences he wants the reader to have.

"Stories are constructed. You may hear talk of 'discovering' stories, of them writing themselves… I implore you, ignore such nonsense. Writers who say such maybe excellent, geniuses even, but that does not make them any less misguided. The moment any of us is first told a story we begin to absorb the principles of fiction, unconsciously perhaps, but that does not make them any less real. A writer may choose to continue to make use of them that way, unconsciously, they can work that way, but personally I cannot endorse such wilful ignorance. Fiction is far too important to leave to chance, to blindly bumble into creation.

"Over the coming weeks you will each begin to write a novel. You will strive to employ the four pillars of the novel: theme, plot, character and prose. You will seek to craft something that says something about life in a way life itself cannot. If you do it well, you will almost certainly learn something about yourself along the way."

Beth wasn't sure what to make of the author. He certainly wasn't wishy-washy in his views. When it came to the business of writing he clearly had strong ones, and no doubt plenty to teach, even if his impassioned oration did call to mind a minister of the faith. There was an undeniable magnetism in it too, for sure, but then with zealots there so often was. Listen up heathens…

Dermot O'Shea let his eyes rove over each of them in turn, turned, plucked a marker from the desk and wrote in large block letters on the whiteboard with the whip-sharp stokes of a conductor wielding a baton before an orchestra: THEME.

"Right, let's get to work shall we?"

Chapter 8

With a trembling hand, Mrs Gordon lifted the glass and took another gulp.

The man standing at the foot of her bed watched. His face was a quiet threat, as was the weapon in his hand. When she took too long with the next he prompted her.

"All of it."

Shaking, Rose Gordon emptied the glass. It was the fifth such tumbler of whisky, each one had shaven an edge from her fear, but there was still enough left for her to be terrified. He nodded to the bottle. She knew what to do, and obediently refilled the tumbler.

This man had somehow got into her house without her knowing. She had just finished in the bathroom and was heading to her bedroom to turn in when he had appeared from nowhere and clamped a hand over her mouth. A whisper spat in her ear had made it clear if she so much as a squeaked she would regret it. A knife blade had appeared in front of her face to underline the point.

The man commanded her to drink again; Rose was not a stranger to it. She and Ralph had both enjoyed a nightcap, but since his passing the nightcaps seemed to find their way into earlier and earlier hours of the day… Her tolerance for alcohol was not low, but five big glasses, almost two thirds of the bottle now sitting on her bedside table was plenty enough for anyone.

She finally emptied the glass. Instead of instructing her to refill it as she expected the man told her to get up out of bed. She didn't argue, but the weight of the drink suddenly bore down on her.

The room wanted to spin but she got to her feet. The man waved the knife, indicating she was to go out onto the landing, and then toward the stairs. Where were they going now? She started to take the steps down—

Two hands slammed into her back, thrusting her forward and down. She shot forward, hit the steps hard. Her body crashed upon their edges like an old and fragile boat against cruel and jutting rocks, her head thumped off one. Stars exploded in her vision.

Then, like the last firework in a display peeling into darkness, there was nothing.

–

The phone was ringing. It was late in the evening, almost eleven o'clock. Greg climbed out of bed. The day had been a testing one and he had been happy to turn in. He padded into the front room and picked up the handset.

"Hello?"

"Red paint. Paved path. Rusty gate. Four and a half minutes."

The line went dead. He set the handset back in its cradle.

Greg felt an ill feeling wash through him. He thought back to the similarly abrupt and inexplicable phone call he had received the previous week. Was someone pranking him? If so it was an odd one, unsettling. Giggling kids were one thing, a string of weirdly whispered random nonsense was something else.

He returned to bed, tried to settle back down, unease his unwelcome bedfellow.

Chapter 9

Locking up took ten minutes, longer even than usual. The mortise lock was the sticking point. Greg's fingertips tingled from the pressure he had applied to the head of the mortise lock key during the last few minutes. Standing outside his front door, he had locked and unlocked the thing thirty times, rotating the key clockwise until it wouldn't go any further and his fingertips blanched white with the force, but the feeling he sought was elusive. By the time it arrived and he was confident the front door was secure he had missed his intended bus and had to wait for the next.

Greg didn't relish trips into the city. But sadly Pete and the other local shops didn't sell everything he needed. Occasional sorties into the city were unavoidable, and his monthly pilgrimage to collect his comic books was worth the strain, once he got to where he was going.

He always caught the bus comfortably after morning rush hour, which meant he did not contend with more than a handful of fellow commuters. Even in the late morning, though, the city centre was busier than he liked, and being less familiar with the terrain walking on the city pavement quickly grew taxing. There were parts of the city centre he avoided all together. They had renovated the area he used to cut through to reach the bookstore. A nice stretch of plain tarmac had been lifted and some nightmare patchwork of geometric slabs taken its place. They gave him the sweats even to look at, never mind contemplate traversing.

The city was stressful. Greg was aware almost anything could be bought online these days, especially books, but it was something he couldn't do. Computers, smart phones, keypads and keyboards in general caused him to feel panicky and sick with dread. The matrix of digits, grids of numbers, the sprawling plethora of buttons… Patterns were dangerous, because they invited him to layer his own patterns on top. He lived in constant fear his line provider would cease to support his old rotary. He had tried a keypad type more than once, but quickly fell into having to dial from nine to zero before dialling the number he really wanted. Then doing this once wasn't enough, a few attempts quickly spiralled into half a dozen until it became almost impossible to call anyone.

Thankfully, he didn't need anything but his books today, and the bus terminus was only a short walk from the store, even after the detour to avoid the new paving.

Greg loved Comics & Cool, always had. It used to be a huge store when he was a kid, two whole floors of books and stuff, posters, figures, character t-shirts, but the nineties comic boom was ancient history, and now it was half the size. As a kid it had felt vast.

Greg's mum would wait patiently while he wandered the seemingly endless shelves of new issues, US imports, Marvel and DC, Vertigo, all the British stuff, Warrior, 2000AD, even fanzines, before moving upstairs to where the owner kept the long boxes full of back issues in their plastic bags.

If the whole family were there they would often agree to split up and meet again later for a bite to eat. His stepdad Colin and brother Adrian would go look around some sports shops. If it was just his mum and stepdad, though, and Adrian was off somewhere with his mates, Colin would wait with his wife. Not quite tapping his foot, Greg nevertheless felt the clock ticking on his visit in a way he never did when it was just him and his mum. The pleasure of looking at all the new comics was reduced to a race to choose which two or three his pocket money would allow him to buy. He inevitably left fretting he might have made the wrong choice

His stepdad never actually said it out loud, but his whole bearing seemed to voice the opinion comics were stupid. Who needed superheroes when real life gods walked among us, premiership footballers, boxers, test match cricketers and Olympic athletes? These were Adrian and Colin's Spidermen and Batmen. While Greg's heroes fought their battles on New York rooftops and alien worlds, their heroes fought theirs on the football, cricket, and rugby pitches in edited highlights on the evening sports report. It was all score draws and aggregate points, transfers and signings. Greg much preferred his radioactive spiders, grapnel guns and adamantium claws.

There was something undeniably appealing about all those neat comic book panels too. Life laid out in tidy boxes that flowed one to the other. Logical. Ordered. Not messy. Not like real life.

He picked up his current regular reads, Kirkman's Invincible and the new run of Squirrel Girl, and looked over the trades. The books were increasingly expensive these days, thinner too. He couldn't really afford to follow more than a handful of current releases a month. On the other hand, as far as luxuries went, comic books were about as crazy as things got for Greg.

He walked the store, looked for long enough to realise he had actually stopped looking and started tidying, paid for his comic books and made his way back to the bus station. He was back at the foot of Kettle Street just short of an hour later. The tension of the city slipped away. Familiar street, familiar pavement, bag of comics in his hand, he couldn't wait to settle down, get the kettle boiling and read.

He was perhaps a dozen doors from home, nearly ready to cross, when he heard a banging coming from somewhere nearby, down the street. Mrs Gordon's house? He drew close and saw a young woman, a blonde, hammering on the door. She looked ruffled. She bent and opened the letterbox flap, started to yell through it into the house.

Greg paused at Rose Gordon's small, rusty, iron gate and called down the path, "Is there a problem?"

The girl turned. She was very, very pretty.

"I'm worried something might have happened to the lady who lives here," the girl said. "Rose? Do you know her?"

There was something odd about the way the girl spoke, and when she advanced upon him, moving a little unevenly, Greg thought immediately about Mrs Gordon's pull-along shopping trolley, the clink of bottles. He was certain Mrs Gordon liked a drink, or five. Was this girl drunk? Was she some sort of drinking buddy? Seemed unlikely but…

"Erm, yes," Greg mumbled. "I live across the road there. I'm her neighbour."

"I'm worried she might be sick, or…" the girl slurred.

"What makes you think that?"

"She's not answering, but I can see her walking shoes through the letterbox. Unless she has another pair I can't see her leaving the house without them."

"I see." Greg finally twigged, the girl wasn't drunk, she was… well, he wasn't sure, but there was something going on with her, some kind of disability thing. MS, ME? What was that thing Stephen Hawking had? Maybe something like that.

"Take a look," the girl commanded. Greg obeyed. Slipping through the gate, he negotiated the seams of Mrs Gordon's path to where the girl had again crouched to peer through the letterbox. She moved to let Greg take a look. He pushed the flap open again, stared through, and he did catch something now.

A smell carried through, not a pleasant one. It was decay.

Then he spotted something else. At the foot of the staircase, just peeking out, the tip of a few toes.

"I think I see something. There, at the bottom of the stairs?"

The girl swapped places with him.

"Oh no." She shot up. "We have to get in there."

To Greg's surprise the girl took a step back and gave the door a hard kick. Nothing. She tried again. Still nothing. Rose's original 1930's red-painted timber door was solid.

"Together," the girl barked. "Ready, one, two…"

Without thinking Greg readied himself to kick the door.

"Three!"

He and the girl kicked in unison. There was a crack and the door flew open as the lock gave. The whiff of deterioration Greg had smelt though the letterbox wafted over them; the warmth of the day had captured it inside the house. Greg swallowed, nausea spiking his stomach. He didn't want to look like a complete flake in front of the girl. She was already inside the house, advancing to the foot of the stairs. He caught her up.

Mrs Gordon lay crumpled in the corner. There was a mask of ugly purple black bruising on her forehead, the girl was feeling her wrist, but there was no way she was still alive. Her neck was bent up against the wall in a way that made Greg want to wince. He looked at her face, the thin skin, the red and thread-veined drinker's nose, the bruising… Next to her a bottle of Grant's whisky, two thirds empty. A glass tumbler lay on the bottom step.

Chapter 10

"Tragic really," said the police constable. "I imagine the old girl had a few too many, lost her footing on the stairs, and... Well, that's for the coroners' office. Given the circumstances I don't anticipate any issues arising from your forced entry."

Beside her Beth heard the man, Rose's neighbour, stammer, "Eh? Forced entry?" We were just trying—"

"Of course sir, which is why I don't anticipate any issues."

The man didn't look very reassured. "So we're free to go?"

"I'd like to collect your contact details in case we need anything else."

This took a few minutes, and Beth learned the man's name was Greg. By the time the PC was done Greg looked exhausted, and clearly agitated. Beth already had the impression something was up with him. Now she was sure. She followed him to the road.

"Thanks," she said, "for stopping to help."

"No problem," he replied. "I liked Mrs Gordon. She was nice."

"She was. Did you know her well?"

"Not really. We were neighbours, I used to speak to her in passing, but no, I can't say I knew her well."

"Me neither. She used to volunteer at the library where I work, but left soon after I started. I think it got a bit much for her." Before she could stop herself the question slipped out, "What's up with you?"

"Pardon?"

Beth prided herself on her powers of observation. Greg had done a number of things that had, even under the circumstances, struck her as unusual. "Hm. There's something, isn't there?"

"I have OCD. Obsessive compulsive disorder?"

"Right."

"You?"

"CP. Cerebral palsy?" Under different circumstances Beth might even have smiled. They appeared to have stumbled upon a new game, the What's Wrong With You game, where the answers had to be given in acronyms. In a world all too keen to categorise and label such a game show might have legs. OCD, CP, MS, MD, ADD, ADHD, IBS…

"And you work at the library, the one up the road?"

"Hm."

The man cast a glance across the road, like a tired man eyeing his bed. Beth could sympathise. The day had thrown up an unexpectedly upsetting and stressful surprise. "Well, I think I'm going to get going. Bye… Sorry, I didn't catch your name."

"Beth."

"Bye, Beth."

The man, Greg, smiled. It was a nice, open and genuine smile, like Rose Gordon's, and as with Rose Gordon, she felt she recognised the shadow of loneliness in it. Rose Gordon's loneliness had resulted from being elderly, widowed. She wondered how long Rose would have remained crumpled at the foot of her stairs if Beth had not chosen to drop by. Days, perhaps, weeks, months, even? The thought was sad. To reach the end of your days and the world not even notice?

OCD.

She had rubbed shoulders with enough disabled people in the course of her life to know they too often invited isolation, those disabilities of a psychological nature perhaps even more so.

She was half way home when she finally latched onto something that had been niggling at her. She turned around and walked back to Rose's house. She searched out the recycle bin to the side of it and flipped up the lid. Among the jars and tins were a half a dozen empty whisky bottles.

The label on the front of every single one was Bell's.

You really can't beat a drop of Bell's.

Not a bottle of Grant's to be seen.

Chapter 11

They had settled quickly; done that thing people so often do in classes, which was sit in exactly the same seat they had in the first one. People were, Beth observed, creatures of habit. At least they had all returned; the dropout rates in evening classes were high, especially ones with no formal qualification attached. Perhaps the assorted Google searches starting with 'Dermot O'Shea' in the box had brought them back, hoping to find out the reason for the writer's decade away from publishing, or maybe they were, like her, genuinely attracted to the idea of writing a novel.

"Everyone ready?" O'Shea asked.

There was a brief affirmative mumble from the class.

He nodded, picked the marker pen from the lip beneath the library's white board and block printed a new word upon it:

GENRE CONVENTIONS.

"We discussed some of the core principles of story last lesson, about what sorts of stories we enjoy reading, which genres and which you might choose to tackle yourselves. To this point, beyond the fundamental expectations of story, you may want to be aware of some further issues and reader expectations when dealing with genre. I'm talking, of course, about conventions, those elements which serve to help define a genre. Most of the major ones have them, and the reader is apt to be aware of them, consciously or unconsciously.

"Let's take my own chosen genre, the cosy murder mystery as an example. What are some of its conventions? There are many, but let's focus on the strongest of its roots, established by its early masters, Poe, Christie, Sayers... Can someone tell me a common convention of the murder mystery? Anyone?" O'Shea let his sober grey eyes roam. "You, David."

They had learnt quickly that O'Shea was good with names, details. He seemed to have a very sharp memory, had all eight of his small class's names locked down before the end of their first lesson. David, the middle-aged bearded man who had been called out, seemed surprised to be put on the spot.

"Erm... Someone is murdered?"

There were a few chuckles, but O'Shea simply nodded.

"Indeed. Someone is murdered, commonly early in the tale, and in a suitably contained well-defined location, a Manor House, a ship, a train, a village, even a locked room. Anyone else?"

A thin lady who Beth recognised as a frequent visitor to the library's much molested Contemporary Romance shelves offered a tentative suggestion, "The suspects are limited in number?"

"Correct. The suspects will be few, and presented to the reader, directly or obliquely, early enough in the tale to qualify as being 'fair' suspects, a crucial point. The reader will simply not accept a killer who appears, previously unmentioned, late into the tale. Aspects of the killer's character or background may be revealed later, but the killer himself or herself must be presented early enough to be viewed as a valid suspect by both the reader, and the protagonist tasked with solving the case. Next! The classic cosy detective will most often be..?"

Beth dived in, "An amateur sleuth?"

O'Shea fixed her with a pair of storm grey eyes, "Yes. An amateur sleuth, and often an outsider in

59

some respect, present at the discovery of the murder or called in to crack the mystery by someone close to the victim. He will then take charge, because the authorities are either absent or incompetent. The detective will often be eccentric, an interesting character, but essentially static, and not very deep. The story is first and foremost a puzzle to be solved. As such, the clues and suspects must be there for the puzzle to be solved, red herrings may be liberally employed to disguise them, but they must be there. If the reader fails to discern the killer before he or she is revealed by the detective the evidence or clues must, in hindsight, appear obvious. The puzzle must be a fair one.

"Our useless, arrogant or near-sighted authorities will of course instantly seize upon the most likely suspect, accepting the obvious evidence over subtler clues. It is these contradictions or inconsistencies the amateur detective will know point to a different culprit, and the canny reader too will know the most immediate and likely suspect is unlikely to be the perpetrator. During his investigation the detective will assemble and make note of a series of seemingly insignificant details—"

Beth frowned, for some reason she thought again of the bottle of Grant's Whisky beside Rose Gordon's cold and crumpled body, the Bell's bottles in her recycle bin… A crazy idea fluttered through her head momentarily.

"You. Beth?"

Beth frowned, realised O'Shea was talking to her.

"Yes?"

"Sorry, am I losing you?"

O'Shea was eyeing her like a headmaster faced with a deficient student.

"No. Actually I was just considering something you said, about seemingly insignificant details."

"And?"

"Well, I was just thinking how the sort of clue that would be used in fiction would probably mean nothing in real life. In real life inconsistency, randomness isn't all that unusual is it?"

"No, but then fiction is far more exacting than real life. In fiction, especially in a genre like the classic cosy murder mystery, choices, details, events should never be random, cause and effect must be both discernible and logical, if only after certain other information has been revealed. Everything must mean something."

Beth considered the empty Bell's bottles in Rose Gordon's recycle bin again. The most likely explanation for the incongruity in the old lady's choice of brand the day she died was that the local off-licence had simply run out of Bell's, nothing more mysterious or sinister to it than that.

"In fiction, the murder mystery perhaps most of all, even misdirection must be adequately explained. Every red herring must make sense in hindsight," stressed O'Shea. "The puzzle is a game between you and your reader, a battle of wits. How close can you come to revealing your plan without being found out? Can you brazenly dangle the truth right before their face and still not have them see it? Can you commit foul deeds, nefarious schemes and even cold-blooded murder while giving them all the evidence they need to expose your villainy, if only they can piece it all together… Get that right and by God and Jimi Hendrix, they will love you for it."

—

Beth closed up. Since she was taking the class herself, she had volunteered to spare Hailey the unnecessary caretaker duties, and lock up and set the alarm instead. When she was done she found a couple of fellow students lingering outside, talking to O'Shea. They must have caught hold of him before he left. The three were chatting.

From his bearing in class, she wouldn't have taken O'Shea as someone willing to hang around and chat, he looked too serious, too austere, but here he actually seemed happy to engage, relaxed, nodding animatedly to something, laughing and smiling. The contrast to the gravely intense tutor she had just spent the last hour and a half listening to struck her as stark, as different as she could imagine, almost like he was a different person entirely.

That was when O'Shea spotted her watching. She felt his gaze linger.

As she passed the trio she shot them a goodbye, which they bounced back. Again she locked eyes with the author. This time his stare was balder, and she was almost sure she detected the ghost of a smile.

Chapter 12

Greg woke to a feeling of dread. Anxiety sat anvil-like on his chest. He lay, feeling much the same as he would were his bed a makeshift raft on an unfriendly ocean with no land in sight, surrounded by fins which cut through the surface of the water in ever tightening circles.

Mornings were like this sometimes, the agitation, the tension, the pervading sense of impending doom arriving with consciousness, too impatient to wait for any of the usual triggers. Anxiety, it seemed, was tidal. It washed in and out, tied to the indecipherable orbit of some invisible black moon.

He tried to recall if he had dreamed. He often did. Long and tortuous home movies in which his treacherous psyche assembled a greatest hits of his worst triggers, a carnival of cup handles pointing every which way, a world paved in nothing but cracks, telephone keypads with jumbled numbers, roads where he could never quite count down to zero without making a mistake…

It was exhausting.

He struggled to recall a time when dread and anxiety had not been constant companions. He knew the things he did, the compulsions, were his way of easing them, dealing with them, and the rules and ritual worked, to some extent. He also knew that in the long term they only made things worse. The checking, the counting, all of it, they were akin to the salt water the marooned mariner drinks to stave off his thirst, which only serves to make him thirstier still. That was what people like Adrian, and Martin and all the others couldn't appreciate, because they didn't have to feel what he felt. The dread, the knot in his gut and the gnawing in his chest… It crushed him, relentless, so most often he cracked and did whatever he had to do to escape them. He counted and checked and organised, and he felt better, if only for a while.

Greg envied normal people. He saw them going about their lives, unencumbered and carefree. Sure, they probably had their stresses and strains too, not constantly though, and probably usually for a reason they could point too. Money worries. Relationship worries. Health worries. Greg suffered few of these, but still somehow lived with the dread and fear anyway.

He thought of the girl, Beth, again. He recalled the way she had taken charge of the situation at Mrs Gordon's house. She had been amazing.

He stared at the ceiling, wished he could step outside his body, leave all the bad feelings in this one and become someone else.

Downstairs in the kitchen cupboard his cups were squeaky clean and facing the correct direction. Despite this he knew taking them all out and setting them back would make him feel better. He knew just as certainly that this made no logical sense at all.

He swung his legs out of bed.

Chapter 13

Beth was sorting through the reserved pile with Hailey. People often reserved books and promptly forgot they had, or just got fed up of waiting for them and purchased them from a bookshop or Amazon instead. The library system wasn't perfect, but people weren't either. Many failed to return books they had taken out by their due date, and so the date they should consequently become available slipped by days, weeks and even months, which meant they weren't available for others to take out, or the next reservation in line was kept waiting unnecessarily.

The gardening book that had been on top of poor Rose Gordon's romance novel was still yet to be collected. It was being held for a Bernard Brocklehurst. Beth couldn't put a face to the name. Perhaps Mr Brocklehurst was not a library regular. She put the book to one side. They were having a quiet day of it, so Hailey was calling the outstanding reserveds, or at least those who were happy to leave a contact number or email address. Once contacted, they could either come collect the book within a few days, or decide they had changed their minds and leave the library free to set the book in question back on the shelves. Beth was still sorting and manning the desk while Hailey ran down the current list, which meant Beth was close enough to overhear her calls.

"Hello? Mr Brocklehurst?" asked Hailey.

There was a pause, a hitch in Hailey's voice.

"James?" Hailey said slowly, nodded. "No, I'm afraid I was trying to reach Bernard Brocklehurst. No. I'm not a friend as such; I'm calling from

Northcroft Library. We have a book reserved for your father. Would you know if he's still interested in—"

Beth watched Hailey's face change, and her cheeks colour.

"Oh, I see. Please, forgive me. I had no idea," Hailey said. "I'm really very sorry for your loss. I never intended to... Of course. Again, my sincerest condolences. Goodbye Mr Brocklehurst."

Beth stared at her. "What?"

"How awful," said Hailey, sliding the reserved ticket from the book. "It seems our Bernard Brocklehurst passed away a few weeks ago."

For no reason she could really identify, an hour or two later, Beth checked on Bernard Brocklehurst's library record. He lived on Kettle Street. The library had lost two of its patrons in a matter of weeks. Rose lived on Kettle Street too.

Beth placed the gardening book with the others awaiting return to the shelves.

Chapter 14

The killer watched from the right-of-way behind the houses, invisible in the gloomy shadow of an apple tree, binoculars trained on the conservatory. Tacked onto the back of the house, its large windows and light pouring through the glazed roof offered an excellent view of the youth, red-faced, pumping a barbell above his chest. He lay on his back, arms and chest flexing as he completed each repetition. After perhaps half a dozen he settled the barbell on the rack built into the bench. From where the killer was located the top of the man's head faced him. The youth wore his hair cropped short; the neat spiral of his crown glistened with sweat.

He sat up, legs planted each side of the bench, rested his elbows on his knees, breathing hard.

The killer stared at his back. He wasn't too much of a threat, in good shape, but no professional body builder. The killer was confident he would be able to deal with him when the time came. This was the one. The package was sitting on Greg's doormat right now, waiting for his return. After watching him leave for his morning expedition to the local shop, the killer had arranged to have it delivered, always careful not to be the one who actually posted it through the letterbox. Random strangers could be remarkably helpful.

In the conservatory the youth once again rolled onto his back and grasped the bar, lifting it from the brackets and above his chest.

One, two, three, four…

Chapter 15

…Five, four, three, two, one.

Greg waited for a suitable gap. Nothing had passed during the count, but now a string of vehicles seemed to have appeared from nowhere. If a gap didn't come soon he would lose the feeling and have to start counting down from one hundred again before he could cross.

The last of the clump of cars passed and a gap opened up. Greg crossed the road. A woman had been walking on the other side, as she neared he could tell she had been watching him. There was an expression that fell part way between mild concern and curiosity on her face. As she passed him Greg could see she was torn between wanting to take a peek at what he was doing, and not wanting to attract the attention of a potential weirdo. He was used to the reaction. His road-crossing process usually took several minutes, if not longer. It wasn't uncommon for someone to notice him standing at the kerb, clearly intent on crossing but stationary, not a car in sight. He could see them thinking, 'Go on then, cross!'

He knew the things he did often looked odd to others, but he could no more cross the road without counting down from one hundred to zero than blindly stroll across with his eyes closed. The count was not optional. The dread would build the instant he reached the kerb. Counting stopped everything in its tracks, eased the tension, and got him ready.

He had tried to explain to Adrian when they were kids, but he never got it, until one day. They had taken a day trip to Alton Towers theme park. Greg wasn't one for roller coasters, but Adrian and Colin went on every single one. There was one which did a double loop, The Corkscrew. Adrian and Colin had been seated and ready to go when everyone but Adrian's harness had lowered. For an instant Greg saw the look on his face and knew what he was thinking—what if the roller coaster just goes without me being locked in? That didn't happen of course. The ride attendant performed the usual pre-ride check, simply gave the harness a tug; it immediately lowered over Adrian's shoulders and chest, pinning him in place, but for those few seconds before... Later, Greg had told Adrian that was how he felt at the roadside. The counting, waiting for the feeling it was safe, was like waiting for the harness to lower. Adrian had never asked him why he had to do it again.

His nearest supermarket was two miles away, just a couple of stops on the bus. Pete had a lot of stuff, but just as he was sadly without comic books, he also did not stock enough for a proper grocery shop. Every couple of weeks the supermarket was a necessity, and as with his occasional trips into the city, Greg preferred to go mid-morning, after the school kids and rush hour commuters had dried up. He was running late today.

He hadn't had the best of mornings. Getting out of the flat had been a trial, and this was his second trip to the bus stop. He had missed the first bus, having abandoned the bus stop and hurried back home, convinced he had not actually closed the front door properly. The moment he imagined he hadn't closed the door, he knew he would end up going back to check. He tried to resist, but the possibility gnawed at him. The more he thought about it the more likely it seemed. What if the mortise lock hadn't actually turned all the way over, and the Chubb lock catch not quite clicked home? What if the door, which had just looked closed, was now hanging wide?

He had let the bus go, gone back to check. It was locked.

By the time he actually reached the supermarket he was already fraying at the edges.

He didn't enjoy the fortnightly supermarket shop. It was stressful. The store was full of potential triggers. Already anxious, Greg hadn't shopped long before he got snagged by one. Collecting his packet of frozen burgers he found his regular with-a-hint-of-onion ones were mixed in with some new chilli-flavoured ones. Greg had found himself sorting them without even thinking about it. Seeing them all jumbled in the freezer bay that way made him feel uneasy, and sorting the burgers into two halves wouldn't take more than a few seconds.

The job had taken a little longer than a few seconds, though, long enough for a fellow shopper to notice. She reached in past him, took a packet, and practically scurried away. Greg tried to hurry, get it done before one of the supermarket's staff noticed. When he slid the freezer closed on two neatly segregated varieties of burgers he at least felt a little better, but was keen to finish the rest of his shopping and get home.

Even though he wished he could do all his shopping at Pete's shop, he knew going out was important. Which was why he neglected to buy certain things, precisely to give himself a reason to leave the flat every morning. Greg liked people, knew many of his neighbours because he made efforts to chat when he bumped into them. Managing the OCD was easier when he just stayed in the flat, but after a while he seemed to reach a tipping point where he suddenly felt isolated, which lowered his mood, which in turn fed into his anxiety and encouraged the intrusive thoughts, which made his compulsions worse in an effort to regain control. It was a spiral he tried to avoid. That many of his neighbours were aware of his issues to some extent made venturing out locally easier too.

Once the business of filling his trolley was done Greg prepared himself for the ordeal of the checkout. This went better than expected. He only had to conduct one audit of his shopping against the items on his receipt. A quarter of an hour later he was out of the door and heading for the bus stop. The subsequent journey was blessedly uneventful too.

Greg stepped off the bus and watched it pull away. He shuffled the shopping bags so each side was similar in weight and headed home. Turning into Kettle Street he encountered a familiar face striding up the road, Maurice Cooper. Mr Cooper saw him and waved, took a detour to intercept him.

Maurice Cooper was the founder and chairman of the KSRA, the Kettle Street Residents' Association, an acronym that to Greg's mind always conjured the ominous image of some post-Cold War KGB splinter group. To be fair, at times, Mr Cooper's surveillance felt only slightly less oppressive. If something was going on in Kettle Street, Maurice Cooper usually knew about it. Very little appeared to escape his notice.

"Gregory. How are you? I heard the news. You discovered poor Mrs Gordon? Awful shame, and after losing Mr Brocklehurst so recently too. Not to speak ill of the dead, but her fondness for the drink wasn't perhaps the best kept secret in the world…" Maurice shook his head ruefully. "In hindsight one can't help but feel it was an accident waiting to happen. I tried to look in on her occasionally, but... Well, she was quite a private person. She tended to make one feel as if one were poking one's nose in where it didn't belong. "

"She did?"

"I suppose this means new neighbours, always a concern. You never know who you're going to get do you? That big, tattooed chap who's moved in recently, for instance? Have you seen him? Looks questionable to say the least. Might almost be better for old Mrs Gordon and Mr Brocklehurst to be spared the heartache of seeing what might become of the street if his type keep moving in."

Hearing Maurice refer to Rose and Bernard as old struck him as odd. Greg realised he viewed Maurice Cooper as being old himself, but he wasn't, not really. Technically he was late middle-aged, but he dressed like he came from an older generation. Trousers and cardigans were Maurice Cooper staples. Greg suspected he was one of those people who'd seemed old even in his teens. There was something mole-like about him. It was the short build and the thick-framed glasses. Not that he didn't look fit. He was sturdy-framed and a big walker, always out and about, striding from somewhere to somewhere else.

"I went to see that new chap shortly after he moved in, to say hello, you know?" Maurice continued. "Welcome him to the street. Want to know what he said?"

Greg wasn't sure he did, but that didn't deter Maurice.

"Said he didn't like people he didn't know knocking on his door. I tried to explain I was just being neighbourly and he told me to clear off. Called me a nosey—" Maurice censored the exchange. "Well, let's just say he wasn't what I'd call friendly."

Greg thought back to how the man had looked at him in Pete's shop. No. Not friendly. Maurice was nosey, though. He clearly put a lot of time and effort into heading the resident's group, but he was self-appointed. He kept the street's residents informed of things that might impact them, but Greg got the impression this perhaps led him to believe he was entitled to know more about everyone's business than was strictly necessary. Regarding the street's new resident, however, Greg found it hard to disagree with Maurice.

Most people on the street were long standing. Greg was one of the newer ones. A lot of the council-owned properties at the top end of the street had been purchased by their former tenants, who still lived there. The street's denizens weren't completely ignorant of one another. A new arrival didn't go unnoticed. Greg could easily believe his new neighbour might be trouble. It wasn't just the tattoo and hard look of him, his body language alone threw off a distinctly unfriendly vibe. He reckoned Maurice wouldn't be knocking on his door again anytime soon.

Talking of Maurice, he had already moved on to some other local issue; apparently 'they' were talking about widening the junction and adding more traffic lights at the top of Northcroft High Street. Maurice was concerned this might have the effect of deterring traffic from using the main road and encouraging them down the side streets, including rat runs though Kettle Street...

Greg nodded diligently in all the right places before finally managing to escape. By the time he neared his flat his arms felt like they had stretched an inch with the weight of the shopping bags.

He glanced across the street, to his new neighbour's flat. Kettle Street's unsavoury new resident.

To his surprise and mild shock the man was in the window. For a second Greg was sure he was staring straight at him, had been staring at him, watching... But then from his front window how could he not be staring straight at him, there was scarcely anything else he could be looking at. In truth, Greg had wandered into the scene presented from the man's window, and there was hardly anything menacing in that, was there? Still, Greg kept moving, fumbled his keys from his pocket, let himself in and set the shopping bags into his flat's hallway, closing the door behind him, and then again five times more.

Done.

He felt a huge wash of relief, until he noticed the white envelope sitting on the mat.

The sight of it sparked a stab of anxiety. This made the third such package he had received now. On their own the first two had seemed innocuous, odd but nothing sinister, just junk, the contents so random, but a third... He bent and picked it up, turned it over in his hands, feeling the weight and rough shape of the contents. He looked at it. An anonymous white bubble-pack envelope.

Hand-delivered.

He tore it open, tipped the item inside into his hand. At first he thought it was a chocolate bar or some sort, a Mars Bar or Snickers. It was the right size and shape, but then he read the wrapper. The word MuscleBuildPro blazed from the front, with the bicep flexing in the centre of the O in Pro. He read the smaller text below. Nutritious and low in carbohydrates—packed with 24g of quality protein.

He literally had no idea what to make of it.

Who had posted it though his door, and why? Was someone messing with him? It didn't make a lick of sense. Even so, something about just holding the envelope and protein bar made him feel bad. He walked to the kitchen and placed it onto the table, stared at it, trying to discern its meaning. After a few minutes, instead of tossing it into the bin like the previous two, he slipped it into a kitchen drawer.

Chapter 16

With the brisk application of the marker, Dermot O'Shea stabbed four heavy letters onto the whiteboard:

PLOT.

He was dressed casually this week. In place of the trousers and jacket were a pair of jeans and a plaid shirt; the sleeves rolled up his forearms a little. O'Shea's six-foot frame was solid and lean. Was he unmarried, single? Beth saw no wedding ring.

"When writing a work of novel-length fiction one must have a plot," he began without preamble, and with the sort of gravity the captain of a sinking ship might employ to tell passengers that, if forced to abandon ship, they must have a lifebelt.

"While plot isn't, as some readers appear to think, the be-all and end-all to a story, it is a vital component. Plot provides the frame in which you will express your theme, test your characters, reveal something of their complexities... Plot will force your characters to make choices, and the choices they make will show us who they truly are, and during the course of the story how they may change. A plot is best planned, and like any plan it is wise to know your goal. And yet, like any good plan, it's wise to leave room for improvisation along the way too."

One of Beth's fellow students had his hand up.

O'Shea paused. "Yes?"

"But don't lots of writers just make the story up as they go?"

O'Shea pursed his lips, exhaled, "Indeed they do, although unless they are gifted with preternatural foresight, or are prepared to go though many tangled drafts, they are unlikely to be mystery writers.

Granted, some stories rely far less on plot than others, in literary fiction: prose, character and other thematic elements may take precedence… But the cosy mystery is in its finest form a puzzle in which the pieces slot together like oiled lock and key, and that's extremely difficult to create without planning, especially for the novice. You may choose a different genre for your own novels, of course, but whether it be romance, science fiction, comedy, action adventure, erotica, horror, however light a part plot plays, for the purpose of this class I demand you outline your story.

"So, how do we begin to plot? Where exactly do we start?" O'Shea swept his gaze around the room. "Anyone?"

"At the end," said Beth.

"Indeed. We begin at the end. What's the problem? How is it resolved? Or perhaps not resolved? The goal. The plot. The plan. What is it? We need to know because this will be the story's central conflict, and without conflict there is no story. You can have everything else, the richest of settings, complex characters, the most sublime and evocative prose, but without conflict… It's like holding a match, but with nothing to strike it on. Conflict provides the friction."

For the following thirty minutes O'Shea talked about composition. He outlined the three-act structure and recommended they begin with it, straying only if it truly failed to fit their tale. They were to begin by identifying the source of the conflict in their story and the obstacle it presented to their protagonist or protagonists. How attempting to tackle it should only serve to make the problem worse, and worse still until they learnt, though their trials and encounters with other characters the knowledge or lesson they needed in order to resolve the conflict truthfully, that was to say in a way that struck at the heart of what the conflict represented.

Beth was fascinated. She felt like Dorothy pulling back the curtain to find the Wizard, or in truth simply a plain old carnival magician, stranded balloonist, busily pushing buttons, twisting knobs and pulling levers. Listening to O'Shea talk about 'inciting incidents' and 'story beats' she realised some part of her instinctively knew these things existed in the books she read; it should have diminished the magic, but it didn't. It just made the prospect of crafting her novel feel more realistic. Here were principles, guidelines, tools she could understand, utilise, nuts and bolts techniques.

This approach was a far cry from one espoused in a creative writing class she had taken some years back, where the tutor seemed to insinuate the creative process was somehow a mystical and indefinable state, one her students should simply relax and attempt to tap into, like dowsing for water or attempting to see someone's aura… Beth could only imagine what O'Shea would have had to say had he stumbled in.

This sentiment obviously wasn't shared by all. One of her fellow students, a thin-faced young man called Paul, began to harden. Eventually, almost with disdain, he said, "So you're saying writing a story is like following a formula?"

O'Shea regarded him. "When did I once mention a formula?"

"You said structure, rules—"

"And you think these are the same thing?"

"They're not?"

"Not at all. I believe 'story' possesses inherent laws. You can try to break those laws, but only at your own peril. You could, for example, resolve to write a story entirely free of conflict, and you might even manage to fool yourself you've succeeded, but I promise few readers will be fooled. Like a piece of wax fruit that looks the part, mouth-wateringly rich and firm, a bite will expose it as the facsimile it is."

O'Shea looked serious, and far from ready to let the point go. "Rules, laws, principles, do not inevitably lead to formula. Like an architect you can use them to build something as basic and functional as four walls and a roof, or exotic palaces of words with soaring spires and chasm-spanning bridges, or towering hard-edged marvels of steel and glass that scrape the sky... But that first element is crucial: Your creation must be functional. Tens of thousands of words, incident, characters spouting dialogue, these no more make a novel than a stack of timber, brick and glass do a building. How you put them together makes it one. A roof will always work best on top, foundations beneath, windows on the outside. Do you understand?"

Paul nodded. If he disagreed he decided to keep further comment to himself, although Beth wondered if he was also thinking what she was thinking. If O'Shea was really as serious, as passionate as he appeared about the craft of novel writing, why had failed to produce one for the past decade?

At the end of the lesson O'Shea set them their first homework. They were to think of an idea for a story and the following week they would begin writing it. No excuses.

Voyage of Death: A George and Kathy Franklin Mystery
by
Beth Grue

Chapter One

Port of Southampton, 1924

George and I insisted upon overseeing the overseas conveyance of the model. It had been well packaged, but was still delicate. Were it to be dropped or treated with carelessness it could still be easily damaged. Meticulously based on the real building's blueprints, it was the product of many months of intricate design and construction.

When my husband had been a Scotland Yard detective, he had solved many a crime with his famous eye for small details, quite possibly a skill derived from his boyhood hobby of crafting bespoke scale model creations. Upon early retirement, fearing he would become bored with the hum drum of retired life, it had been I who suggested he turn his hobby into a small business.

Its rapid success had taken us both quite by surprise. One might well be astonished to learn how many industries require such pieces: for planning, for impressive props employed to secure capital for construction ventures. In a few short years Franklin Scale Models had grown into a busy full-time enterprise, serving companies all over the country and, as in this present instance, beyond.

The commissioned model we were shepherding was of a brand-new New York City skyscraper, called the American Radiator Building. It was to feature in the tower's opening ceremony, pride of place in the centre of the foyer. One of the men heading the project was a fellow Englishman who had been an early Franklin Scale Models customer. When someone suggested a centrepiece for the opening ceremony, naturally he had known just the man for the job.

If the ocean liner had looked large from the dockside, it struck one as positively immense from the passenger deck. A flurry of activity designed to get the ship ready to depart on schedule lent the area around me the flavour of a bustling city market rather than the beginnings of a luxury cruise.

While George oversaw the crate's passage to the cargo store, I saw to the accompanying paperwork. I signed the consignment note and handed it back to the gentleman in charge of the men labouring to transport it. He asked me a question and I was required to perform that action most familiar to me: Placing my fingers over my lips I executed a small shake of my head. The man looked perplexed for a moment, before understanding dawned.

"Dumb?" he asked, politely enough.

I responded with a curt nod.

"That will be all then, madam. Good day and a pleasant voyage."

I smiled, and offered a second nod, thankful the man was enlightened enough not to confuse dumb with dumb.

Only moments later I spotted George emerging from below deck. He tipped each of the labourers in turn. My husband, the man I loved with both body and soul, was sharp of mind and generous of heart, intelligent, but unlike so many men who found themselves burdened with considerable intellect, he was never less than saintly patient with those less cognitively well-endowed.

He moved to join me, and invited me to the vessel's starboard side. We approached the rail and looked out over a rippling ocean. In eight or nine days we would be in New York City. We would spend three nights in the New World's most impressive city before sailing home to England.

What could possibly go wrong?

Chapter 17

It was just a few days later as Beth walked home from work, that the incongruity of the whisky bottles got the better of her.

She was following her usual route down Foster Street, left at Greenfield Road, and then onto Kettle Street when she passed Rose Gordon's house, and she couldn't help but cast a glance. Locked up and empty. Her mind served up a flash of the old woman's fragile body crumpled at the bottom of the stairs, the empty bottle whose contents had been instrumental to her demise lying beside her...

Beth first slowed, and then stopped. She looked across the street. The guy, Greg, lived in one of the nearby houses. She had heard him say he lived across the street. The thought had been nagging at her on and off; the discrepancy of Grant's when Rose clearly preferred Bell's.

You really can't beat a drop of Bell's.

She paused at Rose's path. Then she turned down it, walked to the recycle bin and lifted the lid. Empty, probably collected days ago. Had there really only been Bell's bottles in it? She felt sure there had. She looked across the street again.

One of the houses across the street. Time for a little trial and error.

—

Greg was staring again at the open envelope and protein bar when the doorbell rang, startling him. He had removed them from their kitchen drawer multiple times, not really sure what he hoped to achieve.

He opened the door to find the blonde girl from the other day standing there, the one who had found Mrs Gordon.

"Greg?" she asked.

Her voice had a loose quality which softened the R's. She was very attractive, which somehow rendered the soft R's strangely sexy, which made him instantly nervous. He didn't cope well with attractive women. A thought popped into his head, from nowhere, with all the delicacy of a SWAT team visiting a dangerous criminal. Had he looked at her breasts? He didn't think so, but in his head the image of him opening the door and staring right at them flashed up in vibrant widescreen in his head. He hadn't, but the image was so convincing it led him to look down at her breasts to reassure himself he hadn't actually done so already. She was wearing a pale blue shirt over a white vest top, the swell of her cleavage disappeared into the scoop. And now he realised he was actually staring at her beasts. His face suddenly began to burn—

"Hi. I'm guessing you remember me?" she said, seemingly having failed to notice the breast-staring or the fact that his face felt ready to melt. "This is going to sound weird, but did anything strike you as strange about Rose Gordon's accident?"

His face was about to burst into flames.

"Erm?" He struggled to get a grip, and scrambling to recover safe ground he looked her in the eyes, as best he could. They were gorgeous, bright hazel and heavily lashed. "Strange?"

"Yeah. Was there anything that seemed out of place, not right? It's just... as far I gathered, Rose used to drink Bell's whisky, and the bottle we found next to her was a Grant's. It seemed odd, so I checked her recycle bin; all the empties in it were Bell's."

Greg suddenly had the image of another white package, tearing it open to find a miniature bottle of whisky. The recollection shunted thoughts of breasts and hazel eyes violently to one side. He met Beth's gaze levelly.

"This is going to sound strange too, but…"

–

Beth stared at the white envelope and the protein bar.

"And the last package contained a miniature of whisky? A few days before Rose's accident?"

Greg nodded.

"And the one before, the first, the insect sting cream, when was that?"

"About a month before?"

"Hm. But you threw them away?"

"I don't drink, or get stung by insects very often either, and I'm not sure I'd use a tube of cream someone just posted through my door out of the blue even if I did, so yeah."

"And the packages both looked like this? Same padded envelope? No address written on them? Nothing? You're sure?"

Greg nodded.

"And do you remember what brand of whisky the miniature was?"

"Grant's, I think."

Beth frowned. There was something more here. It lay just out of reach, a connection… Then a name popped into her head, prompted by two books kept on reserve for two Kettle Street residents who were now dead, one for Rose Gordon and…

"Did you know a Bernard Brocklehurst? He lived on this street. He passed away a month or so ago."

"I did. Not, well, but we'd chat when we bumped into each oth—" Greg stopped, stared at the white package again. "No…"

"What?"

"A tube of sting cream…"

"So?"

"Mr Brocklehurst? He died from an insect sting, anaphylactic shock. He was allergic to wasp and bee stings. You don't think…" Greg let out an uneasy laugh. "It has to be a coincidence, right? Right…?"

—

Beth sipped her coffee. Greg was a tea drinker.

They sat at his kitchen table, the bubble-pack envelope and protein bar before them.

"So, what now?" Greg asked.

Beth wasn't sure. If this guy Greg was telling the truth about the other packages, the whisky miniature, the sting cream, the protein bar, that hinted at some dark goings-on indeed. Did she believe him? Should she? She only had his word that there were other packages, or even that this one had actually been posted through his letterbox by some unknown person. Greg Unsworth clearly had issues. Watching him make coffee was like watching a lab technician handle a flask of Ebola. He certainly had OCD, even if she hadn't been told she might have worked it out by now. Looking around the kitchen told Beth something else: Greg lived alone, and was almost certainly single. The kitchen was clean and tidy, scrupulously so, but there wasn't a feminine touch anywhere, no candles, flowers, it was a Ychromosome-free utilitarian space from top to bottom.

Greg would want things tidy, neat, then, and surely there are fewer things messier than lies. There was something else too; if she only had his word about the other packages, he could say as much about her claim regarding the empty Bell's bottles. Rose's recycling bin had been emptied, and who else knew her chosen tipple had been Bell's? She had mentioned it to Beth, but that hardly made it common knowledge. She had decided to drop in on the old woman precisely because it appeared few other people did.

What now? She wasn't exactly sure.

"How about we say out loud what we're both thinking," she said.

Greg swallowed, his eyes on the white package and protein bar. "Maybe Mr Brocklehurst and Mrs Gordon's deaths weren't accidents?"

"Which would make your packages, what? Clues? Warnings? A threat?"

"Unless it is just a crazy coincidence," Greg said.

Beth heard Dermot O'Shea's Irish accented oration in her head.

Life is random, shapeless, woefully lacking in definitive beginnings and endings, and is full to the brim with coincidence…

"It could be," she said, feeling like she was echoing the famous author.

"And if it isn't?"

"Then someone murdered two of your neighbours, but only after sending you a message they were planning to. Which means," Beth eyed the protein bar, "this may be a message too."

"So we should tell the police?"

"And say what?"

Good question. Beth imagined for a moment walking into a police station with a white envelope and a protein bar, and a story about two dead people, a recycle bin with empty Bell's bottles and two packages that were now on some landfill, with only a guy who clearly had more issues than a magazine collector to back her up.

She could imagine the response, but preferred not to. And maybe they'd have a point? She had been thinking of murder mysteries a lot lately, had murder on the brain perhaps? She had already started the novel for O'Shea's class, having sailed past the outline that wasn't even due yet, and she had found Rose Gordon's dead body, a shock in itself. So this Bernard Brocklehurst lived on Kettle Street too, had died recently too, but nothing about his death suggested anything but bad luck. She took a mental step back.

This Greg claimed to have received two packages with odd items inside, but hadn't kept them. Beth hadn't seen them, and furthermore only had his word they had been posted through his door before Rose and Brocklehurst's deaths.

She did, in fact, believe both these things; she felt she was a good judge of character, but the police tended not to operate on blind trust. They might prove picky about what might or might not be viewed as evidence.

"Look," she said, "I think maybe we might have got a bit carried away here. Life isn't an episode of Murder She Wrote. The stuff posted through your door might well be random junk, Rose probably intended to buy a bottle of Bell's the day she died and the off-licence had run out, or the Grant's was on special. I very much doubt there's actually anything to this."

"And we'd look like crazy people striding into the police station and screaming murder?"

"As a bag of badgers."

—

Greg stood at the door. The girl, Beth, thanked him for the coffee.

She seemed a little embarrassed, keen to go, like she regretted ringing his doorbell in the first place. Greg wasn't sure what to think now. For a moment there it had seemed like they had stumbled onto something, and then like the shape glimpsed in the dark that looks 99 per cent knife wielding Michael Myers, and upon closer inspection reveals itself to be 100 per cent coat hung on back of door, it had evaporated. Logic, rationality and common sense, three things Greg wrestled with on an hourly basis, had prevailed.

Beth turned at the foot of the path, smiled and offered him a parting wave.

He closed the door behind her, and then opened it a little, and closed it again.

And again, and a few more times.

Logic. Rationality. Common sense.

Adding two and two and coming up with five.

Overactive imaginations.

Still, she had told him not to throw the package and protein bar away.

Chapter 18

The class had all dutifully handed in a thin outline for their proposed novels.

O'Shea spent the first half of the lesson reading them aloud, inviting opinions. Everyone was naturally generous and positive, not least because their own ideas and outline were up for debate too.

The outlines comprised an eclectic selection. Beth and another couple of students had plumped for murder mysteries. Beth couldn't speak for the others, but she just liked the genre, and it seemed a waste to have a tutor who specialised in them and not take advantage of his specific expertise. Of the remaining six outlines there were two romances, one of the Catherine Cookson variety, one which sounded much more E.L. James, riding crops, silk blindfolds and handcuffs; a Western; a daft-sounding Dan Brownish, Knights Templar-style action-adventure in which the Grail was really some sort of hi-tech gadget; an Enid Blyton's Famous Five spoof; a sprawling space opera in which several unpronounceable races battled it out for control of a black hole; and a contemporary tale about the strained relationship of a mother and daughter from the eighties to the present day, told first through letters, then emails, then texts—each medium more condensed and cramped than the last, illustrating their increasing estrangement and inability to express their individual grievances.

O'Shea was encouraging of them all, offering ideas, and pointing out limitations, genre clichés, books that had tackled similar themes or structures. Most of the class had walked in with a few hundred words and an idea, as close to a novel as a few lines scratched on a sketch pad was to a wall-sized oil painting, some, like Beth a page or two of prose, but they didn't feel that way anymore. It felt like they had embarked on a journey, their outlines merely the first step on the adventure.

O'Shea asked them what all their story ideas had in common, setting aside heaving bodices, kinky gazzillionaires, sentient armour-clad reptiles, and premeditated untimely deaths.

After a few half correct suggestions, characters, plot, and so on, O'Shea turned, picked up his marker, and jabbed eight block capitals on the white board.

CONFLICT.

"This is what your stories should and will share in common. We covered conflict in relation to structure and plot last lesson, but its place in fiction is so vital, so connected to every other element, it behoves me to labour the point. You see, story is conflict. Internal, external, interpersonal, environmental, imagined, physical, psychological, man versus man, man versus nature, or a value, a belief, his own desires or unfulfilled desire, a deadline, a mystery... Conflict is compelling." O'Shea punctuated each word with a tap on the white board, "It's untidy, uncomfortable, discordant... The desire to see the world, or your character's world, set right is at the thumping heart of storytelling.

"Three among you have chosen to write murder mysteries, where the conflict is, in essence, a dearth of information. Acquiring it is what allows the protagonist to identify the killer and bring them to justice. Will this be easy? No, because the hero will meet further obstacles, not least in the form of misdirection; the protagonist, and of course the reader, must learn to sift good information from bad, weigh one suspect's possible motive against others, all in search of the answer to one question: What drives a person to kill?"

O'Shea's grey eyes stared from under a questioning brow.

"Is it an act of revenge, of jealousy, to keep a secret from being exposed? What do they have to lose, or to gain? Or are they simply crazy? Surely the poorest of motives in fiction? Sadly, in real life, murder without a complex motive is all too common. Sociopaths and psychopaths do exist, but…" O'Shea looked at them, and when it became clear he did not intend to continue Beth supplied the answer she felt sure he was waiting for.

"Fiction is not life?"

O'Shea nodded approvingly. "Exactly. In fiction, a murder mystery without a motive is unlikely to be satisfying. Even Hannibal Lecter killed for more reasons than just to have something to accompany his fava beans and his fine Chianti.

"To offer a satisfying resolution to the conflict, the clues the protagonist unearths and the motive they indicate must make sense and, in the killer's mind, at least, justify the act."

—

The class emptied. Beth was last out of the library, locking up as usual.

Outside, on the library's small car park, she found Dermot O'Shea. He was just pocketing his mobile phone, and spotted her approaching.

"I'm really enjoying your class," she said.

"Good to hear. I wasn't sure what kind of tutor I would make to be honest. You imagine yourself doing something, but you never know what you're capable of until you actually try, do you?"

"I suppose not. Are you enjoying it? Teaching?"

"I am. It's something I've thought a lot about over the years, and when I decided I was finally going to get my hands dirty, here somehow seemed the right place to do it."

"You used to live around here?"

"Yeah, just a few streets over. Kettle Street?"

Kettle Street, thought Beth. She had passed through it on the way to work thousands of times and hardly considered it, now she couldn't seem to escape the place.

"Happy memories?"

"Mostly. The first novel I sold was written in that flat."

"The first Lumiere mystery?"

"Yeah. The first Lumiere mystery, only it was never meant to be a series, not back then. That was my agent's first question; I was still floating on cloud nine from even having got an agent. He made it pretty plain, though. 'When will the next one be ready?' he says. I thought he meant my next novel at first, but he set me right there and then. When would the next Lumiere book be ready? So Lumiere got another murder to solve, and another, and another... I got tired of it, of Lumiere. It wasn't his fault. I just got fed up of having him around. Familiarity breeds contempt."

"So you stopped writing altogether?"

"I never intended to. I suppose I just needed to stop for long enough to remember why I started in the first place."

"You're working on something right now, then?"

"Yep."

"What is it?"

92

"My masterpiece. The greatest murder mystery I'll ever craft!" O'Shea smiled.

"What is it about?"

O'Shea didn't answer. "Can't say."

"A secret?"

"All men have secrets," O'Shea said enigmatically and stared at her with an intensity that for the briefest instant actually made her uneasy.

"Is that Shakespeare?" she asked.

O'Shea smiled, cracked another grin. It was a good smile. He really was quite attractive. In class he was so serious, out of it he seemed like someone else entirely.

"Nah," he said. "Morrissey."

Voyage of Death: A George and Kathy Franklin Mystery
by
Beth Grue

Chapter Seven

I tapped George lightly on the arm. In the deep shadow of the cargo store something had caught my eye and chilled my blood. It was a hand, white as alabaster protruding from the back of a huge chest.

George followed my gaze and saw it too. We hurried over, rounding the chest to meet with a truly horrifying sight, and our second cadaver of the voyage. It was the woman we had seen haranguing Captain Coleridge yesterday at breakfast. She was not so animated now. She lay in a pool of crimson, her dress ripped wide and her belly sliced open. The organs were missing, an empty cavity where they should have been.

George was still, and hadn't said a word. I knew him well enough not to interrupt. His keen mind was assessing the scene, drinking in the details both large and exceedingly small. After a spell, he knelt, careful not to encroach upon the pool of thickening blood beneath the victim's body.

I watched as he reached for the woman's blanched hand. He turned it over, stared for a moment before beckoning me closer.

"Kathy, look."

He pointed, and I saw it. Like the last body we had stumbled upon, a hair, blond as midsummer straw, had been wound around the ring finger. George unspooled perhaps half an inch of it and rolled it between his thumb and forefinger as he had with the last victim. He seemed to contemplate for a moment and then grunted, as though something of note had been extracted from the study.

"Dry…" he said. "I think we should alert the captain, don't you my love?"

I nodded.

Two victims. One with his throat sliced from ear to ear, one with her belly opened and her organs purloined. Both with a blond hair wound around their ring finger. What did it mean?

Chapter 19

Brett shifted the dumbbell to his other hand, set his elbow over his knee and started his final set of curls.

He squeezed the juice out of the whole range, letting the weight drop until his arm was fully extended and then curling until his bicep tightened into a hard knot. By the time the last repetition arrived that knot burned nicely, and the bicep looked thick, swollen with blood. The pump. You couldn't beat the pump.

He returned the dumbbell to the rack and set the barbell ready for bench-press. He slid the plates on and secured them with the locking springs. 40K each side plus the bar made 96K. He could sometimes do three sets of ten reps of this, with someone spotting him; Gaz came over and trained with him at the weekend, but when alone he stuck to five reps for safety's sake.

He paused to check himself out in the French door's glazing. He looked good, lean and pumped. He flexed his arms, shifted sideways on to assess and admire the definition of his muscle.

Kayleigh was going to Ibiza with the girl's group. Brett had her firmly in his sights.

There were ten of them from work going. Five guys, five girls. None of them were couples. Kayleigh's best mate, Jill, wasn't going to win any beauty contests for starters, but she was a laugh. She fancied Gaz, it was pretty obvious, but Brett knew damn well that like him, Gaz had his sights on Kayleigh.

Brett reckoned he had the edge, though. Girls liked Gaz, he had the looks, but Brett was in better shape by far, and he had been laying the ground carefully. Banter, he never missed the chance to swap a bit of banter when he bumped into Kayleigh. She worked in the offices mostly. He worked shop-floor, but Burgess's Fixtures & Lighting wasn't a big firm. Their paths crossed often enough.

She had never seen him with his shirt off, and like a magician whipping off the sheet to reveal some marvel, he quietly imagined this might be the final nudge which pushed him into boyfriend material in her eyes. Showing off his body, lean, tanned (even oiled!) on holiday wouldn't just be possible, but expected. The beach and the pool, the water-park, the club foam parties… And for his part, he was very much looking forward to seeing Kayleigh sun-pink and in a bikini.

Four weeks left to train. No sweets, no chocolate, no simple carbs, no crisps, just lean meat, protein shakes for breakfast, protein bars for snacks. He rolled back onto the bench, grasped the bar and hefted it from the rack.

Shoulders flat, elbows square, perfect form, lowered until it almost kissed his pecs…

Then up, arms straight, deep breath.

Second rep.

Shoulders flat, elbows square, down until it almost kissed his pecs…

The shadow fell over him, giving him a jolt. Who the fuck—

The shadow, cut from the light pouring through the conservatory windows, grasped the bar, threw his weight down onto it. Brett dug deep, called upon his very decent upper body strength to force it back up, lock his arms straight…

But the man had gravity on his side, the bar came down, landed heavily on Brett's chest, winding him, and then bounced onto his throat. The shadow bore down.

Brett felt 96K plus some crazy bastard crushing his windpipe. He couldn't breathe.

He squirmed, tried to roll out from under the bar, but the shadow had him blocked in. His head felt like it was about to pop and his throat was agony, the muscle and cartilage in his throat buckling under the weight of the bar. He fought to slide free, but he was pinned. It wasn't a matter of strength. The shadow could have been half Brett's weight wringing wet, it still wouldn't have mattered. He had leverage, gravity and the advantage of surprise on his side.

The shadow swam above him, bearing down. Brett couldn't get free. If he could just draw one breath…

Brett's brain just had time to bet himself the guy probably couldn't bench 70 before its oxygen-starved cells expired.

–

Greg frowned and picked up the eraser. He gently removed the curve of Spider-man's left thigh. It was too high; he had been going for a classic McFarland look, but overcooked it. There was a fine line; some of McFarland's best stuff hadn't exactly observed the rules of practical human anatomy, but you knew wrong when you saw it, even on old web-head.

He swept a new arc and felt immediately better.

Web-line grasped in one hand, Spidey's right was reaching forward, first and fourth fingers outstretched, middle two curled back, about to press down on the web-shooter trigger. His torso curled, left leg kicked straight at a forty-degree angle, the right folded back in a now pleasing ball. Greg sketched in his foot, pointing down.

More pencil, more detail, some shading... As he went a little Humberto Ramos style crept in. Ramos's work on Slott's Spiderman was Greg's favourite in recent years. Ditko would always be king, the first and best, but Ramos's art was what Greg saw when he thought of Spiderman now.

Greg set his pencils down, rolled his neck. Adrian had offered to buy him a board more times than he could remember, but drawing on the kitchen table was the only thing that worked. A board was more comfortable for sure, but he couldn't lose himself. Drawing on the kitchen table swallowed him up, everything was forgotten for a blessed spell.

The phone began to ring. Greg set down his pencil, went to the lounge and picked up.

"Hello?"

A voice came back brisk, low, whispery, business-like and utterly baffling.

"Four minutes. White PVC. Tarmac. Oil stain."

The line went dead. What was all that about? A wrong number? A prank call? Greg set the phone back down. He returned to the kitchen table and picked up his pencil. He tried a few lines but it was no good. The spell was broken. He collected everything up, methodically returning his pencils to the plastic box that housed his art supplies and slipping the uncompleted sketch into his zip-up portfolio.

Chapter 20

"Remember our previous session?" said Martin, "when we covered the stimulus threat matrix?"

Greg wasn't sure he did. A lot of what Martin said struck him as needlessly complicated. If Martin was anything to go by, most NLP practitioners would rather call a spade a soil displacement facilitator.

"We were discussing phobias, the subconscious taking some experience or stimulus and attributing a disproportionate level of threat or danger to it? I'd like to talk about some of your longer running issues and habits, try to identify a potential trigger for them, some underlying cause."

Greg wondered how much Adrian had told Martin before he hired him a couple of months back. Enough, was his guess.

"You mentioned crossing the road was an issue, having to count down from one hundred to zero, sometimes several times? Can you think of any obvious negative experiences connected to crossing the road?"

Greg felt the familiar unwelcome feeling. Even the thought of standing at the edge of a road prompted it. It began to spread through him. Of course Adrian would already have told Martin how their father died. It was an obvious thing, a trauma easily pointed to. Too easily.

Greg had no memory of the accident; he was, after all, just three years old when it happened. He and his dad had been returning from the playground on the local green. His dad must have been distracted, or in a rush, or just not seen the car coming when he had stepped out to cross the road, because while under the legal speed limit (as the inquest determined) it still hit his father fast enough to kill him on the spot.

Greg, it narrowly missed. He had been holding his dad's hand tightly, just a step behind him. He had instead been catapulted in his dad's wake before the grip broke, thrown far enough for the subsequent landing to break his arm and put him in a plaster cast for weeks, something else he had absolutely no memory of.

It seemed a slam dunk, neurosis-wise, every one of Adrian's conveyor belt of therapists seemed to agree. It didn't seem to matter that, like any honest recollection of his father, Greg remembered nothing about the incident. Could something you didn't even remember really sit in your subconscious like that? Lodged there, messing you up, but invisible? And if not remembering it caused so much trouble, would digging it up and dragging it out into the light make him any better? Greg couldn't imagine it would. He had nightmares enough about trivial activities like orderly cupboards without nightly action replays of a car smashing into his father, of unyielding metal crushing tender flesh and shattering bone…

He felt clammy suddenly, and a little panicky. Just the topic of roads and crossings was usually enough make him feel tense. No, this couldn't possibly be helping.

"Can we maybe focus on one of my other issues today, something smaller?"

Martin looked at him, seemed to think about it, and then think about it some more. Finally, he said, "Of course. How about shutting off the tap, the cooker knobs, or your door closing issue, the towel folding and sorting, maybe, or this behaviour where you arrange the cups in your cupboard so the handles face a specific direction?"

The session lasted an hour. Greg tried to articulate why it was so important that the mug handles all faced the window. He knew it sounded crazy, knew there was no logic to it, as surely as he knew not doing it made him feel anxious to the point of nausea. Arranging them right made him feel better, made the awful tension go away, and setting them right was so easy. He knew the theory. The other therapists had subscribed to it too. If he fought it, weathered the anxiety, it would subside eventually. The compulsion to set the cup handles just so would diminish, maybe even go away completely. But they didn't have to do it. These same therapists probably didn't feel like they were going to die if the cups weren't arranged right.

That was the problem with trying to explain how bad the feelings were, you had to believe the person you were telling had enough empathy to be able to understand, and Greg wasn't sure Martin did. A lot of what Martin said sounded great, about how if one human being could do something practically anyone could too if they modelled their method, or how what people believed was true was more important than what was really true, how the whole notion of reality was not always 'useful'...

Martin seemed to believe people could be perfect if only they tried hard enough, believed hard enough... but then why was the world so full of fuck-ups? Martin always looked so together, groomed, tanned, smartly-dressed and self-possessed; Greg didn't want to be the way he was, but he wasn't sure people were supposed to be perfect either. Wasn't history littered with wonderful fuck-ups? He remembered reading an article about famous people with mental health issues. Winston Churchill suffered from bouts of deep depression,

Isaac Newton too, most people think Van Gogh was a genius, and he cut his own ear off and gave it to a prostitute... Even the best of humanity was messed up. Okay, so he wasn't instrumental in preventing Fascism from conquering Europe, or painting incredible pictures, or formulating a theory of gravity, or even coming up with inventive gifts for sex workers, but he did wonder how much of him was his OCD and how much was separate. As much as he hated it, a tiny part of him feared what would be left if someone took it away.

The session lasted its hour, and Martin began to wrap up. Greg walked him to the front door, already anticipating Martin would take note of how many times it took him to get it closed. He imagined the therapist at the foot of the path, watching him struggle, seeing the door open a crack, and click closed, open and click closed...

"I'm meeting with my mentor this evening, Daryl Carlton," said Martin. "I'd like to discuss your goals with him, would that be okay with you? He's a master practitioner, a remarkable individual, very experienced. He's sure to have some extremely valuable perspectives and strategies to contribute. He's overseeing the final stages of setting up a UK based NLP centre of excellence and development right now. It's very exciting."

"Whatever you feel will help."

As Martin was on his way out, Greg noticed a small commotion a short way down across the road. He accompanied Martin to the end of the path to get a better view. An ambulance was parked outside number 45. A guy called Brett lived there. A few people had gathered; a man was standing outside talking to a police constable. Greg thought he was a friend of Brett's, he had spotted them together before.

Brett was a fitness fanatic. Greg saw him running occasionally. They would chat if Brett's run had ended, if not Greg and he would just exchange a neighbourly wave as Brett flew past, a blur of pumping arms and legs.

Greg was getting a bad feeling.

A moment later Brett's white front door swung wide and two paramedics wheeled a bodybag out, the trolley rumbling over the tarmac drive to the waiting ambulance.

As they pushed it into the rear of the ambulance Greg looked at the muscular-looking shape filling the bodybag.

Then he thought about the protein bar and white envelope in his kitchen drawer.

Chapter 21

Beth stepped out of the staff room and saw Greg at the library's front desk. Pale and practically vibrating with agitation. He was talking to Hailey. Hailey saw Beth coming, shot her a guarded look.

"There's a gentleman here looking for you."

"Hi Greg. What's the matter?"

Greg's eyes flicked to Hailey, then back to Beth.

"It's alright, I'll take the desk."

Hailey nodded, and left them alone.

"There's been another."

"What?"

"My neighbour, Brett. He's dead. The protein bar!"

"You're not making any sense. Slow down. What happened?"

"I just saw them wheeling him into the back of an ambulance in a body bag. Brett, he lives up the road from me—"

"On Kettle Street?"

"Yes. He's keen on fitness, running, lifting weights. His friend was there. I went and spoke to him while the police were busy. He was the one who called them. He said Brett hadn't been to work, wouldn't answer his phone. They found him in his conservatory. He used it as his home gym, kept his weights and stuff in there apparently. He was pinned under a barbell, choked to death by it. That's the message I was sent: the protein bar. See?"

Beth did.

Three was a pattern, and it looked like this.

Bernard Brocklehurst was dead. The apparent cause? A wasp sting.

The contents of the blank white package? Sting cream.

Rose Gordon was dead. The apparent cause? Too much drink and a tumble down the stairs.

The contents of the blank white package? A miniature of whisky.

Now this Brett, a fitness fiend, was dead. The apparent cause of his death? Strangulation by barbell, by the sound of it.

The contents of the blank white package? A protein bar.

Three tragic accidents… The packages, however, suggested a whole different story.

"You believe me, don't you? We have to go to the police. You saw the package."

She had. Which left two explanations. Either Greg was lying and had made them himself, shown them to her, and killed three of his neighbours, or someone really had posted them through his letterbox and then committed the murders.

Even aside from the state he was in, and that he was proposing they alert the authorities…

Greg didn't look like a killer.

–

Beth had got off work early. Hailey agreed to cover for her. She had gone back to Greg's place with him, sat in the kitchen once more, the protein bar and white envelope on the kitchen table. After talking it through, they agreed. They would take the package, the protein bar and their suspicions to the police.

It was a decision Beth was already beginning to question.

Arriving at the local police station, they had asked to speak to a detective. They had information which suggested foul play involving the deaths of three people. The desk sergeant had told them they would be happy to take all the details and deal with them, but Beth had insisted. The desk sergeant had said he would see what he could do.

That was twenty minutes ago. In the interim Greg had gone from fidgeting like a four-year-old who needed to pee, to pacing the police station's reception area. He was now fussing with the seats, apparently intent on making sure they were arranged in perfect alignment, the spacing and orientation identical. In Beth's handbag the envelope and protein bar nestled in the sealed sandwich bag. Never exactly a smoking gun, they now felt more like a bad joke.

The desk sergeant was busy observing Greg, who seemed momentarily absorbed to the point of oblivion. Beth wasn't stupid, Greg's behaviour was obviously a result of his OCD, but she had somewhat underestimated how severe his issues were.

She was almost ready to grab him and tell him they might want to rethink their approach when a side door to the reception area opened and a squat man in a suit wearing a serious expression stuck his head in.

He let his eyes rove over Greg's chair business and then Beth.

"Miss Grue? Mr Unsworth? Detective Inspector Dingle. I believe you wanted to share some information with us?"

—

The sandwich bag with its evidence sat on Detective Dingle's desk.

"And this came when?"

"Monday," Greg repeated.

"And this Mr…" Dingle scratched his chin and checked his notes. He looked like the kind of man who would need to shave twice a morning to escape a 5 o'clock shadow before noon. "Brett Foster, he was found deceased this afternoon?"

"You can check this, surely? His friend got worried when he didn't come into work and wouldn't answer his phone," Beth added.

"His friend told you this, Mr Unsworth?"

"Yes."

"But Mr Foster's death looked like an unfortunate accident. As with the deaths of…" Dingle again referred to his notes, "Mr Brocklehurst and Mrs Gordon?"

"Yes."

"And you say you received similar envelopes containing items days prior to their passing?"

"Yes."

"But you threw them away."

"Yes. I thought they were junk."

"Did anyone else happen to see these envelopes and items?"

"No."

"And you, Mr Unsworth, did not see the empty Bell's bottles in Mrs Gordon's recycling bin? Forgive me, but I'm just trying to establish what we actually have, evidentially speaking."

Beth felt sure Dingle almost smiled. She had been patronised plenty in her time; it wasn't a tune she liked, but she knew the notes when she heard them. Dingle thought he had a couple of nut-jobs on his hands.

"Excuse me?" Greg was pointing to a biro on Dingle's desk. "Would you mind if I moved your pen?"

A look of pure bafflement washed over Dingle's face.

"Pardon?"

Beth could see Greg was almost dying. His face was growing bright red.

"I have OCD, obsessive compulsive disorder... Your pen? I'd really like to move it. I'd feel better if it was parallel to the edge of your desk."

Dingle looked at Beth, then at the pen and then back to Greg.

"Feel free."

Greg reached out and rotated the pen so it ran parallel with the edge of Dingle's desk, made a slight adjustment and set his hands in his lap. His face was still burning. Beth wondered if the clarification, his OCD, had made things better or worse.

"Sorry," Dingle said, "where were we?"

"Evidence," Beth replied.

"Right," said Dingle. "Evidence. I'll be honest, nothing in what you've told me suggests anything beyond mere coincidence. Which isn't to say I don't appreciate you coming forward with the information. I will be making some phone calls, to the coroner's office and such, to enquire about anything suggestive of foul play."

Beth immediately regretted using the phrase. When the desk sergeant had asked what they wanted to report, she had said they "had reason to believe three recent deaths in the same street might not be accidents but the result of foul play". Out of Dingle's mouth the phrase sounded silly, verging on melodramatic.

Dingle continued, "Rest assured, if anything looks suspicious I'll most certainly be in touch."

Greg looked stunned. "That's it? But the packages—"

"Are very likely a random coincidence. Trust me, Mr Unsworth, I've investigated murders. Rarely are they complex or puzzling. Tragic, yes. Brutal, often. Needless and ugly, without doubt, but rarely are they a Byzantine puzzle to be solved. To be sure, there are sometimes attempts at deception, but they're most often crude and hastily cobbled together at best. In movies, books and on television murders are always fascinating and intricately planned. In real life, even when premeditated, they are most often just depressing and violent."

–

"Sorry. I couldn't help it," Greg said. "I'm not good under pressure. I thought I could manage. I should have warned you."

They stood together outside the police station. All in all things hadn't gone spectacularly well. Beth wasn't exactly sure what she had anticipated, but feeling daft and slightly embarrassed wasn't it. And no, although she would never have said it out loud, Greg's strange need to rearrange Detective Dingle's stationery hadn't exactly helped bolster their credibility.

She looked at him, took him in. He wasn't strange to look at. He was quite attractive in fact, big blue eyes, dark chocolate brown hair, unkempt but still kind of pleasing. Tall, just over six foot tall? Nice build, lean, but then the way he was wired he probably burned calories faster than a hummingbird. On the surface his issues were not readily apparent.

What she saw most, though, was that what he had said was true: He couldn't help it.

Like most people, she knew a little about OCD, knew it was an anxiety-related issue, but she hadn't really stopped to consider what wheeling someone with the disorder into a police station to report the suspected murder of three people would go like. The reception had given her a clue, his fussing with the chairs, but by then it was too late. Dingle's office had been too much. She was accustomed to having to overcome initial impressions; the occasional dim person slow to grasp that despite an odd vocal delivery and the occasional unruly limb, she wasn't mentally disabled. In some ways, though, Greg had it harder. While he looked and sounded perfectly ordinary, a little interaction and his issues started to emerge. She had spent time with him on home ground, likely seen him at his best, most at ease and in control. The mistake had been hers.

"It's okay, really. Look, we told them."

"So, what now?" asked Greg.

"We pray our Detective Dingle is right and we're wrong."

Chapter 22

O'Shea handed her back the opening chapters of *Voyage of Death: A George and Kathy Franklin Mystery.*

"I like it." O'Shea smiled. "It has real promise and certainly hits the ground running. Although, maybe a little too quickly?"

Beth felt a tiny pang of disappointment. She had, of course, hoped O'Shea would be blown away. She'd worked hard on the chapters all week.

He must have read something in her expression.

"Relax. You're on the right track, but the change in pace with chapter two is maybe too hard a swing? The discovery of the body at the end of chapter one gives you some great momentum, but then we get chapter two's exposition... well, not quite dump, but there's a lot to take in and you lose a lot of forward motion. I think a little of it might actually work fine peppered into chapter one, and some might benefit from being pushed out into chapter three or later. The part where Kathy has a flashback to her childhood and her father's attitude to her disability, her being mute? It's good, works well, but might work even better once we've got to know her adult self in the present a little more."

Beth thought about this, and immediately saw where some of the stuff he was referring to could be slipped in, with a little editing.

All but one member of the class had arrived with at least the opening scene of their novel. The empty-handed student, Anita, had offered an excuse, something to do with her car breaking down and requiring three separate trips to the garage before the issue was resolved. O'Shea had nodded, but made no

112

comment. Beth got the impression he wasn't best pleased.

O'Shea read excerpts from the rest of their work, insisting he wasn't going to ask for permission. If they were embarrassed to share, they might as well quit now. Once their novels were in the wild, no matter how brilliant, there would be critics. He advised developing a thick skin as soon as possible.

Beth thought most of what he read out was okay. And they were a gentle crowd, all in the same boat; there would be no savage critiques coming from the assembled.

O'Shea offered each pointers on where he thought improvements could be made and opportunities explored, and encouraged the others to suggest what they would focus on and develop if the story was theirs. It was fun, and one or two suggestions for her own story did point out aspects she might never have considered alone. The class wrapped up with a positive vibe, everyone raring to get back to their respective tales. Once the last student was out of the door, Beth began to close up. She armed the alarm and locked the library's big green doors.

When she turned, she found O'Shea still outside, leaning against his car. He looked to be waiting for her. There seemed no other reason for him to be hanging around. She walked up to him. A lazy smile loitered on his face.

"You have cerebral palsy?" he said, before she could respond he added, "I have a cousin back home. He has it bad, not like you. Wheelchair, harness, my aunt and uncle provide full time care. Nice kid, though, big reader."

"Sorry to hear that."

"Yeah, sucks." O'Shea pressed the car-key fob in his hand. The car's central locking obeyed with a little thump. He sighed. "Well, I'm off for a drink. Don't suppose you'd like to join me?"

"To talk writing?"

"If you like," O'Shea said, smiling affably, "but I was thinking more to get nicely drunk, have a few laughs, follow that up with some wild sexual intercourse if the mood takes us?"

Beth laughed. O'Shea didn't appear offended.

"I'm taking a break from men for a while, but thanks anyway... for the offer of intoxication and wild sexual intercourse and whatnot."

It was O'Shea's turn to laugh.

"Perhaps I can just offer you a lift home in lieu then?"

"It's only a short walk."

"Then it'll be an even shorter drive."

O'Shea still wore the affable smile. Beth wasn't sure what to make of him, but was curious to find out.

"Okay. Thanks."

A few minutes later she was directing him to turn right and pull up outside her flat.

"Thanks."

"Ah, think nothing of it. Guess I'll see you next week then. Don't forget: I want an outline up until your inciting incident, however thinly sketched, and a thousand words too please."

"Yes sir. Wouldn't want to get into trouble for not doing my homework." She got out, quite deftly to her relief. No stray lurch or inconvenient wobble to spoil her confident exit.

"Bye."

"Bye Beth."

She swung the car door shut and O'Shea drove away. It was growing dark. His car's tail lights cut through the gloom. Seconds later they swung left at the foot of the road and he was gone.

She fished her house keys from her bag and started down the path to her front door. She'd half expected him to take another shot. Pull the old 'how about a coffee' card. She would have been disappointed if he had.

Maybe even as disappointed as she was that he hadn't.

Chapter 23

Greg spent the rest of the week on tenterhooks, expecting to find another package beneath his letterbox, but as the weekend rolled around without incident, little by little Dingle's sober perspective proved a powerful lure. The detective's calm assurance the whole business was simply a coincidence was comforting. Greg wanted to believe it. It let him off the hook, made the whole business go away.

Adrian had dropped by earlier in the week, persuaded him to go out with him for a meal at the weekend. Greg didn't like eating out. Restaurants, especially good ones, had enough rituals of their own without fitting his in, but felt he owed it to Adrian to make the effort. Adrian booked a table in a nice Italian place in the city. Greg liked Italian. He tried not to view it as a test of how his sessions with Martin were going and just a chance to spend time with his brother. He'd had a good day, and was almost looking forward to the evening as he got ready, only having to iron his shirt twice.

Adrian collected him in a taxi at six and they reached the restaurant bang on time. The maître d' led them to the table, where everything curdled.

Greg spotted Colin first, but Colin was only a second or two behind. Greg actually saw the expression on his stepfather's face sour in recognition, and then scarcely a second later he was out of his seat, pulling his coat on.

Greg just had time to register shock. Colin looked tired. He had aged some since they had last set eyes on one another. Apparently, though, on the inside nothing had changed. Greg was willing to bet that like a conker soaked in vinegar, the intervening years and only made him harder, more unyielding than ever.

"What's he doing here?" Colin hissed.

Adrian held his hands up. "Dad. Please, sit down."

"Is he staying?"

"I was hoping you both would."

Greg didn't even bother waiting for Colin's response. "I'm going," he said. "You two enjoy your meal."

Adrian grabbed his arm. "Stop. Wait, both of you. Can't you just sit down, for a few minutes at least?"

"If he's stays, I'm going." Colin went to put his coat on.

"Don't bother," Greg spat.

The maître d', spying the beginnings of a commotion, appeared like magic at Greg's side and accompanied him as he left. Greg was probably on the street before any of the other diners even noticed there had nearly been a scene.

He set off, shaking, heart hammering in his chest fuelled by exasperation and anger, making a beeline for the bus stop, eyes down, furiously planting his feet between the seams of the paving before him. What the hell had Adrian been thinking? What exactly had he hoped was going to happen? Greg felt the shock of the confrontation still thrumming through him. He wanted to get on a bus and get home, right now, but the unfamiliar paving in the city was slowing him to an awkward stomping pace. To anyone watching he was sure his gait would look odd, that he would look odd, scowling, staring intently at the ground ahead, not quite like a manic person playing hopscotch, but close enough. At the moment, though, he didn't really care. Train. Home. Bollocks to Adrian and his stupid meddling.

He heard the footsteps racing up behind him, knew they were his brother's before they even reached him.

"Stop."

Greg didn't. He didn't even acknowledge Adrian's presence.

"Greg! Please?"

Adrian had suddenly scooted in front of him, blocking his path. Greg tried to dart around him, but Adrian gripped his arms.

"I'm sorry. Okay? I just thought—"

"What Adrian? What did you think?"

"I thought I might take one more shot at reuniting what's left of my family. He's our dad, Greg. The way things are… It's not right."

"He's not my dad, Adrian, and he isn't yours either. He's our stepdad."

Adrian snorted, shook his head. "Oh, come on. Do you even remember him, our dad? I know I don't." He pointed back toward the restaurant. "That man back there is who raised me, and you."

"More you than me. Excuse me, I want to go home."

"We're family, Greg. The three of us. All that's left. This business between you and him, this stupid rift, I refuse to accept there's no way to fix it. I know if only you'd both sit down, talk it out—"

"I don't need him. And he doesn't want me."

"I don't believe that."

"Don't you? Remember the last thing he said to me? 'You're not my son'. Got to say, it doesn't look like he's changed his mind."

"Come back in," Adrian begged, "we'll talk to him. He'll come around."

"I don't need him to. I'm done with him. Fuck, Aid, I feel bad enough most of the time anyway, I'm not looking for anyone to help me feel worse."

"You ever stop to think you might feel better, possibly even get better, if you quit feeling so sorry for yourself?"

Greg was stuck for words. There it was: Adrian's view, a moment of pure, freshly hewn honesty. For a second Greg wanted to say something hurtful back. In the end he settled for honesty too. "You're right. You are his son. I'm going home. Let go of me."

Adrian, who still had hold of his arms, looked about to say something else. Instead he let go, held his hands up, palms out, fingers splayed, like a man surrendering. Greg sidestepped him and headed in the direction of the train station. Hating the way his stilted progress must look. He couldn't even stride away with dignity. Fucking OCD. Fucking pavement seams. Fucking Adrian. Fucking Colin, the miserable, bitter old bastard… Home, he just wanted to get home, shut the door and be surrounded by a corner of the world he could control.

Adrian's voice, a parting shot, followed him there.

"You're wrong. He cares about you, I know he does. Deep down."

Greg almost shouted back.

No, he cares about you.

I'm not sure he ever cared about me.

–

…three, two, one.

Greg tried to cross but it didn't feel right. He worried he had missed a number in the twenties, but had ploughed on regardless. He should have known to just quit right there and then and start over. Now

119

he had just wasted another half a minute. His stomach was a wet knot pulled tight, unpicking it felt impossible, but he wanted to be home, door closed behind him.

He went again. More deliberately this time. Fighting the frustration of just wanting to be done, wanting to cross.

One hundred, ninety-nine, ninety-eight, ninety-seven, ninety-six, ninety-five, ninety-four, ninety-three, ninety-two, ninety-one, ninety, eighty-nine, eighty-eight, eighty-seven, eighty-six, eighty-five, eighty-four, eighty-three, eighty-two, eighty-one, eighty, seventy-nine, seventy-eight, seventy-seven, seventy-six, seventy-five, seventy-four, seventy-three, seventy-two, seventy-one, seventy, sixty-nine, sixty-eight, sixty-seven, sixty-six, sixty-five, sixty-four, sixty-three, sixty-two, sixty-one, sixty, fifty-nine, fifty-eight, fifty-seven, fifty-six, fifty-five, fifty-four, fifty-three, fifty-two, fifty-one, fifty, forty-nine, forty-eight, forty-seven, forty-six, forty-five, forty-four, forty-three, forty-two, forty-one, forty, thirty-nine, thirty-eight, thirty-seven, thirty-six, thirty-five, thirty-four, thirty-three, thirty-two, thirty-one, thirty, twenty-nine, twenty-eight, twenty-seven, twenty-six, twenty-five, twenty-four, twenty-three, twenty-two, twenty-one, twenty, nineteen, eighteen, seventeen, sixteen, fifteen, fourteen, thirteen, twelve, eleven, ten, nine, eight, seven, six, five, four, three, two, one.

Greg waited, it was okay. He was good to go. Now to hurry before doubt crept in. He looked both ways and crossed.

Harassed, emotional and hungry he finally turned into Kettle Street. It was dark and the streetlights had woken. Their light pooled over parked cars, transforming the street into a tunnel of silhouettes with the occasional light from a window.

He kept his head down and hurried, stepping between the paving seams. Home. Not far now. He saw the boots too late and stopped just short of colliding with someone coming in the opposite direction. He looked up and met with the grim and grizzled face of his newest neighbour, the sketchy guy from across the road.

The man stared at him.

"You want to be careful."

Greg looked down and saw the man was holding a peculiar-looking case. It was wooden and appeared handmade. It was stained jet-black and looked well-used, scratched and knocked about, but as solid as the individual carrying it. The man had swung it out behind him, protectively. Greg looked back up, to find the man nakedly studying him. Then he took one languid step aside, held out his hand in an exaggerated fashion, offering Greg ample space to pass by.

Greg mumbled a 'thanks' and got moving, only after a couple of dozen steps he couldn't help stealing a glance back. The man was yet to move on. He was standing where he had stopped, watching Greg leave, a strange sardonic smile on his hard face.

A minute later Greg was finally home. Pushing the door wide, he stepped inside and felt for the light in the hallway, but before he found it his foot fell on something.

He switched the light on and saw the white envelope. Without even thinking he picked it up and tore it open, shaking the contents into his palm.

An old keyring with a Rover motorcar logo stamped into it.

Just looking at it made him feel sick.

Chapter 24

"Please, Greg, you need to calm down. You're almost hyperventilating."

Greg brandished the keyring again. "There's going to be another one. I know it."

Beth looked about the library. It was quiet, just a couple of people, one using the computer and another browsing the compact disc music library. Beth knew she needed to calm Greg down. He had come in looking agitated, but he was starting to get really worked up. Apparently he had been up all night. She didn't doubt it. He certainly looked like he had been, ragged and wild-eyed. She didn't even allow herself to think about the implications of what he was saying yet, what the keyring might mean.

"Hold on. Wait here," she said. "Don't move."

She found Hailey and asked if she could take a short break. Then she returned and herded Greg into the staffroom.

"This came last night?"

"It was waiting on the mat for me when I got home."

"What time?"

"Around nine? I'd been out, into the city with my brother."

"And it was in a white envelope like the others?"

"Yeah. We need to tell Detective Dingle, before something happens, then if someone else winds up dead he'll know, right? It will prove the things in the envelopes are clues, that the deaths aren't accidents."

Beth wasn't so sure. She was fairly sure Dingle had taken them for a pair of weirdoes, and presenting him with nothing more than a story and a keyring probably wouldn't change his mind. But if something did happen, if someone else on Kettle Street was found dead… would that vindicate them? Possibly, but he might just as possibly chalk it up to coincidence, or worse he might believe the death was perhaps a murder, but turn his attention on them.

Beth looked at Greg. He was sitting in front of her, literally wringing his hands. She envied Dingle his ignorance. The empty Bell's whisky bottles in Mrs Gordon's recycling bin flashed into her mind's eye. She wanted nothing more than to believe it was all coincidence, but… There was really no choice at all.

She exhaled, blowing a weary whistle of breath through her lips.

"Okay. This is what we do. We call the station and leave a message for Detective Inspector Dingle. Tell him you got another package. Tell him what we're afraid this might mean: that sometime soon there's going to be another fatal 'accident' in Kettle Street. We leave our contact details, again, and ask him to call us back if he wants to talk. How does that sound?"

Greg thought about it.

"What if he doesn't call back?"

"I don't know. I would have thought he'd have to. Although, I seriously hope we are wrong. The alternative is what? Someone's not only killing your neighbours and staging the deaths to look like accidents, but they're intent upon you knowing they are? Why? Why would they do that? To prove how clever they are? To feel like they're giving someone the chance to stop them?"

"I don't know. But if they want someone to stop them they'd have been better choosing someone else. Some days I struggle just to get out of the house."

Beth frowned.

Maybe, she thought, that was exactly it. What had she just said? To feel like they're giving someone the chance to stop them? To feel like… She'd read her fair share of crime fiction, from the clockwork puzzles of Poe, through Christie and Sayers, to the psychological thrillers that dominated today. She remembered reading Thomas Harris's The Red Dragon and The Silence of the Lambs back when criminal profiling was still novel… Now it was the staple of many crime books, criminal psychology, tales that thrived on exploring the minds of cold-blooded killers.

Displacing responsibility. Was that it? Was the Kettle Street killer seeking to absolve himself of guilt or blame by providing clues to someone so they might stop him? Only by choosing someone ill-equipped to truly stop him, he got to have his cake and eat it? Amateur psychology to be sure, but if someone was really murdering the residents of Kettle Street and feeding Greg clues prior to the killings, he had to be pretty screwed up. Clues.

Sting Cream. Bernard Brocklehurst.

Miniature Whisky. Rose Gordon.

Protein bar. Brett Foster.

A Rover keyring—?

"The keyring?" she said. "What does it mean? Who does it mean?"

Greg looked pale.

"I hadn't even got that far…"

"Think. Does anyone on Kettle Street drive a Rover? Think."

Greg tried to. He wasn't really a car person. He didn't drive himself, and had never even come close to learning to. Cars were just cars to him. He could name types, Ford, Fiat, Volkswagen... But Rover? Did Rover even make cars anymore? Hadn't they folded years ago? "I'm not sure. I can take a look about though, check."

"Okay. Let's call Dingle, and then you go try to see who drives what on Kettle Street."

Greg nodded, seemed to settle a little.

Beth called the station, asked to leave Detective Dingle a message, gave her own and Greg's names and said Dingle would know what it was in relation to. She said Greg had received another package, feared it was a clue, and that another 'accident' might be imminent on Kettle Street.

"There, done," she said, setting down the phone. "Right, you get to work. I want a complete list of house numbers with the car manufacturer of any vehicles belonging to the people who live there. There's a good chance some will be out at work until later this evening, but do what you can. Meet me here at library closing."

Greg nodded again.

—

Mornings, post rush hour, Kettle Street was usually a quiet place, just the occasional vehicle and pedestrian passing through, the rare resident coming or going.

Greg had gone home and fetched a notepad. He was now walking down one side of the street cataloguing cars on drives, and cars outside houses. These were more questionable. People parked on Kettle Street and walked the few minutes to the High Street rather than pay to park in the shopping centre. So far he had found just one Rover parked at

125

the top end of the street outside number 17. He didn't know who lived there. A round trip up the other side of the street, the side Greg's own flat lay on, failed to produce another. Some of the houses on Kettle Street had garages, though. There could be more Rovers hidden from view. It struck Greg how little he actually knew about the majority of his neighbours. He recognised many of their faces, even knew a good number well enough to offer a hello in passing, but the farther their houses got from his, the more vague things got. Did anyone know all the residents of their street that well? He imagined streets were like a Venn diagram, some at number 50 might know neighbours from 40 to 60 quite well, and someone from 60 people from 50 to 70, but unless they made it their business to get to know people from one end of the street to the other…

He stood for a moment, and suddenly thought of one person who did make it his business.

Greg rang the bell fixed to the front of Maurice Cooper's glazed porch and waited. Maurice Cooper appeared a short while after, and opened the door, the original timber variety, painted in an almost brazenly unattractive sage green. He was dressed in his usual sober attire, the trousers and cardigan combo.

He saw Greg and smiled.

"Good morning Greg."

"Hello, Maurice."

"What can I do for you?"

"I don't suppose you can think of anyone who owns a Rover on the street can you?" Greg had his excuse for asking ready. "Only I found this on my way to the shops earlier." He produced the Rover keyring.

Maurice's eyes examined it for a moment, before turning on Greg.

"May I?" Greg handed Maurice the keyring, who looked it over. "This looks old, the logo is an older one they had years back. The two thousands? Nineties, even?"

"So you think it might belong to someone who drives an old Rover car?"

"Can't say anyone springs to mind who does."

"Oh."

"Sorry. Maybe it's just litter. I wouldn't lose any sleep over it."

Greg said goodbye and walked back onto the street. For some reason he glanced back and caught Maurice peeking at him from behind his net curtains. But only for an instant. Maurice must have realised he'd been caught watching because his shadowy face suddenly vanished.

—

"One Rover?" Beth repeated. Greg had returned to the library at closing as instructed, Beth was waiting for him outside.

"And we can't even be sure that belongs to anyone living at number 17."

"Okay," Beth said. "We'll check to see if it's still there."

They walked together back to Kettle Street. When they got to number 17 the Rover was gone. The street was busier than the morning. There was a steady stream of cars, people journeying home from work. One such vehicle shot past them, heading in the opposite direction, far too quickly for a residential road. The speed limit was meant to be thirty miles per hour, but at rush hour some people could be more interested in shaving a few minutes off their commute than observing the law. The car speeding down the road must have been doing fifty at least.

A moment later they heard the screech of tyres on tarmac, and on top of this an awful thump. An engine roared and they heard the squeal of tyres again, this time as a result of someone hastily tearing away.

The whole thing had taken seconds. They turned and made sense of it all at the same time.

A shape lay sprawled in the road. Not a something, a someone.

They weren't the first to reach the man who the car had hit; a small group of people had already emerged from nearby houses. The victim lay motionless in the road, still, a pool of blood spreading out under his head. He let out a small groan.

Among the fast growing crowd, Beth and Greg shared a look, both thinking the same thing.

Chapter 25

"Attempted murder?" Dingle repeated slowly, from behind his desk.

"Check your messages," Beth said. "We left you one this morning, about the clue, the Rover keyring? Nearly eight hours prior to a hit and run on Kettle Street. I bet you anything if you can find the car it's a Rover."

Dingle regarded them with a steady gaze.

"You two wait here. I need to check some of this out."

Beth caught Greg's eye. At last they were being taken seriously. The awful burden of stopping a cold-blooded killer would shift to the authorities where it belonged.

Dingle returned a short while later. To his credit, Greg was pretty contained; he had straightened his own chair repeatedly and Beth's once, but thankfully was sitting when Dingle came in.

"Well, I have good news. All round."

Beth was puzzled.

Dingle sat down before them. "To begin with the victim involved in the hit and run is doing okay. I just finished speaking to the officer with him at the hospital. He has some broken ribs, lacerations, but nothing life-threatening. And, the driver of the car that hit him called to report his involvement forty minutes ago. It appears he panicked and drove away. He soon after called an ambulance and then us. He's in custody as we speak." Dingle paused. "The car was a Ford Focus." In a manner hovering somewhere between avuncular and patronising, he added, "See? No mysterious Rover-driving killer. No grand scheme. No attempted murder. No foul play.

Just a common road traffic accident, some poor judgement, swiftly followed by regret."

Beth wanted to protest, but how could she?

They had been wrong.

It seemed impossible, but the facts were the facts. The driver had turned himself in, and most conclusive of all, he hadn't even been driving a Rover. She looked at Greg and saw the same expression on his face as was likely on her own.

They had been so sure, as close to certain as two people could be. The result? They again looked like a pair of nutters, a couple of crazy fantasists. At a stroke, and at their own hand, their credibility was toast. What could they possibly say now that wouldn't make things worse?

There was only one thing they could do.

"Come on Greg. We don't want to waste any more of Detective Dingle's time.

Chapter 26

They sat back in Greg's kitchen. Greg sipped a mug of tea, Beth a glass of orange squash. It had been a strange day to say the least, eventful in a whole bunch of unwelcome ways, and almost dizzying. They had gone from theory, to certainty, to empty-handed in a matter of hours... Had they just got swept up in the moment? Was that all it was?

"Is it possible Dingle is right?" Beth said. "Are we just chasing shadows?"

"I honestly don't know. I'm not sure I feel sure of anything right now."

"Me either." She recalled Dingle's calm delivery, his steady assurance, delivered almost in the way a tired parent might tell a small child there were no monsters in closets or under beds; there was no Kettle Street Killer, no dark and deadly scheme. He didn't state the next part, he didn't need to; that they should stop dreaming up the whole business and stop wasting his time.

Greg looked at the Rover keyring in the sandwich bag on the table. They hadn't even given it to Dingle in the end. Greg suddenly swept it up and walked to the bin in the corner.

—

Steve wrestled with the locking nut. It wouldn't budge. It was seized, caked in a crust of grime and rust. Not an uncommon occurrence; the car was over thirty years old after all. The old motor had probably seen her last proper service over a decade ago.

He had picked her up on eBay, and what a find, bought off a chap who had inherited his very old and recently deceased uncle's house, savings and other belongings. The car had been in the garage, thick with dust, not driven for years. Perhaps the uncle's eyesight had got too bad to make him safe on the road. It looked the business though, the bodywork showing a few tiny patches of rust, but not a single dent.

The nephew clearly wasn't interested in the Rover so Steve had bought it for a song. Steve was interested, very interested. He loved the Rover SD1 like Bogart loved smokes, as his dad was fond of saying. A little time, dedication and elbow grease and the SD1 would be like new when Steve was finished with it.

This would be Steve's sixth SD1. The first he had purchased as a teenager, his first set of wheels. There was something magical about the first car you owned. His lifelong love affair with the Rover SD1 had survived long after all his other teenage passions had faded, bands that used to make him want to dance and sing along, old girlfriends who made him hot and stupid, Crombie hats and stay-press trousers.

In the summer of 1984, after two years of working at his dad's garage through holidays and weekends to earn the money (although his dad had cracked and chipped in to make up the full amount in the end), he had registered his first motor with the DVLA, a two-year-old (one careful owner) silver grey Rover SD1.

Weekend trips all around the country with his mates had followed, tunes blasting from the Blaupunkt car stereo (speakers front and back), equaliser lights on the stereo's face plate rhythmically jumping from green to red… Happy days. Maybe the happiest of days.

His dad would have loved this, restoring the car to its former glory. Had his old man's passion for motors infected him, or was it just there, buried in his DNA? Either way it was a bond they shared until his dad's final days. When he finally met his end there was a stack of car magazines a foot high beside his hospital bed.

Steve had spent most of the last fortnight under the car. There was a lot to do: while the bodywork was mostly fine, the car was still over thirty years old, the last bunch of those years sitting still. That created a lot of work.

The track rod ends were seized, the fuel lines corroded, the bushes shot, the exhaust… Well, actually the exhaust wasn't too bad, but it would be replaced anyway. Secretly, Steve was in heaven, even if he was presently cursing.

He had given the rod ends a second shot with penetrating oil, but the bolts didn't want to budge. It was looking like he was going to have to resort to heating them.

A noise at the end of the garage caught his attention. It had sounded like the side door opening; Marg must be returning early from her Pilates class.

"Marg? That you sweetie?"

He paused, listened.

Nothing.

He gave a mental shrug and returned his focus to the seized rod end. If he could just—

There was a loud clang and the SD1 suddenly shifted. His eyes darted to the jack. It was leaning. He scrambled to get clear of the car.

He first saw a pair of boots, and then a lump hammer striking the foot of the jack for what he now realised was a second time.

The jack shot free.

With the tyres removed for easier access and nothing to hold it up, Steve experienced the full weight of the SD1 crashing down on him, the sill landing across his chest. His ribs cracked and the air was driven from his lungs. He tried to draw breath, but over a ton of classic vehicle, quite literally, weighed against him doing so.

Denied the breath to even scream he died several minutes later, hands grimed with grease and oil, heart still as a seized engine

–

Beth watched as Greg dropped the keyring into the belly of the swing-top bin. She had been on the verge of telling him to stop, and then thought, why?

The lid snapped shut with a small finality that actually prompted a stab of relief. It was over.

In Greg's front room the phone began to ring.

"Sorry. Give me a second. Probably my brother."

He went to answer it. From the kitchen Beth heard him say, "Who is this? Hello?" There was something in the quality of his voice that made her leave her seat.

By the time she reached the lounge doorway he was setting the phone back in its cradle. It was an old rotary style one where you put your finger in a hole in a disk on the face and dragged it to the start to dial the number. She didn't think she had seen one for years, since her childhood. Greg was staring at it strangely. He looked over to her frowning.

Beth wasn't sure if he was speaking to her or himself when he said, "Four minutes. Royal blue.

Blocked. Black alarm box. What kind of crank call is that? That's the fourth one in the last couple of months."

Then he must have caught the look on her face. "What?"

Chapter 27

"Slowly," Beth said. "It's important. You're sure that's the fourth?"

Greg was looking at her. He appeared to see she was thinking something, but he hadn't caught up. She hoped she was wrong, she really did.

"Including that one? Yes."

Her eyes flicked to the kitchen clock. She really hoped she had got it wrong.

"You're sure?"

"I'm sure."

"And the dates? Think back, would each of them happen to have come before one of Kettle Street's 'accidents?'"

She saw the penny drop. Now he understood. She saw the colour drain from his face and his mind begin to race.

"Oh, no..." He swallowed. "Yeah, I had one the night before we found Rose Gordon, and the morning Brett was found, I'm almost certain. Was the first before Bernard Brocklehurst was discovered dead in his garden? I think it might have been. You really think—"

"And the times, the amount of minutes and seconds the caller stated, they were different?"

"Yeah. I don't remember exactly, but I think so. The first time he said six minutes, I think, another four and half... and a bunch of random stuff."

"Like what?"

"This time? Royal blue. Blocked. Black alarm box."

"I'm getting a bad feeling, Greg."

He nodded. "If the things in the packages are clues to the next victim, the phone calls are what?"

"More clues? Letting you know long you have to stop him?"

"Or catch him?"

Four minutes. They both looked at the clock now; at least two had already passed.

"Come on."

Beth hurried outside. Greg followed but got caught up fussing with the front door. She guessed the issue, and grabbed his hand. She gave the door a firm push and said, "It's shut. It really is. Okay?"

He nodded, and she pulled him onto the street.

"Royal blue. Blocked. Black alarm box. It has to describe one of the houses. You check that side. I'll do this side. Quickly."

She scanned the houses and flats. Feeling the clock ticking, she heard Greg's shout. He was pointing to a house across the road, number 27. It had a double block paved drive, a royal blue painted door behind a porch and what Beth was fairly sure was a black dummy alarm box on the wall beside one of the upper windows. She sprinted across the road and pressed the doorbell.

No answer.

She tried again, snapping the letterbox flap as well, just in case the bell didn't work.

Still nothing.

She continued to try, to no greater result.

Eventually Greg appeared beside her. "Anything?"

"No."

"There are no other houses that fit? Royal blue, block-paved, with a black alarm box?"

"I don't think so. Let me go check again. You keep trying here."

She walked the length of Kettle Street scanning the properties. There were other block-paved drives, other blue doors, other alarm boxes, two of them black, but not all on the same house. She rejoined Greg, still periodically trying number 27's bell and knocking on the door. He saw her coming and she shook her head. This was the house.

Four minutes was long gone, and it seemed no one was about to answer the door to number 27 Kettle Street.

"What now?" Greg asked.

"We wait?"

–

The confirmation came two hours later. A police car and ambulance arrived outside number 27. A short while before this, from Greg's bedroom window that faced the street, he and Beth had watched a woman pull up onto the drive and get out, dressed in powder pink gym gear. She had entered the house and run outside not long after, hysterical and hammering on the next door neighbour's door.

Together with the neighbour she had gone back inside. It was shortly after this the ambulance and cop car arrived.

Greg had seen the pink woman around, with her husband: a middle-aged couple with a daughter in her twenties, who seemed to have moved out a year or so ago. The woman in the pink gym gear was called Maggie, or Margery, or maybe Margaret? Greg was fairly sure her husband was called Steve. He was even more sure Steve was dead.

From his window, he and Beth watched as the front door opened and a pair of paramedics entered with two police officers. The pink woman, Steve's wife, was at the door. She looked in deep shock. Another woman was with her now. She had arrived just prior to the paramedics and the police. The neighbour looked relieved to be dismissed. The new woman looked like an older heavier version of the newly widowed woman. Greg's guess was they were sisters. A small crowd had gathered outside, neighbours come to see what had happened. At Beth's suggestion, they ventured out to join the group.

Maurice was there, gently interrogating those among the assembled for details. Greg and Beth stood close enough to overhear as he quizzed the dazed next door neighbour. Steve had been restoring an old car he'd picked up. He was working under it when the jack either slipped or failed. The neighbour, still obviously in shock, excused herself, no doubt disappointing Maurice who looked ready to pump her for more details.

As she passed by Greg couldn't help himself.

"Excuse me, but the car? It was an old Rover?"

The neighbour frowned, but nodded.

Beth gave his arm a sharp tug; it was time to leave.

As they left the small crowd Greg glanced up the street, and something snagged his eye. Standing at the end of his path, watching those gathered outside number 27 at a distance, was Kettle Street's newest resident, the man with the web and spider tattoo on his thick neck. For an instant, before Greg hastily averted his gaze, he could have sworn the man was staring not at the crowd, but at him.

Chapter 28

Greg slept poorly; his mind had been on a fast spin cycle of facts, fears and supposition. When fatigue had overwhelmed him in the small hours he finally slept, and his dreams had picked up the baton and run with it, all ringing phones, speeding cars and corpses, nothing coherent, just his poor brain's attempt to deal with the previous day's insanity.

Beth was coming over after work. The plan was to get their heads together. If they were going to contact the police again they both knew it was going to take more than news of a few crank calls and the sincere assurance that, 'No, honestly, this time it really, really was a murder!' to get anywhere.

They needed to chart the facts, the dates, the evidence…Go through all of it and make sure they hadn't missed something, and Greg wanted to check a few things out too. The more he thought about it the more one thing seemed to stick out: the date his new neighbour had moved in across the road, and the date they suspected the killer had claimed his first victim, Bernard Brocklehurst. If pressed, Greg would estimate the former and latter lay no more than a month apart.

He wanted to see if he couldn't find out a little more about his new neighbour, and where Kettle Street intelligence was concerned two immediate sources presented themselves.

—

Greg slipped into the shop accompanied by the familiar ding of the bell on the door. Pete spotted him entering.

"Hello Gregory, my friend!"

"Hi Pete."

Greg went through his usual business, unhurriedly collected a litre carton of milk, a packet of chocolate digestives. He was all good for teabags. He wanted to keep things regular and relaxed. He wanted to quiz Pete about the gorilla with the spider tattoo, but wanted it to come across as idle curiosity rather than an interrogation. He walked around a bit longer, just to underline he was in no particular rush, and then he took the milk and biscuits to the till.

He and Pete exchanged the usual pleasantries while Pete scanned the items and put them into a plastic bag. Greg thanked him, but as he handed him the money to pay he casually asked, "Do you remember that man who was in here a few weeks ago, Pete? He moved onto my street a few months ago, stocky build, tattoo of a web and a spider on his neck? It was the morning you told me about Mr Brocklehurst's… passing."

"Dennis Crompton."

Greg was surprised. "That's his name? How do you know?"

Pete smiled. "I hold a copy of The Racing Post for him, so I write it on the top of the cover every morning."

"What do you think of him?"

Pete shrugged. "He just comes in and collects his paper. Not a chatty fellow, but he's not given me any trouble." A shade of concern suddenly crept onto Pete's face. "Is he bothering you, Gregory? Causing you trouble?"

Greg thought, but didn't say, Aside from possibly killing my neighbours?

"No. no… He just… I bumped into him a few nights ago walking home, or nearly did. He told me I should be more careful."

"Like a threat?"

"I don't think so."

"But you felt intimidated?"

"He looks like someone I wouldn't want to upset."

Pete nodded. "If he does threaten you, you must call the police. You can't let people get away with that sort of behaviour. Never."

"Do you remember when he moved in around here? When he first started to come in for his Racing Post?"

Pete mulled it over.

"A couple of months ago?"

Greg paid for his biscuits, carefully checked his change, carefully checked it again, accepted Pete's offer to double check the receipt, and set off for the next stop on his intelligence-gathering mission.

–

The sage green door behind Maurice Cooper's glazed porch opened and Maurice Cooper appeared in the gap. He had eschewed a cardigan today, instead opting for a knitted vest, shirt and tie combo. There was a small notice tucked in the corner of the porch window that read, 'No Salesmen Thank You'. Cooper didn't appear to mind Greg's intrusion though. He seemed quite ebullient.

"Greg? Two visits in as many days? Something of an eventful day on the street yesterday, a hit and run and then the terrible business with Steve Holt down the road. Awful. His poor wife finding him like that? You know that makes four deaths in the last two months?"

"Does it?" Greg should have guessed Maurice would be the last person not to have noted this. When it came to Kettle Street there didn't seem to be much he missed.

"I believe Mrs Holt has gone to stay with her sister. I'll put something in the forthcoming newsletter, remind people to keep an eye on each other's properties? I don't actually hold neighbourhood watch meetings anymore, the turnout used to be too patchy, but vigilance really is the best deterrent to the opportunist thief. I'd hate the thought of Mrs Holt returning to a break-in, given what she's already going through. There are always unsavoury types on the prowl, looking for vulnerable properties. I attended a talk given by a local crime prevention officer recently. He said it was common practice for gangs of burglars to travel around scouting out streets, targets to hit in quick succession over a few days—"

"Talking of unsavoury types… There's something I wanted to ask you. Do you know anything about that guy who moved into number 41 a couple of months ago? The one you tried to welcome to the street? Dennis Crompton?"

"So that's his name is it? Dennis Crompton?"

Maurice leant out his front door and looked down the street toward Crompton's ground floor flat.

"Do I know anything about him? Can't say I do, apart from he's rude, abusive and far from neighbourly. And there's that odd-looking case he carries around."

Greg perked up. "What case?"

"This boxy wooden thing. I've seen him pass by here, carrying it, in the evenings. Heaven knows what he keeps in it, or where he's off to. He doesn't seem to have many friends, just a young chap who visits him on Wednesday afternoons, and if they're friends they make an odd pair. Looks to me like someone checking up on him more than paying a friendly visit."

This was what Greg was hoping for. For someone who didn't know much about Crompton, Maurice seemed to have gathered plenty from his routine curtain twitching. Greg got the feeling that Maurice had started the resident's association to keep him busy after he had retired. He wondered if it had become close to a full-time job in itself, and the street's inhabitants were under Maurice's benevolent surveillance more often than they knew.

"Who would be checking up on him?"

Maurice seemed to hold the answer back for a moment, like a juicy treat he would prefer Greg beg a little longer for. "Well, I'm only guessing, but it's not the district nurse so…"

"So…"

"Given the look of the chap…"

"Yes…?"

"I wouldn't be surprised if he were his probation officer, that people who've recently been let out of prison have?"

Greg felt a chill run through him.

"And this man visits every Wednesday afternoon?"

Juicy suppositional morsel dispensed, Maurice seemed to lose interest. He simply nodded.

Today was Wednesday.

"Do you remember around what time in the afternoon?"

144

"Around two thirty?"

"Thanks Maurice." Greg went to leave.

"Not going to tell me what this is all about then?"

The tone was jokey, but the curiosity, thought Greg, was very real. Glad to have come away with something, he hoped he hadn't piqued Maurice's interest too much in the process.

"Just wondered what kind of person had moved in over the road from me. Thought it might be wise to try and find out."

—

Greg was set. He had made a thermos full of tea (good for three mugs) and was sitting in his bedroom, on one of the chairs from the kitchen. He had the radio on to help kill the time and his eyes directed though his window at Crompton's flat. Two thirty came and went, but then just before three a car drew to a stop in front of Crompton's flat. Greg watched a lean man in a shirt and tie under an anorak emerge and walk down Crompton's path. He knocked, the front door opened and he entered.

Greg was out a few minutes later. His front door slowed him down, the mortise lock refusing to feel right. He had to stop and wait, relax before a fifth run at it got the job done. Fortunately, his count to cross the road only took three attempts.

He strolled as casually as he could manage down Crompton's side of the street. When he reached Crompton's visitor's car he ducked behind it and peeked through the passenger side window. It was a mess. The man was a slob. A bunch of empty Red Bull cans and chocolate bar wrappers littered the seat and foot well. Pay and display parking tickets, and a couple of magazines joined the detritus, and

145

then Greg saw it. It was tucked into the open shelf above the glove box, a laminate pass on a lanyard. Greg could see enough of the legend: -OBATION SERVICE.

Maurice was right. Crompton was an ex-con.

The question was, what crime had he served time for?

Chapter 29

Beth dropped by as soon as she left work. What she found was a very excited Greg. After her shoes had been removed and set neatly on the mat near the front door, perpendicular to the wall, Greg led her through to the front room and told her what he had discovered.

She was impressed by his initiative, and his detective work. A prison record was hardly a smoking gun though.

"Just because he served time in prison doesn't mean it's him. For all we know he might have been convicted for theft, or fraud, or not paying his TV licence…"

"Wait until you see him. Over six foot tall, India ink neck tattoo, shaved head, arms thicker than my thighs…"

"His name's Dennis Crompton?"

Beth took out her phone. She opened the browser and tapped 'Dennis Crompton convicted UK' in the search bar. A few seconds later a bunch of hits appeared.

She scrolled down.

"I thought the first thing you'd have done is hit Google."

"I don't have a computer, or mobile phone. I have issues with keyboards. Patterns."

"Right…" Beth tapped the screen of her phone, and swallowed, looked up at Greg, "Bloody hell. Here. BBC news online, 2002."

Greg moved to look over her shoulder, scanned the story.

Youth Jailed After Being Found Guilty of Murdering Two Neighbours

Dennis Crompton, aged 17, was convicted yesterday of beating a neighbouring couple to death with a hammer at their home in the West Midlands last July.

The bodies of Geoffrey Jacobson, 47, and his wife Jackie Jacobson, 36, were discovered after another neighbour saw Crompton flee their house via the back garden. The youth was described as being covered in blood and still holding the murder weapon.

The court was told Mrs Jacobson had befriended the teenager, and employed him to carry out casual gardening work.

Crompton pleaded guilty to two counts of murder in the face of overwhelming evidence, and Mr Justice Kenneth Westgate sentenced him to detention for life.

The Jacobsons' family were in the public gallery with friends and other relatives as the verdicts came in.

Westgate described the murders as "frenzied", and Det Supt Steven Keely, who led the investigation, called the attack one of the most brutal murders he had ever dealt with, adding that, "Unless Dennis Crompton chooses to tell us, we may never know for certain why he committed this horrendous crime."

They read slowly though the story. Beth paged back and tried to find other reports. Coverage of the murders was sparse. Local papers of the time would have carried the story, and probably in greater detail, but their archives weren't online. Fortunately Beth knew where those archived papers could be found. She checked her watch.

Greg must have caught the look on her face.

"What?"

She got up from the kitchen table. "You up for a little more detective work?"

—

The big library in the city centre remained open until 8.30 p.m. mid week. Beth and Greg were there by 6:30. Beth had anticipated it would be quiet, meaning they wouldn't be required to pre-book use of the microfiche readers as they would during the day. Northcroft Library had nothing like this. If someone wanted a novel or such, or to use one of its three computers to access the internet, she was covered, but the city library was something else: a cathedral to Northcroft's quaint parish church.

They had taken the train. Greg hadn't been on one for years, and found he actually preferred it to the bus. It was cleaner, made fewer stops, and the longer walk to the station had been more than offset by the speedier journey.

The library was situated to the north of the city centre, about ten minutes from the central station. Greg liked walking with Beth, there was something liberating about being with someone who walked in an unorthodox fashion too.

The area around the library was pedestrianised, had been redeveloped a couple of decades back and expanded. A theatre lay to the left, with a conference centre and concert hall opposite.

The library was the newest of the buildings; a huge modern edifice that resembled a three-tiered, box-shaped wedding cake. It was only a few years old and still divided opinion. Built to replace the old library, a huge concrete thing which people had actually tried to save from demolition because it was a notable example of brutalist architecture, some thought the new library was brave and contemporary, quirky and fun, others an awkward and ridiculous eyesore. Personally, Greg liked it.

As they reached the plaza where the library stood, Beth suddenly slowed. "Oh, are you going to be okay?"

Greg didn't understand.

"The block paving, are you okay to cross it?"

Greg realised what she meant. The area around the new library was block paved in an expanse of tight herringbone brick. He was about to explain the difference, how the seams between these were different, they weren't like the ones between paving stones, because… Here he began to struggle. They were different because, well, they just were. The thought of stepping on them didn't spark the same dread, the bad feelings. Like many of the things which caused him to feel anxious, logic wasn't a great deal of help. It was like Martin had said about spiders. Tons of people were freaked out by them, the thought of being near one, touching one, enough to make them not just uneasy but genuinely fearful, but why? Britain wasn't Australia. The infamous red-back might offer you an agonising ticket to and through the pearly gates, but in Britain the worst thing most spiders could do was leave a web in the corner of your ceiling. Logic and reason had nothing to do with it, so in the same way many would happily let an ant or beetle crawl over their hand but would freak out if an arachnid did the same, he found the seams between block paving no problem, and the ones between paving slabs a major one.

That was just the way it was. He considered trying to explain about spiders and whatnot, but instead said "I'm fine. It's not the same."

He wondered if she would quiz him, but she just shrugged.

"Great. Come on then."

—

The trip was Greg's first time inside the new library, and while the exterior divided opinion, the inside was unlikely to. It was spectacular, sprawling, towering, open and modern, with seamless sweeping pathways. No cracks or obvious divisions, no steps to count, someone couldn't have designed a more welcoming route to the fourth floor where the library's archives room lay. The room, nearly half the size of Northcroft library alone, housed a huge repository of archived local newspapers on microfiche going back over thirty years, journals, and reference only texts.

They took the escalators, ascended through the floors, up through the barrel-like architecture and curving shelves full of books, and entered through a set of glass doors. Beth took charge. She spoke briefly to the girl manning the desk. She allocated them a station, and Beth led Greg to a computer by the window. She used her library card to log in.

"Right," she said, "we have the date, so let's go look."

Greg followed her to several rows of glossy white cabinets labelled with dates and the names of local papers. They started with The Mail. Beth found the relevant drawer and pulled it out on its runners.

Inside were line after line of black boxes with blue and white stickers on top bearing dates. There was a box for each month of a particular year. Beth ran her finger along them until she reached the one she wanted and plucked it out. Greg marvelled, it was all so neat, so organised.

She repeated the process for the month Crompton was sentenced, and then, moving to the cabinets holding archives of the other local papers, went through it all again, before returning to the computer and its attached microfiche reader. Beth slid the reader's tray out, removed the roll of microfiche from the black box and fixed it onto the prong, fed the first length through the runners, and slotted the tray back into place. A window opened on the computer monitor with a mess of frozen white noise.

She took a deep breath, and said, "Here we go."

Beth clicked one of a series of icons in the corner of the screen and the white noise whizzed past, replaced with page one of a decade old copy of The Mail.

And there it was, the front page story reporting on the Crompton murders. Greg leaned in, and shoulder to shoulder with Beth began to read.

COUPLE HAMMERED TO DEATH

Police were called yesterday to the scene of a brutal murder in Calder Avenue in Hoseley, in which a married couple were viciously beaten to death in their home with a claw hammer.

A neighbouring man alerted police, after witnessing a suspect fleeing the rear of the home, and a local youth has been arrested in connection with the murder. Enquires into the circumstances surrounding the incident are ongoing.

Police have appealed for other witnesses to come forward.

A police spokesperson said, "Calder Avenue is a busy thoroughfare, and it's possible people will have seen events prior to or after the incident that may provide us with valuable information. We urge such individuals to contact us."

The victims, Mr Geoffrey Jacobson and his wife Jackie Jacobson, were found dead in their home. Police are guarding the property, which remains cordoned off by tape.

Beth found another story reporting the murders in the second local paper.

TEEN KILLS TWO NEIGHBOURS WITH HAMMER

A seventeen-year-old youth was arrested by police yesterday in the wake of a seemingly unprovoked attack upon two of his neighbours. Mr Geoffrey Jacobson and his wife, Jackie Jacobson were found dead in their home. The authorities believe the boy took his father's claw hammer and forced entry to the Jacobsons' home, killed the couple and fled the scene via the back garden.

The Jacobsons' next door neighbour heard sounds of a struggle and witnessed the blood-stained youth scaling the back fence. The Jacobsons' discovery by the police resulted in a manhunt which located the boy hiding in a nearby underpass several hours later. An investigation is underway.

Beth proceeded slowly, day by day, through both archives. The next significant stories relating to the murders covered the court case and Crompton's conviction.

YOUTH CONVICTED OF BRUTAL HAMMER MURDERS

Eighteen-year-old Dennis Crompton was convicted yesterday of the murder of neighbours Geoffrey Jacobson and his wife, Jackie Jacobson, and sentenced to detention under her Majesty's pleasure. Due to his age at the time of the offence, Crompton was sentenced to serve a minimum of 12 years.

During mitigation and sentencing, the court heard that he was well known to the couple, particularly Mrs Jacobson, with one witness describing Crompton as a 'quiet, intense youth, and something of a loner.' Mrs Jacobson had offered Crompton odd job work, mostly gardening. The prosecution alleged the Jacobsons were murdered by a volatile, emotionally blunt youth in a fit of rage. What prompted Crompton's rage remains unclear, what is known is that he had presence of mind enough to collect his father's claw hammer from a tool box kept in the family's shed, cross the street to the Jacobsons' home, force entry and kill Mr Jacobson in the front room and Mrs Jacobson on the property's upper landing. He then sought to escape via the couple's back garden.

When the youth was located a few streets away he was arrested and confessed to the killings the following day.

Beth saved images of all the stories relating to the crime, emailing herself copies. Greg helped her return the spools of microfiche to their glossy white cabinets, before finally she logged out of the computer and they descended the library's escalators. Once outside, in the dimming evening, Beth asked the question occupying both their minds.

"So," she said, "do we think it's this Crompton guy?"

Greg recalled a passage from one of the newspaper stories. Repeated it out loud. "Volatile, emotionally blunt and prone to fits of rage?"

He fixed Crompton in his mind's eye. Big, hard-looking inside and out, that ugly tattoo. You want to be careful. Had that been a veiled threat? And what was in that curious black wooden case he had been carrying?

"Maybe he's still volatile and emotionally blunt," Beth replied, "but prison has taught him to keep a lid on the rage part, be more careful?"

They started walking, from the expanse of block paving into the city.

Beth continued. "Either way, this isn't enough. If we're going back to the police we need more. The fact that he killed two people in a fit of rage over a decade ago doesn't explain why he'd be bumping people off now like this, methodically, carefully, ensuring the deaths look like accidents. We don't have any proof."

They made their way back toward the train station. The orange ember glow of light pollution hung over the city, the breath of thousands of street lights, of windows, car headlamps, traffic lights and electronic billboards holding the darkening evening at bay. Beth pulled out her phone and checked the time.

"Crap."

"What?"

"That took longer than I expected. I'm meant to be at my writing class at eight." She paused; the thought seemed to have prompted another. "Maybe… My tutor is a murder mystery writer. He must have done his share of research in his time. If I posed all this as a hypothetical thing I bet he would have a take on it. You know, about how a detective would approach trying to finding out more about Crompton? Think I should ask him?"

"I think we could do with all the help we can get."

Chapter 30

"Let's imagine then," said O'Shea, "that we've reached the end of our first act, delivered our inciting incident, leaving our protagonist or protagonists in a position where turning back is no longer an option. The central conflict of our story is clear and the burden of resolving it squarely on our characters' shoulders. What's next?"

O'Shea raised a questioning eyebrow. "We enter the wild and twisted terrain of our second act. You'd be wise to tremble with fear, as this is where it's all too easy to get lost. Dangers abound, false trails and pitfalls litter every avenue, shadows and phantoms all too prepared to lead us into darkness and despair, eager to derail our tale...And should this happen, should we find ourselves lost and afraid, our handy trail of breadcrumbs scattered to the four winds? What do we do?"

O'Shea turned and collected his trusty water soluble marker. Jabbed five block capitals on the white board, dotting a period with a brutal flourish:

THEME.

"We stop. And we remember why we wanted to write our story in the first place, we remind ourselves what we wanted to say. This is at the heart of our venture. When things get tough, and in my experience they invariably will at some point, and you begin to question why you're doing what you're doing, when doubts and fears intrude, you must remember this one thing, because if it's strong enough it will carry you forward, no matter what obstacles you meet along the way."

The class was lively. O'Shea was clearly enjoying himself and everyone seemed convinced that writing a novel was firmly in their grasp.

Beth had to lock the library up at the end as usual, but caught up with O'Shea before he left, asked him if she could have five minutes to talk about her work in progress before he headed home.

O'Shea suggested they might like to chat over a quick drink instead. There was a nice quiet pub on the high street, less than a two-minute drive. This time Beth agreed.

—

O'Shea returned from the bar and set their drinks down, Beth's a Diet Coke, his looking very much like a triple whisky. The Black Horse bar and grill, an impressive mock-Tudor building, was quiet and comfortable enough on a Thursday evening. They had taken a table by one of the lounge's large windows.

O'Shea took a big slug of his drink, followed by second that nearly emptied the glass, followed by an audible sigh. Beth smiled to herself, suspecting it was purely for her benefit. O'Shea was definitely the type to fancy himself the tortured artist, a complicated man, a raw nerve to the world's truths, burdened by insights less perceptive souls than he were spared. A man who, quite understandably, sought relief and escape through dulling his sensitive faculties with the application of hard liquor. She suspected just as strongly that O'Shea simply liked a drink.

He was looking at her, openly, appreciatively.

"You really are quite stunning you know. Sure, you might slur your words some here and there, look a little unsteady on your feet when you walk sometimes, but," O'Shea knocked back the slim remains of his drink, "catch me on the way out of here at closing time some evenings and you might say the same of me." He beamed his best scoundrel's smile. He was very nearly handsome and charming enough, and crucially self-aware enough, to actually get away with it.

"I thought we had agreed to talk writing?"

"Of course. A quick refill first, though?"

Beth had hardly touched her Coke.

"I'm good thanks."

O'Shea returned shortly with a second large whisky.

"Please tell me you don't plan to drive home?"

"Of course not. What kind of man do you think I am?"

She smiled. "You really want me to answer that honestly?"

"No, perhaps not."

"So you're going to leave your car and get a taxi, then?"

"Good gravy no." O'Shea pointed to the window behind them. "See that row of flats over there? I'm renting one." He fine-tuned his pointing finger, "Top floor, that one there. I'm working on something new, and I wanted to come back here to finish it. This was where I wrote my first novel you know? Just a few streets from here. I had a romantic idea about renting the old place again, but rather inconveniently, someone is already living there. So no 11 Kettle Street for me."

Beth frowned. O'Shea saw.

"What?"

"Eleven Kettle Street, the downstairs flat?"

Now O'Shea was frowning too. "Yes?"

160

"It's just, well, the person who lives in it is a friend of mine."

"Wow." O'Shea shook his head, smiled, "Coincidence. Real life is bloody full of them. Don't dare use too many of them in your writing though. People will squeal, trust me. 'Contrived!' they'll yell, like that isn't the whole point." O'Shea paused for a few seconds, seemed to reflect, "Eleven Kettle Street, that's where it all started for me, though, that cosy little flat, where Joseph Lumiere was born, for good or ill. Shame, I'd hoped to end it there too."

"To end it?" Beth asked.

"Relax. I'm not terminally ill or anything. The work I mean. This will be the last murder mystery for me. My finest I hope, my last word on the genre. But we're supposed to be here to discuss your project, aren't we? Go on, please, I'm all yours." He smiled.

Beth smiled back.

O'Shea definitely had something. He was attractive. Maybe it was the fact that beyond his religion of writing he didn't seem to give a toss. Maybe that was the attraction, the mixture of severity (and there was no doubt, when it came to the business of story, and how to write fiction, O'Shea was prescriptive, devout and militant) juxtaposed with the thirsty bohemian.

Beth wondered if she had ever met anyone quite so incorrigible. "Sorry." He prompted her, as she hadn't responded yet. "Please, ask away."

"In my story, Voyage of Death, let's say George Franklin has a suspect he knows has committed murder in the past, someone who has been convicted and released, someone he thinks might be killing again. How might he go about gathering more information, outside of newspaper reports?"

161

O'Shea considered the question. "To naturalise the information in your story, there are three things you need to consider. The first is the practical one, how does your protagonist acquire the information, the second is how to present it in the most dramatic fashion for the reader, and the third is who do we want to have the information? The reader and your protagonist, or the reader alone? The latter is easy. You're using third person, past tense, no? Which means you could even switch viewpoint to the murderer himself if you wanted, have him reflect on his past crimes, provide some nice insight about his inner life while you're rummaging around in his head."

"What if it's more important how my protagonist acquires the information?"

"You need a mouthpiece. A witness, a journalist, a police officer or authority figure intimate with the case, someone who knew the man and his crimes first hand, someone who had contact with the suspect, or his victim or victims."

"Yes, that would be perfect…"

"Beware though. What we're talking here about is exposition, dangerous stuff."

"Dangerous? Why?"

"Because exposition, by definition, deals with events that have already occurred, that lie in the past. That means going backwards. Plot wants to go forward. If your exposition doesn't immediately forward the plot, tread carefully. Murder mysteries are afforded more leeway, though. Someone has been killed. The truth naturally lies in the past." O'Shea was becoming animated, but also more serious, the way he was in class. "Detective stories are built around revelation and accruing information. Delving into the past to understand why and sometimes how something happened are at the heart of them, one of the joys of them, no?"

"Why did you stop writing?" The question had just popped out. Beth had been thinking it, but the moment it was said she knew it was one too delicate to have just blurted out.

It seemed to take O'Shea by surprise. Before she could apologise, and take the question back, he answered.

"I had nothing left to say. I'd lost sight of what made me want to do it in the first place. I was dangerously close to writing books I not only didn't like, but may even have come to hate."

"Oh."

"That wasn't even the worst part." O'Shea snatched up his glass and threw back the rest of his drink. He looked not just unhappy, but a little angry. "I wondered if my readers would even care, if they mightn't just carry on reading the books and not even notice. I think my best Lumiere book was my first, but the last one, the one I like the least, sold the best. There's something deeply unsettling about that, discovering your keenest readers may just be the least discerning." O'Shea stared at his empty glass. The momentary flush of anger had evaporated as quickly as it had appeared.

"I'm sorry," Beth apologised. "I shouldn't have asked."

O'Shea looked deflated, but even this didn't last long. "There we were, having a nice chat and I ruined the moment, didn't I?" he said and with a slow smile, like the flip of a coin, the serious O'Shea vanished and the libidinous goof returned. "And just when you were teetering on the brink of begging me to take you back to my bed and ravage you."

163

Chapter 31

Long ears or short? Kelley Jones's Batman had ones almost a foot long, Miller's bulky, aging Dark Knight had blunt and stubby fins scarcely an inch high. Greg's own renditions of the caped crusader plumped for something in between, although like Miller he definitely favoured the fabric suit. Greg didn't hate the newer, more armour-clad interpretations of Bruce Wayne's dark alter ego, but the classic Lycra look would always be his preference.

The picture was still only half complete, but shaping up nicely. Greg was bent over it, as lost in drawing it as the costumed vigilante beneath his pencil was in the shadows of his cape. Sometimes, especially with Batman, what you didn't show mattered more, planes of deep shadow, throwing focus on the details emerging from them, that pointy-eared mask, white eyes, mouth biting a growl above a jaw square as a kitchen tile. Evil-doers beware! The cowl and the cape…

Drawing had always offered respite, a blessed escape hatch from reality he could sometimes climb through and isolate himself from the chaotic world and its demands, the symmetry that begged to be recognised and obeyed, the odious disorder that whispered unfocused but dire warnings lest he set things right, the resulting rituals that ground him down… When he got lost in a drawing it all melted away, if only for a time.

It was the doorbell that wrenched him rudely from his refuge this afternoon. He set down his pencil and padded through the hall. He opened the door to find Adrian, carrying a large plastic bag.

Greg noted the familiar logo of his preferred art and crafts shop on the side of it.

"Hey," Adrian said. "Got you some things."

Greg recognised a peace offering when he saw one.

—

They sat in the lounge, Greg sipping tea, his twelfth mug of the day. Adrian had requested his usual glass of tap water.

"I settled the business with Dad's neighbours' trees. Hired a landscaping and gardening firm to replace them, and threatened him not to touch them. Since I paid for them I reckon he'll leave them alone. I think he's struggled since retiring. He needs a hobby or something."

"Think he'll behave?"

Adrian shrugged and conceded Greg a small grin. "Probably not. He's a stubborn old git isn't he? I'm sorry you felt ambushed at the restaurant. I suppose I just can't understand why you and Dad can't just sit down and work out your bloody differences. If you could just cut each other some slack—"

"I didn't feel ambushed. I was ambushed," Greg said, but he wasn't angry anymore, not really, just frustrated. "What does it matter if we never speak again? I'm not sure I care. And I'm fairly certain he doesn't either. Why can't you just let it go?"

"Because I'm stuck in the middle. I can't spend time with either of you without being made to feel like I'm taking sides. I feel that way when I'm here, and the same when I'm over his. It's alright for you two, you can just go on ignoring each other, but where does that leave me? I have a brother, and I have a father, but I don't have a family."

"He looked old."

"Why shouldn't he? He is a pensioner, Greg. He'll be eligible for his free bus-pass and winter heating allowance soon, still fit as a butcher's dog, though. Still walks miles and does his push-ups before breakfast same as ever."

Greg recalled what living with Colin had been like. An infantry soldier who had eventually left the army and joined the police, swapping one uniform for another, and like many uniformed types he carried regimentation into his personal life too. Their mum had softened many of his harder edges, mellowed him, but he was still a creature of order and discipline. There would be no child nor teenager lying in bed past 8a.m. under Colin's roof. No lazing around, only in Colin's mind anything that meant keeping remotely stationary was lazing. Drawing was certainly tantamount to lazing. Kids should be outside, kicking a football around or climbing trees... The irony of the situation was almost funny. In any other household Colin would have been viewed as the obsessive one.

Adrian never seemed to mind, though. Quite the opposite; he took Colin's ethos to heart, flourished under it. He attacked life like a series of obstacles just begging to be scaled, astonishingly good GCSE grades in school, clubs, star player in sports, amazing A-level grades, university, more clubs, a solid respectable, financially rewarding profession... Adrian was Colin's dream son.

Even without his issues Greg could never have been his favourite.

"So," he said, keen to change the subject, "how's work at the moment?"

"Good, great. Looks like I'm in line for a promotion."

"That's great," Greg said, before noticing Adrian's expression had scarcely changed. "Isn't it?"

"I suppose. I can look forward to spending even more of my time there. Speaking of which I'd better get going in a minute, I've got a presentation to give in the morning and I've still got some material to put together."

Adrian had always been very career focused, but something seemed to have changed. Adrian didn't look excited about his forthcoming promotion. Was this a new development, or something Greg had missed? He couldn't deny he had a tendency to drift off when Adrian talked about his job. He was debating whether he should ask if something was wrong when the doorbell rang. He excused himself, and went to answer the door.

It was Beth.

"Okay, so I have a plan," she said. "Want to hear it?"

Greg cast a look back. Adrian was following him out. Caught between his brother in the hallway and Beth on the step he felt uneasy suddenly.

"Adrian, this is my friend, Beth. Beth, Adrian is my brother. He's just leaving."

Beth smiled, removed her shoes and set them perfectly straight and aligned on the mat.

Greg could almost see Adrian's mind whirring as she slipped past him heading for the kitchen.

"Adrian?"

"Huh?"

"You have that presentation to prepare for?"

Adrian looked like someone who'd had a puzzle tossed at him, and no idea where to begin solving it.

"I was?" he said, "I mean, yes, I was. I mean, have. Well, nice to meet you Beth."

"You too," she said before vanishing into the kitchen.

Adrian appeared to slip his shoes on with some reluctance.

"I'll call you in a bit, yeah?" he said on his way out.

"Sure," Greg said closing the door behind him. Four further tries finally did the job, by which time Adrian was long gone.

–

Beth was at the kitchen table studying the drawings when Greg walked in. A large zip-up portfolio had been open on the table. Curious, she had taken a peek.

"You drew these?"

Greg nodded awkwardly.

She was a slightly taken aback. She turned the pictures over in turn, taking each in. In the present one a kid wearing a sheriff hat too big for his head stared out over a street full of milling zombies.

She looked to Greg. "They're amazing."

"Carl."

"Pardon?"

"In that one? That's Carl. From The Walking Dead?"

"Like the TV show?"

"It was a comic book first."

"Really?"

She continued looking. A giant half-man half-lizard in a lab coat was emerging from an alleyway. The next one featured two characters she did recognise. Even if she had never seen them in comic book form she would have known them from the movies. The picture had Spiderman battling the

168

Green Goblin on his flying glider thingy. The Goblin had his arm pitched back, holding some sort of pumpkin-shaped bomb. Spiderman had him by the throat; the pair looked on the verge of toppling from the speeding glider.

It was the next picture that stopped her short, though. She heard Greg stammer something. When she managed to take her eyes from the picture she saw his face had gone blood red.

The picture was of a woman in a black skin-hugging outfit. Again, Beth had seen the movie version of the character. She was one of The Avengers, the Black Widow. In Greg's picture she was vaulting over one Hydra agent to kick another in the face. The goon's face was snapped toward the viewer, spittle flying from his lips. In the movie, Scarlet Johansson had played the character, but in the picture the face was not Scar Jo's… In the picture it looked startlingly like the one she met in the bathroom mirror every morning. It was stylised, sure, but quite definitely her face. Even the tiny mole on her chin was present and correct.

"Greg, is this… me?"

"Well," Greg swallowed, his face looking ready to go supernova, "I might have, erm…"

"I like it. It's cool."

"It is?"

"Hell yeah. I mean, who wouldn't want to kick a Hydra agent in the face?" She smiled.

"Would you… like to keep it?"

"Very much."

Greg looked both delighted but still a little mortified.

"So," he said, "you were saying you have a plan?"

"Last night? I spoke to my tutor, Dermot O'Shea; he's a murder mystery writer. He said something interesting. I think I know what we should do next, the next step in our investigation."

"Our investigation?"

"If we intend to approach the authorities again and expect to be taken as anything but a pair of loons we need to build a case. We need evidence. If this Crompton guy is our prime suspect we need to know more about him, get something on him. We need to be sure it's him, and have enough to convince others he's the murderer, build a picture of who he is and why he's killing again."

Chapter 32

There was really only one way to do what she needed to do, and as much as she felt bad not including Greg, after seeing him under pressure in Dingle's office she knew it would be considerably less complicated done alone.

She needed to speak to someone who had been around when Crompton committed those first murders, someone who knew Crompton and his victims personally, who maybe knew the sort of stuff not found in the local newspapers.

Greg's comfort zone seemed far from expansive; talking to strange people in a strange place would test him. She needed someone to talk, and felt they were much more likely to if faced with a woman alone, even one who moved and talked a little funny. The important thing was to acquire information. If she came up empty-handed, she could choose not to mention the trip to Greg at all. If she came away with something useful, he might, she hoped, be too interested in what it was to be offended she hadn't invited him along.

Decision made, she had booked a train ticket and travelled to the place where Crompton had helped two people shuffle off their mortal coil with the assistance of a claw hammer, just an ordinary suburban street to the north side of the city. It looked not unlike Kettle Street.

Beth had racked her brain for a cover story to explain why she wanted to know what sort of person Dennis Crompton had been prior to violently taking the lives of two of his neighbours. Staying as close to the truth as possible seemed the best bet. She would simply approach the residents on Crompton's old street and ask if they had been around in 2002, recalled the murders, remembered Crompton, and were willing to talk. When the obvious question surfaced, she would tell them Crompton had just moved in nearby and, after inadvertently discovering what he had done, wanted to know if she should be afraid.

Over a decade and a half is a long time, and at first things didn't go all that well. The residents she spoke to had either moved onto the street after the murders had occurred, or were there at the time, but weren't really that familiar with Dennis Crompton, his family or the couple he had killed. Many remembered the crime, but that was about it.

Resolute, she worked methodically from the bottom of one side of the street all the way to the top, and then back down the other side, and was close to running out of houses when she eventually struck gold.

When the man opened the door, Beth repeated her line. Like many of the other houses she had tried, there was an awkward spell, where he attempted to work out what Beth had going on. It was something she was well used to, but in this case, for a change, possibly quite useful, disarming enough to make people forget they were being door-stepped. Terry Parsons admitted that, yes, he did indeed remember the event, and the people involved, all too well, sadly. When Beth explained her concerns about her new neighbour Parsons seemed sympathetic, and invited her in.

"So Dennis Crompton's out then is he?" he said. "Moved in near you? And you want to know if you're safe sleeping in your bed at night?"

"That's pretty much it," Beth replied.

172

"Just ten years for two lives, not much is it? Hammered to death. Nobody deserves to die like that, even if Jackie Jacobson was playing a dangerous game."

Beth wondered if she had missed something, but didn't prompt. Terry Parsons, the neighbour, seemed to want to talk, so she let him.

"She was a one, Jackie, the wife. Nice enough, wouldn't want to speak ill of the dead and all, but maybe a bit too friendly when she chose to be… If you know what I mean."

Beth was not sure she did.

Thankfully Parsons elucidated.

"Men."

"She cheated on her husband?" said Beth.

"If even half of the rumours were true, although some reckoned the husband was every bit as bad. They both must have known, but neither seemed upset. To meet them, they seemed happy enough. Never appeared at odds, nothing like that. Dennis used to take care of some gardening for them, weeding the borders, mowing the lawn and whatnot. He did a few other houses in the street too, for a bit of pocket money. As he got older, shot up the way young lads suddenly do, and filled out, I think Jackie took a liking to him. You'd see her chatting to him while he worked, bringing him a drink or a snack."

Beth nodded.

"He was a fit-looking lad," Terry continued, "good physique, from the gardening and his boxing. I remember him when his family moved into the street. He was just a quiet, scrawny little thing, but by the time he hit his late teens he was already bigger than most men.

"I saw him fight once, a charity event at the local legionnaires club. He'd have been around, oh… 15

173

then? Dangerous enough, though. A natural he was, a nice mover and fast too. He made mincemeat of the other lad. Put him down in a single round. Boxing's supposed to be about controlled aggression, that's what they say isn't it? There was nothing controlled about how Dennis finished off the other kid that night." Parsons stopped himself. "The other lad was the more experienced, and he clearly wanted Dennis to know it. He came out all showy, bouncing around the ring, all cocky, like. The fight starts and he goes at Dennis like it's the last minute of the last round rather than the first, both barrels, full on, clocks Dennis with a bunch of good ones. Only then he goes back to showboating, dancing around Dennis like he's just playing with him. He must have had a big crowd supporting him, because you could hear them all hollering and shouting encouragement. Well, that was it. Dennis didn't like it. You could see it in his face. The other lad saw it too, not that it did him any good. Less than a minute later the fight was over, Dennis had put the kid flat on his back, and his supporters, mouthy enough before, were suddenly quiet. The other kid tried to get up but you could see he was done. The ref stepped in and stopped it.

"So when Jackie started fooling around with him, and it seems pretty clear to me that's what was going on, she should have known it wouldn't end well. I mean what woman sleeps with a boy of seventeen and doesn't expect it to end badly? Maybe not in murder, but still… Playing with fire."

"What do you think made him do it?"

"Jealously. I think he fell in love with her, and then realised he was just a bit of fun as far as Jackie Jacobson was concerned, she was actually happy enough with her hubby. Or maybe she got tired of him and gave him the brush off? Whatever it was, it upset him enough to go fetch the claw hammer from his old man's tool box in the garage and kill. Hard to know who to feel sorriest for isn't it? Two people dead and a young man's life ruined. Ten years. He'd be coming up thirty now then? Not too old to make a fresh start maybe."

"So you don't think I should be worried he lives across the road from me?" Beth asked.

The man seemed to think about it.

"Have you upset him?"

"I don't think so."

"Well," The man shrugged. "then I expect you're probably fine."

Chapter 33

Greg had actually forgotten his session with Martin. It was only when the doorbell rang that he remembered. He let Martin in and waited while he removed his shoes. Greg had to arrange them properly. Martin had just dumped them down on the mat. Greg wondered if he had done it deliberately, to test him, but as they got themselves ready Greg got the impression Martin was distracted; outwardly he was doing his totally-in-control act, but as someone who rarely felt totally in control Greg wasn't buying it. Something was up. He thought his therapist looked flustered.

They were conducting the session in the front room as usual, Greg sitting, Martin standing. Before they started Greg had to ask.

"Martin? Are you okay?"

"I'm fine, thank you Greg."

Martin was doing his pacing thing again, but it seemed even more contrived than usual. He dispensed with any preamble too.

"Are you sure," said Greg, "because—"

"Why don't you tell me about your mother?"

Greg felt a stab of annoyance. "She's dead."

"I know. Your brother told me, but I'd like you to tell me in your own words. How did she die?"

Greg wondered if Adrian had shared this too.

"I'm not sure I'm ready to—"

"Greg," Martin said, really quite abruptly, "if you seek to make progress we need to start actually addressing things. A simple thing like talking is simple unless we choose to not make it simple. You agree, yes?"

This was another of Martin's NLP things; you were never to utter negative adjectives. Something was never bad, it was not good. An experience was never difficult, it was challenging. Greg got the idea: he was meant to try to frame things in a positive way, but it made for some awkward phrases and was something that veered into feeling vaguely oppressive, just a small hop from the thing in that book they had made them study at school. 1984? There was a language Big Brother wanted everyone to speak. Newspeak? Ungood, doubleplusgood, all that... It was meant to stop the people thinking freely, to not even think wrong thoughts. Thought crime...

"I'll try. It's diffi—" Greg corrected himself to spare Martin the job. "It's challenging."

"I understand, and that's why it's important to do it. Except, don't try. *Trying* acknowledges failure as an option."

Greg was afraid they had just taken a sharp detour past Orwellian Newspeak; what Martin had just said sounded dangerously close to 'Do or do not. There is no try!'—motivational philosophy as dispensed by Yoda from *Star Wars*. Greg collected himself, tried to believe Martin was helping him get better (and he did want to get better), took a deep breath and tried to do and not just try.

"My mother died six years ago. We were on our way home. We'd been to the city to do some Christmas shopping..."

—

The city had been busy, but not as crazy as it would become in the weeks ahead. It was still early enough in December for plenty of Christmas gift-buyers to be leaving the job until later. It was a weekday too. Greg could usually deal with visiting the city during the week, and his mum was always a calming influence. She never rushed him, never tutted or pushed. They had finished up before the rush hour, jumping on the last off peak train home.

It had grown dark early, and the temperature had plummeted. Suddenly spared the meagre warmth of the dazzling, low winter sun keeping them at bay, patches of frost lurking under the shadows of buildings and trees all day crept out to claim what they could. The ground underfoot was akin to an ice-rink in some places.

He and his mum each carried multiple shopping bags, containing the last of Colin and Adrian's gifts. They were nearly home. It was only a short walk from the local station. They had cut through the heath, which was dark and empty. The cold had driven most inside early. They didn't quite live in the deepest countryside, but far enough outside the city for it to feel like it sometimes.

His mum was playfully complaining how the cold got into an old lady's bones more easily than a boy's. Greg protested. At 44 his mum was hardly a pensioner yet, and at 24 he was hardly a boy anymore. The path was icy but tarmacked so at least seamless. They were laughing at how the other was walking, taking exaggerated almost comically deliberate steps to avoid slipping.

Greg loved to see his mum laugh, she had a silly streak which she only really let loose when it was just the two of them; Colin wasn't completely humourless, he appreciated wit and jokes, but simple silliness wasn't in his vocabulary, and Adrian preferred to think his sense of humour had a more sophisticated bent. Were either present, Greg knew his mum would have felt daft playing up her Bambi-on-the-ice act for added comic effect, but not with him. So she wobbled, grinning, raising her arms like a tightrope walker. Goofing she was going to slip.

Only then she did.

One moment she was upright the next she was gone, laying on her back, her head crooked against one of the kerb stones edging the path. It was so fast, for a second it was almost funny. Greg immediately dropped his bags and crouched down to help her up, and suddenly it wasn't funny at all. Her face looked all wrong. He tried to help her sit up, but she couldn't. He realised there was blood on his hand from where he had cupped her neck. An instant later she vomited all over herself. That was when the panic had really combusted. He rolled her into the recovery position, tried to look into her mouth, listen, afraid she might be choking. He heard her groan, and felt her breath on his ear. Their house was close, around the corner, over the road and just down the lane. He ran, as fast as he could, not caring if he slipped and fell.

The ambulance ride and the accident and emergency room were lost in a blur. He sat with Adrian and Colin in the family room while the doctors did whatever they were doing. Soft-spoken medical staff parcelled out the details: a fractured skull, bleeding on the brain, swelling, neurological damage, talk of an induced coma and life support, and then the news that rendered it all pointless. The MRI scan came back, showing Greg's mum had sustained profound damage to her brain and was deteriorating quickly.

The doctor switched off life support at 2 a.m. She was declared dead eight minutes later.

Chapter 34

While she had been inside his place on a number of occasions, today was the first time Greg had been inside Beth's flat.

She lived in one of the new builds on Ladle Lane. Some still looked a little identikit, exactly as the developer had left them, but many had been given a personal touch. Beth had put her stamp on hers. The default cream door had been painted punchy fire-engine red, and she had swapped out the plain chrome effect knocker for an ornate brass one. There was a bird feeder in the small front garden and the grass was edged into a neat circle around it, bordered with perennials. It had charm.

He liked the inside of the flat too. It was neat, tidy and clean (even by Greg's standards), but cosy too.

She had erected a small cork board on the wall. The board's front was covered in four sheets of copier paper taped together. At its centre was a blown up a map of Kettle Street. Above one house on the map was the name Dennis Crompton in block capitals. There were several push pins with twine tied to them; each length of twine radiated to another push pin. Beside these pins were more names.

Under each name was written the cause of their deaths.

BERNARD BROCKLEHURST
CAUSE OF DEATH: WASP STING, ALLERGIC REACTION.
CLUE: INSECT BITE CREAM.

ROSE GORDON

CAUSE OF DEATH: FELL DOWN STAIRS, DRUNK?
CLUE: MINIATURE WHISKY BOTTLE.

BRETT FOSTER
CAUSE OF DEATH: PASSED OUT WEIGHT TRAINING, CHOKED BY BARBELL.
CLUE: PROTEIN BAR.

STEVE HOLT
CAUSE OF DEATH: JACK SLIPPED, CRUSHED UNDER CAR.
CLUE: CLASSIC ROVER KEYRING.

Beth stepped back and studied her handiwork, hands on her hips, staring at the map and the names like they were some sort of puzzle to be solved, which they very well might have been. What connected the victims? Why were they chosen?

"You're not going to like this," she said, "but…"

She walked to the board and picked up the marker, found the appropriate spot on the map and wrote GREG UNSWORTH: WITNESS?

She pushed a pin into the board beside Greg's name, but left the twine alone, so his name hovered below the threads, like a fly caught on the periphery of a spider's web. Seeing it laid out this way, he wondered how long it would be before he twanged a thread and joined the others.

"We need to think in terms of patterns, opportunities, motives, psychology, methodology, and weaknesses. I take it you see what I see here?"

Faced with the incident board one thing snapped into sharp focus, something they had both missed.

Greg nodded. It was hard not to.

All the victims lay on one side of Kettle Street, Greg lay on the other.

"He's making you face them? Is that it? Laying them all out before you, one by one?"

Beth had pinned a blank sheet of paper beside the map. She wrote MOTIVE on it. She reflected upon O'Shea's viewpoint regarding motive, how had he put it? 'An act of revenge, jealousy, to keep a secret from being exposed, what do they gain? Or are they simply crazy?'

"Crompton's murders were down to jealousy last time. Is that what we think?" offered Greg.

He had been surprised when Beth had told him what she had done, and what Terry Parsons had told her. She had, of course, done her best to play down not asking him to come along. Crompton's old neighbours would be more likely to talk, she felt, to a woman on her own. He agreed and nodded. She was almost certainly right. Two people would be more intimidating. Their recent encounter with Dingle was still fresh in his mind, though. And it was unlikely to be any less fresh in Beth's.

Beth mused, "His neighbour said he had a hair-trigger, maybe prison simmered that down into something colder and controlled as he matured? Anger held close, the patience to nurse a grudge, for a while. These murders must have required careful planning. And then there's the actual execution of them, staging them to appear like accidents... How does he know so much about them? Is he watching them? How? And why these people specifically? Did each of them upset him in some way?"

"Like how?"

"Dunno, just thinking out loud." She tapped the pin next to Greg's name. "This is what makes least sense. Why you? Why would he single you out? If you upset him too, why not just kill you like the others…" Beth turned from the board. "Do you remember the first time you met Crompton, saw him, or perhaps more importantly the first time he met you?"

Greg tried to think. The very first time he had seen Crompton? That would be shortly after he had moved in, a couple of months ago? The flat he lived in had been empty for a spell prior to that, the couple who had lived there, Debbie and Ben, had moved. He had discovered the place was occupied again after seeing Crompton step out of the door one morning. Greg had been on his way to Pete's shop as usual. Taking Crompton in he had noted many of the things he expected a lot of people did, details that were hard to miss. Crompton looked big, weathered, well-built, and hard. In short, he seemed like trouble.

Too late Greg had become aware not only was he looking at his new neighbour, but his new neighbour was looking at him, had almost certainly caught him staring, and possibly even read some of what he had been thinking from his face? Crompton's hard, cold stare appeared in his mind's eye…

Had it happened that way, though, really? Or was he just thinking that now in retrospect, his memory embellishing the moment? Either way he knew he had been quick to avert his gaze. That much he remembered. You don't stare a mean dog in the eye, unless you're itching to get bitten. No, he'd looked away alright.

He related the moment to Beth.

"The first murder was around a month after Crompton moved onto Kettle Street then?"

"Sounds about right."

"Long enough to take offense, long enough to develop a grudge and plan a murder?"

Voyage of Death: A George and Kathy Franklin Mystery
by
Beth Grue

Chapter Twelve

Resigned as I am in such situations to listening rather than attempting to converse, I perhaps caught the slip when others around me had not.

Mason Rutledge had previously said he and his sister, Charlotte, had family roots in London and their father was an artist. I was certain of it, but now he had just declared his late father a surgeon. I would mention the incongruity to George later, although I suspected he had likely caught it too.

The Rutledge siblings made for a striking pair, beautiful and intense. During our first encounter with them I had been struck by their resemblance to one another, as close in appearance as two individuals of differing genders could be. The pair were, we had learned, fraternal twins, and yet not only did they share the same blond hair, so pale as to be almost white, their features were near identical too, save for Mason Rutledge's heavier jaw and broader nose.

Meeting them for a second time I noted how the resemblance went beyond the physical. It was underscored in other ways. They dressed similarly. Mason's slate grey suit and olive shirt appeared to be tailored from the exact same fabrics as his sister's dress and blouse. Mason wore his hair long for a man (perhaps a style more common in the New World) and his sister short, for a lady.

But even this was not the full extent of it: they shared similar mannerisms too, something both uncanny and disconcerting.

The steward broke the gentle murmur of the after dinner conversation with an announcement, delivered with a direction and force worthy of a drill sergeant.

"If the captain's guests would like to retire to the lounge?"

As we all began to rise from our seats I noted someone staring at me, as I had just been studying Mason and Charlotte Rutledge.

He was the quiet bearded man, Alexis Demidov, the Russian land baron whose muscular build suggested he worked the fields rather than owned them. Still staring at me, he wiped his lips with a napkin.

He rose as I did, and joined the others as they filed from the room. He cast me a final parting glance before he disappeared from sight.

Chapter 35

The moment he saw it his heart lurched in his chest and a chill ran through him.

Greg had emerged from his bedroom, half way through a yawn. His mouth snapped shut.

The white rectangle sat on his doormat like a threat.

He had already come to dread what he found there. As much as he had hoped it would all simply stop, he feared it was just a matter of time before someone else was marked for death. Eventually another blank package with some item inside would arrive, a cryptic death sentence. If he and Beth were right, a killer was even now planning to take someone's life.

And yet, the strange thing was life was continuing to just go on. Greg was used to living with a sense of dread hanging over him and waking up day after day anyway. He knew better than anyone how even under the shadow of crushing fear, the world didn't stop. Things that appear intolerable are commonplace. People live on the streets in destitution, with sickness, with terminal illnesses, with loved ones with terminal illnesses, in sometimes unimaginably hostile conditions, warzones, the aftermath of natural disasters... Here Greg was living with a killer haunting his street, a man literally getting away with murder. But a new day had dawned nonetheless.

As had a new delivery.

He knew his options. He could run away, or he could try to stop the murderer. The only thing necessary for evil to triumph is for good men to do nothing.

He didn't want to do nothing. He swallowed and approached the package.

Only as he neared it he saw it wasn't a package, it wasn't even an envelope. It was simply a sheet of copier paper folded in two. He unfolded it, relief flooding through him like a balm. It was simply one of Maurice Cooper's residents' association newsletters.

Feeling the dread slink a few paces into the background he scanned the text.

Kettle Street Residents Association Newsletter
Autumn
Welcome Councillor
Maurice Cooper (and residents of Kettle Street)

A warm welcome to Kevin Hayes, our newly elected Northcroft ward Councillor.

Attempted Burglaries
Maurice Cooper

Over the past fortnight two attempted burglaries have taken place, into sheds belonging to residents of the odd-numbered side of Kettle Street. The would-be thieves appeared to have gained access via the common. While both sheds remained secure, damage was done to the doors and locks. The incidents have been reported to the police. Please be vigilant!

Street Lighting
Maurice Cooper

At last some positive movement. I've again been assured the remaining columns (including the badly dented one outside number 72) will be replaced with the new models under the next contract year, which runs from January next year until the following January. A request for a more specific start date has been sent to Mr Paul Dyer, the relevant Highways Electrical Asset manager.

Many thanks to Councillors Bob Birch and Terrance Sidebottom for their support in this matter.

Uneven Pavement Slabs
Maurice Cooper

It has been reported that amongst other locations, a handful of uneven pavement slabs are present among the path skirting the green at the top of the road intersecting with Hereward Road and Badger Street. An incident occurred where a local woman tripped and badly grazed her knee. I'm aware, as always, there are monetary considerations, but surely people's safety must be given the highest priority. I shall continue to converse with the relevant council departments and report back.

Security Gates and Rear Access Drives
Maurice Cooper

The security gates connecting rear access of the right-of-way behind the even-numbered sides of Kettle Street and Greenfield Road are still unsecured. I would really like to urge residents to remain keen to keep this right-of-way more private and secure. If you agree, contact me so we can appeal to newer residents to contribute to a fund to purchase new padlocks and keys so we can again lock the gates at both ends and thereby deter undesirables and criminals.

In addition, there still appears to be a good deal of refuse littering the area. Our property case deeds do state the ground in the rear access within our land boundaries does belong to us and is our responsibility and should be kept clear and open by us.

Newsletter

The deadline for the next newsletter is the 30th of next month, for distribution the following week. Any items for inclusion should either be emailed to me (MauriceCooperKSRA@digimail.com) or posted through my letterbox at 48 Kettle Street before the 17th. Once again please don't let it all be me.

Greg folded the newsletter neatly in two and put it in his kitchen drawer.

—

Going outdoors, even just to Pete's, always took resolve. His flat was safe, manageable, a corner of the world he exercised control over; out there was the Wild West, a potential three-ring circus of unpredictable, random, stress-inducing chaos. Venturing out made him anxious, some days a little, some a lot, which was precisely why he made himself do it, even when he didn't actually need anything.

The reason was simple. The only thing more terrifying than what lay out there was what might happen as a consequence of trying to avoid it. In short, he was afraid of becoming a shut-in.

There was a very real danger of this. He liked his own company, always had. He could exist for long stretches alone. His mum had been the one to nudge him outside to play, or invite school friends over, but solitude was comfortable too. Hours were easily consumed drawing or reading comic books or sometimes novels, listening to music, or watching television or movies… Deep down, though, he knew he needed other people. Human contact was like one of those trace minerals your body required, measured in some tiny zero point zero something microscopic amount, but vital all the same.

Enough to make you sick if you didn't get it.

He walked the familiar path, negotiating the cracks and paving seams, but slower than usual. He had started to study the houses across the road, all the different doors, the different colours and styles. He took in the furniture outside each, plant pots, hanging baskets, house numbers, some brass cast, some moulded plastic, a few painted on plaques… The gardens, the driveways where gardens used to be, some properties were fronted by walls, some hedges, some not at all… Unlike the homogenous blur of many modern housing developments, the majority of the dwellings on Kettle Street were old enough to be distinctive in all sorts of ways.

With just a few choice details a property might be easily identified.

He would have liked to believe there wasn't going to be another package, another call, that a whispery voice wasn't going to present him with a trio of these distinctions and challenge him to a perverse game of Guess Who while someone lay dead or dying, but he couldn't afford wishful thinking. He needed to be prepared.

When the dreaded call came, accompanied with its meagre deadline, he wanted to be ready.

–

A loaf of bread and packet of sliced ham and Kettle Street property frontage reconnaissance complete, Greg embarked on the next phase of his mid-morning mission.

A wide alley ran behind the far side of Kettle Street. Around the mid-point it intersected with a spoke which emerged on Badger Street, which swept in a horseshoe behind Kettle Street. Back in the 1930s, when the first houses had been built, the right-of-way had been intended to provide alternative access to the rear gardens. As more houses were built and car ownership grew more common many residents erected garages at the foot of their gardens, and the right-of-way became more of a narrow shingle-studded road than a foot path.

At some point security concerns, the potential for the right-of-way to offer easy access to burglars, had resulted in residents of both streets chipping in to erect galvanised steel gates. These probably worked as intended for a while, but as time wore on and people moved in and out of the street the business of obtaining keys to the padlocks became more hassle than anyone wanted to be responsible for, and now the gates were more often than not unlocked.

In response, many residents had fenced off the back of their gardens and allowed nature to oblige with its own defences. As Greg approached the rear of Crompton's ground floor flat this was exactly what he found: an aging timber fence covered in a sheet of thorny bramble.

He approached, trying to look casual and as invisible as possible.

He paused as he passed. If he strained up on his tip toes he was just able to make out the top of Crompton's bedroom window. He wasn't sure what he was looking for precisely, what he expected to find, he just wanted to—

"He ought to get that back window frame fixed."

Greg almost leapt out of his skin. He whipped around to find Maurice Cooper standing right next to him, close enough to reach out and touch.

"Sorry," said Cooper. "Didn't mean to give you a start."

"What are you doing here?" Shock had caused the question to sound blunter than Greg intended.

Maurice stiffened. "I could ask you the same thing."

Greg felt exposed. He scrambled for something plausible. He viewed honesty as the best policy in general, but doubted 'Checking on someone I think might be killing our neighbours' was the way to go on this occasion.

"I was just taking a stroll."

"Do you often have a stroll through here?"

Greg didn't appreciate the tone. Maurice Cooper might like to think he owned Kettle Street, but he didn't.

"Not often, no. Do you?"

"I pass through here now and again, to keep an eye on things. Neighbourhood Watch? I know most people can't be bothered these days, but I'd still prefer Kettle Street not become a soft target for thieves. It's how they operate you know, why you hear about a spate of burglaries. Gangs pick a street, case it, watch to see when people come and go, which houses are empty and when, vulnerable points of entry, doors, windows, determine if anyone is keeping a watch over things… And then they strike! One house here, another there. By the time residents wake up to what's going on, maybe get around to finally installing that expensive house alarm system they've talked about having fitted for years, the scumbags have moved on to robbing houses in some other street miles away."

"I see."

"There." Cooper pointed over Crompton's fence. "See? That window frame has been broken for over a year now. All a thief would have to do is climb over this lot, pull it open and climb in. They might even be able to open the back door from inside and walk out with whatever they liked."

Greg looked. Maurice had a point. A piece of dumped furniture, an old TV cabinet, leant sadly against Crompton's back fence. It would be easy enough to use it to scale the fence and walk down the garden to reach the damaged window.

He wondered how many other people left easy avenues for entry, open windows, unlocked patio doors, or older ones that could be lifted off their runners…

Was this how Crompton got to his victims? Was it how he watched them? It offered the opportunity to access rear gardens from a place that was often quiet and not overtly suspicious for someone to pass though. Anyone at all was free to stroll through the right of way, especially residents who inhabited properties on this side of the street.

"Asking for it," Maurice mumbled, shaking his head in weary disbelief. "Honestly. If only people cared more, were a little more interested in protecting where they live. Makes me livid sometimes, I mean, look at this place…"

Greg did. The right-of-way wasn't a pretty picture. Quite apart from the overgrown bramble and scrubby wild grass, Crompton's TV cabinet, fibre-board warped and swollen where it had soaked up heaven knew how many rainy days, wasn't the only rubbish to have been dumped by those too lazy to take a trip to the local council tip. There was a stack of fencing panels a few houses down. Clearly a new set had been slotted between the concrete posts the old ones once occupied, and instead of disposing of the former ones properly, they had been left slowly disintegrating into bleached grey fragments. More detritus lay behind other back fences, too. It seemed more than a few residents subscribed to an out of sight, out of mind philosophy.

"People should be ashamed. Don't they realise what all this leads to? You get too much of this and a street can go to the dogs. The value of houses begins to drop, good people move out and undesirables move in. The value plummets further. What then? I'll tell you: noise, disorder, dilapidation, litter! You have to take a stand. I for one am not prepared to just sit idly while the place where I live is ruined."

Greg nodded. He knew a zealot when he saw one, and knew just as well not to argue, but he also felt sorry for Maurice Cooper. Until he retired he probably never had the spare time to work himself into a froth over litter and untidy rights of way.

Maybe these days he had nothing but time to patrol and obsess. Greg knew better than most the dangers of obsession.

Maurice looked almost pained. "Honestly, some people don't deserve to live in a nice street like this."

Chapter 36

Greg had risen early. An interminable sorting dream had put him through the wringer. He had been in a supermarket surrounded by towering shelves filled with cornflakes. Only someone had mixed the crunchy nut variety in with the regular ones. The boxes were all mixed up and begged to be separated and restacked. The repeated moving and sorting only to find a crunchy nut box had suddenly appeared on the standard cornflake shelf and vice versa had been so frustrating and stressful he had woken with a headache and stiff shoulders.

The alarm had gone off at 5.30, by which time he was already up anyway. He had set it to ensure he was awake well before Crompton became active, but forgotten to turn it off, was in the shower when it sounded, and so had to endure a couple of minutes of its high-pitched squawking before he rinsed off, and dried off, enough to hit the quiet button.

He was dressed and on his way through the hall to the kitchen to make a second cup of tea and resume keeping watch on Crompton when he heard the letterbox snap shut. He looked around in time to actually see the white package hit the mat.

This time there was no doubt. The white bubble-pack envelope had landed face up and it was blank, just like the others.

He ran, fumbled out his keys and unlocked the door, threw it wide, to catch a figure just at the head of the path. He shouted.

"Hey! You!"

The figure actually jumped a little, and looked back.

Greg stared him in the face.

197

And had not a single clue who he was.

The youth, 15, maybe 16 years old at best, was black with a design clipped into the side of his hair, a backpack was slung over one shoulder, a dark blue blazer, black trousers, shirt, stripy tie, shoes that looked like they could wear a polish… a typical school kid. He was looking at Greg, warily.

"Did you just post something through my door?"

The boy nodded. "Yeah, he asked me to."

He looked to the road, started to point, and then seemed surprised to find no one there. "The guy was in a van, parked up there. I just was passing when he pulled up and asked me if I'd be good enough to just pop a package through your letterbox, said he was already running late, but he'd promised he would to get it to you this morning."

"You didn't know him?"

The youth shrugged. "Sorry mate, not from Adam. Just trying to do a guy a favour. Look, mate I gotta get moving, be late for school, you know?"

The boy moved to leave.

"Wait! The man, what did he look like?"

Again the boy just shrugged. "Glasses, had a woolly hat on? Just a guy."

"How old? Tall, short…"

"Wasn't really paying attention, and he was sitting down, so hard to say, you know? Look, I really do need to go."

"How old? What did his face look like?"

The boy seemed to think. "White guy. Thirty, forty? Maybe fifty? I only saw him for a second. I was passing, he asked if I could post something, save him getting out his van, I did." The boy was starting to look uncomfortable; Greg was aware he was making him feel uncomfortable. "Sorry I can't be more help."

The boy started again to leave, and for a moment Greg considered asking him for his phone number, or offering the boy his own in case some detail came to him, but a strange man asking for or offering phone numbers to a school boy would be open to all sorts of misunderstanding. He let the boy go. Whoever had been in the van knew exactly what he was doing. Pull up and wave a passing pedestrian over, ask them to take a momentary diversion to do a busy man a favour... How many people would actually say no in the moment? And how many would remember much about the driver, especially if he didn't want to be recalled? A hat, glasses. Things a person would be most likely to remember, and things that, rather conveniently, best concealed the man beneath.

Greg closed the door.

Then closed it again.

And four subsequent times.

—

Greg was wearing a pair of brand new, searing yellow rubber dishwashing gloves, and holding a pair of tweezers Beth had sterilised in boiling water. A sheet of sketching paper lay on the kitchen table, on which rested the latest package.

Part of him had known it would only a matter of time before another would arrive. It had turned out to be six days. Eventually, amid the utility bills, and double glazing and pizza delivery leaflets, and Maurice Cooper's newsletters, a white bubble-pack envelope would silently slip through his letterbox— Greg was only surprised that he'd managed to see it happen.

Greg had slipped the package, unopened, into a sandwich bag. He was following the plan—he and Beth had discussed the procedure should another package arrive. Calling her was the very next thing he did. In less than a quarter of an hour she was sitting across the kitchen table from him.

She gave him a quiet nod to proceed.

Greg peeled the package's adhesive flap open with the tweezers, slowly, so as not to tear it. The package was evidence, they needed to preserve the integrity of it, be 'forensically aware' as Beth put it. If the package's flap was dry gum sealed there could be saliva on it. There could be a stray hair that had found its way into the package, fingerprints… Hence the sheet of paper, rubber gloves and the tweezers.

"Steady."

He caught Beth's eye, and nodded, suddenly feeling like someone from a movie attempting to disarm a bomb. Which wire, red or blue, red or blue…? Except he was no movie hero, and was holding a grooming instrument instead of a wire clipper, and whatever was inside was only deadly by implication, if they failed to identify who the item pointed to and act in time to stop them becoming the killer's next victim.

Greg had teased the package's flap open. He set the tweezers down and tipped the contents onto the sheet of paper.

They both stared at it.

"Is that a dishwasher tablet?"

Greg nodded. "I think so."

"So?"

"What?"

"Any idea who it relates to?" Beth asked.

"Absolutely none."

"I was afraid of this," Beth said.

"Of what?"

"I wonder if maybe you're not supposed to know who the item points to. Maybe it's not a clue to help you catch him. Maybe none of them were."

"So what is it then?"

"Did you know Bernard Brocklehurst was allergic to wasp stings?"

"No."

"Did you know Rose Gordon was fond of whisky?"

"I was pretty sure she liked a drink, but whisky in particular? No."

"Brett Foster. You told me he was a fitness junkie. I remember that."

"I used to see him run, and he was in good shape."

"Steve Holt. Crushed under his classic Rover. Did you know he'd bought the car, was working on it, that he was a classic Rover fan, even?"

"No. I had no idea."

"Then how can they be clues? They're too obtuse. This here, a dishwasher tablet... How many people on Kettle Street must have a dishwasher? Dozens at least. Sting cream, a miniature bottle of whisky, a protein bar, a Rover keyring, they're nowhere near enough to point to a victim, until they're dead, until you know how they died."

"So why's he doing it? Why is he risking getting these to me?"

"To show you it was him. The phone call, that's your chance. That's when the real clues come, the ones that point to the victim, and the time limit? It has to be to catch him, not to save the victim. How can it be? A few minutes? He can't be calling you then killing them, there's not time. It's how long he's giving you to come catch him."

201

"But that means…"

"The person this dishwasher tablet relates too is as good as dead, they just don't know it yet."

"Is it Crompton? It has to be, right?"

"Right now we have to view him as our prime suspect. The only thing we can do is keep watching him, night and day, as often as humanly possible. We'll take shifts, because if he's preparing to strike, we need to be ready, catch him at the scene." Beth reached for her phone, pointed it at the window and took a picture. The phone made an electronic camera shutter noise, "And get solid evidence even our Detective Dingle can't ignore."

Chapter 37

Greg's bedroom was situated to the front of his flat. Entering through the front door into the hall, it lay to the right, with the kitchen directly ahead, and next to this his modest lounge. In short, Greg's bedroom window offered the best view across and up the street to Crompton's flat.

It was their third evening of such surveillance. Outside the light was fading. The bedroom lights were off, rendering Greg and Beth as good as invisible behind the net curtains to anyone passing by; conversely the evening offered more than enough light for them to see Crompton if he emerged from his home.

Sitting on a couple of kitchen chairs set in front of the window, they were watching his flat. Watching, and watching, and talking and watching, and drinking tea and eating chocolate digestives, and watching… Beth set the binoculars down. Since catching a few glimpses of Crompton through his kitchen window an hour ago, there had been no further visible activity. She took a sip of her third cup of tea of the evening (she was ordinarily a coffee drinker, but at Greg's… Well when in Rome) and set it down on Greg's bedside table.

They had been discussing their families.

"Oh, no doubt about it," she continued, "university was as much about escaping my mum and dad's clutches as getting a degree. It's not that I don't love them, I do, to bits, I just knew I had to get away if I was ever going to learn to fend for myself. I imagine most parents are protective of their kids, but the older I got the more I felt the weight of it, you know? They were afraid the world was going to hurt me, and I was afraid enough all on my own. I wanted to be more independent, and I saw that wasn't going to happen if I continued to live at home.

"I knew going to university in another city would force me out of my comfort zone, force me to try new things, make new friends, without the added stress of having my mum and dad watch over me like I was walking a high-wire without a net.

"And actually it was great. I did make friends, and learned to fend for myself. I had a ton of fun too, fell in love along the way… and experienced disappointment and heartbreak in the process, but maybe that was important, too. We are forged in adversity, right? That's true enough, isn't it? Pass me a biscuit."

Greg grabbed the packet and held it out. She plucked a pair of chocolate digestives from the neck.

"Either way, I think I emerged stronger, more self-reliant. I'm not sure that would have happened if I'd chosen to remain living at home, tucked under my mum and dad's wing. Aren't you in some sense always a child until you leave home? No matter how old you are."

"I moved out after my mum died. I was in my mid-twenties, more than old enough to be leaving the family home, but it didn't feel the same without her there anyway. It felt like that was all the house was, somewhere she wasn't anymore. I had to get out. Adrian did soon after. That says something. He hadn't before, and let's face it living with me isn't easy. I know I'm messed up. Somehow my mum made it work, though. She was like the oil and the rest of us gears, she stopped us all from grinding. Me, Adrian and Colin on our own, it wasn't the same. Too much friction."

"Everybody is messed up, I think. Some people just don't know it, or are good at hiding it."

"You seem pretty together."

"You mean apart from being a spaz?" Beth smiled.

"Come on, you know what I mean."

"So you have your OCD stuff going on. You're working on it, though, right?"

"Without much success. Maybe if I didn't feel trying to get better was as much for Adrian as me... It's like you were saying about getting away from your mum and dad. I know Adrian cares, only wants the best for me, but that creates a lot of pressure, which doesn't really help."

"Adrian? He's your little brother, right?"

"Yeah. Mr Perfect."

"Mr Perfect?" Beth pulled a face. "Why do you say that?"

"Successful career, financially comfortable, organised, driven, athletic, well-educated, well-travelled, well-dressed, well-groomed, well-adjusted, well-intentioned... I was a picky kid from day one by all accounts; my peas couldn't touch my meat; I used to sort any multi-coloured sweets into piles of the same colour before I ate them, that sort of thing. The older I got the worse it got, but it was always there. While I hid in my room drawing superheroes and reading comic books, Adrian was busy being brilliant, being moved into all the top sets at school, scoring the winning goal on the school football team or something. He was sporty, popular, he got good grades…"

"Do I sense some sibling rivalry here?"

"Ha. No, no rivalry. I'm happy to admit it; Adrian was always the clear winner. And I never wanted to compete. The only person who saw us as equal was my mum. I'm not sure Colin ever much liked me."

"Your dad?"

"My stepdad. Adrian's too. Our real dad died when I was a toddler and Adrian still an infant. He was hit by a car. I was with him, we were crossing the road. I don't remember anything about it, though, too young. My mum met Colin a few years later and remarried. He wasn't a bad father I suppose, and it was probably easier for him to form a bond with Adrian. I was a little older, seven, and... well, already had all my stuff going on. Adrian was practically still a baby. He did try with me. I'll give him that, maybe even beyond keeping my mum happy. When she died... It was hard for all of us, but things between Colin and me kind of broke down, so I moved out, managed to get this place from the council. Adrian moved out a few years later. If I had to guess, I'd say living with Colin might not have been a party for him either. Not that Aid would ever admit it. It certainly hasn't stopped him from trying to patch things up."

"How did you lose your mum?"

"She slipped on an icy path one evening, simple as that. Hit her head, fell funny, landed in just the wrong spot. A fall that should have meant a bad lump and a headache fractured her skull and caused serious brain injury. She died in the hospital the next day."

"That's awful, Greg. I'm sorry."

"Me too."

"He wants you and your dad to make up? Adrian does?"

"Yeah."

There was a spell where Beth said nothing. Greg was happy to let the topic go, but then she said, "He's married, your brother?"

"No."

"He has a partner though. He's in a good relationship?"

"No. He's single."

"Hm. I wonder then."

"Wonder what?"

"If he's so perfect, why has no one snapped him up?"

"He travels a lot, works all around the country. I assume that makes relationships hard."

"Plenty of other folk seem to manage it."

"I'm sure if he wanted a partner he'd have one. He's the can-do sort." Greg half smiled. "I'm more the can't-do sort."

"Don't sell yourself short. You have some good stuff going on."

"Yeah? Like what?"

"You're an amazing artist, kind, and kind of good-looking."

"You think I'm—"

"Shhh, look." Beth had suddenly snatched up the binoculars. Greg followed her gaze through the window all the way to Crompton's front door. He was pulling the door shut, carrying something. Greg identified it almost at once. It was the same curious wooden case he had been carrying before. There was something about the case that called attention to it. Part of it was that it was clearly one-of-a-kind, made by hand, and not by some master craftsman, but someone with more rudimentary skills, a talented schoolboy woodwork project level of craft. It was black and solid, and quite large, not quite as tall and wide as a briefcase, but deeper, boxier in shape.

"He had that before."

"What, the case?"

"Yeah, when I almost walked into him coming home that night."

"Right." Beth was already on the move. She grabbed Greg's shirt and pulled him with her. "We're going to tail him. See exactly where he's going."

They hurried into the hallway, and grabbed their coats and shoes.

Beth was at the door. She turned to stare him right in the face. "I'm going to close this okay? I'm a door closing expert, practically a champion in the door closing department. You can trust me. You will not need to check it. Okay? Got your keys?"

Greg nodded dumbly, trying to catch up with how fast events were suddenly moving. And like that, Beth pulled him outside and closed the door. She held the knocker, stared at him, and gave it a firm tug.

"Closed. See? Secure."

Then she was pulling him down the path. He had just left his flat faster than on any occasion since moving in. He negotiated the path's paving and then the street's, hurrying to keep up.

"There he is," Beth whispered.

Crompton was already a good way up the road, but didn't appear to be in a hurry. Beth hadn't stopped moving. She still had Greg's hand, too, and they were going at a healthy clip, even if it did require him to practically skip along to avoid the paving seams. They closed the distance, Crompton wasn't so far ahead now, but they needed to cross, get onto his side of the road.

Beth appeared to select a spot and swerved to a stop.

"Close your eyes."

"What?"

"Don't argue. Just bloody close them."

Greg did as he was told. Knowing full well what she was about to do, and working just as hard to avoid thinking about it.

"We are not crossing the road, okay? We're just going to walk along the edge next to the kerb. There are no cracks. It's all tarmac. Good?"

Before he could even respond she pulled him over the kerb. In his head he resisted, but his feet were moving. He knew they were crossing, but that wasn't what he saw. What he chose to picture was what she had described; they were simply tracking the road, just hurrying along the gutter parallel to the path, and, for a few seconds it worked.

Then the panic hit. The klaxon in his head started up. They were crossing, without the count. Shock licked a strip of cold sweat up his back and laid frost on his bones. Dread sluiced through his veins like iced water.

He opened his eyes to find they were already across the road. It didn't help.

Beth either wasn't aware, or was too focused on Crompton, because she was still pulling him on. He scrambled to avoid the cracks on the pavement. Crompton was at the head of the street now, about to turn and vanish from view. Beth quickened their pace. Greg tried to get a rein on himself, but it wasn't easy. His heart was hammering faster and faster in his chest, smashing blood through his arteries rather than pumping. He could actually feel the veins in his neck and ears throbbing. If this continued he knew with a conviction that had precious little to do with common sense that he would die. Conversely, while he feared his heart was going to explode, his chest felt like it had suddenly shrunk. When he tried to breathe he seemed only capable of drawing in tiny hitches of air into his lungs. It wasn't enough, so he was forced to breathe faster just to get any air at all…

He needed to get control, stop, count and cross back over the road, set things right before he dropped dead on the spot, but Beth wasn't quitting. She still had his hand and was dragging him on.

They reached the top of the street to find Crompton had stopped a short stretch ahead. He was standing at the bus stop with his back to them, preparing to board the bus even now slowing to a stop. They watched as its door wheezed open and he stepped in and dumped his money into the pay box. Seconds later the bus pulled away and sailed right past them.

Greg threw up on the pavement.

–

It took over half an hour before they were again sitting in Greg's flat.

Beth felt awful. She just hadn't appreciated Greg's OCD would be such an issue. No, that wasn't right. She had expected it would be a problem, but not such a large one. She had mistakenly believed if she got him moving fast enough they could get around it. The moment it became clear they would have to move quickly and cross the road to tail Crompton she had known: there just wasn't going to be time for Greg to count to one hundred umpteen times, so she had improvised. And it had worked, sort of, for a while. What she hadn't really considered was the fallout.

After Crompton's bus glided past and Greg had relocated his dinner plus several digestive biscuits diluted with tea to the pavement, she had belatedly realised he was teetering on the verge of a full-blown meltdown. He looked awful, white as bone, sweating profusely, visibly shaking. It was the look of caged panic on his face that caused her to feel the most shame though. She had guided him to a wall fronting one of the houses nearby and sat him down.

Almost hyperventilating, he had explained he was having a panic attack. After mumbling to himself several times that he was 'not dying' and repeatedly checking his pulse, he had closed his eyes, and they just waited. Beth fought the urge to keep asking if he was okay. Eventually he had climbed to his feet. He still looked shaky but his breathing was almost back to normal and some colour had returned to his cheeks. He'd handed her his keys and told her to go back to his flat. He would join her as soon as he could. She didn't argue.

Standing at the bedroom window, she tried to resist, but she couldn't help stealing a look at him crossing, or attempting to cross the road again and again. It took him almost fifteen minutes.

–

"Are you okay?"

Greg nodded. "You mean apart from feeling like a massive useless idiot?"

"Don't do that. You can do plenty."

She meant it. While loathe to admit it, there were things she found tricky or frustrating because of her CP, but so what? There were lots of so-called able-bodied people who were more 'disabled' than she was simply because they chose to sit around, letting

211

their health suffer, watching television or playing videogames twelve hours out of every twenty-four. How many people couldn't write a coherent sentence, not because they had learning difficulties, but because they just couldn't be bothered to learn, and were content to have the only book they owned be the Argos catalogue?

She wanted to tell Greg he was a fighter, someone who did things even though they were hard. Like her, he faced ridicule from ignorant people every time he left the house, walking in his irregular gait as he dodged the cracks between the paving, every time he crossed the road, tried to close his front door, moved an object to make it fit neatly into whatever invisible order his mind commanded as he had in Dingle's bland little office…

Beth wanted to tell him all this, but she didn't, because this was the wrong moment. It would sound patronising. She'd had her fill of that over the years, too many condescending smiles and gushing 'you've done sooo well's…

She took a different route.

"So," she asked, "what now?"

He thought about it for a moment.

"We wait. We watch. He has to come back sometime, right?"

Chapter 38

 Night crept over Kettle Street until one by one the flats' and houses' lights switched on and the streetlights awoke, spilling pools of light down onto the road and paths. Beth spotted the large figure strolling down the path, case in hand, first.

"Hold on! He's back. Look."

Greg had spotted Crompton immediately. Even though the street was dark and he was scarcely a silhouette, his body language, the hard swagger of his locomotion was unmistakable. The case, gripped in his right hand, swung at his side. He reached his flat, turned down the path and let himself in.

Greg grabbed the binoculars and trained them on the kitchen window. A minute later a light came on and Crompton appeared at the sink.

Unzipping his jacket, Crompton hurled it onto the table behind him and began fussing with the front of his t-shirt. A large dark stain was clearly visible on the front. He mouthed what could only have been a string of curses, judging by the expression on his crudely carved face, and peeled the t-shirt off. There were deep red smears where the stain had soaked through to the skin. Naked from the waist up, muscular, tattooed arms flexing, he stared at the garment. For a moment Greg thought he was going to turn on the tap and start to rinse it.

Instead he spun and flung it into a linen basket in on the work surface above his washing machine. He grabbed the box of detergent on top, shook it, peered inside, mouthed more colourfully silent profanities, and strode over to the swing-top bin on the other side of the room, slamming the empty box into its belly.

He walked from the kitchen, switching the light off behind him.

Beside him, he heard Beth's voice.

"Holy fuck, Greg. We need to get that shirt. That was blood or I'm America's Next Top Model. If we go to the police again it has to be with something concrete. We need evidence. I want that shirt."

"And how exactly do you suggest we get it?"

"What you were telling me how the killer could be using the right-of-way… You think Crompton's back window frame is still broken?"

Chapter 39

Greg carried the mugs of tea from the kitchen through his bedroom door and set them on the bedside table. Bathed in morning light, Beth was watching Crompton's flat through the binoculars.

"It's seven-thirty. He should be leaving soon. You said you usually pass him fetching his Racing Post and on the way to the bookie's around eight?"

They had taken turns keeping watch. Greg had taken the first shift, while Beth had napped on the bed (or attempted to) for a few hours. Crompton's lights had gone off at midnight and remained off. Greg had woken Beth at three to take over when, eyelids drooping, he was afraid he might fall asleep himself without meaning to.

He hadn't slept much better himself, just drifting in and out. He would surface, steal a moment to watch Beth keeping vigil, drink in her beautiful profile in the darkness. A girl in his bedroom; there was a novelty.

The thought of invading Crompton's flat was not a calming one. On the other hand, the prospect of securing a piece of evidence that might bring an end to the whole horrific business sounded pretty good.

Beth had filled him in on what he had missed. She had witnessed no further activity during the night. Once dawn broke she had checked; the blood-stained shirt was still in the linen basket in the corner where he had thrown it. Through the binoculars it was even possible to spot part of it spilling over the lip.

Beth, elbows leant on the chest of drawers in front of the window, binoculars still trained on Crompton's flat, suddenly sat up. Greg hurried forward in time to see Crompton's front door open wide and the man himself stepping out. They watched him amble down the path and up the road. He was empty-handed; the squat case was still in his flat, then.

Beth stood up and set the binoculars down.

"Ready?"

Greg sorely wanted to admit that, as it happened, no, he wasn't even close to ready. The prospect of breaking and entering (okay, technically just entering, seeing as Crompton's back window was already unsecured) filled him with dread.

"Greg? It's now or never."

As tempting as never sounded, he knew there was no backing out now. If another body turned up and the blood on the shirt matched the victim, it could be over. Crompton would have the full glare of the authorities on him. The resulting investigation would surely unearth something else to connect him to the other deaths.

Crompton was already a tiny figure at the top of the road before they hit the end of Greg's path. He and Beth had discussed this already. If Crompton followed his usual habit, picked up his Racing Post at Pete's and on to the bookie's, they might have an hour or more, but Greg had no intention of spending anything like that long in Crompton's flat, wanted to get it done as fast as possible.

They hit the kerb and Beth went to cross.

Greg cleared his throat. "I need to…"

Beth paused, opened her mouth to say something, closed it, then opened it again. "Of course you do. Sorry. Take your time."

Greg took a deep breath. One hundred, ninety-nine, ninety-eight…

Beth, to her credit, simply waited beside him patiently, as if there was no hurry.

Once he was done, he winced. He hadn't skipped a number, or even stumbled, but it didn't matter. It felt wrong. He started over.

One hundred, ninety-nine…

Around half way in he felt Beth's hand slip into his, give it a little squeeze. She continued to hold it.

He reached zero, waited for the part of him that held sway to respond. Was it good?

Yes, good. Only two counts was very good. Was it having Beth next to him? He thought maybe it was. Before he could dwell on it, risk opening the door to doubt, he looked both ways a final time, saw no traffic approaching in either direction and stepped out into the road. Once across, they hurried to the end of the street and turned into Badger Street, where the entrance to the right-of-way lay. The tall, pointy topped metal gate was, as usual, unlocked. They slipped through and hurried to the fence at the rear of Crompton's flat. The discarded TV cabinet was still propped against the fence, but hopefully still sturdy enough to serve as a step up. Greg placed a testing foot on it to check it would hold his weight, and then clambered onto it. From here, he swung a leg over the top of Crompton's fence and dropped down into his back garden. In under a minute Beth was standing next to him. Her technique was a little awkward but surprisingly athletic. He had managed it no faster.

The convict had done nothing to his wild garden since Greg's last reconnaissance sortie, and neither had he fixed his bedroom's broken window frame. They cut quickly to the back of the property.

"Me first?" Beth asked.

Greg considered gallantry for a moment, wondered if going first or second was better. When gaining illegal entry to a convicted killer's property the correct etiquette was murky, but on balance probably not a case of ladies first.

"No," he said at last. "Me. Just in case."

Greg wasn't exactly sure what he would do if Crompton came back and caught him climbing into his house, but it at least sounded good when he said it.

He lifted the window and hoisted himself up so his elbows rested on the lip. A little clambering and half his torso was in. He leant forward and gravity took care of the rest. In an instant he was lying in a heap on the floor of Crompton's bedroom.

He found his feet quickly enough to help Beth through the window a little less clumsily. So going first had been a good call after all.

"Right," Beth whispered. "Let's get that shirt."

They crept from Crompton's bedroom into his hallway and from there through into his kitchen. Through the window Greg could see his own flat across the road. The linen basket was still on the work surface above the washing machine, the shirt, stained with dark crimson, part of it draped over the edge. They began to make their way over when something stopped them in their tracks.

Behind them from the hall came the sound of the front door being opened.

Greg felt sick. Beth stared at him, panic on her face. She mouthed at him, Whatthefuck?

Greg looked back, mouthed, Hide?

They looked about the small kitchen frantically. There was a large cupboard in one corner. Beth dragged him over and opened the door.

Greg tried to take in what amounted to a case of storage disorder bordering on insanity…

Ironing board, bucket and mop, bottles, jars, rags, boxes, books, tools, magazines, DVDs, shopping bags, cleaning rags, drying rack, containers, rolls of bin liners… The cupboard had shelves but nothing jammed onto them appeared organised. The whole lot was just piled haphazardly everywhere, no discernible order at all. Greg became tangentially aware Beth was pushing at him. She wanted him to hide in the cupboard, amid all that mess…

He was about to tell her he couldn't, simply could not, when the door in the hall clomped shut, and it became a moot point because Beth all but heaved him forward and threw herself in after. She pulled the door closed and darkness swallowed them whole. They kept stock still, listened.

They heard the kitchen door bump against the wall, footsteps, and then something scraping on linoleum, a series of clicks followed by a muffled bump… Why had Crompton returned so soon? What hadn't he gone to the bookie's after Pete's shop like usual? Had he even got as far as Pete's shop? Either way he was back now, and where did that leave him and Beth?

At best they were indefinitely trapped in a killer's messy cupboard, trapped with Crompton's junk spilling all over them, piled from their feet up to their necks. Greg didn't suffer from claustrophobia, no more than the average person, but the mess? The mess had got into his head immediately. He felt it all around him, smothering him, intolerable; the confluence of darkness, dirt, dust, disorder was too much. He had to get out. The chaos surrounding him, unseen in the blackness, captured fleetingly as Beth had propelled him into the cupboard, was

219

ballooning, multiplying, seemed to be breeding, if not in the cupboard, in his head, claiming space reserved for logic, and certainly something as mundane as self-preservation.

"I can't do this!" he hissed. "Beth I can't—"

He felt her hands on his face. She was close. She couldn't be anything but close in the tight confines of Crompton's kitchen cupboard, but this was more. Deliberate. He felt her press against him, her warm breath, her breasts squished into his chest, and then... from nowhere her lips on his.

Then there was only her mouth, her lips, full, lovely and warm, fused with his and moving, and everything was, in an instant, different. It was like she had thrown off the switch to the great thrumming machine vibrating and grinding inside him, the current had stopped dead, the instrument fell quiet and utterly still.

Some distant corner of his mind registered the sound of a door banging closed.

He had no idea how long the kiss lasted, just that when it ended it felt like both forever and not nearly long enough. She broke away, and in the dark of the cupboard, the machine wound back into motion, its infernal ungreased gears grinding and grating and vibrating. Greg felt himself become Greg once more.

Beth whispered in his ear, "I think he's gone."

They waited just a little longer, still nothing. Beth opened the cupboard door a few inches and peeked out. A moment later she opened it, looked back at Greg, finger pressed to her lips, and crept out. He was on her heels, glad to be free of it.

Crompton had gone.

Behind them the rhythmic whirr and the sound of filling water already told them what to expect. They turned and, sure enough, saw the washing machine full of soapy water, the empty linen basket in front of it, suds sloshing back and forth, rinsing any evidence they might have hoped for away…

Chapter 40

Greg had, of course, put the kettle on. Beth suspected a box containing the words MAKE TEA? Y/N would appear frequently should someone ever make a flowchart of his core decision-making process. She recognised a stress reflex when she saw one, and if tea got Greg sitting, thinking and marginally more relaxed, then her view was 'white, one sugar please'.

On the way back he had asked her, as she knew he would. He crept up to the question like a sprung trap that might take off a finger.

"Why did you—"

She had the answer ready, a half truth, if only because she was only half sure why she had done it.

"I figured it was either kiss you or slap you. Kissing you was quieter."

And they had larger concerns to consider. The evidence they had hoped to secure had been destroyed. It was hard to know what else they could have done. They had gone as far as anyone could have, further than most. They had illegally entered another person's property, a very dangerous person, if their suspicions were correct, and had almost been caught. Crompton must have gone to Pete's shop, bought a fresh packet of detergent and come straight back to wash the evidence out of his blood-stained shirt. If they had only got their hands on it just it a few minutes sooner…

While Greg boiled his kettle, positioned two mugs, spooned two meticulously level teaspoons of sugar into them, poured in the water, let the teabags steep, removed them and deposited them into a swing-top bin clean enough to eat off, added milk and stirred, she was already thinking what to do next.

Beth hadn't taken long to conclude they needed to be a lot more prepared. If Crompton went on the move with his curious case again, she wanted to be ready to follow him, move quickly and with a little more ease, and maybe circumvent some of Greg's issues. She reckoned she had the answer.

–

Beth revealed her solution later that day. It had taken just a phone call, a debit card payment, digging out her licence and a trip to collect it. It was parked a little way down the road from Greg's flat, where, she explained, it would remain, ready to be utilised at any moment.

Greg looked it over.

"You hired a car?"

Beth nodded.

The small Fiat was dark blue and modest. The sort of car no one, particularly someone you might want to follow, would likely even notice was there.

"You can drive then?" Greg asked.

Beth frowned. "Yes, Greg, I can drive. This way if Crompton moves, catches a bus again, we'll be ready to follow him. Quickly, immediately and discreetly."

"Right."

She wanted to let it go, but she couldn't help feeling slightly annoyed. She hated it when people simply assumed she would be incapable of driving. Worse still, this car wasn't even a manual shift. It was an automatic, practically idiot proof. Park. Drive. Gas. Brake. Indicate. Steer.

She had learnt to drive over a decade ago, in her late teens. The lessons had been a gift from her

223

grandparents, and she had even passed the test first time, no sweat. Her CP had never got in the way one bit. She was somewhat wobbly on foot, but in a car she had no real issues. She decided to let it go.

Then decided not to.

"Why would you assume I can't drive?"

"I didn't."

"The only reason I don't have a car right now is because I don't need one. I live close enough to work to walk, and if I need to get around, public transport is more than adequate, and on the very rare occasions it's not I can just call a taxi."

"Right."

"For your information I drive very well. Besides this is an automatic, not far off driving a bumper car."

"Beth—"

"Just shift into drive and put your foot down. Any idiot could drive it."

They stood for a moment looking at the little car. It was Greg who broke the silence. He was wearing a strange smile. She wondered why.

"Not me. I've never been behind the wheel of a car in my life."

Chapter 41

The following few days passed without incident. Greg kept watch on Crompton throughout the day, going as far as to follow him to the corner shop for his Racing Post and on to the bookie's.

Crompton's timetable was remarkably predictable.

Greg and Beth had discussed the practicalities of their surveillance. The simple truth was they could not watch Crompton twenty-four seven. Furthermore, even when one or both of them were watching him, they couldn't guarantee he hadn't slipped from their sight. Crompton could exit his flat from the rear and clamber over the fence should he choose to and they might never know. The best they could hope for was a something to link him to the murders, some uncharacteristic behaviour that signalled he was preparing to go after his next victim, hope to catch him scoping his target out, making plans, collect some evidence to pin on him if he slipped up... It sounded thin, and desperately hopeful when laid out, but what other options were open to them? The police thought they were kooks, and Crompton had covered his tracks, left nothing to convince anyone the series of deaths on Kettle Street was anything other than a random clump of tragic accidents.

This was the thing. Greg got the impression many of Kettle Street's residents were blissfully unaware there had even been a string of fatal 'accidents' throughout the past weeks, let alone potential murders. Maurice might mention them in his next newsletter, but how many residents bothered reading them? Many probably filed them in the bin along with the junk mail. Most worked full-time jobs, had

225

children, and plenty of other things to keep them busy. Many might struggle to put names to neighbours who lived more than a few houses along. An ambulance half way down the street might catch their interest if they saw it in passing, but life went on. They might never hear that a man at the bottom of the street got stung by a wasp and died, or an old lady eleven doors down fell down the stairs drunk and died, or a young guy screwed up and choked himself with a heavy barbell or with his own Rover....

The whole business only seemed out of the ordinary once you stacked these accidents up, and to someone like Detective Dingle, who insisted upon irritating details like hard evidence, maybe not even then. Certainly a dishwasher tablet in a polythene bag in Greg's kitchen drawer wasn't about to mobilise a crack squad of CID officers to descend on Crompton. For now, it seemed he and Beth were all that lay between the residents of Kettle Street and an untimely death.

She came over after work; Greg cooked, they ate and watched Crompton's flat together, which, Greg had to admit, was nice. Beth was funny and smart. Sitting beside her, watching, discussing theories, talking about movies and music and themselves, made him realise how much of his time he spent alone. After his mum had died, it hadn't been the same. Somehow the absence of one person removed not a quarter of the warmth in their family home, but almost all of it. Leaving wasn't a difficult choice. His mum's life insurance policy, and her provisions for him and Adrian in her will, provided enough for him to get by. He lived frugally by most people's standards; teabags and comic books were about as decadent as his tastes reached.

In the past weeks he had seen more of Beth than any human being in years. Adrian had dropped by a lot when he first moved out, but over time his visits became less frequent, and felt motivated more by obligation than the genuine desire to see and spend time with him. Greg had convinced himself he liked his own company, or at least was comfortable with it, but talking with Beth, swapping stories, having a conversation that didn't just feel like killing time....

Then, ultimately, he would remember exactly why Beth was there, and it wasn't because time was being killed. It was because people were.

Chapter 42

Leslie Yates was up early, too early, over an hour earlier than she would have liked.

Dean had woken her on his way out to work, not intentionally, but because he appeared to find the simple act of closing the front door quietly impossible. He virtually slammed it behind him every time.

So she had lain awake, irritated, staring at the luminous digits on the alarm clock, far earlier than she needed to get up for work, too late to be able to relax and fall asleep again. It was the perfect imperfect timing.

Resigning herself to the fact her day had started whether she like it or not, she elected to get up and get ready, have a leisurely breakfast and get a few chores done before she had to leave for work herself. Not quite ready to eat, she had decided to shower first, see if some hot water might help rinse off the leaden feeling left from losing an eighth of her night's sleep.

Feeling marginally less zombified, she drew back the shower curtain and reached for her towel, only to find it wasn't there. The heated rail had just a single towel on it: Dean's. It was tossed carelessly over the top, was close to sopping wet, twisted and bunched up, meaning glaciers would melt sooner than it would dry. The annoying embers of being woken early due to sheer selfishness flared again. Even if simple common sense failed him, why couldn't Dean just do what she asked, do what anyone with half a brain would and just fold his towel in half and hang it over the rail so the heat could get through it? By the time the boiler went off at nine it would be dry.

For an instant she couldn't decide which riled her more, the stupid and lazy manner in which the towel had been abandoned, or the fact that it was the only one there.

When she set the towels out, she got two, one for herself and one for Dean, removing the old ones and putting them in the linen basket. When Dean's Neanderthal brain recognised he needed a fresh towel he had no trouble fetching one, except he did exactly that. He fetched one, for himself, which right now meant she was left, well, not high and dry exactly, more wet and cooling by the second. It felt like yet another inescapable sign of her new man's selfishness. She was supposed to be his lover, but outside of the bedroom it felt like she was fast becoming his mother.

She stared at the twisted, sopping wet towel. She would have to tramp, cold and dripping to the linen cupboard on the landing… Then realised she hadn't put the dry ones out of the tumble dryer away yet. They were still piled atop the dryer in the utility room—downstairs.

Hissing an inventive construction consisting of one proper noun, three adjectives and an expletive Leslie couldn't actually remember using before, she plucked Dean's gross, wet, lukewarm towel from the rail, wrapped it around herself and stepped out of the shower.

How could such small things, she wondered, make you want to kill someone?

And to think she had imagined Dean perfect once. No, not merely once but alarmingly recently.

They had met at a Halloween party thrown by one of Sharon's friends. Dean was dressed as Dracula and 'recently' divorced, which by his definition meant he and his wife had split some three years ago. Leslie had been single for approaching a year, since Iain had communicated their marriage wasn't in the best of shape through the medium of screwing a work colleague, a mousy stick insect called Fiona who worked in HR.

To her shame, she had been oblivious anything was even wrong. When Iain had taken her out for a meal (her favourite local Italian, Gino's, somewhere public, where he knew she wouldn't make a scene) and told her he A) was leaving her, and B) no longer loved her, and C) loved someone else he had been 'growing close to' for a while now, it had come as a bolt from the blue. He had moved out the same evening. He had rented a flat, he explained, to give them both 'room to adjust'.

The following months had been a humiliating trial, during which Leslie discovered Iain had not in fact rented a flat, but immediately moved in with his plain, half-woman-half-wafer lover, Fiona. Soon after this he had informed her he wanted to sell their four-bed home. It was around this point she had slowly realised all their friends had known about the affair for ages, but were too embarrassed or afraid to be the one to share the information with her.

This, the silence of people she had believed cared about her, hurt almost as much as Iain's betrayal. People she imagined turning to for support had not simply watched her made a fool of, but in their silence had been complicit in Iain's long-running deception. Too many of her close friends were Iain's friends too it appeared, and didn't want to take sides, but while Iain had the skeletal Fiona, she had no one.

She couldn't recall ever feeling so isolated and alone.

Then she met Sharon.

Sharon had started work at M&S three weeks after Iain moved out. She was middle-aged, like Leslie, single (as Leslie now was), friendly, fun, sympathetic and kind. She also, it turned out, had a busy social calendar, and was happy to make Leslie part of it.

Leslie went from a humiliated wife to a fun and sexy singleton overnight. She and Sharon got on like a house on fire. Sharon said she was better off without Iain. The world was full of better men. Why would a strong, smart woman like Leslie want to share a four-bedroom house with a selfish tosspot likely as clueless with a clitoris as he was with a washing machine or a cooking range?

Take your half, Sharon told her, buy your own house, a little smaller maybe, but all your own.

Then Sharon had met Trevor. She hadn't dumped Leslie, in fact she had made an obvious effort not to, but Trevor suddenly took a big slice of the time they had been sharing together. There were not just evenings out with Trevor, but evenings in. Sharon's social calendar became a lot thinner, which mean so too did Leslie's.

So when she had met Dean the timing had seemed perfect. To begin with the relationship was all passionate sex and glorious attention. Dean was spending so much time at the new two-bed house she had bought on Kettle Street, him moving in had just seemed to make sense. Why pay rent on his bedsit when he was hardly ever there? So what if they had only been seeing each other for four months?

Perspective and context are funny things. When someone is your guest you don't seem to see their faults quite so starkly. When Dean had been a visitor in her home and bed, she had never really expected him to pick up after himself, or help out with the housework, but once he was a permanent fixture and still didn't feel obliged to pitch in it suddenly chafed.

They had begun to have… not arguments, but spats.

Would it hurt him to tidy up a bit?

Could he not leave wet towels on the bed?

Could he not leave pubes on the soap?

Could he please close the toilet when he was done, or not leave coffee rings on the furniture, or possibly put the washing machine on now and then or peg the washing out on the line to dry, not leave crumbs on the sofa, empty the bin when it was so crammed full the swing-lid refused to swing, and god forbid, would it kill him to cook her a meal once in a while?

What annoyed her more than any of these things, though, was hearing herself complain about them. It made her sound like a nag. That had been one of Iain's retorts when he 'worked late', that he sometimes chose to even when he didn't have to just to escape her nagging. Why did men seem to think not wanting to live in a hovel equated to wanting to live in a show home?

Leslie stomped down the stairs and through the hallway into the kitchen and pulled up short.

She frowned.

The dishwasher door was lying open, the rack stacked with dirty dishes and cutlery. Had Dean filled it before leaving for work? Was this meant to be some sort of half-arsed peace offering? Had she finally got through to him? It seemed so, but even then it was too much to expect him to do it properly.

She stared at the open dishwasher, trying to see a glass half full.

Why if you loaded a dishwasher would you not take the extra thirty seconds to throw in a dishwasher tablet, close the bloody door and set it to wash?

She sighed. If you wanted something done properly, you really did have to do it yourself…

She advanced, and noticed he had put the cutlery in the bins with the knives facing upwards. Leslie knew you had to be more careful, if you put them in pointed end down you had to check they didn't poke through and interfere with the hot water spinning blaster thingy, but that was the way she always did it. They looked lethal pointing up like that, and for some reason Dean had decided to wash all the knives in the drawer, clean or dirty.

As she moved to flip the dishwasher drawer shut she saw something from the corner of her eye, something behind her, a shape looming from behind the kitchen door.

And then suddenly her feet were swept from beneath her, and she was shoved forward.

The dishwasher drawer raced to meet her.

A bed of sharp blades, razor-sharp, and Japanese, (only £199, a bargain deal from the QVC home shopping channel back when Iain's salary had made impulse buys a staple) slid effortlessly into her. She tried to scream, but as two of the many knife blades had punctured her lungs, instead of a cry, only a hoarse whistle and bloody foam burbled from her mouth.

Another blade had run straight through one of her heart's pulmonary arteries, the biological equivalent of pulling a hose pipe from a fast running tap. There was blood, a lot of it.

233

Leslie opened her mouth, forgot why she had done so and died shortly after.

The figure standing above her took a phone from his pocket and began to punch in a number. As it started to ring out, he took a step back, before the expanding pool of blood could reach his shoes.

Chapter 43

Greg had scarcely shut the door behind him when the phone rang. Aware it couldn't be that call (Crompton was after all in the bookie's scanning the day's races and placing his bets) his heart nevertheless began to thump.

He had been keeping watch over Crompton. He had glimpsed him eating breakfast and a short while later followed him to Pete's shop, watched him go in, come out with his Racing Post and continue to the bookie's. This was where he had doubled back, slipped into Pete's too, collected some milk, bread and a packet of chocolate digestives (with Beth around he had actually been in danger of running out rather than running low) and hurried home. If Crompton stuck to his routine he would be back in an hour.

He went to the living room and snatched up the phone. The whispery voice was unmistakable.

"Four minutes. Cream door. Lawn. Leaded windows."

The line went dead.

Crompton was in the betting shop. This couldn't be happening, not right now. Only Greg knew it was, and the clock was ticking. He ran into the hall and started pulling his shoes on. He flung his front door wide and practically leapt out, yanking it closed. He gave it a push to check. Shut.

He turned, but had he really closed it? Or just thought he had? Maybe he hadn't closed it as firmly as he had thought? Or had he not truly pulled it all the way shut? The part of his mind from where these doubts issued grew louder, warnings so deafening they threatened to crowd all other considerations out.

He didn't have time for this now. The seconds were ticking away, across the road behind a cream door and leaded windows someone's life had been taken, yet he still couldn't seem to move. Even knowing the killer might be standing over their body made no difference.

Cream Door. Lawn. Leaded windows.

There simply wasn't time to get caught up checking the door.

Because how did he check a door was properly closed? He did it until he was sure, took as long as it took for the voice inside him to be satisfied. If necessary he might have to go back inside, close the door behind him and start over, clean slate, because the door had to be closed, absolutely, definitely, demonstrably, definitively, closed. He had to feel it in his marrow, because otherwise he would be half way up the road or even on the bus or train and have to turn around and go back, heart pounding, sweat drenching his back and armpits, feeling the dread, the horrible all-consuming dread that coiled in his torso, took the place of his lungs, sucked in dread and anxiety and exhaled peace and comfort…

Cream door. Lawn. Leaded windows.

A person was dead. If Greg didn't catch the killer, he would slip away unseen and there would be another, and another until someone stopped it.

He looked back to his front door, and quite to his surprise he started backing away from it.

He plunged down the path, searching his memory. Which house? Which house had a cream door, a lawn out front and leaded windows? He was at the top of his path now, scanning the other side of the road. The hour was early, Kettle Street was deserted.

236

Cream door. Lawn. Leaded windows. Cream door. Lawn. Leaded windows. Cream door. Lawn. Leaded windows. Cream door. Lawn. Leaded windows...

He spotted it, down the far end of the street, ran bounding between paving slabs until he drew level with it, met the kerb and was pulled up short as surely as if he'd been wearing a tether.

He tried to step out—

Nothing happened.

He tried again, feeling the dwindling time limit ticking away as he stood paralysed at the edge of the deserted road. And knew there were some battles he couldn't win. If he was going to cross it was only after the count, but he knew that if he did it quickly and only once, there might still be time. He closed his eyes, tried to forget why he needed to cross, and began to count.

One hundred, ninety-nine, ninety-eight, ninety-seven, ninety-six, ninety-five, ninety-four, ninety-three, ninety-two, ninety-one, ninety, eighty-nine, eighty-eight, eighty-seven, eighty-six, eighty-five, eighty-four, eighty-three, eighty-two, eighty-one, eighty, seventy-nine, seventy-eight, seventy-seven, seventy-six, seventy-five, seventy-four, seventy-three, seventy-two, seventy-one, seventy, sixty-nine, sixty-eight, sixty-seven, sixty-six, sixty-five, sixty-four, sixty-three, sixty-two, sixty-one, sixty, fifty-nine, fifty-eight, fifty-seven, fifty-six, fifty-five, fifty-four, fifty-three, fifty-two, fifty-one, fifty, forty-nine, forty-eight, forty-seven, forty-six, forty-five, forty-four, forty-three, forty-two, forty-one, forty, thirty-nine, thirty-eight, thirty-seven, thirty-six, thirty-five, thirty-four, thirty-three, thirty-two, thirty-one, thirty, twenty-nine, twenty-eight, twenty-seven, twenty-six, twenty-five, twenty-four, twenty-three, twenty-two, twenty-one, twenty, nineteen, eighteen, seventeen, sixteen, fifteen, fourteen, thirteen, twelve, eleven, ten, nine, eight, seven, six, five, four, three, two, one…

He searched for the feeling, already knowing it was no good. He wasted no time and went again.

One hundred, ninety-nine, ninety-eight, ninety-seven, ninety-six, ninety-five, ninety-four, ninety-three, ninety-two, ninety-one, ninety, eighty-nine, eighty-eight, eighty-seven, eighty-six, eighty-five, eighty-four, eighty-three, eighty-two, eighty-one, eighty, seventy-nine, seventy-eight, seventy-seven, seventy-six, seventy-five, seventy-four, seventy-three—

He focused only on the count, running through the familiar sequence as fast as he dared—

Seventy-two, seventy-one, seventy, sixty-nine, sixty-eight, sixty-seven, sixty-six, sixty-five, sixty-four, sixty-three, sixty-two, sixty-one, sixty, fifty-nine, fifty-eight, fifty-seven, fifty-six, fifty-five, fifty-four, fifty-three, fifty-two, fifty-one, fifty, forty-nine, forty-eight, forty-seven, forty-six, forty-five, forty-four, forty-three, forty-two, forty-one, forty, thirty-nine, thirty-eight, thirty-seven, thirty-six, thirty-five, thirty-four, thirty-three, thirty-two, thirty-one, thirty, twenty-nine, twenty-eight, twenty-seven, twenty-six, twenty-five, twenty-four, twenty-three, twenty-two, twenty-one, twenty, nineteen, eighteen, seventeen, sixteen, fifteen, fourteen, thirteen, twelve, eleven, ten, nine, eight, seven, six, five, four, three, two, one.

He waited for the feeling to come. It didn't.

He took a step, already knowing it was futile. He couldn't. Stepping out into the road was like trying to step off the top floor window ledge of a skyscraper. He took a breath, refused to unravel.

One hundred, ninety-nine, ninety-eight, ninety-seven, ninety-six, ninety-five, ninety-four, ninety-three, ninety-two, ninety-one, ninety, eighty-nine, eighty-eight, eighty-seven, eighty-six, eighty-five, eighty-four, eighty-three, eighty-two, eighty-one, eighty, seventy-nine, seventy-eight, seventy-seven, seventy-six, seventy-five, seventy-four, seventy-three, seventy-two, seventy-one, seventy, sixty-nine, sixty-eight, sixty-seven, sixty-six, sixty-five, sixty-four, sixty-three, sixty-two, sixty-one, sixty, fifty-nine, fifty-eight, fifty-seven, fifty-six, fifty-five, fifty-four, fifty-three, fifty-two, fifty-one, fifty, forty-nine, forty-eight, forty-seven, forty-six, forty-five, forty-four, forty-three, forty-two, forty-one, forty, thirty-nine, thirty-eight, thirty-seven, thirty-six, thirty-five, thirty-four, thirty-three, thirty-two, thirty-one, thirty, twenty-nine, twenty-eight, twenty-seven, twenty-six, twenty-five, twenty-four, twenty-three, twenty-two, twenty-one, twenty, nineteen, eighteen, seventeen, sixteen, fifteen, fourteen, thirteen, twelve, eleven, ten, nine, eight, seven, six, five, four, three, two, one.

Please…?

This time it came, the feeling, like a piece sliding neatly into place.

The road was thankfully still empty. He broke into a run.

He reached the front door of the house and jammed his eyes to a lifted letterbox, saw nothing but a stretch of coffee-coloured hallway. The cream door was solid timber. He wasn't sure he would have been able to kick it in if he tried. He thought immediately of Crompton's broken frame, perhaps the rear of the house… He ran around to the entry way and found the gate open, praying to find an open window, or unlocked patio door.

He reached the back garden, saw a set of glazed French doors and hurried to peer through them. The handles wouldn't budge. Locked.

Half of the kitchen floor was dark and glossy. Greg jammed his face to the glass. From behind the work surface trailed a pair of naked legs and the lower half of a torso wrapped in something deep red. It took a moment to make sense of what he was looking at. What must have been the door to a dishwasher was open. It sagged under the weight of the body upon it.

Greg felt numb with shock.

What now, call the police?

The garden looked untouched, there were no footprints in the grass, although a path snaked from the patio to the far end, beyond which ran the right-of-way. Had Crompton scaled the fence, hopped over and made his escape? Greg hurried down the path, grabbed the top of the fence and pulled himself up, peering down the right-of-way, half expecting to see a figure fleeing. The right-of-way was deserted. He dropped back down, and something snagged his shirt. The fabric had caught on the fence. One of his shirt buttons pinged off and landed on the grass.

He instinctively reached out to pick it up, and as he did a thought sidled into his head.

What if he hadn't seen the button come off? What if it had just sat there in the grass waiting for someone to find it?

He stared back up to the house. The early morning light fell on the French door's glazing and he saw something clear as day: two hand prints and a blob where he had pressed his face to the glass.

He picked his way back up the path. The killer would have been careful not to leave evidence, nothing that might suggest anything but an accident was responsible for the demise of this Kettle Street resident any more than the previous four.

Yet in less than a minute Greg had almost left a shirt button, ten fingerprints and a quarter print of his stupid face. Right now there was far more to tie him to the dead person lying in a slowly spreading pool of blood in the kitchen beyond the French door than anyone else. A question presented itself:

Why was the killer trying to get Greg to the scene of the murders immediately after they had happened? Did he really want to be stopped, or maybe, just maybe was he hoping to frame someone else for his crimes?

Greg suddenly had an image of himself sitting in Detective Dingle's interview room, not as a witness, but a 'person of interest'. That's what the police and the news always called people who they suspected of being guilty of something, but who hadn't been caught or charged yet.

He backed away from the glass, panic rising. Without a second thought he stepped forward again, tugged his sleeve over his wrist and began to scrub at the glazing, erasing every last trace of his hand and face prints. He stared at the result. Fortunately the windows must have been cleaned recently, because instead of the porthole clean patch Greg suddenly feared finding, he faced nothing but a squeaky clean, unblemished, window.

He looked around, checking he hadn't left any other trace of his presence. He needed to get away. He needed to call the only person who might understand and he could trust. He needed to call Beth.

Chapter 44

"Greg, you're going to need to slow down. I can't even hear you properly."

"There's been another, and I don't know what to do. I think he might be trying to frame me."

Greg explained about the call, the body, and his handprints on the French door's glazing.

"What? No, why would…" Beth had been about to tell him that was crazy, but then the sinister logic of it dropped neatly into place. Commit a murder, make it look like an accident, leave no evidence, but engineer it so someone arrives at the scene soon after you're gone? Let them go bumbling around leaving all manner of contamination in their wake, DNA, footprints, fingerprints, fibres…

And who might you choose for this job? Maybe someone who lives on the same street as your victims, someone easily identifiable as 'odd', someone hampered by a condition which leaves them ill-equipped to actually stop you, someone who will reach the scene but not too quickly, safely after you've departed? Then if someone were later to view the deaths as suspicious, start looking for evidence, witnesses…

She didn't tell Greg it was crazy.

"Wait there. Don't move. I'll be right over."

She found Hailey in Books on Tape/CD, and arranged to take her lunch early. It was becoming at bit of a habit, but Hailey was a good egg, and knew Beth wouldn't ask unless it was important. For the same reason she had to be beginning to wonder if something was up.

"Are you feeling okay? You don't look so great."

"No. I'm fine, honest, I just need some fresh air."

"Hm." Hailey looked less than convinced. "If you need the rest of the afternoon off just take it."

Beth nodded, thanked her. Five minutes later she was striding down Kettle Street, only to find five minutes was plenty of time for events to have moved on. An ambulance and a police car were parked outside a house near the bottom of the road. A white van was parked nearby. Beth slowed her pace.

A man was sitting on the kerb, looking very much like he was in shock. A female police officer was crouched beside him, and appeared to be doing her best to comfort him. Beth joined the dots. Whoever the stricken-looking man was, it seemed very likely he knew the latest victim. Whether husband, partner, brother, or friend he must have dropped by the house and found the body after Greg had left.

The question of what to do next had suddenly grown more complicated.

–

Beth had expected to find Greg agitated, stressed, maybe even wrestling with a panic attack, but if anything he looked angry. After opening the door to her he had turned and stormed into the kitchen.

She slipped her shoes off, squared them up on the mat and followed. The sandwich bag with the package and dishwashing tablet was on the kitchen table.

"I took too long, just like he knew I would. I tried to get there. I really did—" Greg shook his head, Beth could see his jaw clenching. "Four minutes. I nearly made it, can't have been more than five, six… I tried to hurry…"

243

"I know," Beth sympathised. Greg had every right to be angry. The killer was playing with him, but she wanted to make sure his anger was directed squarely where it belonged, and that was not with himself. "This is not your fault, hear me? Whatever game this is, you never chose to take part, you didn't get to pick the rules, set the pieces or weight the die. This is not your fault. These people's deaths are not your fault."

Greg's eyes fell on the package, the clue that only made sense once another body provided the context. Then he looked at her.

"He thinks I can't stop him, but he's wrong," he said. "I don't know how, but I'm going to, I swear it."

For a moment she thought she glimpsed a shadow, a Greg who crossed roads with nothing more than a glance left and right perhaps, who walked away from his front door confident in the knowledge doors didn't spontaneously pop open, who could, if he chose, leave a tap dripping, or set the mugs in his cupboard without considering which way their handles faced, who stepped on seams and cracks in paving with reckless abandon... Someone shaped by different personal circumstances might have mistaken this glimpsed shadow for a normal Greg, a Greg with the OCD excised, a carefree, obsession-free Greg, but Beth knew better.

In the same way there was no Beth Grue without CP, there was no Greg Unsworth without OCD.

People were not machines, with component parts you could simply swap out or remove, and even if you could, only a fool would expect what was left to remain unchanged. People were the sum total of all their parts, fundamentally indivisible. The things that shape someone into who he or she is cannot be

244

sifted through, bits kept or thrown away. It all matters. Nothing escapes. It's all there, sometimes front and centre, sometimes buried deep inside, informing views, shaping choices.

Are qualities like kindness and empathy sparked by acts of cruelty or generosity? Is apathy birthed by privilege or want? Is it our strengths or our weaknesses we owe to our encounters with adversity? How are we to know? Which experiences should we thank and which should we curse? To Beth's mind the answer was rarely clear.

All the times she recalled being made to feel like a freak, grotesque and broken inside and out, by girls so seemingly perfect, so popular and pimple-free they treated school less like a place of learning and more like a party, somewhere to rule, to flirt and to hurt. To enjoy the attention of boys they liked, and trample the girls they branded losers, the less fashionable, less pretty, or like her, less 'normal'…

Would she change that?

Not for one second. She wasn't sure if she agreed with the whole what doesn't kill you makes you stronger philosophy, but those experiences had shaped her, had made her who she was, and she liked who she was.

In the same way she believed there was really only one Greg, and OCD was part of the package. So, no, the shadow she had glimpsed was not some other Greg, because no such thing existed. The shadow was thrown by the Greg she knew, the same one who had just sworn to catch a killer.

"We need to stop playing by his rules," she said.

Greg nodded. "Find an edge, be ready in case he slips up, stop him before someone else dies."

Chapter 45

Beth had been tempted to skip O'Shea's class, but after some internal debate had elected not to. She needed time to think, and that meant space to think. She and Greg had watched Compton and still not prevented another death. And something didn't add up. Maybe because of the writing classes it was hard not to view the real life murder story unfolding through the lens of a fictional murder mystery. If this were a story Crompton would just be too obvious a suspect. That bothered her.

She again found herself staring at the homemade incident board, staring at the names, dates and other details, convinced some vital clue was staring right back at her, the sneaking suspicion she was missing some larger obvious point. Despite everything it was this that convinced her she needed to get away, if only for one evening.

She needed time to clear the mental decks, see clearly, and as Greg had yet to receive another package that meant they had time.

The class would be the ideal distraction, help her mind stop going over and over, stuck on a loop, perhaps let her come back to look at the Kettle Street murders with a fresh eye, and besides, for what it was worth, Greg would be watching Crompton.

O'Shea didn't mess around; less than a minute after the class started he was delivering his beliefs about the mechanics and principles of storytelling as he saw them, in full and impassioned flow.

"…indivisible from plot, prose, and theme. These four pillars must work together, be woven so as to strengthen your story, and unify it into a whole.

Each element should draw from the others, to seek resonance! How does your plot illustrate facets of your theme? How does your theme inform the rhythm, pace and tenor of your prose? What do your cast of characters bring to the tale? Do they reflect your theme, or contrast it? What skills or aspects of their background or personality do they afford you when constructing your plot?" O'Shea poked a passionate finger at the white board, at the chunky capital letters he had left there. Beth's mind was briefly yanked back to the collection of words printed in block capital letters on her incident board at home.

CHARACTERS.

"So let's say we have our central protagonist, let's call her…" O'Shea looked at Beth, and very nearly smiled, "Bess. She is…" He paused to think for a moment. "Beautiful. Sensual hazel eyes, full lips that men daydream of kissing. Her body is athletic without being too lean, still sporting enough curves to keep an alpine mountain road happy… Bess is our central character." O'Shea stopped pacing. "Except she's not, because as yet, she has no character at all. She is a physical description, nothing more. We know nothing about her, nothing of her character, her thoughts, feelings, fears, prejudices, dreams, preconceptions, talents, neuroses, ambitions, triumphs and failures… She is, as people are in life, opaque, until she takes action. What she does is what will show us her character: her choices, as with us all, will reveal who she is.

"And here, yet again, we find fiction better equipped than life to expose essential truths about the human condition, because we have the opportunity to discover, in definitive black and white, exactly what Bess thinks. Whereas, of course, in real life every single other person on the planet is to some extent a mystery, their true nature akin to an image on a movie screen. We do not see the motor that moves the gears, and levers, the celluloid that speeds through the beam of light at 24 frames per second… We see only the action, the distillation of all the hidden machinations. Only through fiction can we know another human being with true intimacy, know them fully, laid bare, all their secrets exposed. Admittedly a fictional human being, but what more do you want? Blood?"

–

As she had half come to expect, O'Shea was waiting for her by his car.

"Fancy grabbing a quick drink? I've been reading through your George and Kathy Franklin murder mystery. There's a scene, when George notices the captain's tattoo… I think you're onto something, but you run the moment a little too long. I promise not to proposition you again, I swear."

"You swear?"

"On my life, although, obviously, the invitation remains, unspoken, that I am a remarkably sensitive, considerate and athletic lover, capable of delivering carnal pleasures the like of which you have never experienced. Should you change your mind."

"Unspoken, eh?"

O'Shea extended his arm toward his car.

"Diet Coke wasn't it?"

–

The pub was quiet enough and they grabbed a table by the window, offering a view onto O'Shea's flat. O'Shea had his laptop open on the table, he was scanning Beth's work in progress.

"Here," he said. "This one, the one where George follows Captain Coleridge to the bar and asks him about the passenger manifest." O'Shea began to skim, his eyes flying over Beth's words, assessing what she'd typed. "You reveal the tattoo and hint at its meaning, but then you run on with the business with Mason Rutledge. I think you should get out there, and pick up the point about Mason later. It is very good though. You're bringing yourself to the material, not putting yourself in it, but providing a prism. The first meeting with Mason and his sister Charlotte, where Mason reacts to Kathy being mute and the whole time George is busy Sherlocking him... That's a genuinely nice moment. Don't get me wrong, the rest is good too, very promising, but it feels less unique, almost like you're writing the scenes the way you would expect to find them in a book you picked up. That one, though, is a Beth Grue scene. It feels alive."

Beth wondered if O'Shea was just buttering her up. She didn't think so. While she was fairly certain he was serious about wanting to get into her knickers, when it came to the craft he spoke with the same gravity as a priest would his religion. O'Shea could be funny, but when he was talking writing it was all writing. You could see the shift. O'Shea the writer was deadly serious. O'Shea the man almost never was. He seemed happy to treat real life like a joke.

Almost as though to demonstrate the very thought, O'Shea the writer snapped his laptop closed, and disappeared to the bar for a refill, and O'Shea the man returned.

"About my offer of passionate and athletic lovemaking?"

"The unspoken one?"

"The same. I said you could still change your mind at any time?" O'Shea gulped back half his fresh drink. "If you think there's any danger of that, for an optimal experience you might like to give me the nod before I imbibe too many more of these."

"Well, as tempting as your spoken unspoken offer is," Beth responded, "I think I'm attracted to someone else, I'm afraid."

"I see. Well, that is most disappointing."

"Sorry."

"This someone, can I at least ask what this incredibly fortunate individual has than I don't?"

"I'm not sure attraction has much to do with logic."

"No, fair point. I find it rarely does. Does he at least know?"

"I'm not sure. Maybe?"

"Have you considered telling him?"

Beth shrugged. She didn't want to say. Unfortunately she forgot whose company she was in. O'Shea didn't miss much.

"Oh dear, are they still tender?"

"What?"

"Your burnt fingers?"

Beth saw O'Shea was teasing her a little, but not unkindly.

"Who was he?" O'Shea nudged. "Or her. Forgive me, one shouldn't presume."

Beth hadn't intended to rise to the bait, but for some reason she answered anyway.

"His name was Neil."

"Was it serious?"

250

"Enough that I thought I was going to be Mrs Neil."

"So did he die or something?"

"God no. Why would you think that? He just got cold feet."

"Ah." O'Shea nodded to indicate he understood. "Funny how the looming prospect of standing in front of a room full of people declaring you want to spend the rest of your life with someone suddenly makes you consider whether you really want to."

"Have you ever been married?" Beth asked, then another possibility occurred to her. "Are you married?"

"No I'm not. But yes, I was. Divorced. Twice. Love paves a rocky path sometimes, no? I believe you were telling me about the boy with the chilly feet?"

Was I? thought Beth. And then, why not?

"I met Neil at university. He was very popular, very smart, very good-looking…"

"Very, very, very?"

"Very."

"And?"

"He noticed me, started paying me a lot of attention, in a good way. I wasn't used to that. My parents thought it was crucial I attended a mainstream school. That wasn't always easy. The world has no shortage of dickheads. I had the common teenage problems, face full of acne, my boobs took forever to appear… only I had cerebral palsy too. Sixth form was better, my spots cleared up, my chest was suddenly filling c-cups. The other kids were older and a little more mature, the hyenas were mostly gone… I enjoyed it a lot more, and came away with good results, got a place at Liverpool Uni."

"Where you met Mr Cold Feet, you looking a lot more like the gorgeous creature before me now?"

"He asked me out. I was flattered, and very attracted to him. After that everything became easy. Despite both of us having started Uni at the same time, he somehow seemed to know everyone, and so soon enough I seemed to know everyone. We studied, and partied, and studied and partied. It was great. He was my first lover, and my first love. Shortly before we graduated he asked me to marry him. I believed I'd met my soul mate. I really did."

"So what changed?"

"He did. Almost the second we set the wheels of actually getting married into motion, arranging the church, where we would have the reception, my dress, who my bridesmaids were going to be, who his best man would be… he changed, got twitchy. We had never really argued before, but suddenly we were bickering over the smallest things, almost all the time. I told myself it was just the stress, the pressure of arranging everything, the mounting cost, all that. You have no idea what an operation and how expensive getting married is until you start.

"The wedding date was only four months off when he dropped the bombshell. He didn't want to get married anymore. Okay, I thought, trying not to freak out, the time wasn't right. Maybe we were too young, look what the pressure had done to our relationship already. We had all the time in the world, marriage would wait. Except it didn't take long before I realised it went deeper than that. It wasn't just marriage he had cooled on, or even being married to me, he had cooled on being with me at all. He suggested a break, time to get our bearings, not a break-up as such… I was so stunned. I actually thought he meant it, at first. It took a couple of months to see it for what it really was. I would call him, just to chat, but he was always on his way out, busy, sullen. It was like talking to a stranger. I got it, eventually. It was a hard time for me."

O'Shea nodded. "When it comes to affairs of the heart, the worst injuries we inflict often result from indifference more than cruelty."

"Very eloquent."

"Hm. I can't claim credit. Not one of my lines, but my first wife's. She was, is, a poet." O'Shea took a gulp of scotch, knocking back the last of it. "A word of advice? Never marry a poet, every damn thing you do from making love to washing the car is apt to be regurgitated into some baroque linguistic confection. She hurled a vase at me shortly after that line. I still don't know which hurt more. Few of us like to think of ourselves as heartless or cruel, do we?"

"No," Beth concurred. "My fiancé? It was my CP I think. The reality of being married to someone others would view as disabled for the rest of his life dawned on him. It became real, you know?"

"And what about this new chap? He's different, you think?"

Beth thought about Greg, repeatedly closing his front door, turning off the tap and checking, checking, counting from one hundred, his cup handles so precise you could measure them to the millimetre…

And then she thought of the Greg who saw her brave and smart, some smoking-hot, ass-kicking super-secret agent, the Greg she had kissed because she knew it might save them from a killer returning home unexpectedly…

And because she had wanted to.

"Different? You have no idea."

Chapter 46

All of his therapists seemed to concur it was the catalyst. Early childhood trauma: the root of all his issues.

Greg was familiar with the concept of the subconscious and all that, but he still found it hard to believe something he couldn't even recall could be responsible for how he was. Even his mum, when quizzed, had admitted he had been a child who liked things to be a particular way almost from day one. As a toddler, before the accident, he'd had his tics and kinks. He liked baked beans and he also liked toast, but should the sauce from the beans touch the toast, well, that was one Scooby-doo decaled plastic plate full of food destined for the bin.

His OCD had always been there, Greg felt, but had it always been destined to run rampant, to creep and sprawl like vines tangling up his life and impeding progress at every turn?

He had constructed the incident in his head too many times, thousands, lights, camera, action... but what he saw wasn't memory. Versions of this grim home movie wanted to stick, replayed so many times they threatened to become fixed, but he was never in any doubt reconstructions were all they were, assembled from the blunt facts of the tragedy and storyboarded into a scene, projected in horrible sight, sound and feel-o-vision onto the canvas of his imagination.

The angle, viewed from first person of course, was always low, looking up. How tall is the average three-year-old? Two, two and a half feet tall, something around there?

They are on a street, approaching a road, and he is holding his dad's hand, because that's what one of the witnesses described seeing moments prior to the accident. The day is dry, bright and sunny, the seventeenth of July, just past 4 p.m.

There are cars parked along the road, the parking on the high street is inadequate, everyone seems to agree on this point. His dad is impossibly tall, a giant whose legs go up and up and up…

Greg couldn't actually recall his father's face. All he had was an amalgam from various photographs, faded square Polaroids. There weren't many, and only a couple from the year his dad died. The modest collection, split between Adrian and himself, showed their father sporting an audacious variety of haircuts and clothes. Their dad looked like he could be a different person in each one, the disparities as large as the similarities. The only constant appeared to be his smile, big and easy. It was the same in every picture, as seemingly definitive as the loops and whorls of a fingerprint. It was a smile Greg would very much liked to have grown up seeing, a smile he could easily imagine his mother having fallen in love with.

They are walking down the street (even 3-year-old imaginary Greg cannot step on seams in the paving) until his dad suddenly doglegs and turns into the kerb. In some versions of the reconstructions the giant above him looks both ways, in others he steps straight out. The truth is no one will ever know if it was carelessness or distraction or some freak blind spot that prevented his father from seeing the van coming up the road.

Either way the giant steps out first, Greg a pace behind him.

255

The impact is sudden and brutal. Again, the facts (his dad was thrown some twenty-five feet down the road) inform the reconstruction. Before his father's hand loses purchase on his, Greg is torn off his feet and hurled far enough to land and break his arm. He does not even remember the plaster cast he wore for six weeks.

A road, a father, his son, and a van doing a perfectly legal thirty miles per hour.

He was 3, Adrian just eight months old, their mother suddenly a widow at 23.

Chapter 47

Greg opened the door to let Martin in. He was eight minutes late. Martin was never late. This, however, was not the only change.

Greg couldn't help staring. "What happened to your face?"

Martin stepped though and sharply tugged off his loafers, tossing them onto the mat. Greg tidied them so they were straight and square.

"It's nothing. One of my hobbies happens to be mixed martial arts. I was sparring with another student last night, should have kept my guard up."

"Looks tender."

"It's fine. Sorry I'm late, I've been a little bandwidth limited."

"Pardon?"

"Busy. I've been busy, Greg."

While he checked the door was properly closed (seven times. Not bad.) Greg stole another couple of glances at Martin's battered face and wondered. His therapist had a split lip, a long graze down the left side of his jaw and a swollen cheek with a cut in the centre of it. Determining if anything Martin said was untrue was tricky, partly because of his view that reality was apparently in the eye of the beholder, and partly because every word he said, true or untrue, seemed to pass through some complicated filter in the same way a lie would anyway.

"Well," Martin said, "let's not waste any more time. I'd like to see if we can enable you some today, reconfigure some limiting boundaries."

"Okay…"

"Your mug handles issue? I'd like to work that. How does that sound?"

"Erm, sure…"

—

They retired to the lounge, where Martin asked Greg to recline on the sofa while he slowly explained how they were going to spend the following fifteen minutes, Martin coaching him with a series of associative imagery, utilising hypnotic language patterns and conditioned response. He was absolutely not *going to be hypnotising him right now*. He would simply be assisting him to identify a series of locations, real or imaginary, where he felt *completely at ease*, and *totally relaxed* and *confident*, places where he felt *supremely confident* and *in control*…

Once Greg had vividly visualised these places, Martin would instruct him to firmly pinch together his thumb and index finger. This action would then be *powerfully bonded* to this unique emotional state, such that when they progressed to the kinaesthetic portion of the session he would be free to utilise this conditioned response to *immediately feel calmer and totally in control*. It was possible, Martin said, that just by understanding how *this process was going to be effective* it might already be *producing positive changes within him*.

Greg closed his eyes and Martin commenced the exercise.

The scenario Martin encouraged him to visualise was of being one hundred feet tall, walking confidently across a featureless landscape. Brilliant tracers of pure white light sailed like swooping birds through a brilliant cloudless blue sky, and whenever he chose to, Martin said he was free to reach out and touch the tracers. Upon contact the light would be absorbed into his being, each additional beam causing him to feel calmer and stronger, so much so that he was able to turn his eyes to the sky and just let his feet fall where they pleased…

Greg kind of got into it. After a while the living room fell away and he seemed to actually feel the tracers relaxing him as he brushed them from the sky and absorbed their light. Each time he did so Martin would instruct him to wait until the positive feeling peaked and then firmly pinch his thumb and index finger together.

He imagined himself striding over Kettle Street, towering over Lilliputian-sized houses, the brilliant white tracers circling him like gulls…

Martin was still calmly talking in his languid, sing-song way. "In a moment I'm going to ask you to open your eyes, Greg. People often find themselves very relaxed and confident after the exercise you just completed, they find the association of the imagery and the powerful kinaesthetic bond has become permanent. Simply by pressing thumb and forefinger together they are taken instantly back to a calm, confident state of mind. Once it pleases you, you can open your eyes to feel totally relaxed, totally confident, totally in control."

Greg opened his eyes.

"You're ready to join me in the kitchen now, yes?"

"Erm, yeah, sure."

Greg sat up and then stood up. Martin led the way through into the kitchen. Once there he opened the cupboard, revealing the neatly positioned mugs, lined up like soldiers on a drill. He moved several of them, shifting them out of alignment, twisting them so the handles poked out here and there. Greg felt a familiar tension rise in his chest.

Martin stepped back, and invited Greg to stand before the open cupboard, while he stood close behind him.

"I'd like you to just look at the mugs for a moment, Greg. *You can do that*, yes?"

"I can try—"

"Greg? Remember what we say?"

"Sorry. Yes, I can do that. I think."

Greg looked into the cupboard. Staring into the space was like staring at a child playing beneath a precariously balanced bucket of hot tar. He itched to reach in and set things right, to quell the rising anxiety and feel safe again.

"How do you feel right at this moment?"

"Tense."

"Really? Then please, feel free to pinch your thumb and forefinger together. Just don't feel surprised if *it immediately makes you feel calmer and more in control.*"

Greg followed Martin's instruction. He tried not to think about the chaos in the cupboard for a moment and pinched his thumb and forefinger together. He felt the pressure travel up the digits, and then something amazing happened. It did make him feel better. He caught a flash in his mind's eye of the white tracers sinking into his giant body in the visualisation, and the calm but invigorating feeling touching them brought.

But it didn't last long.

The mug handles were still all over the place. The itch to set them right washed back in, the tension returned to his chest, the dread rolling in like storm clouds overhead.

"It's not working."

"It is," Martin crooned from over his shoulder. "Take a moment. Relax and do it again. Commonly people feel the *sensation of relaxation and calm becomes even more powerful the second time* in close succession."

Greg pinched thumb and forefinger together once more. This time he felt nothing. How could he relax when the mugs were everywhere like that? They might as well be on their sides and upside down and…

"I'm sorry, it's not working. I need to put the mugs back how they belong. Maybe we can try again next session?"

"No," Martin said. "You can do this, other people can do this, other people can do this very easily. If they can you can. I can help you."

Greg heard the exasperation in Martin's voice. He was surprised. He had never heard him speak in anything other than his near-sedated drone. He started to turn around to look at him.

"Really, I'm not ready—"

"You *can* do it."

Suddenly Greg found himself in a headlock, one arm pinned behind his back. Martin spoke directly into his ear.

"Look at them, Greg. They're *just mugs*. It doesn't matter which way they face. It doesn't even matter which cupboard you put them in. They're just mugs. Nothing will happen depending on where and how they are put. You *must see this*. If I am to help you, you must see it. Look, and say, 'It doesn't matter.'"

Greg was doing his best not to panic, but he could feel himself beginning to hyperventilate. He wasn't sure what was making him feel worse, the mugs or the fact that his so-called therapist had him in a half-nelson. He felt his head perform a barrel roll, felt panic take hold. He tried to throw Martin off.

"LET GO OF ME YOU FUCKING LUNATIC, I'M GOING TO PASS OUT!"

Suddenly the grip was gone, Greg lunged to the doorway and bent over, panting, trying to breathe and control the thumping in his chest. When dizziness subsided enough he stood upright, and strode to the cupboard, barging past Martin who still stood there, looking now a little uneasy.

Greg plunged into the cavity and frantically rearranged the mugs until every last one was set as it should be. He immediately felt better, more in control.

He turned, suddenly furious.

"Get out!"

"Greg…"

Greg glared at him. "Get out of my home before I call the police."

"If we don't push your boundaries—"

"GET OUT!"

Martin nodded quietly, turned, padded down the hall and collected his loafers from the mat, jamming in his feet and opening the front door. He looked back.

"I'll call you. I know today's session was testing… We'll talk when you've had a chance to reflect."

Like fuck we will, thought Greg. Once you're the other side of that door it's the last time I ever see you, you bloody nutcase.

Voyage of Death: A George and Kathy Franklin Mystery
by
Beth Grue

Chapter Seventeen

Under questioning the steward remained steadfast and most adamant in his recollection.

"It was Mr Rutledge I saw. He was on the portside, at the bar, reading a book, by lamplight. He was enjoying a pipe. I didn't disturb him, but that was the time and it was definitely him, sir."

"You're sure? Absolutely sure?"

"I am, sir. He has quite the fairest hair."

George pursed his lips, as he always does when perplexed, a small mannerism that for some reason I find incredibly stirring. I could almost read his mind. He obviously believed the steward to be telling the truth, stating events as he recalled them, but then how did this tally with Madam Proust's equally assured testimony of having seen Mr Rutledge slip out of the verger's office at almost precisely the same time, half past the hour?

We had all heard Lady Garbutt's scream as she discovered the body only minutes later.

And yet, a man cannot possibly be in two places at the same time now, can he?

George pursed his lips again (Good Heavens, Katherine, focus!) and ruminated.

"Would you be as kind as to take us to the exact spot you were standing in when you saw Mr Rutledge reading his book?"

"Of course sir. If you'll both follow me."

We followed the steward to the portside deck. The bar was at this hour most quiet, as it would have been at the time the steward saw Mr Rutledge immersed in his book and smoking his pipe.

"He was sitting over there, he was." The steward pointed to the table by the bar.

It was, I felt, a gloomy spot, ill lit for reading. Many more suitable locations presented themselves.

"He was facing you?"

"No sir. He was facing that way. It was him though, definitely him."

Again George pursed his lips.

I would quite simply have to ravish him later.

Chapter 48

It had arrived in the night, was waiting for Greg when he got up.

The alarm had roused him at 5.30 am, and as he stepped from his bedroom it had been there waiting for him on the mat. He had immediately called Beth as agreed.

The package lay open on the sheet of paper, and what had been inside it, a single sheet, folded into four.

She stared at the residents' association newsletter.

Greg still had the rubber gloves on.

She had come straight over, called Hailey to tell her she might be late for work, again. Something had come up. Hailey had said no problem, but not like she usually did. Beth got the feeling her erratic lunch juggling and early finishes might be wearing thin. Not that she could explain to Hailey, but right now there were larger things to consider, like someone's life.

They had discussed ways of catching whoever delivered the next package, and arrived at the conclusion it would do them little good anyway. Even if they installed a security camera it would likely be useless. Greg knew for a fact the previous one had not been posted through the letterbox by Crompton himself, but a passing schoolboy who had no idea of the significance of what he had just done.

And even if Crompton were careless enough to be caught posting it, hoisted up in a big cartoon net or on video, there was nothing inherently damning in slipping an unmarked envelope containing some innocuous item through a person's door. The items and packages proved nothing in isolation.

No, they had to catch Crompton. If not in the very act of murder, then prove beyond doubt he was planning to commit one.

To some extent they had, in truth, been waiting for the next package to arrive.

"It's Maurice Cooper," Greg said. "He's next. There's nothing else this could mean." He stared gravely at Cooper's two-month-old newsletter, dated and delivered the same week Rose Gordon had 'fallen' drunk down her stairs with fatal results. It was even possible the newsletter had been taken from her house.

When they had opened the white package and tipped out the sheet, Greg had initially been convinced opening it would reveal a letter, a message from the killer himself. For a second or two he half expected to find a series of letters crudely clipped from random newspapers and magazines, movie ransom note style…

Instead he had found it was one of Cooper's newsletters, exactly like the one Greg already had himself.

Innocent enough all on its own, in this context it reeked of menace, blunt as a painted crosshair.

Greg checked the kitchen's wall clock.

"Crompton will be leaving to get his Racing Post in twenty minutes. From now on I'm not going to let him out of my sight. I want to know where he is every single second of the day. I'm going to catch him if it's the last thing I do."

Beth nodded, and got her phone out, ready to construct a fib about some family emergency. She hated lying to Hailey, but when it came to eight hours of understaffed library and a man's life, local municipal services were going to have to take the hit.

"Right," she said. "Let's catch this arsehole."

266

–

They sketched out a plan, of sorts. Beth remained at the flat, keeping watch on the front of Crompton's flat, ready to follow him. Greg left to acquire something that would make the plan possible. He was sure he had seen a set in Pete's shop.

The bell dinged as he entered.

Greg caught Pete's eye at the counter, raised a hand in greeting as he usually did. Pete smiled and waved back, delivered his familiar hearty greeting, "Hello Gregory, my friend! How are you this morning?"

Greg offered his usual response and headed to the back corner of the shop. They were still there, in the small carousel of pocket money-priced kids' toys, plastic laser pistols that flashed and buzzed, race cars, fighter jets, garish robots that were absolutely not Transformers (no sir, these were entirely different, these were TechoMechFormers). The walkie-talkie set was cheap, but so long as using one didn't require him to scroll through menus or punch numbers into a keypad, and when he spoke into one it came out of the other across a single street, they would do the job.

He took them to the counter.

"Pete, can I get a pack of double AAs to go with these?"

Pete plucked a packet of batteries from amid the cigarettes and vaping gear. Greg paid and Pete gave him his two pence change. Greg counted it to confirm he had paid in full. Pete, as he always did, waited patiently.

"Would you like me to check too, Gregory?"

"No, it's all right, but—"

"And check all the items are on the receipt?" Pete smiled and began to double check the transaction. Walkie-talkies, £7.99. AA batteries, £1.99. £10 tendered, change, £0.02. Greg took the receipt.

Outside the shop he removed the walkie-talkies from the bubble pack, installed the batteries and disposed of the packaging in the litter bin on the corner. He pressed the trigger on one and mumbled "Testing." His crackly voice cut through the hiss and issued from the other walkie-talkie. He adjusted the volume slider and repeated the test. Less hiss and squawk and much quieter too. Perfect. He started back to the flat, and spotted Crompton coming in the other direction when he reached the head of Kettle Street. He kept his head down and kept moving.

Crompton was on the opposite side of the street. If he followed his usual routine he would stop by Pete's first, pick up his Racing Post and then continue to the bookie's, where he would remain for the next three quarters of an hour.

A second familiar figure was approaching too. Hanging back, her asymmetrical gait unhurried, Beth was tracking Crompton from the other side of the street, Greg's side. They locked eyes, and as they neared she mouthed, You get them? He nodded, slipping her one of the walkie-talkies as she passed. He continued in the opposite direction.

Half a minute later he heard "Testing?" come out his walkie-talkie. He pressed the talk button on his end and replied, "Roger." The word had just come out, and he immediately regretted it. He needed Beth's help, and would rather she didn't feel she was allied with a complete goof who thought they were playing spies with the aid of a cheap plastic toy. A man's life was at stake. Stick to the plan.

"He's in the shop," said Beth's crackly voice.

He pressed the talk button again. "I'll be in the right-of-way. You stay on him until he returns."

There was a brief pause before the speaker spat white noise once more, and Beth's voice came back.

"Roger."

—

When Crompton had left his flat, Beth had been ready and waiting for him.

She tailed him, staying far enough behind on the opposite side of the street to remain inconspicuous, having passed Greg and received her walkie-talkie. She followed him to Pete's shop on the corner and on to the betting shop a few streets on.

Greg had returned to the flat to collect the things required for his cover story. As he had predicted, Crompton left the bookie's under an hour later and walked back to his flat on Kettle Street.

They agreed Beth would watch the front of Crompton's flat from Greg's bedroom while Greg took care of the back. A roll of refuse sacks and a pair of rubber gloves in hand, he could, under the pretence of cleaning litter from the right-of-way, keep watch over the rear of the property for as long as he liked.

Greg was willing to bet hardly anyone passed through the right-of-way in the course of a day, and even if someone did they'd be unlikely to find anything odd about someone tidying up. It was a tip precisely because few of the street's residents used it or seemed to care what went on there.

If Crompton left his flat they would know about it.

The day ground along slowly. Keeping one eye on Crompton's back fence, and stopping only to check in with Beth every hour or so, to confirm the walkie talkies and batteries were still working okay, Greg actually did quite an effective job, filling over two dozen refuse sacks with a mixture of litter, pieces of rotting discarded furniture, weeds and dead bramble, but the light was starting to fade now. The hour was getting late enough that tidying or no tidying, he would start to look a little conspicuous to anyone who happened upon him. He would loiter as long as possible before discarding the pretence, and finally seeking a spot to lurk in. If it was dark enough—

"What are you doing here then?"

The voice startled Greg; he turned to discover Maurice Cooper standing a few feet away, as though he had silently materialised from nowhere, like a cardigan-clad ninja.

"Maurice." Greg thought he did a fair job of sounding causal, which wasn't easy when part of him wondered if he was addressing a dead man. Maurice Cooper, neighbourhood busybody and letter-writer, association group avenger, reporter of faulty streetlamps and nemesis of local planning, the man who took it upon himself to keep the streets clean, or at least the one he lived on. Greg felt guilty suddenly, he was being unfair, even if the residents' association was more of a hobby than anything else, it proved Maurice cared, could be bothered. Greg deployed his cover story.

"Just clearing up back here. After we spoke about it the other day? I just thought, why not? I have the time. I thought I'd see what I could do."

"That's very… commendable."

Greg had expected Maurice to be on board, more than most people who might have stumbled upon and quizzed him. Maurice more than most should have been delighted to hear someone was making the right-of-way look more presentable, but that wasn't the vibe he was getting. Not at all. Feeling defensive, he went on the offensive.

"What are you doing back here?" Greg asked. At least under the pretence of clearing up he had an excuse for loitering in the right of way with darkness encroaching. What was Maurice doing here again?

"Just taking a stroll."

Cooper was still staring at him oddly. Examining him, or that's how it felt.

It was at this moment Beth's voice issued from the walkie-talkie.

"Greg?"

Greg looked at Maurice, who looked surprised.

"Excuse me." He turned and pressed the walkie-talkie's button, whispered into the microphone hole. "I can't really talk right now." There was a blip of static before Beth's voice came back.

"Tough. You need to get back here, now. He's on the move, and he's got the case."

271

Chapter 49

Greg didn't even try to explain himself to the bemused Maurice Cooper; he just abandoned the black bags, turned and ran, peeling the rubber gloves off as he went. He rounded the right of way and plunged down Kettle Street to find Beth waiting in the Fiat on the nearside of the road, the door to the small hire car already open. Beth leaned over from the driver's side.

"Get in. He's nearly at the top of the road."

Greg threw himself into the passenger seat.

Beth pushed the stick from P to D, indicated, and put her foot down. The car pulled away and she moved over the road into the correct lane. Just like that. Greg looked up the road and spotted Crompton's hulking figure turning the corner. As they neared the head of the road they were able to catch sight of him again. He had come to a halt at the bus stop, that strange wooden case dangling from one meaty hand.

Beth pulled in. From across the street they had a clear view of him idling.

"What now?"

"We wait for his bus to arrive, and then we follow it until he gets off."

A couple of minutes later the bus crested the hill, and drew to a stop. Crompton climbed on. The doors folded shut and it pulled away. Beth once more moved the stick into drive and pulled away, turning left at the junction to follow the bus.

They trailed its tail lights through the darkening evening roads, pausing when it did to collect passengers or let others get off. If anyone were paying attention they might have wondered why the small car behind didn't just overtake, but it was very unlikely anyone was paying attention. It was well past rush hour, the roads were quiet and they were holding no one up.

The journey lasted ten stop-and-start minutes before Crompton disembarked, stepped off and started to walk back down the road. Beth used the next turn off to double back.

They watched him walk for a short stretch, the black wooden case banging lightly against his denim leg, before he reached a pub, The Coat of Arms. He disappeared inside.

Beth turned into its small car park and parked up.

"What now?" Greg asked.

"We go inside, try not to let him see us. Hope there's more than one man and a dog in there."

Luckily there was. For a weekday the pub was surprisingly busy. Greg looked around, trying to locate Crompton among the patrons, and eventually spotted him, headed for a set of glazed double doors at the far end of the room. It took a little manoeuvring for him to open the door with a pint in one hand and that enigmatic case of his in his other, but he managed it, slipped through the doors into the corridor.

Greg and Beth edged forward.

Through the door's windows they saw Crompton turn and begin to scale a staircase. Greg performed a brisk assessment of the terrain, for potential obstacles. Nothing jumped out. Having the upper hand for once felt good, lent him confidence.

"Wait here. I'll go take a look."

"You sure?"

Greg nodded.

He slipped through the doors and entered the corridor and looked about. At the far end was a door that read Staff Only, two doors with Gents and Ladies plaques to the right, and the staircase Crompton had taken leading up. Greg followed. A sign with an arrow was affixed to the wall. It read Function Room.

The staircase brought him to a door. He teased it open and peeked through the crack.

And for a moment struggled to make sense of what he saw.

The function room had a number of large tables covered with what appeared to be miniature hills and mountains. Looking closer Greg saw tiny fortifications and figures. There were twenty or more men in the room, many grouped in pairs around each table. He tried to spot Crompton among them.

"No need to be shy. New are you?"

For the second time in under an hour Greg almost leapt out of his skin. A man was standing behind him. Only it wasn't Maurice Cooper this time, but a bespectacled man, carrying a stout case reminiscent of Crompton's, except instead of being wooden it was made of chunky black plastic.

"Erm, yeah." Greg saw no choice but to wing it.

The man held out a hand. "Barry."

Greg shook it. "Greg."

"Come on then, Greg," the man said, reaching out and pulling the door open. "Saw the ad in the local paper I suppose? That was Reg's doing. Reckons we could do with some new blood. Do you already play, or are you just curious?"

"I'm… curious?"

Barry smiled and guided Greg into the function room.

"We hire this place out couple of nights a week. We all chip in. Midweek. If we book a couple of months ahead the landlord gives us a reasonable discount."

A few people looked up from their tables and greeted Barry, who introduced Greg as they went, telling them he had seen Reg's ad.

Greg smiled at the serious men huddled around the tables, peering with intense concentration at the masses of intricately painted figures doing inanimate, dice roll fuelled, battle. Tabletop wargaming.

"So," Barry asked, setting his black plastic case down and flipping the catch and opening the lid to reveal an army of miniature green orcs in foam lining. "You drawn more toward Warhammer, or 40K?"

"Erm…"

"You?"

The voice was close, deep, and familiar.

Greg was suddenly aware someone large was standing beside him. He turned and looked up to find Crompton's grizzled face assessing him with an expression of ill-concealed surprise. Fortunately Barry was still in full flow.

"Might have ourselves some new blood here, Dennis."

Crompton frowned. "You into tabletop wargaming, then?"

Greg swallowed. "Erm, more curious? I'm looking for a new hobby and… well, it sounded interesting. You play?"

"Now and then, but I mostly paint."

Barry seemed to finally pick up on the vibe. "You two know each other?"

"We're neighbours," said Crompton, still looking at Greg.

"Oh, I see. Well there you go then, Greg! Got pretty much our finest figure painter on your doorstep. Dennis's work is something else. Go on, show him your Tyranids, Dennis."

Crompton looked unmoved.

"I'd love to see them," Greg prompted, hoping he didn't look as caught in the headlights as he felt. To his own ears his voice had at least sounded even. "If you don't mind?"

And like any enthusiast invited to share his passion, Crompton surrendered. He set his squat wooden case on the table and unlatched it. When he flipped the lip open it revealed rows of strange alien creatures in myriad poses. They were all intricately painted in mind-boggling, almost microscopic, detail. The predominant colour scheme was a deep bloody red.

Barry marvelled at them. "He's doing these for Dave over there. Incredible, eh?" he said, addressing Greg.

"They are. They're so detailed."

Barry issued a strange amused snort. "Dennis is so fond of the old Battle Crimson he painted himself last week."

Faced with Greg's puzzled look, Crompton rolled his eyes wearily, while Barry elaborated.

"Dennis spilt a whole bottle of Battle Crimson over himself last week." Catching Greg's still baffled eye, Barry added, "Paint. Acrylic. Once it dries there's no getting it out. Looked like that scene with John Hurt from Alien, or like someone had tried to eviscerate him!" Barry giggled girlishly.

Crompton took charge. "Come on," he said quietly, maybe just a little uncomfortable, "I'll show you around. Tell you what's involved an all that. See if it's for you."

Greg's tour involved interrupting earnest men engaged in methodical turn-by-turn conflict, some with traditional orcs, elves and humans, some with exotic Xenomorphs and hulking men in massive armour which appeared to fall somewhere between futuristic and medieval. The former was apparently regular Warhammer, and the other Warhammer 40K. Crompton explained a little about how the game was played, and how for some, like him, the craft aspect of the hobby was the main draw. Crompton led him to a couple of tables set up just for painting and crafting.

He removed a handful of partially completed figures.

Some of the ones he had seen on the tables were spectacular, but Crompton's really were something else. The closer Greg looked the more he saw, tiny patches of rust, or grime carefully layered into creases on the figure's armour, or patterns streaking alien scales and skin, like exotic lizards or deep sea creatures.

"You're very good."

"Thanks. I had a lot of time to practice." Crompton paused, checked there was no one in immediate earshot. "In prison."

Greg said nothing.

"Look," said Crompton, "I know you know, okay? I saw you poking around my probation officer's car. I doubt you're the only one to notice him dropping in on me. I'd bet one of my kidneys that bloody busybody Cooper up the road has. And now you're wondering what I what was in for, aren't you?"

Greg wasn't sure what to say. He was busted, had been for weeks.

Crompton gaze held firm, "Well, let's just say a long time ago I did something bad. Very bad."

Greg didn't answer.

"Call it a crime of passion. Not an excuse, but I was young, stupid and angry. Believe me, if I could go back, not do what I did, I would, but I can't. I served my time for it, and now I'm trying to start over. That's not turning out to be easy. See that bloke over there, Stewart? He works at the Warhammer shop in the city. He's trying to get the owner to give me a job. That would be nice, get off job seekers allowance, pay my own way. See, I'm not out to mug anyone up or rob their house, no matter what that Maurice Cooper bloke thinks. Prison shapes you, inside and out. People take one look and think they know who I am." Crompton averted his eyes. "Look… I'm sorry."

"You are?"

"I'm not always good with people, especially when I think they're judging me. That night, when I bumped into you, weeks back, I think I might have tried to scare you a bit. Bad habit. Like I said, prison shapes you. I'm still dealing with being on the outside. I'm trying to adjust, but it's hard, you know?"

Greg did. He was the reigning champ of finding things hard.

"I get it. I'm used to people making assumptions about me too."

Crompton nodded, "You only step on the centre of paving slabs. I've seen. Problems crossing the road too?"

"Yeah. OCD."

"Right. That can't be easy."

"No."

Crompton nodded again.

"So," Greg asked, "how did you get into all of this?"

"Inside. One of the last blokes I shared my cell with was into it. When he got out he was good enough to keep in touch. He liked the playing side more, so he'd send me sets to paint and come visit me every now and again to collect them."

"You have real skill."

"Thanks."

Crompton nodded slowly. "Fancy trying your hand at it?"

"I'd love to."

–

It was half an hour before Greg felt able to tell Crompton he needed to go. He hurried downstairs and found Beth where he had left her in the pub's lounge.

"I followed you up, took a peek through the window. What are they all doing up there?"

"Playing games," Greg said. "It's not him, Beth. Crompton's not the killer."

Chapter 50

"But if it's not Crompton," she said, "then who?"

Greg had finished explaining about the case, Warhammer, the tiny model orcs and Space Marines, and Crompton's accident with his red Battle Crimson paint they had mistaken for blood. With the contents of the mysterious black wooden case exposed, and the chilling shirt stain explained, the confession he was an ex-con and the unvarnished regret he had displayed for what had put him there, there was nothing left. Coincidence, prejudice and misunderstanding, that was what they had been going on.

"I have no idea."

All their efforts and sleuthing had added up to nothing at all.

Beth pulled in just up from Greg's flat, thought about the homemade incident board she had constructed, and suddenly felt foolish. How many times had she stared at it these past weeks, convinced it must hold some hidden connection? Was it just a joke, like the walkie-talkies, a stupid toy created by a pair of fools playing detective? What had they actually achieved? They had saved no one, prevented nothing. Was the next victim even Maurice Cooper? Was the killer so many steps ahead of them they didn't stand a chance of doing anything more than incriminating themselves? Was Greg right? Was his role to be nothing more than a contingency plan patsy, to take the role of prime suspect if the authorities actually did take note of Kettle Street's rising body count?

Greg opened up. Beth removed her shoes and set them carefully next to Greg's, then went through, waiting for him in the kitchen while he completed his door check.

"Tea?" He said quietly, when he eventually joined her, already charting a course for the kettle.

She followed him through to the kitchen. It was increasingly dawning on her that they had nothing, were back at square one, the weight of it settling more fully now. She sat down at the kitchen table while Greg went through his traditional and not infrequent tea-making ritual. Tea bag, sugar, boiling water, stir, squeeze tea bag against inside of mug with spoon, stir, squeeze, stir, squeeze, remove, pour in milk… It was how many people made a cup of tea, only she was willing to bet this was exactly how Greg made one, down to the precise detail, the specific timings. Were she to record a video of him doing it twice the two clips would likely be indistinguishable from each other.

He returned, set the drink in front of her, but remained standing.

His eyes were on her. "You know this means we have no idea who he is, the actual killer? I was so sure it was Crompton." He began to pace. Twice his eyes flicked to the window. He looked like he wanted to say something.

"What?"

"I'm feeling a bit… worked up. I need to do something, okay? It will help me relax, help me think. The mugs in my cupboard, if I arrange them…"

"Don't mind me."

And so he did, and she realised it wasn't the window he had been eyeing but the cupboard there. He opened the door and began to remove all the mugs from the shelf, setting them on the work surface below.

"Not Crompton. I was just so sure it had to be him," he repeated. "The real killer is probably laughing at me right now. What if I was right, what if he picked me precisely because he knows I can't do what a normal person could, stacked the odds so far in his favour he can't lose?" The cupboard was empty. He started to replace the mugs, almost mechanically setting one right at the back in one corner and then rotating it a little. A second mug was soon meticulously positioned next to it. Again he gave it a small twist and a tweak, and she immediately saw how each of the handles was perfectly aligned. A third mug confirmed it. He was still staring in the bowels of the cupboard when he spoke.

"I'm not like you," he said. "You're strong. I'm not."

When she didn't answer he turned.

It wasn't self-pity she saw. He wasn't whining, feeling sorry for himself or making excuses. He really believed it. Like a blind man explaining he simply couldn't see, he felt he was stating a fact. He wasn't.

"That's bollocks. You're a million times stronger than most people."

"Beth, I know you're trying to—"

"No, I'm not. Other people do what they do without having to even think about it. They go about their day, turning off their taps, using their stupid mobile phones and computers, closing their front doors and walking down the street without a second thought as to where they plant their feet—but not because they're strong, Greg, because it's easy for them. It's not a fight. They're not wrestling with anything. Not like you. For you every day is a battle, and yet every day you still march out to face it." She

282

stood up. "How can you not be stronger than them?"

Greg frowned, as though she had offered not an opinion but a conundrum, the kind you fear might be hard because the answer is hiding in plain sight.

She walked over to where he was, picked up a mug from the work surface and handed it to him. He took it and set in next to the previous one. With a slight adjustment the handle perfectly reflected the others.

"If I'm strong," she said, "it's because I've had to be. Being able to do what someone else can? I can't get away with that shit. If I want to be taken seriously, I need to be better than the next person, and even then more often than not I won't be seen as normal." She handed him another mug. He took it, but his eyes never left her. "Do I care? Excuse my French, but no, I don't, because normal can go fuck right off. You know what another word for normal is, Greg? Ordinary. Seems a dumb thing to aspire to when you put it like that, doesn't it?"

"You're right." He swallowed. "You're not normal, or ordinary. You're amazing."

She recalled the sketch. The Beth Grue he had drawn: beautiful and fearless. She liked that comic book Beth, smoking hot and kicking ass. She liked that he saw her that way. It was the Beth she wanted to be. Why then when he looked in the mirror couldn't he see that better version of himself?

The truth was Greg was good-looking. Tall, with intelligent eyes and a mouth that always seemed a moment away from a shy grin. He was handsome, no doubt. She had not noticed so much at first, but over time it had emerged. There was plenty to like, even before you got to know him, before you discovered he was funny, and kind, and thoughtful.

283

True, from a certain perspective, he was easy to view as a train wreck that had derailed carrying a dozen carriages of hot mess, and to get involved with him was to enter into a world of right angles, numbers, checking and double checking and triple checking…

She remembered sharing the cramped dark of Crompton's cupboard with him, feeling his tension and recognising her desire to smother it.

Not normal.

No, any normal girl would run a mile.

—

Greg was finding it hard to escape noticing Beth was very close and looking at him. Not just looking, but looking.

She tilted her head and just as he was about to ask if something was wrong she moved forward and kissed him, and he was kissing her right back. Just like it had the first time, everything else seemed to melt away. If anything, safe from the danger of being discovered hiding by a serial killer, it was even more deliriously pleasurable.

Beth had plunged her hands into his hair. He felt her fingers behind his skull, and this felt good too, her mouth on his, her tongue darting, flashing against his own.

Then she broke off, drew away just far enough to seemingly study his face for a moment, then gripped his hand and pulled him through the hallway toward the bedroom. His mind was reeling but his feet were on board. Still looking into his eyes, she began to unbutton her top. She peeled it off and tossed it to the bedroom floor. Greg felt a stab of anxiety cut through his excitement, and it was quite a lot of excitement to cut through. The lump in the crotch of his jeans testified to it, but a glimpse down, seeing Beth's top lying splashed in an untidy heap on the carpet… It was all rumpled up, and probably picking up fluff…

Beth's eyes followed to where his gaze had flashed.

"Don't look there," she said reaching her hands behind herself like some circus contortionist, except Greg realised the action must be one most women performed at least twice a day. "Look here."

Beth's bra joined her top on the carpet. Before his eyes could track its position she guided one of his hands, placed it on her breast. "Here," she said, and then she moved his thumb and steered it to brush over the areola and the pink and perky nipple…

The lump in his crotch strained against its moorings.

Then her mouth was on his again, her hands at his belt. Somewhere in the delirium of the following few minutes his jeans and trunks ended up at his feet and his t-shirt was peeled over his head. Beth pushed him back onto the bed, and slipped out of her skirt and knickers. Both naked now, she moved over him. Her skin felt toasty warm, smooth as velvet.

She found him, took him and straddled him.

What followed was like some delicious out-of-body experience. She rocked atop him, and he reached for her, pulled her down, wanting to have her mouth on his again. Good gravy it felt amazing… He began to moan…

She pulled away.

"Not yet." She twitched her head, her eyes falling toward the carpet.

He understood, glanced over at the clothes scattered on the floor, the untidy heap that demanded to be picked up, folded...

It was enough. The needle in the gauge fell from red to orange.

She drew back, rocked back, set her hands on his chest, moving faster, let out a moan of her own. Hearing it, Greg knew that all the untidy clothing in the world wasn't going to do a damn thing this time, someone could have discharged a tipper load of landfill through the bedroom window and it wouldn't have done the trick.

She leant forward again, her breasts meeting his chest, her hot breath mouthing a word into his ear.

"Now…"

–

They lay together for a while, her head on his chest. It felt nice, but it wasn't enough. In the end he had to ask. She seemed okay with it, though. He collected up their clothes and neatly folded them, placing them over the wardrobe door.

He tidied the bed sheets too, tugged the ends back where they belonged and folded back the top. Happier, he was able to slip back in beside her. And it was enough. For a while all thoughts of clothes, bed sheets, road crossings, pavement seams, correctly locked doors, definitively tightened non-dripping taps, murderers and mug handles were forgotten…

Chapter 51

"I have a plan."

He was giving her a gentle shake, although she had been half awake already. Okay, maybe not half, but at least a third. She had been dimly aware of Greg getting up, heard him moving around, heard the kettle boil and him brushing his teeth. She opened her eyes properly, looked up at him sitting beside her on the bed.

"I've been thinking," he said. "We might not know who the killer is, but we still have something. We know who he intends to kill next: Maurice Cooper. If we watch Cooper, same as we watched Crompton, we can still catch him. The difference is this time we already know where he's going."

Beth thought about this. It was so obvious that in the aftermath of discovering Crompton wasn't the killer, the confusion and shock, they had missed it. Greg was right; if Maurice Cooper was the next victim they could still catch the killer, hopefully before another Kettle Street resident lost their life.

She sat up. "I like it. It's a good plan."

He smiled.

"I watch the back of his house. I'll do it from the car. I'll park nearby." She swung her legs out of bed and got up, collected her clothes from where Greg had neatly folded them. "You watch the front from here with the binoculars. You have fresh batteries in the walkie-talkies? The second we see someone entering Cooper's house who shouldn't be, we call the police, alert Cooper. It's our best chance, isn't it?" She stepped into her knickers. Greg was trying to look like he wasn't watching. She walked to where he was, pulling on her shirt. Kissed him. "We can still do this."

This was the plan. Beth would take the car, drive home, grab some fresh clothes and come straight back. Greg would keep an eye on Cooper's house with the binoculars as best he could, and when she returned, twenty minutes tops, they would begin their surveillance proper.

–

Greg watched Beth drive away and closed the door, and closed it three more times.

He walked to the bedroom and was about to pick up the binoculars when in the lounge the phone began to ring.

No, it couldn't be. Not yet...

He felt an icy dread slalom down his neck. His heart began to thump. The phone's ringer sounded more like an alarm. He moved through the flat, grasped the handset and brought it to his ear like the nose of a loaded pistol...

He waited without speaking for the whispery voice to speak first.

"Hello?" Not a whisper. The voice was familiar, but it was not that one.

"Adrian?"

–

Had he been less wired he might better have handled telling Adrian he was done with Martin's 'therapy'. Adrian might even have agreed the therapist wasn't a good fit, but all that tension had to go somewhere. The information had unfortunately come out sounding like a criticism directed at Adrian for hiring such a weirdo in the first place. Built for adversity and winning, Adrian didn't cope well with criticism. He slid from defence to attack almost immediately. Maybe, he suggested, Greg just wasn't trying. It didn't help.

"He's unhinged, Aid! Didn't you hear me? He had me in a headlock!"

"Are you hurt?"

"No, but—"

"That's how these guys operate. It's what makes them so effective. They'll do whatever it takes to affect change. They're unorthodox, flexible, result-oriented."

Adrian was working out of town at short notice, covering for a colleague who had fallen sick. That was why he had called, to say he wouldn't be dropping by during the next few days as usual. Greg had meant to call him about Martin, but with everything that had been going on had forgotten.

"Including physical assault? Is that frequently part of his unorthodox, flexible, result-oriented approach? Where the hell did you find him anyway?"

"He and his partner ran a series of training sessions for our sales team. Their results were up seventeen percent for the next quarter. They're a new set up. The other guy, Martin's partner, is American, one of the leading lights over the pond. He studied directly under Richard Bandler, apparently, the guy who created this NLP stuff."

"Is he deranged too?"

"Like I said, the Neurolinguistic Programming as a methodology is results-based. The whole philosophy is not to be dogmatic, but creative, prepared to try things other therapies won't, think outside the box—"

"Well, I can assure you, Martin Mangham is definitely out of his box."

"I know some of it sounds odd, but it can work. Want to know what the American guy had the sales team do?"

"Go on."

"He got them selling balloons in the street. Made them all throw in £25 and gave them each two dozen red balloons, the one who could sell the most in an hour got the pot, and the kudos. These are educated people, Greg, experienced. Some make six figure deals on a regular basis, and suddenly they're seeing how many bloody red balloons they can shift in an hour. To begin with some of them weren't happy, but they got into it soon enough. Strip away all the contacts, the reputation, the expectations… Could they still sell?"

"I don't care. That lunatic is not stepping foot in my house again."

There was a pause.

"I mean it, Aid."

"Don't you want to get better?"

The exasperation in Adrian's voice bordered on anger. It was Beth's voice in Greg's head that answered.

"Yes, that would be great, but a close second would be not feeling like I'm useless as I am."

"I never said you were useless."

"No, you just think it. I wish you could spend a day in my head, Aid, I so wish you could, just so you could understand what being me is like, how hard getting through every single day is."

"You're right. I can't know, but I do try. I know you hate it, that's why I want to help."

"But you still think I just don't try hard enough. Like Colin. He always thought it was for attention or something. I thought you at least understood."

"You're not being fair. I do, or I've always tried to."

Greg felt tired. What was the point?

"Call that lunatic of a therapist. Tell him he's fired."

There was a long pause.

"Okay," Adrian said at last, "I'll tell him you're done."

"Okay."

"Bye."

"Bye."

Greg set the phone in the cradle. He was half way to the kitchen when the phone rang. He walked back and fetched it to his ear, wondered what Adrian had forgotten. Maybe even an apology?

"Adrian?"

"Greg?"

The voice wasn't Adrian's. Talk of the devil, thought Greg. The voice belonged to Martin Mangham.

"Martin? Look I really don't think—"

"Please, hear me out. I want to apologise. I think maybe I pushed you too hard too soon."

"By grappling me in my kitchen?"

"We have to be prepared to wade into uncharted waters to discover true change. And… It was too soon perhaps. I think it's vitally important not to view the exercise as a failure. No experience is negative if something positive can be extracted fro—"

"Martin—"

"I'm sorry, okay. I've been facing challenges of my own recently. It was important to me you made progress. When I take a client on I pledge to myself I'll do whatever it takes to make that happen, that's my promise, but I never meant to lose your trust."

"Look, Martin I'm not sure this is working for me."

"Give me a chance to explain. Let's meet up. We can discuss how best to progress. Please, I want to help you, and despite how we left things last time I think we're close to making real strides."

"I don't think so. Goodbye Martin."

Chapter 52

The killer waited patiently in the spare room, listening to the intermittent clack of a laptop keyboard, the irritating peck of a two-finger typist.

Maurice Cooper's residents' association newsletters, the impotent ramblings of someone without the courage to do something beyond begging or complaining, the drivel of a passive, lifelong whiner…

Can't someone do something? Can't someone intervene? Can't someone tidy up, change their ways, do the right thing and be considerate…? But never Cooper himself, apparently. He stopped at bleating about it in writing.

He had checked. Maurice Cooper had never been married. His whole house was evidence enough. The room he hid in even now was no exception; one look screamed it had never enjoyed a woman's touch. No flowers or scented candles to soften the space, no floral prints, textured fabrics. He bet the musty and dry room's windows hadn't been opened for years…

The spare room seemed emblematic of Maurice Cooper's bachelor existence, stale and cold, made for visitors, when there was likely no one to visit. The single bed, the bedside table, the single-width wardrobe, everything was plain, cold, hard or purely functional, and slightly grim. When Cooper's body was discovered no one would be too surprised. A lonely man, who had known only loneliness, had gotten tired of being lonely.

As far as he could see there wasn't much of a life here to take.

Down the landing the keyboard's clacking ceased. He tightened his grip on the nylon rope, poised for when Cooper's footsteps reached the edge of the staircase. He had practiced the manoeuvre umpteen times in his own house, stepping out, ready with the noose, the grab, the lift…

The landing met the stairs, which turned, and turned again, looping back so the stairs ran under the landing, creating a nice eleven-foot drop. The killer had measured the drop and rope carefully. The drop and the five-foot rope, combined with Cooper's pudgy, approximately five-foot-eight frame would leave a good two feet of fresh air between the man's feet and the stairs below.

A muffled creak of floorboards betrayed Cooper rising from his desk.

The killer readied himself.

The footsteps neared. Cooper passed the spare room door, and the killer sprang. Practice made perfect. He hooked the noose over Cooper's head before the fool even knew what had happened.

The killer looped one arm under Cooper's armpit and his other under his thigh, and one swift motion carried him up and over the head of the banister rail.

Cooper fell for a second and the rope snapped tight. The killer dropped to his knees and reached through the banister rails, gripped Cooper so he faced outwards, held fast with his latex gloved hands to his cardigan to prevent him from turning. If he succeeded in grabbing the rail and was able to take the weight off the noose around his throat, things might get messy and drawn out.

Cooper flailed, but the drop had been long enough and swift enough to draw the rope tight around his neck. He seemed torn between batting at the banister for purchase and clawing at his neck to pull the rope free, but he did neither for long.

He kicked a bit, gurgled, issued a few unintelligible gasping throaty noises and eventually hung still.

The whole operation had been gratifyingly swift and efficient, over in minutes. Very neat.

The killer released his grip on Cooper's cardigan and stood up. He walked to the study, pleased to find Cooper's laptop still on. Half a newsletter filled the screen.

The killed added six words at the foot of the litany of complaints, warnings and notices. They read:

What's the point? No one cares.

This done he drew down the zipper of the disposable paper suit he wore just far enough to fetch the phone from his pocket with a latex gloved hand, tugged his face mask beneath his chin and started to punch in Greg's phone number.

–

Greg was almost back at the bedroom door when the phone rang again. He should have known Martin wouldn't give up that easily. Unorthodox, flexible, results-oriented... Greg had had enough. He was fresh out of patience, and had larger concerns at present. He needed to be watching Cooper's house. He would be polite, but firm, tell Martin he didn't want him to call him again, and if he persisted he would file a complaint of assault against him with the police. That should do it.

He snatched the phone from the cradle and brought it to his ear, resolved to end any further discussion right here.

"Look, Marti—"

The whispery voice spilt into his ear and chilled his brain, the ice travelling down his neck and spine.

"Glazed porch, puke green door. No Salesmen Thank You sign. Two and a half minutes."

The line clicked dead.

Greg stared at the phone in his hand. He saw Beth's mobile number scratched on the pad beside the phone. She had to be back at her flat by now. How long would it take her to get in the car and return? Longer than two and a half minutes? Probably. How long would it take him to reach Maurice Cooper's house and kick the door in? Under two and a half minutes?

Then he realised the clock was even now ticking, his two and a half minutes already closing in on two. He moved to dial Beth's number, hovered at the phone for perhaps two seconds more and then plunged into the hall. He jammed his feet into his shoes and almost fell out of the front door in his urgency, and got around four strides down the path…

What if the door hadn't actually slammed shut. Greg grimaced and swore, while across the street Maurice Cooper was likely dead or dying and the killer was begging to be caught next to his cooling body.

But the door…

It would only take a few seconds to check, longer than he had already hesitated. He ran back, tugged at the knocker. It was shut.

He gave it another firm tug.

It was definitely closed.

He turned, and before his treacherous, malfunctioning mind could whir doubt back into his thoughts he hurried into the path, and actually set a foot on the empty road. Cooper's house lay across the road only a dozen or so doors up the street.

He tried to take another step, but hit the familiar wall. He felt anxiety spike, threaten to ignite into full-fledged panic. Instead of another step forward his foot somehow rejoined the other behind the kerb.

He knew there was no time to count, there hadn't been before, but again that knowledge seemed locked away in a separate compartment of his brain, one with thick sound-proofing. Right now all he could think about was how he couldn't cross without a count…

A woman with a buggy rounded the top of the road. The child in the buggy was idly kicking its legs. The woman pushed the buggy with one hand, her other hand was holding a phone to her ear. She was talking into it. Greg hurried toward her up the road, hopping between the paving slabs in his hurry.

He yelled at her.

"You! Call the police! There's a murder being committed over there!" He waved toward Cooper's house. "In that house! Now! Right now!"

The woman stopped dead. There was a spell of perhaps two seconds where she took Greg in. Like expressions drawn into a flip book Greg recognised, surprise, then alarm, then suspicion, and finally fear. The woman backed away from him, drawing the buggy back too, as if he were some animal escaped from the local zoo.

And in her frightened gaze Greg saw what she saw: a wild, crazed man, pale, desperate, babbling and yelling like a lunatic.

She swung the buggy around and began to hurry in the opposite direction, casting intermitted glances over her shoulder to check Greg wasn't in pursuit. The clock was ticking.

He stepped back to the kerb, tried to fight the rising panic, started to count…

One hundred, ninety-nine, ninety-eight, ninety-seven…

He reached Cooper's house sweating and breathing hard. The porch door with the now tell-tale 'No Salesmen Thank You' sign tucked in the corner of the window was unlocked. He threw it wide and took a pace back. Two hard kicks at the original hardwood door beyond sent the sage green body of timber crashing in. He plunged into Cooper's downstairs hallway, and spotted a set of slippered feet and corduroy trousered legs dangling over the last few steps of the staircase.

He ran to the staircase and climbed the first few steps, seized Cooper's legs and waist and lifted him up. An upward glance rewarded him with Cooper's pop-eyed stare. He head was a ghoulish shade of purple, the blue nylon noose biting cruelly into his neck.

Greg tried to take the weight off the rope, gripping Maurice with one arm while fumbling for his hand. His fingers searched his wrist, trying to locate a pulse.

If Maurice had one he couldn't find it.

It was around this point Greg began to bellow, "Help!" over and over like a looped audio clip.

By the time someone heeded his call, saw what was going on and called the emergency services, Greg had cut Maurice down with a knife from the kitchen and removed the noose from his neck. The paramedics found him administering a bout of inexpert and almost certainly futile CPR. When they took charge he flopped back against the wall of

Cooper's hallway, arms and shoulders burning from the chest compressions, with the taste of a dead man on his lips and the weight of failure dragging him down.

Chapter 53

The interview room looked exactly like they did on TV. So bland as to be featureless, just a few chairs, a table and recording device to provide a dash of character.

Greg felt weirdly calm. His body had not long ago manufactured a party-sized dose of adrenaline. Now that it had bled away he felt almost sedated, and while the room might have seemed oppressive to many, its sparse nature afforded Greg's obsessive eye little to latch onto. Even Dingle's colleague's notepad, surely only by accident, was neatly aligned with the table's edge.

Greg had spent the past hour telling Dingle how he came to have found Maurice Cooper hanging from his banister rail in what looked very much like an attempt to take his own life, and more besides. He chose to leave out breaking into Crompton's flat, and how Crompton had been his and Beth's prime suspect. He wanted Dingle to take him seriously, and pointing how wrong he and Beth had got things just twenty-four hours previously was unlikely to help his case. In fact Greg downplayed Beth's involvement as much as possible. And yet, even as he laid it all out he suspected he knew what Dingle's assessment would be.

He wasn't wrong.

"The problem I face here, Mr Unsworth, is there's nothing to suggest any of the admittedly unusually high number of deaths in your street lately are more than what they appear to be, an unfortunate mix of accidents and in Maurice Cooper's case, suicide."

"I told you. The packages, the phone calls. We tried to tell you before."

"Yes. The phone call." Dingle glanced over at the other detective's notes. "If you'll extend me some patience, just so we're absolutely clear, this is why you were moved to check on Mr Cooper, because you had another of these anonymous phone calls?"

"We've already been over this."

Dingle checked his notes, "I know. The information, 'glazed porch, puke green door. No Salesmen Please sign. Two and a half minutes', this was enough information to prompt you to race across the street and kick in your neighbour's front door?"

"Thank you."

Dingle frowned. "Excuse me?"

"The note on Maurice's door reads, 'No Salesmen Thank You.'"

Dingle cast a glance at his colleague, made a small expression with his eyes. The man drew a line through 'please' and wrote 'thank you' above.

Greg tried not to think, just to answer Dingle's questions as best he could.

"It was like the other calls," he said. "I knew what it meant. It meant someone was probably already dead and whoever killed him was giving me the chance to catch him."

"And why would they want you to do that?"

"How the hell should I know?"

"You seem to have everything else worked out. Someone is killing your neighbours and making the deaths look like accidents. Doing a fine job of it too, as the coroner hasn't found a single thing to suggest this isn't the case. Nothing. You have a series of peculiar calls, some random items posted through your letterbox, and a theory. It's a theory I'm unlikely to be able to convince my superiors to sanction a full-scale murder investigation on the strength of."

"Have they looked? Checked for DNA at all the crime scenes?"

"I've asked them to review the findings again, ensure something wasn't overlooked, but right now the only person we know for sure was in the proximity of Maurice Cooper at the time of his death was you."

"And you don't believe me do you?"

"I'm obliged to take any information relating to something as serious as murder seriously. I assure you the matter will be investigated further, and to that end it's very likely I'll want to speak to you again."

Greg didn't like the ring of that. Not at all. The only person we know for sure was in the proximity of Maurice Cooper at the time of his death was you.

"If you'll excuse me, I need to take a break," said Dingle. "We'll try not to keep you too much longer." Dingle recorded a pause to the current interview, and left Greg to stew.

—

Dingle apologised for keeping Beth waiting, and started asking her his questions.

Beth had never suffered from claustrophobia, but there was something about the small beige interview room that pinched. The air seemed stale, stuffy, the temperature just a little too warm to be comfortable. She tried to ignore all this and answer Dingle's questions to the best of her ability.

Almost twenty minutes in, and one thing seemed to surface as a running theme: It was amazing, and slightly concerning, just how thin all her and Greg's evidence sounded when summarised in the tight, charmless interview room.

"If you'll just clarify a previous point for me again… You were there when one of the phone calls came." Dingle peeked over at his companion's notes. "The one Mr Unsworth believes informed him of Steven Holt's death?"

"Yes, I was there. Greg picked up the phone and began to freak out. That's when we realised the packages were clues, and the phone calls were essentially informing Greg someone was dead, and presumably, how long the killer intended to remain at the scene."

"And you actually overheard the content of the call, what words were actually used?"

Beth frowned. "Well, no. I mean not directly, but Greg told me exactly what the caller said."

"I see."

"Are you suggesting he made it up?"

"I'm not suggesting anything. I'm just clarifying what actually happened. If you didn't actually hear the call, you can't really corroborate what was said. You can attest to a call at that time, and what Mr Unsworth claimed was said by the caller, but…"

"He could just as easily have been lying?"

Beth had intended the retort to be a barb, but Dingle fielded it with nothing but a non-committal purse of the lips.

"Miss Grue, how long, exactly have you known Mr Unsworth?"

Again Beth was almost sure Dingle knew the answer, so she remained silent while he made a show of glancing over at his colleague's notes. "Just over two months," he answered himself. "Forgive me, but that doesn't seem a very long time to trust someone's word about a matter as serious as murder.

Doesn't seem like that long to assess what kind of person someone is at all, deep down."

Again Beth wanted to fire back a dry retort, but something stopped her. Two months, had it really been only two months since they had found Rose Gordon dead at the foot of her stairs? Greg had been near and come to help... He had shown her the packages which had the clues inside. Well, not the packages exactly but the contents, what had been inside the packages. Of course, she had not actually seen any of them delivered first-hand... Greg had told her about the phone calls, the clues... Greg had told her about his new neighbour Dennis Crompton, who they had investigated together, unearthing his violent past. Greg had not known Crompton was a killer; just that he had looked sketchy.

Hadn't he?

What Dingle said was true, Beth had never actually heard one of the phone calls herself, but she had been there when a call came. She had seen Greg's reaction. You couldn't fake something like that.

Could you?

Dingle was still staring at her quietly, his lips still pursed. His manner seemed to shift, the opaque CID detective relaxed, and Beth thought she detected the shadow of real concern.

"Miss Grue... In truth, I don't really know what to make of these deaths in Kettle Street. On one hand they might just be simple accidents, a series of unfortunate deaths, statistical anomaly, unusually concentrated along one street purely by coincidence, and perhaps not. I very much intend to investigate the matter further, but..." Dingle spoke his following words with a softer, but no less serious weight. "Until we're both sure what exactly, if anything, is transpiring here, you might want to consider how well you truly know Mr Unsworth, and whether it's wise to spend time in his company alone."

—

Dingle had returned, but the questioning appeared to be over. He thanked Greg for his cooperation, said he was sure it has been a very distressing morning and told him he would be in touch if they needed any additional information. And like that it was over.

Greg was about to leave the station when Beth emerged from a corridor nearby. They acknowledged each other but didn't say anything, not yet. She had obviously been in another interview room, and must have just wrapped up too. Greg offered her a tired smile, and she smiled back, sort of. He wanted to get clear of the station before discussing what had gone on inside. They exited in silence.

Outside the day was overcast. Right now it was dry, but Greg knew rain clouds when he saw them. He wanted to go home, put the kettle on, make a cup of tea and pretend, if only for a spell, that he had taken part in a less horrible morning, and that it was all over, when he knew it couldn't possibly be.

"He still doesn't believe us," he said. "He said he plans to look into things further, but…"

"He said the same thing to me."

"He asked you to go over it all?"

"Yeah."

"I didn't mention Crompton."

"No," Beth said. "Me neither."

They walked together in silence for a few more strides. Greg found the paving on the path awkward, too big to take two slabs in a long stride, and not large enough to accommodate a short step. He was forced to adopt a short step, long step pattern. He didn't want to, but couldn't help giving voice to the obvious question. "So what do we do now?" he said.

Beth didn't answer at first. He thought maybe she hadn't heard. She seemed distracted. He was about to ask again when she answered.

"I honestly don't know, Greg. But Dingle said one thing I found it hard to argue with: there's no concrete evidence. We've been relying on circumstantial stuff too much. What if we've been feeding each other false assumptions? Crompton kind of proves we have, doesn't he? I think we each need a chance to take what happened this morning in without the other skewing anything…"

"Oh, um… Okay, I guess I'll speak to you later, then?"

Beth smiled, but it was oddly tight, had a mechanical quality to it.

"Is everything alright?" He realised the absurdity of what he'd just said. "With you, I mean, with us?"

"Yeah. Of course."

But Greg wasn't so sure. Beth seemed off, almost evasive.

"I'm going to cut through the park," she said. "I'll call you."

"Okay."

What had Dingle said during her interview? Had he asked something that had upset her, or was it something else? Greg wanted to ask her if everything was alright again, but resisted.

Instead he watched her take off. At speed her gait was almost as awkward as his on the path's too-big-

306

too-small paving. He couldn't shake the feeling she wasn't in a rush to get home, but to get away.

From him.

Chapter 54

Beth studied the incident board on the wall, stared at the spider web of red twine from the pushpin above which DENNIS CROMPTON was etched in block caps. She held a pair of scissors, ready to cut.

They had been wrong about Crompton. He was a killer, true, over a decade ago, but with the true nature of the curious wooden case laid bare, the bloody shirt which had looked so damning exposed as nothing more than spilt paint, all they were left with was the tragic story of a teenage boy who had got involved with an older married woman. Mrs Jacobson had perhaps forgotten how hot young passion and jealousy burn, hot enough to ignite murder. In this context Crompton was nothing more sinister than an ex-con trying to start again.

There had been no murder on Kettle Street immediately prior to spying Crompton the night of his stained shirt, and nothing to link Crompton to the murders beyond this past crime. And, once she discarded the theory the man was simply a murderous psychopath, he had never really possessed any discernible motive either. They had been watching the wrong man from the start, while the killer went about his business right under their noses.

Beth lifted the scissors, snipped at the threads stretching out from the pushpin by Crompton's name. One by one they fell free, dangling untethered, nothing left to unite them. Nothing seemed to connect the victims now.

Well, not quite nothing.

Facts. What were the hard, indisputable facts?

A lot of people had died on Kettle Street recently, too many to be accidents, maybe too many to write off as coincidence as Detective Dingle seemed prepared to. She began to collect each thread and wind each end around to one pin previously unconnected. The web once more spread out from the board, only now a different name lay at the centre.

GREG UNSWORTH.

She picked up the marker and etched more block caps on the copier paper taped upon the board, finishing by drawing a large oval around it and the web.

The letters spelt KETTLE STREET.

GREG UNSWORTH.

KETTLE STREET.

One of these things had to be the key. Was the killer stalking Kettle Street because of the street itself, or because Greg lived there, or both?

If Greg was the key, why?

If Kettle Street, again, why?

If both, then what connected the two?

Chapter 55

Beth needed distance. Even her own flat had proven stifling. She needed to get away from Kettle Street, murders, disbelieving detectives, and even Greg. She had grabbed her coat and caught the train into the city.

From the Starbucks by the cathedral, she watched the late afternoon shadow of an office block creep over the stonework like a dour stain. One question nagged above all others.

How well did she know Greg, really? Just this morning she might have answered quite well, but Dingle had planted a seed of doubt, damn him. She felt its insidious roots burrowing into her head. Could Dingle honestly believe nothing was going on, that the deaths in Kettle Street were no more than unfortunate accidents? He was a police detective, so clearly not a moron. Could so many supposed fatal accidents and Maurice Cooper's apparent suicide this morning really not be sufficient to force him to take a closer look? Maybe, she believed, but he would be practical, ask himself practical questions. In short he would look at the situation like a professional copper. Statistically, what was commonly accepted about murder, murderers and their victims?

In real life murders, the killer is usually known to the victim; Beth recalled a figure of something like eighty percent of them (from reading a recent James Patterson novel admittedly, but Patterson did his research, right?). She pulled out her phone and Googled 'serial killers common traits'. The various hits that came back, upon even a brief skim, were sobering, and a little scary if she were hoping for reassurance Greg couldn't possibly be one.

Such individuals often knew their victims.

In real life serial murders, the killer will often be known to the police, some are even known to insinuate themselves in aspects of the investigation.

Serial killers are often loners with very few social connections, isolated, lonely individuals.

The overwhelming majority are single white males in their twenties and thirties.

They frequently come from dysfunctional family backgrounds.

They are often very proficient liars, extremely convincing.

They are usually intelligent, and will sometimes go to great lengths to fabricate false evidence, and co-opt people to provide alibis, sometimes unwittingly.

They are often victims of childhood trauma, abuse or some other event that desensitizes them, distorts their view of the world, and stunts their emotional development.

Beth didn't like how many of these traits could be applied to Greg.

Because in her heart she knew he wasn't the killer.

He couldn't be. She found it impossible to believe the Greg she knew was an act, that she had been fooled, that he was nothing but an elaborate front for a calculated killer.

Did she really know Greg?

Dingle had said it himself; how well can you truly know someone in a matter of weeks? Enough to know they wouldn't lie to you? Enough to know if the issues they have are real, exaggerated, or faked to cover for some darker purpose? Enough to develop strong feelings for them?

She had to think. Set aside Dingle's insinuations and her own false assumptions polluting everything. The facts, they were what she needed to focus on.

What had she seen purely with her own eyes and ears? What hard evidence could she rely on?

She had found Ruth Gordon's body. Greg had been passing. After, she had gone to him about the whisky bottles. It was only then Greg had told her about the miniature of whisky and the sting cream, and shown her the protein bar from his mysterious packages. True, Greg had come to her after Brett's death, but if he had been acting the part of someone on the verge of freaking out it was a performance worthy of an Oscar.

More than this she fancied herself a good judge of character.

Greg was no killer.

She had worked out what the cryptic information in the phone calls meant. He could have led her to those conclusions, but that deduction was all too dependent on everything else... She couldn't believe Greg was behind anything. He was involved because whoever was behind the murders had involved him.

But why?

That was the biggest question. Why had the killer chosen to involve Greg? Where was the connection, because surely there had to be one? Why had the killer chosen Kettle Street's residents as his victims and then chosen a man who could scarcely leave his flat without it being a major operation to—

Beth pulled herself up short. Something, some glancing connection had darted past and just as swiftly vanished into the dark. She tried to latch onto the shadow, but it was gone. She tried to run through the previous thought, willing it to emerge from the gloom.

It hovered just out of reach.

She stared out of the window; the office block's shadow had fallen almost to the foundations of the cathedral. Evening was upon the day.

She was supposed to attend her final class with O'Shea at eight, but—

"Beth?"

The man passing was scanning the busy coffee shop for a free table, but now he screeched to a stop, staring at her. She had been squeezing out from her seat at the counter at the window, concentrating on not bumping into anyone as she extracted herself. It was his voice that prompted her to look up. She had not heard that voice for years, but recognised it immediately. She turned and came face to face with a ghost from the past. The ghost from the past:

Neil. One-time future husband, erstwhile fiancé, old boyfriend, first love.

He looked older, as one would expect after several years, but rather annoyingly he was no less handsome. He had clearly continued to take care of himself, had gained no paunch, nor even a receding hairline to take solace in, instead he had simply matured, was less boy, more man. He looked happy and healthy. He even had the audacity to be tastefully dressed. He smiled, and to Beth's surprise she spied a seam of nervousness.

"I thought it was you."

Beth found her heart racing a little, like she had received an electric shock, and a solid jolt at that.

To say she never thought of Neil would be a lie. She had indeed wondered on occasion what might happen if she were to bump into him one day. In her head the meeting would ultimately be characterised by proving how little he meant to her now. How completely she had moved on, how their

313

relationship had been jostled and diminished in the context of the following years to a blip, a forgotten chapter of her youth… How confident and independent she would appear, so different from the Beth he had known. Only now it was actually happening she didn't feel so assured.

This man had loved her once, and she him.

She had burned like a hot little sun at the centre of his galaxy for a time, or had been made to feel she did. She could see her place by the movement of bodies around her, the way her gravity pulled at everything, creating complicated and tangled orbits, until one day when the physics of their relationship had suddenly shifted. The laws became unpredictable, and slowly she realised she was no longer the sun, or a planet, or even a moon, but a cold and uninteresting rock spinning into darkness.

She had loved Neil. He had pursued her, won her heart, and then broken it, dumped her.

The consideration and adoration she had grown comfortable with vanished. Suddenly they had been arguing, and afterwards only she had attempted to hold out the olive branch. The person she'd loved seemed to be wilfully creating distance between them, manufacturing arguments that afforded him reason to storm off, to make them both look unreasonable when it was only him, because it was only he who wanted to get away.

She had learned the cruel equation at the heart of all relationships: the power lies with the person who cares the least. In an ideal relationship you'll never know which one of you that is. In a doomed one it is often revealed slowly, and the one who cares most faces a choice. They can put up or get out.

In their case Neil had been the one to finally grasp the nettle she could not. He wasn't ready for marriage, he said. He had made a mistake. He was sorry. He needed to be on his own for a while. Soon enough she had understood what he really meant: I want to be without you, for good.

Now he was standing right in front of her. She had loved this man, and then hated him. Emotions, like the high pressure responsible for a dazzling and deliriously hot summer day, had needed somewhere to go, and for Beth they'd become the next day's thunderstorm. Love had turned to hate, for a while.

There were things she wanted to ask. Why? What changed and when? She had assumed these were questions that would cease to matter in time, but that hadn't turned out to be true. Even now she would have him tell her.

What made you change your mind? What made you see one thing and then something else, someone else, someone you no longer wanted to be with? Was it gradual, or did it happen all at once? What was the first thing you noticed? Where exactly did the rot start? What did I say or do? I used to be someone you yearned to spend every waking moment with, yearned to touch, to make love to, to talk late into the night with, and then you didn't want me around at all. Why did it take you so long to see the real me, and decide that wasn't what you wanted? It was not an original story, she knew, but one so common it was a cliché, first love, followed by heartbreak.

There were still questions, but she would rather gargle deadly poison than ever actually ask them.

No, when faced with an old lover, there is really only one response. She was about to say the words when he got there first.

"You look well," he said.

She found her voice. "Thank you. You too."

315

"So," he scrambled, "what are you doing these days?"

"I'm a librarian."

"That's…brilliant."

"You?"

"Advertising."

"You didn't go into law, then?"

"For a while. It wasn't for me. Money well spent on that degree, eh?"

He smiled, humble, what a mess I am, kind of smile. It suited him.

She had loved Neil, might well have hated him, and finally she had got over him, but that was not, she now discovered, the same thing as not caring. Faced with the reality of him, standing in a busy coffee shop, she discovered she did still care. He had a place in her life, in the woman she had become, and while she wasn't quite ready to give him a free pass, he had acted badly, had hurt her, she found she wasn't angry or sore. Neither, though, did she want him back to rekindle any old flame. Their good and bad times had simply mingled enough for the brew not to taste bitter any more.

There was an interval of silence, not long, but large enough to allow awkwardness to begin to stretch its legs. Beth decided to let it. He had started this. Let him be the one to feel uncomfortable, she was damned if she would.

"I'm sorry." He almost blurted the words out, and seemed to realise it. "About how things ended between us? I really am. I could have handled things better, I know. I was thoughtless, and selfish and immature. You deserved better."

Beth pulled a face, one she hoped would communicate something hovering between agreement and indifference. She shrugged.

316

"All water under the bridge now. Ancient history."

Only it wasn't, because one question elbowed aside all the rest. Why her? When he'd had plenty of options where women were concerned, why had he picked her? A mistake, one he had eventually rectified? As much as she would rather think otherwise, that was her suspicion at the time, and nothing had changed. Why in the first place, though? Why would someone who could have the trophiest of trophy girlfriends choose a wobbly, disabled chick who spoke funny?

Neil almost visibly exhaled with relief.

"You don't know how good that is to hear." He looked like he genuinely meant it too. "I suppose I shouldn't be surprised, after all you always were the strong one."

"I was?"

"Yeah, when I think back to our time in Uni now, well, I was always trying too hard, desperate for everyone to like me. You must remember how I was, always desperate to be in with every clique? It was almost pathological. I loved how you didn't care what people thought. You were your own person, like it or lump it, you know?"

"I… was?"

"I never meant to hurt you. I might never have actually said the words 'it's not you, it's me', I wasn't that stupid, but if I had it would have been true. I've thought about contacting you over the past few years, more than once I've looked you up on Facebook, but… I was confused back then. I wish I could have been braver, more honest with you, with everyone. I was too worried about what people would think of me, not just friends but my parents. You remember my dad, not exactly the most

317

enlightened of men… That's why in the end I did the only thing I felt could do, I got away. I did care about you, though. I really did. I want you to know that."

Beth had to admit, it felt good to hear him say it out loud, but it didn't change the past. Neil admitting her disability was an issue didn't change anything.

He looked about to say something else when a tall and impossibly handsome sandy haired man walked up beside him holding two medium, bucket-sized lattes.

"I saw a table free over there. Got you skimmed, that okay, hon?" He turned to address Beth. "Hello?"

Neil smiled awkwardly. "Chris, meet Beth, an old friend."

Chris offered a friendly nod.

"Beth, this is Chris. My partner."

Voyage of Death: A George and Kathy Franklin Mystery
by
Beth Grue

Chapter Twenty

The upper deck was almost empty as dusk fell over the Atlantic. The moon shone white, like a ball of molten metal, dunked into the twinkling expanse of water. It was not cold, but cool. I did not hear his approach, and almost jumped when he took up position at the rail beside me, joining me to admire the view.

It was the taciturn Russian, Alexis Demidov. He removed a small ring-bound notebook and a pencil from his pocket, scribbled something on a sheet, tore it free and handed it to me.

At such moments I have learnt to be accommodating of other's ignorance and misconceptions.

I removed my own notebook and scribbled a note of my own.

It read: I'm dumb, not deaf.

I handed it to him, my expression neither conciliatory nor coloured with irritation.

The big Russian took my note, and surprised me by smiling. He shook his head, and then he held his fingers to his lips and gave me a small shake of his head. Now it was I who felt foolish.

So he wasn't just quiet, and evidently nor was the English language a hurdle.

Dumb, not dumb. I should expect more from myself.

He scribbled another message. He cast his eyes over the ocean, before looking back to me, where they lingered.

I read the note.

There were four words.

My eyes seek beauty.

Chapter 56

Greg sipped at his mug of tea. Everything was a mess, and worse than ever.

Maurice Cooper was dead. The killer's identity was a total mystery. The longer Greg thought about it the more he believed that if Detective Dingle were ready to believe the deaths on the street were suspicious, it was likely to be Greg he would start investigating first. And Greg feared his only ally had had enough. He couldn't blame her. For him there was no escape, the killer had made sure he was tangled up in his crimes, but Beth? She had chosen to get involved. The difference was if she changed her mind, decided catching a killer wasn't her responsibility, she could walk away.

The doorbell rang. Greg went to open it. As he turned from the lounge into the hallway he did his best to gird himself before looking at the mat beneath the letterbox, but to his immense relief there was nothing lying on the floor.

He opened the door, to find Martin Mangham standing before him.

He was about to protest and demand the therapist-turned-assailant leave, but Martin didn't give him the chance.

"Greg, please? Hear me out? Five minutes, that's all I ask. Just the chance to explain myself and try to make amends? Please?"

Greg looked Martin over. The graze on his cheek and split lip were healing, but the bruise had blossomed into a lurid yellowy purple thing. There was another change, though. For the first time Greg could recall, Martin's body language, bearing and speech patterns actually resembled those of a normal human being. There was no awkward matching of Greg's own posture, no unnatural emphasis placed on words or phrases.

Greg looked at Martin. He looked troubled, and spent.

Greg sighed and stepped aside to let him in. "Tea? The kettle's just boiled."

—

They sat in the lounge, but this time Greg took the armchair and left Martin the sofa. He sat and took a sip of his tea. With his new human mode of operation and his battered face, Martin struck Greg as an oddly vulnerable figure.

"Martin, are you okay? Is something wrong?"

Martin let loose an eerie little laugh. It wasn't funny. Quite the opposite, it was bleak and a little desperate-sounding. Greg suddenly felt uneasy. He had spent a good many hours in Martin's company, and yet he wasn't sure he knew the man one bit. He had met calm, controlled Martin, with his calculated choice of vocabulary, who added emphasis to otherwise casual phrases, seeking to change their whole meaning. He knew the Martin who spoke in psycho-babble, the man to whom every aspect of interaction seemed designed to trap him in a verbal corner or convince him he wasn't actually feeling the things he was feeling. He had even met a version of that Martin ready to push too far, to actually manhandle him, but this Martin was new, this Martin seemed like the old one peeled down to the raw.

What had happened?

"I swear I really did just want to help you. I really did. I might have misjudged how best to do that, but honestly, the goal was always to help." Martin got up, took a few steps to the window. "Fucking hell, what a mess..."

"Has something happened?"

"You could say that. I have a confession to make."

"You do?"

"The truth of it is I've had some difficulties of my own lately."

"You have?" Greg was momentarily left staring at Martin's back.

"Would you like to know how I found my way into therapy? How I came to NLP, to meet my mentor Daryl Carlton?" the other man said, turning now. His face expressionless.

Greg shook his head.

"Seven years ago I tried to take my own life. I'm telling you this so you know I understand how hard things can become. I was depressed and grew unhappy enough that living started to mean nothing to me. My wife had died six months before. We had only been married for six days. She cut her toe on the beach on our honeymoon, just a nick, from a piece of glass maybe. We never really found out for sure. Wasn't anything too serious to look at, so we bought some antiseptic cream, plasters, cleaned it up, slapped 'em on. Job done, right? Only the cut turned ugly. We cleaned it up again, put more cream on. It turned uglier, started to swell up and weep pus. So eventually we went to the holiday rep who pointed us to the local doctor, who in turn sent us to the island's little hospital. They'd sort it, right? We'd lose a few days of our holiday in a hospital while my lovely bride's toe got some treatment.

"Only that's not how things went. Things turned bad, fast. By evening she looked like death warmed up. The doctors looked worried, and you know things are bad then. Septicaemia. Blood poisoning. Antibiotics, talk of amputation and flying her to the mainland… She went into septic shock. Her blood pressure plummeted in the late evening, and her organs started to shut down one by one… She died in the night. She was 27."

"I'm sorry, Martin, I can't imagine…"

"I pretty much fell apart. I wound up losing my job. Not surprising since I rarely went in. That was when I tried to end it, but I couldn't get it together enough to do that right. I spent a while in hospital, got some help. I must have been practically rattling with Prozac. I was getting therapy, but it was useless, and I hated popping pills, always have, but I didn't know what else to do. So I started reading self-help books, courses, videos… and, well, to my surprise they actually helped. I stumbled across NLP and that was it; it seemed to make sense to me, make sense of everything. You behave in a certain way, learn to think in a certain way and you get a different result. I started to feel more confident and in control…And there was so much to learn, so many people making strides in the field. I studied all the big names. I wanted to do what they did, use NLP to help others. So I took the courses, made contacts. That was how three years after trying to kill myself I came to be in LA studying under one of the biggest master practitioners in southern California. Daryl Carlton."

"Your partner? The one you're setting up the institute with?"

"Yes. Daryl was everything I wanted to be: centred, confident, successful, a man ready to do whatever it took to help people achieve the breakthroughs they needed. I've never met someone so persuasive, so in control. I've seen him achieve things with clients you wouldn't believe; watched people with fear of heights bungee jump from a crane after just an afternoon seminar with him, seen people who have suffered trauma reframe the experience into something positive and leave itching to take the reins of their lives again. I've seen him help people with compulsive disorders like yours. It was one of the reasons I was so sure I could help you, if I was prepared to do whatever it took. That was Daryl's maxim; you had to be prepared to do whatever it took, no limits, you had to be ready to cast aside society's convention and rules, be totally open and flexible in your thinking and actions."

Greg felt a creeping dread.

"Martin, what have you done?"

A strange expression flitted across Martin's face.

"You know what."

"I do?"

Martin seemed not to be staring at Greg, but into him.

"Come with me."

"Where?"

"Your kitchen."

Greg swallowed, tried to remain calm, or at least look calm. Martin was already at the doorway. Greg followed him into the kitchen. The packages and clues, all sealed in sandwich bags lay inside the drawers, a police officer was meant to have called and collected them for Dingle at some point. Greg guessed that if Dingle had believed they were actually evidence he would have come and got them himself already.

Martin walked past the drawers to the corner cupboard by the window, the cup cupboard. He reached out and opened it, exposing the matrix of perfectly aligned mugs, handles neatly pointing to the window.

"This? This needs patience and time, but because I was struggling I screwed up. I assaulted you," he said. "Physically forced you to do something I knew would cause you distress. Worse still, I'm afraid I did it not because I was sure it would help, but because I lost control. I was afraid. I was angry."

"I don't understand."

"Right now I have no idea where Daryl Carlton is. What I do know is he has taken two million pounds of institute funds, including my life savings, and the police aren't even sure he's done anything wrong. Apparently the funds were legally classed as donations, a technicality, but one I doubt was a mistake. I remortgaged my house to invest in that institute. I'm flat broke, heavily in debt, and judging by the evidence, a complete idiot and a total sucker."

"Martin, I'm sorry…"

Martin shuffled back to slump into the sofa.

"I should have trusted my instincts. I knew something wasn't right, but by the time I did anything it was too late. The evening before I saw you, I went to Daryl's house and confronted him. Some of his people were there, Americans, from his operation in the US… There's always people around him… I'd never really taken them as protection before, just other practitioners. Things got heated. Daryl was being such a smarmy shit, I lost it, went for him…" Martin wafted a hand at his face. The graze and bruising were still in evidence. "His people worked me over and threw me out, threatened to call the police and make a complaint of assault. What a joke. Just days before the sneaky crook does a runner with everyone's money, he has the brass balls to threaten to call the law on me?"

Martin leant forward, ran his hands up his face. Greg was familiar enough with desperation to recognise someone it has decided to come visit.

"So," he said, "you see? Me telling anyone how they should go about living their life is tantamount to a total fucking joke. I'm ruined, Greg. Boned. Fucked. Cleaned out." Martin's lip started to wobble, and then the tears came. "Only a crazy person would listen to me. I wouldn't listen to me!"

Greg got up, fetched the box of tissues on the bookshelf, handed one to his weeping therapist and placed a hand on his shoulder, gave it a friendly squeeze.

"You know Martin. I might be a complete mess, but I still believe one thing is always true; things are rarely as bad as they appear."

Martin blew his nose, and offered Greg a wan, desperate look.

"You think?"

Greg nodded. "Come on. Let's put that kettle back on to boil. A cup of tea never hurts does it?"

When Martin eventually left a few hours later, after he had talked and Greg had simply listened and tried to reassure him, it struck him that it was perhaps the first real and honest conversation they had really had.

Chapter 57

On Beth's train journey home from the city, the connection, the dark shadow which had briefly flitted across her mind skirted past again, only this time she was able to seize its hem. The forgotten fact, caught like lint in an empty pocket of her mind began to grow. The ensuing churn fast created a dirty fibrous ball of matter, comprised of suspicion, deduction, scant evidence and wild supposition.

Until that moment she had been tempted to skip O'Shea's final class, but suddenly, attending had become quite possibly a matter of life and death. Arriving home, she had again been drawn to her incident board. She scanned the houses labelled with the names of the dead. All on one side of the street, all opposite Greg's flat.

Greg's flat.

This had been the shadow, a half forgotten fact, a solid indisputable connection.

Dermot O'Shea used to live not just on Kettle Street, but in Greg's very flat, 11 Kettle Street. He had looked into renting the place, ideally hoping to live in it while he stayed in the area working on his new project. I had a romantic idea about renting the old place again, but it's a council flat, and of course, rather inconveniently, someone is already living there. So no 11 Kettle Street for me…

Dermot O'Shea, whose life was built on murder, revolved around murder, crafting murders, tricking the observer, being smarter, always one step ahead of his audience…

Dermot O'Shea who had returned to the area around the time Bernard Brocklehurst had died.

True, in O'Shea's own words, real life was 'full to the brim with coincidence', but what if in this case there was none?

She had searched through her drawers for an old gift from her parents, something that until now she had never actually put in her pocket: a small can of pepper spray.

–

The topic of O'Shea's final class was, as the block caps on the white board yelled, CLIMAX AND ENDING.

From behind a desk in Northcroft Library's modest study room, O'Shea was in full flow, the white board behind him. He waved a hand at the block caps again to punctuate his point. His final lesson was drawing to a close.

"The climax and dénouement of your story should do one thing above all else. It may seek to excite, yes, surprise, ideally, wrap up major and minor plot threads, one would hope, but more than all of these it should lead the reader to the ending and tell them what the story they just read was about." O'Shea was orating with his usual intensity, as though writing was all that spared the human race from disaster. "It should, if successful, throw the strongest light thus far onto the heart of your story's theme, expose facets of it, make a stance or a counter argument, encompass all that has come before it. It should say something, and invite your reader to confront that something. If it does not? I would suggest you go back and work out whether your story had anything to say to begin with.

"Most do. All stories, at some level, offer a comment on the human condition, from base emotions like lust, fear, hate and love to more complex emotions and motivations like regret, longing, resentment, suspicion, envy, sadness, shame, indignation, disgust, the craving for redress, justice…" O'Shea placed his hands on the desk before him, stared each and every one of his students in the eye.

The class waited.

"But," O'Shea let the moment gain just a little more weight, "the path from beginning to end is a tricky one. You may have set out to accomplish one thing, and discovered something more important on the journey. It is not difficult for one to lose his way. Life, as we know, is messy, but fiction should not be. When you reach your climax and ending, ask yourself this question: what were you trying to achieve? What was the point?"

O'Shea straightened up. The class and the course were over, and just like that, the serious tutor who treated writing with the kind of gravity most might reserve for a hostage negotiation was gone. By the time he reached the car park there would be little trace of him left, by the time O'Shea reached the pub, none. The relaxed O'Shea, the affable, irreverent flake fond of a drink would already be taking his place.

Beth wondered suddenly, which was the more authentic Dermot O'Shea, the first or the second, or maybe a third only his victims saw?

–

Beth had been the one to suggest grabbing a drink this time. The pub was surprisingly empty, but they still chose the tables beneath the big leaded

330

windows, through which O'Shea's flat could be spied.

O'Shea downed half his scotch in one go. It was his eighth. He had, having become more comfortable in her company perhaps and less concerned about keeping up appearances, begun to fetch two doubles each trip to the bar. Beth's second Diet Coke was still half full. O'Shea was, not uncommonly, in a talkative mood. He resumed his current theme.

"Writers want what all human beings want, only more so," he said, his accent thicker now. "To be heard, to have someone to really listen to us, just for a while without tapping their feet and willing us to shut up so they can take their turn, for the world to recognise we have unique things to say. We want people to see us—for who we really are, and accept us, warts and all. That's it, isn't it?" O'Shea sighed. "Or that's what I used to think, before I realised you shouldn't need to be heard. You shouldn't need everyone to understand. It's more important to know yourself, know what you're capable of, where your limits lie, what you can do, to quit worrying and accept there's no one to prove anything to but yourself. Do something monstrous, brilliant, fuck all the rules…" O'Shea jabbed a hard finger to his chest. "Do what this here tells you to do."

"What do you mean?"

O'Shea stared at her, unwavering. There was a pause so pregnant its feet and lower back were probably giving it hell.

"I want to share something with you. It's time. Someone needs to know, someone other than that useless waste…" O'Shea shut up, chewed his lip.

"What?"

"Not here. We'll need to go back to my flat."

"Dermot…"

He shook his head. "Really, it's not that. This is something important. Something a lot of people won't understand. Maybe you will, though—or maybe you won't. Either way I'd like to see. I'd like to know. Come on." He got up from his seat, wobbled a bit, but eventually found his sea legs. "Before I can change my mind."

—

The door to O'Shea's flat banged open and he and Beth almost fell in. Arm still slung over Beth's shoulder for support, O'Shea wrestled his key from the lock. His flat was nice; untidy, but clean and tastefully decorated.

O'Shea straightened up, swayed little, but remained upright. He winked at Beth.

"What can I get you? I'll be sticking to the old fire water." He waved an errant drinking hand toward the sofa. "Grab a seat why don't you?"

"I'll take a soft drink if you have one, water if you don't," Beth called after him as he stumbled into the kitchen.

She looked around for anything that suggested a double life, the lair of a serial killer, evidence of deeds dark… She ran a hand over her jacket, felt the reassuring bump of the pepper spray.

O'Shea reappeared, a big glass of scotch in one hand, a bottle of Guinness in the other. He offered it to Beth and looked about too, following her gaze as she took in his living room. He spotted his laptop on the desk in the corner of the room.

"There it is," he said. "The dread fucking beast. Think that's a keyboard you see? More like a mouth

332

full of shark's teeth, ready to maul the unwary writer. That's right, I see you, you bastard."

Beth knew the majority of this was for her benefit. Never less than loquacious, when he was drunk she could easily envision O'Shea straying into the theatrical. It wasn't all manufactured outrage, though. She did detect an undercurrent of genuine grievance beneath the performance.

"I thought you enjoyed writing," she said.

"I do. Exactly the same way a masochist enjoys having his genitals thrashed with a cat-o-nine tails. Some of my happiest moments have been at the keyboard, some of my darkest too. When the words come… It's like flying isn't it? You feel like a god, the smartest fucker alive. When they don't…" O'Shea grimaced.

"But this new project, work in progress, you said you thought it might be the best thing you've ever done."

"I do. Which means most people will likely despise me for it. They'll look at it, and then look at me…" O'Shea seemed, for once, lost for words.

"What is it? I won't tell. You can trust me."

He stared at her. All humour gone, his face inscrutable. He suddenly knocked back the entire glass of scotch. Grimaced fleetingly, and sniffed.

"Can I? What will you think of it? I wonder."

Beth couldn't help it now. She pushed on, even though in her head a siren was ringing a warning. She tried to tune out its din, concentrate on O'Shea.

"Dermot, what are you trying to tell me?"

He face was still oddly blank. "Murder, Beth. What else? I've crafted a murder mystery. One to make all my others look like the silly nonsense they were."

Beth felt a brief thrill of fear. Despite it all she kept her poker face on.

"In the drawer." O'Shea, pointed to the desk. "It's all there, the whole thing, not quite finished yet, but nearly, very, very close. Go on," he said, and wobbled drunkenly to an armchair, plopped himself into it. "I'm going to rest my eyes."

Beth stared at the drawer.

She got up and walked over, reached out to open the drawer, half excited, half terrified of what she might find. She imagined discovering the notes for a terrible, horrible plan, records of deeds already committed. Photographs of the freshly dead; Mr Brocklehurst, sprawled on a lawn, eyes swollen, face blue... Mrs Gordon, crumpled and broken at the foot of her stairs, Brett Foster, a heavy barbell crushing his throat, eyes popping, face purple and bent in horror, Steve Holt, crushed beneath the body of a classic Rover motor car, Leslie Yates impaled on a bed of Japanese cooking knives, Maurice Cooper clawing at the rope around his throat, legs kicking...

She stole a glance at O'Shea; sure enough his eyes were closed.

The drawer slid out on oiled runners, bumping to a stop.

But there were no gristly pictures, no notes, no plan, nothing like that.

Inside there was a cardboard folder. Three lines were written on the front in block printed capital letters.

BEGINNINGS AND ENDINGS
A JOSEPH LUMIERE MYSTERY
DRAFT 2.6

She lifted it out and set it on O'Shea's desk, flipped it open, pulled out the half-ream of papers and set them on the desk. A second glance back revealed O'Shea had gone past resting his eyes and fallen asleep. He was snoring quietly, mouth open.

She drew up the desk chair and began to read, and read for the next six hours straight. The pile of sheets shrank on one side and grew on the other as she finished each page and flipped it over face down to join those she had read.

What she found was no blueprint for a series of murders, but something quite beautiful, a poignant story, full of insight, wit and pathos, all wrapped up with a painfully bittersweet dénouement.

It followed the final days of O'Shea's signature character, the great amateur sleuth, the great twentieth-century detective, Joseph Lumiere. The year is 1989, and he is a resident of a nursing home on the south coast of an English town in bleak mid-winter. Born in the closing years of the previous century, Lumiere, now in his early nineties but still painfully sharp of mind, is watching the fall of the Berlin Wall unfolding on a common room television as his fellow nursing home inhabitants cough, wheeze, and slide into decrepitude, senility and death.

He reflects upon the cases he has solved, and the ultimate impact he has made on the lives of others, how the curious perspective he is both blessed and cursed with has enabled him to foil countless murders, but has also been responsible for poisoning many of his closest relationships. The inability to overlook the most minor detail has tainted every romantic and platonic relationship. Old and infirm, he is alone.

The narrative, fractured shards of wounded lovers and lifeless victims of murder, is laced with insight into the human condition and dark humour, including several laugh-out-loud moments where Beth felt sure she would wake the story's dozing author. It has a single thrumming thread, a mystery involving a nurse working at the home, and her simmering vendetta against another resident, a frail sweet-faced gentleman named Horace Kindly.

Hours of phone calls to old contacts, ex-police chiefs and home office types, many old men themselves, to call in old favours, deliver nuggets of information piecemeal, which the elderly Lumiere fits together to uncover the truth. The nurse was a primary school student of the resident, who was a former P.E. teacher, one who repeatedly abused her and many other girls.

Armed with this knowledge, at the climax of the tale Lumiere takes matters into his own hands and does what the nurse cannot bring herself to do. He takes the old man's life, suffocating him in a manner that, due to his extensive experience, Lumiere knows will be taken for death by natural causes. The murder is not driven by vengeance, or justice, but pity. He seeks to end the nurse's torment. The book closes with her leaving the nursing home's employment. Lumiere passes away in his sleep the same evening, an unrepentant killer.

Beth turned the final loose leaf page over, placing it on top of the rest, and then returned the pile to the folder. This was O'Shea's work-in-progress then, his much hinted at masterpiece. Not a series of elaborate real life murders, but a story. Now she had read it, that she could have nursed such an outlandish idea seemed laughable. O'Shea, a murderer?

"So?"

Beth looked around. O'Shea was still in the armchair, but awake.

"How's your head?"

O'Shea paused in thought to make an assessment, the way a master chef might sample a dish returned to the kitchen after a complaint. "Like a gang of demon children sawed the top of my head off, scooped my brain out with a rusty garden trowel, set two coats down on a concrete playground, played a game of five-a-side with it for an evening, then slapped it back in my cranium?"

Beth smiled. O'Shea matched it with a good-natured grimace.

"So?" he repeated, the pained smile fading from his face.

"It's wonderful. A proper book— sorry. No offence, I just meant—"

"None taken." He sighed. "They'll hate it, won't they?"

"Your fans? Lumiere fans? I'm afraid a lot of them might, yes."

"I expect the most fervent ones will utterly despise it, tear it to pieces."

Beth understood. The book was darkly beautiful, but O'Shea was right; many Lumiere fans would hate it with a passion, take it as an affront, which in a way it was. It was everything the previous Lumiere books were not, a complete betrayal of what they represented. It was not the comfy end of a cosy series, one last adventure. It was languid, reflective, wordy, unconcerned with the attention span of its reader, and sparsely plot driven. There was no familiar formula. It was almost a rebuke to the whole concept of long running series. O'Shea's weariness

337

of the form, its restrictions, its conservatism, its genre rails, coloured every word and sentence.

O'Shea had felt trapped. His response was to make his hero a murderer, to take him from quirky detective to a wonderfully complex and layered character, and in doing so had posed the question, who was he to have ever presented himself as judge and jury in the first place?

"You're going to publish it?" Beth asked.

"My useless, spineless agent thinks I should burn it. Screw him. If my publisher won't take it I imagine I'll self-publish. That's all the rage these days, right?"

She assumed the question was rhetorical, and so offered the appropriate response: nothing.

"Right," O'Shea announced. "Where's that scotch? I need a hair of the dog." He rose from the armchair with all the grace of a zombie from the grave and made for the kitchen.

O'Shea was egotistical, verbose, irreverent, wrestling with his legacy, and quite possibly had a drink problem, but exposed to how much he cared about his work, how for him it was all that mattered, Beth saw he was not and could never have been Kettle Street's killer.

She was already up and at the door when he returned to the room.

"Gotta split," she said. "I'll catch you later. Yeah?"

O'Shea considered her for a moment, and then raised his glass.

"Don't forget to grab breakfast," he said. "Most important meal of the day."

—

She stepped out onto the street. The early hour meant it was deserted, like a scene from a movie where everyone has mysteriously disappeared. To walk home was a short enough trip, and the journey would help her clear her head, take stock.

She felt oddly drained. If O'Shea wasn't the killer, the question remained, who was? And on the heels of this thought, why was it her responsibility to find out, to stop him? Greg had been dragged into this murderous game, made to act as some perverse witness, but when had she enlisted? Why exactly was it her job to stop him?

Because of Greg. He was involved and she was involved with him. Shy, awkward, introverted… Her heart had somehow moored its ropes to a fuck-up of epic proportions, a man for whom even crossing the road was an undertaking. Woven between the arcane and convoluted layers of his behaviours was a good man, a kind man, a talented and smart man who saw her like no one else ever had, a man who despite all his flaws she had grown to love.

She felt ashamed suddenly that Dingle's insinuations and suspicion had made her question him.

She reached her front door with thoughts of hot showers and naps. She would go straight to Greg's then. Screw the hour. And in the morning they would take a fresh look at everything. Beth felt sure they had to be missing something, some vital clue, some overlooked evidence, something to connect the murders other than the street they had occurred on.

She slid the key in, gave it the obligatory half-clockwise turn, pushed it open and stepped inside. As she pushed it closed again something moved behind it. She spun around just in time to see something hurtle toward her head and felt the sudden crack as it connected.

Chapter 58

He had left the handicapped girl in her kitchen, gaffer-taped to a chair. She had started to come around, but had still looked groggy. The strip of tape over her mouth would keep her quiet until he returned.

The world was still largely asleep. He parked the white van a couple of doors down from Greg's flat. The vehicle's ubiquity rendered it as invisible as anything on four wheels could be. The licence plates were fakes, but there was no one around to notice him anyway. It was still early, Kettle Street all but empty.

He left the engine running, pulled on a fresh pair of latex gloves, checked the van's mirrors and looked around one last time, collected the white package from the passenger seat.

Jump out. Post the package through the letterbox. One sharp snap so Greg couldn't fail to find it. Sprint back and go. Twenty seconds tops. He would be driving away before Greg even picked it up.

Then Greg would open it. Even for a flake like Greg he doubted it would take more than a few seconds to work out what the item inside meant; he had spied them together umpteen times these past weeks, they appeared to be getting quite friendly.

Then, from the girl's flat, he would use the pre-paid mobile to make the call.

It was the moment of truth. One way or the other he would know. By the time the day was done they would both be damned.

When the police were finally called in they were going to find a terrible and tragic scene, a poor handicapped girl tied up and stabbed to death in her own home, the weirdo responsible present too, having taken his own life straight after he had robbed her of hers. The forensics might look iffy should anyone look hard enough and in the right way, but he doubted they would. The evidence linking Greg to the other deaths on Kettle Street would be too great, and his previous interaction with the police had to mean he would be the first to appear on their radar. As a culprit he was a thousand times more plausible than some mystery killer.

It was almost over. The moment of truth. Today he would have his answer.

Chapter 59

The kitchen clock read 4:34 a.m. Greg was busy; he had emptied the mugs from the cupboard and was in the process of returning them. He was three rows in, fourth mug along. He set the mug in its spot and adjusted it. It didn't look right. He took it back out, set it on the side and chose another. Again it didn't feel right. He tried adjusting this one, too, but even when it looked perfect it didn't click. This was supposed to be helping him feel better, but he was beginning to wish he hadn't started.

He had woken early, from a poor night's sleep. He had given up trying to fall back off again and got up. Beth had not called the previous evening, and he had resisted the urge to call her. He would wait. If by afternoon there was still nothing then he might even go to see her at the library, face to face. He would tell her that if she wanted out, that was okay. The killer had drawn him into his plans, but not her.

He removed the uncooperative mug and was about to swap it for yet another when he heard it.

In the hall the letterbox snapped shut. And he knew. Without even looking, he knew what he would see long before he turned.

For an instant he felt frozen in place, then he realised what he should be doing. The realisation broke the spell.

He lunged and clawed his house keys from the hook on the kitchen wall and sprinted down the hall, fumbling to unlock the front door. He burst outside and ran down the front path and looked around the deserted street, just in time to see a white van turn left at the top into Badger Street.

343

He hurried back inside and closed the door, which in his present state of agitation took half a dozen tries. He fetched his rubber gloves, a sheet of paper and a sandwich bag. Soon the package was open and he was tipping the contents out onto the sheet of paper waiting to receive it.

What slid out was a library card. A slightly worn library card, pale blue and credit card-sized with a magnetic strip running alone the back and a barcode above, and on the front printed in capitals: BETH GRUE.

Greg felt ill, staggered as the world performed a queasy barrel roll, like some awful secret axis had been tripped.

Beth…

In the lounge the phone started to ring.

He crashed through the hall into the lounge and snatched the handset from its cradle. He heard his own voice say hello, and it sounded calm, like someone else's voice.

The voice on the other end of the line filled his ear. It was the voice, but different in one crucial aspect; there was no husky whisper now; its owner was making no attempt to disguise himself. Stripped of the raspy, opaque whisper, the blunt brevity, delivering a few verbal clues describing a handful of tell-tale features identifying his victim's home, and the time limit, he recognised it at once.

"Morning Greg, you piss-poor excuse for a human being."

Greg knew the killer, and the killer knew Greg.

And Greg also knew what he said during the next few moments might, for Beth, mean the difference between life and death.

"Don't hurt her."

There was a pause.

"Why Greg? What will you do to me? Turn all my mug handles the same way? Turn my shoes ninety degrees so they're perpendicular to the wall? Tighten my taps until the bloody thread is stripped to fuck? How many did I have to replace? Remind me, I lost count."

Greg knew he had not been the favourite, even when his mum had been alive to make it all work, but it was shocking to hear the degree of sheer, naked loathing and hatred in his stepfather's voice.

"You've killed people, Colin."

"The first yes, there was nothing you could have done there, but the rest? They're only dead because you didn't stop me. After every single one I gave you the chance to save the next. If you weren't such a pathetic waste of space they would still be alive, like she would be alive. You might have managed to convince yourself her death wasn't your fault, that nothing could have been done, that those minutes didn't make any difference, but I've looked into it, again and again and with head injuries every moment counts. I'm offering you one last chance to face that fact. If I'm wrong your friend will die, if I'm right you can still save her."

This was the closest Greg had had to a conversation with his stepfather in five years. What had happened in the intervening years? What seemed evident was that the often dry, inflexible, unimpressed man his mother married had not flourished in her absence. Without her warmth and light to draw out the best in him he had not just calcified, but clearly lost his mind. He felt suddenly sorry for his brother. Adrian had been dealing with this man? What stories hadn't he shared? What things had Colin done even Adrian didn't know about?

"Colin—"

"How many times Greg? So help me, tell me now or I'll kill the girl right now. How many times did you count before you crossed that road you useless little bastard? How many one hundreds? How long before you got across? Goddamn you, you will tell me. How many?"

"I don't know."

"Oh, I think you do. Come on you useless fuck-up. Be a man for once. How many fucking times? Tell me it or I swear I'll kill her right now."

Of course Greg knew. He would never be able to forget, and yet he had never shared the truth. Not to a single living soul. Colin was the only person to come close to asking, at the hospital after they had been allowed in to see his mum. Two words: "The road?", and Greg had answered.

"I got across."

It was the truth, but not really the answer to the question they both knew had been asked. And Colin had never asked again. Adrian had never even broached it. Not once. Either he knew it made no difference, Greg had crossed as quickly as he could, or he had decided he preferred not to know. It was the sort of information, Greg knew only too well, capable of torturing a person, the sort of information that might drive another man to bitterness, and perhaps even madness.

Like Adrian, Colin of course knew he would not have been able to cross immediately, knew it would have taken more than once, possibly even more than twice…

Greg couldn't rush, because if he made a mistake he would have had to start over, and his mum needed help as soon as possible. So as she lay on the path in the empty park, horribly still, he had

346

counted. One-hundred, ninety-nine, ninety-eight, ninety-seven… Praying for a car to appear to flag down, to get help…

Greg had come to believe Colin had, like Adrian, chosen ignorance. He was wrong. The question had not gone away, it had festered. He could lie now, but he suspected it would make no difference, and part of him wanted Colin to know. Wanted him to understand that once or a thousand times, he had crossed as quickly as he could.

"Ten."

Colin's voice bled across the line, less an echo than a winded croak.

"Ten?"

"I couldn't, I just couldn't. You have to understand, I couldn't. I could no more cross that road until it let me than I could have flown or teleported across."

But Colin wasn't listening.

"Ten? One thousand seconds is what? Over ten minutes, almost a quarter of an hour? No, more… Sixteen minutes? My wife lay on that park path, her skull smashed, bleeding in her head, for sixteen minutes before you finally called for help?"

They had almost been home. They had got off the train, cut through the heath, dark and empty. The path was icy. They were laughing at how the other was walking, taking exaggerated steps so as not to slip over on the icy path. Greg loved to see his mum laugh. One moment she was laughing, the next she had whipped back and fallen fast and hard. Had he added the bone-shattering crack of her skull hitting one of the kerb stones edging the path to the memory or had he actually heard it?

One look was enough to know it was bad, even as he ditched the shopping bags and went to help her up, he knew, then she had vomited and the panic klaxon already ringing in his head reached a new pitch. Home was near, so close, just around the corner, across the road and down the path.

He had started to run, the klaxon ringing, panic and dread driving him on…

And then he had met the road.

His feet stopped moving, as if they were glued to the kerb. He tried and tried just to step out into the empty road, until he surrendered and began to count, that infernal, internal arbiter refusing to let him free, to give permission until he had met its demands. He had wanted to cross, never wanted anything more. Ten counts. That was what it took, what the broken trip switch in his head finally accepted. Colin had lived with him, watched him grow up.

But he had never understood.

The one person who truly had was dead.

And if he couldn't make him understand now, someone else he loved might die too.

"I couldn't. Don't you fucking get it? Don't you think I would have if I could? She was my mum."

"You always were siphoning away her attention, like a little vampire, jealous of any time she gave to me. You couldn't stand it, could you? And finally you were old enough to be moving out, I thought there was light at the end of the tunnel! Just me and Liv. No fucking counting or straightening, or opening and closing and opening and bloody closing… We were meant to grow old together, just the two of us, and then I had nothing. Only work, and then not even that, forced into retirement."

"She was my mum, Colin. I loved her too."

"And you let her die."

"I couldn't—"

"I think you could!" Colin nearly screamed it. "If you'd have loved her like I did, you would! I've had to think about it over and over and over, year after year! I'm alone Greg, because of you!"

"Colin, don't. Whatever you're thinking, don't. Do what you like to me, but don't hurt Beth."

There was silence on the line, then, "Here's the deal. Where I am right now, I timed it. Strolled from the foot of your path in just under eleven minutes. I was going to give you fifteen, but I think I'll give you sixteen instead, more than enough time to save someone's life, enough time to count to one hundred ten times. I counted four roads to cross. Brass knocker. Red door. Bird feeder. I trust you know where?"

"I do."

"Good. And Greg, don't even think about calling the police, I see one flash of blue and sixteen minutes or sixteen seconds, I'll kill her."

The line went dead.

Chapter 60

Sixteen minutes.

Greg looked at the clock. 4:45 a.m. He ducked into the kitchen and seized the kitchen timer from beside the cooker hob. It was red and egg-shaped. He twisted it so the tiny white arrow was under the sixteen-minute mark, felt the whir of its tiny gears as it began to tick down in his hand.

Sixteen minutes.

Brass knocker. Red door. Bird feeder.

Beth's flat.

Still dressed in pyjama bottoms and a t-shirt he sprinted to the front door, jammed his feet into his shoes and threw it wide. He didn't even bother to close it. It was open. He decided to leave it open. It was open. No need to check. Come one, come all, steal and destroy everything I own...

He reached the edge of the path and met the kerb, road one of four. He tried to take a step, willed his foot to take a step, not to count. There wasn't time. His feet wouldn't obey, he felt himself start to shake, breathe too fast...

Stop.

One count per road, he could still do it if he allowed for no more than one count per road. He checked the timer. The red notch was fast approaching the fifteen-minute mark. He tried to keep a rein on his anxiety, panic was not an option. One count per road was all he could afford.

He shut his eyes and started to count. Don't hurry, don't screw it up...

One hundred, ninety-nine, ninety-eight, ninety-seven, ninety-six, ninety-five, ninety-four, ninety-three, ninety-two, ninety-one, ninety, eighty-nine, eighty-eight, eighty-seven, eighty-six, eighty-five, eighty-four, eighty-three, eighty-two, eighty-one, eighty, seventy-nine, seventy-eight, seventy-seven, seventy-six, seventy-five, seventy-four, seventy-three, seventy-two, seventy-one, seventy, sixty-nine, sixty-eight, sixty-seven, sixty-six, sixty-five, sixty-four, sixty-three, sixty-two, sixty-one, sixty, fifty-nine, fifty-eight, fifty-seven, fifty-six, fifty-five, fifty-four, fifty-three, fifty-two, fifty-one, fifty, forty-nine, forty-eight, forty-seven, forty-six, forty-five, forty-four, forty-three, forty-two, forty-one, forty, thirty-nine, thirty-eight, thirty-seven, thirty-six, thirty-five, thirty-four, thirty-three, thirty-two, thirty-one, thirty, twenty-nine, twenty-eight, twenty-seven, twenty-six, twenty-five, twenty-four, twenty-three, twenty-two, twenty-one, twenty, nineteen, eighteen, seventeen, sixteen, fifteen, fourteen, thirteen, twelve, eleven, ten, nine, eight, seven, six, five, four, three, two, one.

Greg tried to take the step out into the empty road.

Only he couldn't. He wanted to scream, but knew what he really needed to do was keep his head. Think, don't unravel. Think.

He checked the timer; the tiny white arrow was halfway between twelve and thirteen.

He had already lost over three minutes. He tried again. His body wouldn't obey, refused to.

If he counted quickly and accurately he could do it in a minute, maybe less. He took a deep breath, tried to quell his rising panic.

One hundred, ninety-nine, ninety-eight, ninety-seven, ninety-six, ninety-five, ninety-four, ninety-three, ninety-two, ninety-one, ninety, eighty-nine, eighty-eight, eighty-seven, eighty-six, eighty-five, eighty-four, eighty-three, eighty-two, eighty-one, eighty, seventy-nine, seventy-eight, seventy-seven, seventy-six, seventy-five, seventy-four, seventy-three, seventy-two, seventy-one, seventy, sixty-nine, sixty-eight, sixty-seven, sixty-six, sixty-five, sixty-four, sixty-three, sixty-two, sixty-one, sixty, fifty-nine, fifty-eight, fifty-seven, fifty-six, fifty-five, fifty-four, fifty-three, fifty-two, fifty-one, fifty, forty-nine, forty-eight, forty-seven, forty-six, forty-five, forty-four, forty-three, forty-two, forty-one, forty, thirty-nine, thirty-eight, thirty-seven, thirty-six, thirty-five, thirty-four, thirty-three, thirty-two, thirty-one, thirty, twenty-nine, twenty-eight, twenty-seven, twenty-six, twenty-five, twenty-four, twenty-three, twenty-two, twenty-one, twenty, nineteen, eighteen, seventeen, sixteen, fifteen, fourteen, thirteen, twelve, eleven, ten, nine, eight, seven, six, five, four, three, two, one.

The feeling didn't come. In his hand the kitchen timer whirred and vibrated, ticking down the seconds. There wasn't time for this. Just take a step, put one foot out. If he could just do that the other might follow. Just one tiny step…

Only he couldn't do it. Trying to set his foot into the road was like trying to feed his foot into the funnel of a mincing machine, every fibre of his being rebelled. Instinct, however misguided, had its boot on logic's throat.

Time was running out; four roads, how was he supposed to cross four different roads in—

He checked the timer. Less than twelve minutes remained. Four roads, when he couldn't even cross this one? There was no way. Even if the crossings were easy the distance would be too great, even as fast as his feet could carry him—

So what if he wasn't on foot?

He spun on his heels, flew down his path and crashed through his open front door, through the hall and into his kitchen. He nearly tore the kitchen drawer from its runner, fumbled in its belly for the key: the key to the hire car. It had been Beth's idea; she would keep one, and they would keep the other at his place, close to where the car was parked. He saw it, and grabbed it. In seconds he was back outside and bounding over the paving slabs as fast as he could run.

The small Fiat was parked a few houses down, where it had been left, ready to follow Crompton at a moment's notice. The key featured a button with a padlock icon. He pressed it and heard the clunk of the doors unlock. He pulled the passenger, kerb side door open, scrambled over into to the driver's side, tossing the kitchen timer into the tray beneath the dashboard as he went. The steady clicking of the mechanism continued, the arrow clicking relentlessly closer to zero.

He slotted the key into the ignition and tried to focus. Beth had said driving an automatic was like driving a bumper car. He prayed she hadn't been exaggerating too much. He grabbed the seatbelt and snapped it in, turned the key and the engine started up. Trying to recall what she had done, he pushed the stick from P into D. The Fiat started to creep forward.

He put his foot to the gas pedal.

The car lurched forward and he quickly steered away from the kerb into the road. He pushed the pedal down some more and the car picked up speed. He was driving, sort of. Colin had set the rules, four roads to cross, except if he pulled this off he wouldn't need to cross a single one of them. The houses raced past, Mrs Gordon's, Dennis Crompton's, Maurice Cooper's…

For the first time since waking, his mind felt deliriously clear. Obsessions did not appear immediately, they developed, and that took time. Driving was not only commanding every ounce of concentration he possessed, it was brand new, blissfully unburdened by ritual, yet. Should he ever attempt to learn, the rituals would come. Given all the indicators, levers, buttons, switches and pedals, it would be inevitable. How long before just checking the mirrors were positioned correctly became a ten-minute ordeal? How many other things would soon choke up the simple act of getting into a vehicle and driving away? Enough, he imagined, that it would become almost impossible, in time.

But right now? Right now he was moving, and at some speed.

All he lacked was a single shred of experience behind the wheel of a car. Perhaps for this very reason he hadn't noticed he was veering toward the kerb until discovering it via a bump, some juddering and an ugly scraping noise. He jerked the steering wheel to correct his course and rather alarmingly found himself in the middle of the road. He course-corrected again, found his lane, suddenly thankful of the early hour and being the only moving vehicle in sight.

Something that was about to change.

The T junction at the head of the street connecting Kettle Street with Badger Street arrived surprisingly quickly, and so did another car travelling along it. Greg jammed his foot on the other pedal and screeched to a halt at the give-way lines, inadvertently performing what those in the driving instructor business like to call an emergency stop. He shot forward, only the seatbelt sparing his face from smashing into the steering wheel. The passing car swerved a little, blaring its horn as it flew past.

Greg collected himself. With the road ahead once again clear, he pressed his foot to the gas and the car lurched forward, forcing him to frantically spin the wheel to make the turn along Badger Street and the direction of Beth's flat.

Brass knocker. Red door. Bird feeder.

He picked up speed again, getting a feel for the car. His steering was less jerky and he was keeping to the middle of his lane, mostly. He had been a passenger more times than he could remember, but actually being behind the wheel was a markedly different proposition. For a start everything seemed to move double speed, and the road seemed a hell of a lot narrower. As a passenger he scarcely noticed the road, he was usually preoccupied with the passing scenery; as the driver, though, navigating it felt like one of those games where you feed a metal loop along a metal wire without touching the two and setting off a buzzer. With the speed and the amount of his attention it demanded, it was difficult to gauge how much time had passed since getting in the car.

Speared by this thought he glanced down at the kitchen timer. The arrow had just passed the eight-minute mark. Beth's flat was just a few more streets away.

The turning for Hereward Road loomed, and then was suddenly upon him. He swung the wheel, realised too late he was going too quickly and took the corner wide, winding up on the wrong side of the road. Heart hammering, he steered hard and got back into the correct lane.

On the right side of the white lines again he stole another glance at the timer.

He couldn't believe it. At this rate he was not only going to make it, but arrive with minutes to spare.

355

The tiny white arrow was only just approaching the seven-minute mark. A whole seven minutes left. He was—

Greg had veered again. The arrow hit the seven-minute mark just as the Fiat's passenger side wheel hit the kerb.

The small car leapt up and mounted the pavement. The kerb wasn't high, and thankfully there was no one walking the pavement. The error might even have been salvageable, were it not for the street lamp. Greg tried to right his course, but whereas one moment the lamppost had seemed a distant feature, suddenly it was right in front of him.

The sound of buckling metal and shattering glass and the cessation of forward motion signalled an abrupt end to Greg's short-lived driving career. An airbag exploded from nowhere like a magic trick, smashing him in the face and breaking his nose, and an instant later he blacked out.

—

It took a moment for Greg to identify the whirring, clicking sound. He pushed the deflating airbag out of his face and peered through a set of fast-swelling eyes to its source.

The timer, miraculously, still sat in the tray below the dashboard, an ovoid omen of death. He tried to parse the signals his gluey eyes were sending to his shaken brain. The tiny white arrow and the numbers swam into focus. The arrow lay between two and one. He clawed the timer from the tray and fumbled for the door handle, threw the door open, and leapt out.

Or at least that had been the intention, but his seatbelt, still locked into place, had other ideas. He jabbed furiously at the release button and a moment later the belt popped free. He stumbled out of the car, one leg throbbing. There was blood, a lot of it, all down his t-shirt and spattering his pyjama bottoms. His face felt wet and sticky and hurt like hell. He wiped a sleeve across his mouth; it came away a dazzlingly bright red. His nose felt like someone had taken a hammer to it, and three times its normal size.

He got his bearings. He was half way up Hereward Road. Beth's flat was just around the corner on Ladle Lane.

He started to run, or more accurately hobble quickly, a smashed-up knee and unfamiliar paving making for a testing combo. He had to hurry, couldn't afford to waste a second.

He rounded the corner.

Beth's flat lay just a few doors up.

Suddenly the timer in his hand stopped its frantic rumbling and fell ominously still. Even without looking Greg knew what it meant. He glanced down and saw the tiny white arrow at rest beneath a moulded zero. His sixteen minutes were up. He flung the timer to the ground and hurried onward.

He tried not to think about the time, tried not to think about hitting the cracks in the paving as he went, or crossings, or doors being really, really shut, or miscounting change or dripping taps, or counting to a hundred, or lining things up so they felt right and neat and adjacent, perpendicular, level and square and symmetrical and tidy and ordered, or dead mothers or dead fathers, or crazy stepfathers or disappointed brothers, about being trapped and hobbled and unable to save someone he loved because he wasn't like other people, normal people

357

who just did things without jumping through hoops of their own creation.

Brass knocker. Red door. Bird feeder.

He ran up Beth's path and didn't even stop, quite the opposite, he threw the last of his energy into a shoulder-barge to the red-painted front door. It crashed open with an impressive crack of splintering wood. He actually saw the lock tear free from the frame as the door slammed into the hallway wall.

He plunged inside, heard a gasp from ahead in the kitchen, and barrelled on, spilled through the doorway, saw the motionless body slumped on the floor.

Only it wasn't Beth's body.

The body on the kitchen floor was Colin's. Beth was standing over him, holding a heavy-bottomed saucepan in one hand and a small can of spray in the other, breathing heavily from exertion. A strip of gaffer tape half hung from her chin and one baggy loop of it dangled from her left wrist.

The kitchen betrayed signs of a struggle. Colin was sprawled on the linoleum, unconscious, a spectacular purple lump developing on his bald pate, eyes swollen and streaming.

Beth looked up, spotted him, and still panting, a puzzled frown kinked her brow.

"What the hell happened to your face?"

Chapter 61

The Accident and Emergency wing was surprisingly quiet. Greg had mentioned it to one of the nurses and she had immediately put a finger over her lips and gently admonished him; that, she said, was exactly what someone always said moments before everything suddenly went crazy.

It didn't though. The craziness, or at least the bit that had led to murder on Kettle Street, was over.

Beth and Greg had been wheeled into adjacent bays, the curtain between them left open so they could see each other and talk. A doctor had checked Greg's nose and knee, declaring the former broken and in need of setting and the latter probably just swollen and on the way to some truly spectacular bruising. Just to be sure they would get an x-ray done. Beth had already been in for a scan; the diagnosis was a contusion and perhaps concussion. They insisted upon observing her for a while.

Colin had been checked over, too, and was presently handcuffed in a side room with two unsmiling police officers watching over him.

Dingle had been to see them, suddenly a lot more interested in what they had to say. Once they had been looked over and patched up and the hospital staff had moved on to other patients, Greg and Beth were finally afforded a moment alone before Beth was taken up to a bed on the ward. Even with a possible concussion Beth was sharper than most.

"You made it."

Greg shook his head. "No, I didn't."

"Okay. But you nearly made it. Doesn't that count for something? Blimey, you even drove a car without as much as a single lesson."

"I crashed a car without as much as a single lesson."

In a way Beth was right, though. He had nearly made it.

Did that make Colin right or wrong? He had always clung to the belief he had done his best to fetch help after his mother had cracked her skull on that icy path, always believed he had got across the road as fast as he possibly could. Now he wasn't quite so sure. Maybe there had been some other way, a way to have turned those sixteen minutes into one or two. Like today, with the car, something he hadn't thought of before. He really didn't know anymore.

He tried not to envy other people, people who were able to go about their business free of the shapeless, nameless dread which so frequently stalked his every move and decision. What did it feel like to be one of them? To be able to act freely, unburdened and unafraid, without double, triple and quadruple checking the smallest things just to create a momentary sensation of what they experienced most of their lives?

Amazing. Did they even realise how lucky they were?

The simple gift of being normal?

He had never known what that was like. Instead, year by year, he had slowly made the devil that jabbed his peace of mind with a hot pitchfork his bedfellow. Better the devil you know. Is there any greater fear than the fear of the unknown? The intrusive thoughts, the obsessive urges they birthed, the irresistible itch on the spot already weeping and raw that demanded to be scratched, as bad as these things were, were they not at least familiar, the devil he knew? If by magic they could be neatly excised, what would be left, how big a hole would that leave,

360

how much of the Greg lying here on an accident and emergency bed would depart with them? He would be so different…

"Don't." Beth was looking at him.

This Greg had nearly made it, but if Beth had been less resourceful, less formidable, less amazing? He met her gaze.

"If you hadn't got free, if he had checked your pockets, if you hadn't had that pepper spray, hadn't managed to grab that pan and—"

"But I did."

"But what if you hadn't? What then?"

"What do you want me to say? You did your best. Sometimes that's enough, sometimes not. That doesn't just go for you, that goes for all of us."

He thought about that, thought about whether she believed it or if it was just a line to make him feel better.

"I'm afraid I'm always going to be like this. However much I try, I'll never be right, never be normal…"

"Normal? That's the goal, is it? Does anything short of that spurious ideal mean you're worth less than someone else? And who the fuck gets to choose what normal even is? I'm not sure anyone really knows what normal is anymore. They've blown right past it in pursuit of some packaged version of perfection. Young girls who think they have to have Mila Kunis's lips and Kim Kardashian's backside… Guys who feel inadequate unless they have a six-pack and a year-round tan, even though they live in a country where a thick coat and an umbrella are a wiser investment than a tube of sun cream … We're all supposed to be well adjusted, smart, cool, beautiful or handsome, have our shit together and steadfastly maintain a positive mental attitude, be revved up go-getters and winners.... Fuck number two, they're the first of the losers, right? It's impossible.

"Can't we just be happy with trying to run a good race? Can't we enjoy our occasional triumphs without beating ourselves up too much about our faults, just be happy with being slightly a better version of ourselves? Is that really aiming too low? Yeah, you have… issues, but bloody hell, Greg, don't we all?" She looked at him. "I think I can live with them."

He wanted that. He wanted to believe she meant what it implied, but the infernal, internal arbiter didn't want him to.

"But what if I can't even manage that, a slightly better version of myself, what then?"

Voyage of Death: A George and Kathy Franklin Mystery
by
Beth Grue

Chapter Twenty-Seven

We had reached an impasse. I felt Charlotte Rutledge's polished steel blade at my throat; one quick slice and my days were numbered. On the other side of the dining room the Captain held her twin brother at gunpoint.

Mason Rutledge was all too aware of the pistol, but it didn't prevent him from glaring at George. He spat the question everyone wanted the answer to.

"How did you know it was us?"

I could see my clever husband assessing the situation, gauging whether revealing his reasoning would inflame the situation or buy more time to find a way to gain the upper hand.

"Two killers?" George answered. "I suspected from the second body. Miss Murgatroyd. It was your calling card that gave it away: the blond hair twisted around the woman's ring finger. She was unmarried, but a far cry from the woman you judged her to be. The blond strand of hair on the first victim appeared almost identical to look at, but when studied in detail revealed itself to be quite different."

Mason frowned. George continued.

"Your sister is a natural blonde, Mr Rutledge, but you are not, are you? The texture of a natural strand of hair and one that has been bleached is quite different. The former will be smooth, the latter coarser by far. You are by nature ginger haired, are you not?"

Mason's frown instantly bent into an indignant scowl.

363

"I knew for certain when the body of Miss Crawley was discovered. We were five days into the voyage by then; your hair had grown just enough to detect your real colouring at the root. There was only a fraction, but enough to confirm my suspicion beyond all doubt. Once I knew I was looking for two killers, the other clues became legion: the sudden change of dinner dress immediately after Miss Pennywinkle's death but before dinner in the captain's quarters, the incident in which Kathy and I saw only one drink beside your twin deck chairs, when you claimed your sister had been with you all afternoon.

"And the cunningly designed alibis; it was not you, Mason, whom Father Turbot saw looking out to sea from the portside that night, as you wished him to believe, but your sister, dressed in a man's suit. Likewise it was not your sister, Charlotte, the steward saw reading by lamplight but you.

"I have learned that it is not method one must seek when getting to the bottom of a murder, but motive. This is at the heart of the matter, and in this case I believe the motive was madness and a lineage of murder and mutilation. Here again you provided the fuel to feed my suspicions, with another slip. Your sister claimed your family's roots lay in London, that your late father was an artist, and yet prior to this you had twice stated his profession that of a surgeon. In your twisted mind, are both not true? Here was the last part of the puzzle, the hand-drawn street maps I found after sneaking into your cabin. How many would be able to recognise those streets without the names attached? Few, I would wager, unless they had walked them for decades as had I.

"The maps had markings, crosses at locations I also recognised. I served for over thirty years at Scotland Yard, beginning my career as a raw recruit at the age of twenty-two in 1889, scarcely a year after one of history's foulest series of unsolved crimes. The horrors were still fresh in the minds of all there, the details known to all who walked those streets and alleyways. The case was still an open wound, and I came to know of the details of the crimes from men still keen to catch the monster who had perpetrated them.

"This was how I came by one of Inspector Abberline's less public theories, that the Ripper had absconded by sea beyond the shores of England, to, it now seems almost beyond doubt, the shores of the New World, America.

"Were those unlabelled maps drawn by your late father's own hand? Did he give them to you so you might continue his work on the streets of Whitechapel, or did you and your sister take that mission upon yourselves?" George shook his head slowly. "When the Ripper left horrors unforgotten for more than thirty years, I shudder to think what you two butchers might have accomplished."

Throughout my husband's steady monologue the knife at my throat had stirred not an inch. With their crimes exposed and her sibling at gunpoint, might my captor not consider surrender? Between the twins they had each emulated aspects of their father's modus operandi. Mason had garrotted and eviscerated his victims, Charlotte opened the throats of four women; I did not wish to be number five.

I saw my husband fix her with his steady gaze. Only I who knew him most intimately would be able to see his fear lurking beneath. "You cannot escape this vessel. The moment we dock the authorities will be waiting for you."

I saw Mason, saw him smile despite the pistol held to his head, saw his lips move and heard the command bellowed from his mouth.

"DO IT, SISTER, CUT HER PRETTY THROAT!"

My husband's face blanched, followed by a sharp nod of his head. My hand flew up, gripped the murderess's hand in a bid to keep the blade from biting into my neck.

And bite it did, but only for an instant. Before it could penetrate deep enough to threaten my life, the mad woman holding it crumpled. I glanced up and saw a huge fist, the same that must have crashed into her face, delivered by a man *who moved as silently as he communicated, and with a speed that quite belied his size and frame.*

Charlotte Rutledge hit the ground like a sack of grain, and remained there.

Demidov stood above me like a colossus. He extended a hand to help me to my feet, his soulful dark eyes asking the question he could not:

Are you unharmed?

I nodded.

The voyage was over. We would be in Southampton within the hour, and Mason and Charlotte Rutledge would face the justice their infamous father had escaped.

Epilogue

Beth woke first. She slipped out from under Greg's arm, reached for her dressing gown and crept from the bedroom. Greg was usually the first to rise. He would make himself a cup of tea, potter about, tidying and cleaning. One of the fringe benefits of living with someone with OCD was that you ended up doing approximately two percent of all cleaning and housework. She wasn't lazy, she had just discovered quickly that even if she did manage to get in first and do it all, Greg would still have to go around and do it all again in order to feel comfortable.

Sometimes she would wake before the alarm, find him gone, and lie back and listen. Hear him moving things and setting them back, plumping cushions and wiping surfaces. He waited until she was up and about to vacuum the carpets. Eventually she would hear the kettle boil, the clink of the spoon, and he would return to the bedroom, set the mugs on the bedside table, lean over and kiss her behind the ear. It was a nice way to be woken, and every bit as nice if you were already awake.

But occasionally, like today, she was first to rise.

She walked into the kitchen and filled the kettle with water.

The past few months had been eventful to say the least. Greg's stepfather, Colin, had confessed to the Kettle Street murders. Beth remembered the moment in her kitchen when his sixteen-minute time limit had expired. He had truly believed Greg would make the deadline, and when he hadn't it had been a savage blow.

Only later had it made sense: what had tortured Colin was the conviction that Greg could have acted faster back on that winter evening which had taken so much. Part of his stepfather had wanted that confirmed, to prove his suffering was Greg's fault. But Greg had not made it in time then, and hadn't this time either. He had done everything he could, on both occasions. The truth of that must have hit Colin hard, but not as hard as Beth was about to.

As Colin was reflecting on how wrong he had been, Beth had taken her shot. She had already worked her right hand free of the gaffer tape binding it, and gone for the pepper spray. She still couldn't believe he hadn't checked her pockets, and the binding job on her hands had been sloppy too. Would he have been more thorough with someone who didn't have CP? She supposed it hardly mattered now. His laxity had enabled her to grab the pepper spray and administer a good dose right in the eyes. He had realised his mistake then, and tried to grapple her. Blind, and yelling like a yodeller on fire, he had tried to get his hands around her throat, but fortunately the saucepan rack had been within reach. She had seized the handle of the largest one and vigorously brained him with it. Greg had come crashing in soon after.

The aftermath had been considerable, but not all bad.

Adrian, Greg's brother, had taken it hard. Part of it was the shock that his stepfather had gone further off the rails than even he had imagined, far beyond the escalating and ever more frequent altercations with neighbours, and part of it was guilt: Colin had not simply fallen out with his brother, but grown to hate him to the point of insanity, and Adrian had somehow failed to see this. Despite fearing the consequences, Greg had told Adrian about the evening of their mother's death, too, about how long it had taken him to get help. To his credit, Adrian said he had always suspected something of the sort; it was the reason he had never asked. Unlike Colin, he had never once doubted Greg had acted as fast as he could.

Kettle Street had begun to heal the wound Colin had inflicted on it, too. The ensuing media attention seemed to force upon its residents an awareness that they should, perhaps, get to know one another a little better. Now that Maurice Cooper was dead everyone seemed to appreciate the newsletters that had tried so hard to keep their street a nice place to live. The turnout at his funeral was considerable, and aided by that remarkable social lubricant of alcohol, many left the wake on genuine speaking terms for the first time after living only a handful of houses away from one another for years.

Even Dennis Crompton had attended. Under the rough exterior, he really was a decent guy, honestly trying to make a fresh start. Greg had taken to spending the occasional evening across the road, painting small resin Xenomorphs and Space Marines with him. It had to be the evenings because Crompton had found a job at the Games Workshop in the city to fill his days and pay the bills. He and Greg benefited from a generous staff discount on paints and figures.

Martin Mangham had somehow fallen into Greg's life, too. Following his mentor's theft and betrayal, Martin had begun to fall apart just a little, at which point he had gone straight to his doctor to seek help. The GP, a young, keen and progressive man, had immediately reviewed Martin's medical history and arranged therapy with a cognitive behavioural therapist he knew from university. The therapist had real talent. Martin asked him if he would be prepared to take on Greg, and after a consultation and referral from Greg's own doctor, he had agreed.

Martin and Greg had both made progress, and caught up regularly to swap stories and encourage each other.

And Beth?

She spent most of the week at Greg's these days. Living with him wasn't always easy, not all kisses behind the ear, sunshine and lollypops and scarcely any housework to do. Sometimes, his habits and rituals did drive her to distraction, like a beautiful pair of shoes one size too tight. It wasn't perfect.

And that was just fine.

She set the half-full kettle on its base and reached into the cupboard to fetch a pair of mugs.

Inside the mugs were perfectly aligned, handles facing toward the window, exactly as Greg had carefully set them after diligently washing up the previous evening. All of the handles faced the window. All except one.

The mug it belonged to was tall and soft pink, and had 'Beth' written on its side in looping cream script. Its handle alone had been set deliberately counter to every other.

Beth plucked it from the cupboard, smiled, and switched on the kettle.

The End

Did you enjoy this book?

PLEASE LEAVE AN AMAZON REVIEW!

Reviews are vital to independent authors like me.
Without the support of a big publisher they're the
best thing we have to encourage others to read our
books.
So, please, spare a moment.

Also by
John Bowen

WHERE THE DEAD WALK

A TV ghost-hunting crew. A haunted house. An unimaginable crime. A past buried deep...

An Amazon US/UK Kindle Store Top 100
Bestseller:
#1 Ghosts & Haunted Houses
#1 Occult
#1 Ghosts
#1 Paranormal
#1 Horror
#1 Supernatural

Also by
John Bowen

VESSEL

Forget all you know.
History's biggest secret was hidden behind legends and lies...

An International Amazon #1 Bestseller in Kindle Thriller and Mystery

Acknowledgements

Thanks to my lovely wife Caroline and my kids, Henry and Freya, Richard Daley my ideas dartboard, and my mom, Carol Thornton.

Huge thanks also to all those who helped out by offering feedback and looking past the clunk of working drafts to the story beneath, the incredible thriller author, Joel Hames, Kath Middleton, Helen Claire, Lou Freya, Loo Elton, Helen Boyce, Tracy Fenton and her amazing THE Book Club, Leanne Cook, Janell Irvine, Steve Moore, Sue Jordan, Shell Baker, Alison Bailey, Kelli Mahan and everyone on the advance reader group.

Extra special thanks as always to my wonderful editor, friend, and kick ass author Joanna Franklin Bell, without whose deft editing skills this book would have featured considerably rougher edges. Trust me, any mistakes you may find will NOT be hers.

Cheers guys

CPSIA information can be obtained
at www.ICGtesting.com
Printed in the USA
LVHW021538250220
648165LV00010B/1026

9 781539 958307

9 781539 958307